"*The Ingredients of Us* is a literary confection filled with multifaceted characters and a compelling story line. Gold's bittersweet look at love will satisfy any contemporary women's fiction reader's sweet tooth."

—*Booklist*

"Come for the story of a baker facing a crisis in her marriage. Stay for the recipes—lush, beautiful things, filled with life lessons. From that very first recipe for passive-aggressive blackberry jam, you know you're in for something special."

—Erica Bauermeister, *New York Times* bestselling author of *The Scent Keeper* and *The School of Essential Ingredients*

"*The Ingredients of Us* is a delightfully original novel filled with love, regret, and recipes that are themselves like little short stories. You'll want to cry for Elle as she navigates the breakup of her marriage and flashes back on the earlier, happier days. And then you want to follow her to her kitchen and feast on her buttery concoctions as she finds healing and strength."

—Maddie Dawson, *Washington Post* and Amazon Charts bestselling author of *Matchmaking for Beginners* and *The Survivor's Guide to Family Happiness*

"Achingly beautiful and emotionally rich, *Keep Me Afloat* explores the heartache of stifling self to put family first. When a marine biologist—broke, jobless, alone—drifts home with a U-Haul of guilt, her past and present merge to reveal her truth in unexpected ways. A stunning novel of love, redemption, and whales."

—Barbara Claypole White, bestselling author of *The Perfect Son* and *The Promise Between Us*

"*Keep Me Afloat* is a rich ebb and flow of human emotion, offering an intimate look at a young marine biologist's journey to finding herself. Set against the extraordinary backdrop of the Pacific Northwest coastline, this engaging story will leave readers buoyant with hope."

—Nicole Meier, author of *The Second Chance Supper Club*

HALF WAY
to YOU

ALSO BY JENNIFER GOLD

Keep Me Afloat

The Ingredients of Us

HALF WAY

to

YOU

A NOVEL

JENNIFER GOLD

LAKE UNION
PUBLISHING

Published by Lake Union Publishing, Seattle

www.apub.com

Amazon, the Amazon logo, and Lake Union Publishing are trademarks of Amazon.com, Inc., or its affiliates.

ISBN-13: 9781662509094 (paperback)
ISBN-13: 9781662509100 (digital)

Cover design by Shasti O'Leary Soudant
Cover image: © Henk Meijer / ArcAngel; © seksan wangkeeree / Shutterstock; © WindAwake / Shutterstock

Printed in the United States of America

For Joseph

ANN

Papeete, Tahiti, French Polynesia
September 1999

Ten thousand miles from home, I realized: *He's not coming.*

I don't remember exactly *when* that realization formed. I'd planted myself at a patio table at our agreed-upon hotel and waited an hour—maybe two?—before my doubt set in.

I'll never forget how the air smelled of plumeria and tropical rain. How the heavy sea breeze sought to extinguish my cigarette. How, beyond my table, the surf of Matavai Bay surged and flowed over the black sand beach.

It was the fifteenth anniversary of our first meeting, and I *knew* Todd wasn't coming.

I also knew that I loved him—a deep certainty that rippled through my heart like the tide. Todd had always been the ocean to my beach, warm and smooth and lovely even as he swept through my everything. He could wipe me clean with perfect devastation. And I was the sand, the sum of a million fragmented, pulverized parts, stirred up in his wake.

Had he never *planned* to come?

I should've expected to be stood up—but then again, when it came to Todd, I never learned. I could never quite reach him. I was always halfway there, trying desperately to close the distance. Waiting in some foreign land and hoping beyond hope that he'd prove me wrong and show up, after all.

But as you know by now, Maggie, it was never quite that simple.

MAGGIE

You can't build trust on a half truth.
—*Excerpt from* Chasing Shadows, *by Ann Fawkes*

Anacortes, Washington State, USA
Friday, January 5, 2024

"Should you be talking while driving?" Grant's voice vibrates through the surround sound car speakers.

"*You* called *me*. And I have Bluetooth." Maggie taps the cracked screen of her dash-mounted iPhone, switching the call display back to Google Maps. "What's up?"

"I thought you'd be there already."

Maggie doesn't bother to scrub the frustration from her voice. "So did I."

The six-hour trip is currently pushing nine. After an early-morning departure from Oregon, Maggie braved a traffic-congested drive up I-5 north and faulty directions that landed her on the *wrong* ferry to the *wrong* island. She's now following a scenic sixty-mile highway to board one more ferry through the glacier-carved islands of northern-Washington-almost-Canada.

As if she wasn't nervous enough already, without the stress of getting lost.

"Did you take a wrong turn?"

"It's almost as if she doesn't want to be found," Maggie jokes.

She's heading to San Juan Island on assignment—her *first* field assignment with the podcast *Stories Behind the Stories*. Tomorrow, she has an appointment to interview her favorite author of all time, an elusive jet-setting one-hit wonder named Ann Fawkes. *SBTS* reasoned that conducting the interviews in Ann's secluded residence would make her feel more relaxed; Maggie has her doubts the plan will soothe Ann's wariness, but an opportunity is an opportunity.

"So," Maggie continues. "Is this a friend call or a producer call?"

"I'm just checking in." Her boss sounds anything but casual.

Maggie waits for his next question, the static road noise consuming his pause.

"Are you nervous?"

"I'm *fine*, Grant," Maggie says. "I have interviewed people before, you know."

"Brit said you were nervous."

Traitor. Brit is a junior sound engineer and Maggie's BFF. After separate internships postgraduation, they were hired by friend-of-a-friend and *SBTS* producer Grant as a duo because of their college radio reporting.

"Of course I'm *a little* nervous," Maggie relents. "This story is a big deal. But that just means I'm even more motivated to do a good job—*all right?*"

Grant chuckles. "Fine, fine. Come to me if you have any concerns before the interview tomorrow morning. I'll check in via text."

"Roger that," Maggie says and ends the call.

The January afternoon is dreary enough for Maggie to switch on her headlights. Everything appears gray—from the rain-heavy sky to the moisture-burdened boughs of evergreen trees to the pavement—except for the solid yellow road lines leading her through the forest. When Maggie reaches a straightaway, the lines break into dashes that blip past at the same quick rate as her heart.

She's about to interview legendary author *Ann Fawkes*. Maggie is *definitely* nervous, but she'd never tell her boss the extent of it—not the fact that she'd practically memorized Ann's novel, *Chasing Shadows*, as a teen nor the flush of starstruck wonder she experiences even now, just thinking about meeting her—no. Maggie is already acutely ashamed, knowing a personal connection to Ann tipped the scales in her favor when she convinced the producers to put a rookie like herself on such an important project.

Granted, Maggie has never met Ann—but much of her family did, way back when, and while Maggie always knew there was an unspoken dislike, she hadn't expected it to run so deep. Her parents had been furious when she told them the exciting news. *She's not a very trustworthy person, dear,* her mother, Tracey, had said, near tears. *Take everything she says with a grain of salt. Be careful.*

No one fully trusts Maggie to run this interview—not the producers, not her parents. And if Maggie's trip up from Portland is any indication, perhaps she is destined to fail. The only reason she hasn't turned around is for the sake of her timid teenage self, the suburban girl whose worn, Post-it-Noted copy of *Chasing Shadows* still endures as her most treasured possession. That, and her dream of one day becoming a producer. Her father, Bob, always says that an opportunity is not something you receive; it's something you seize.

She owes this to herself. So here she is, seizing it, despite her sweaty palms and self-doubt.

When she reaches the ferry terminal, Maggie unlocks her death grip on the steering wheel and flexes her numb fingers. Normally, she would call her mother in Colorado to talk through her worries, but she hasn't spoken to Tracey since she dropped the news of this trip. Maggie always knew that her mother disliked Ann, but it still stung when Tracey tried to convince Maggie to relinquish the biggest interview of her career—without explaining why.

Taking up her phone, Maggie scrolls past her mother's name and Brit's GOOD LUCK MAGS!!! text, pausing on the Whitaker Family text thread to thumb through old jokes and memories. The family stopped messaging each other shortly after Uncle Keith—Tracey's brother—died. The last message is from his wife, Barbara, trying to arrange a family barbecue like Uncle Keith used to do—a plan that ultimately fizzled. He was the glue that held everyone together. Maggie used to text her family all the time—a security blanket—but now all that's left are loose threads.

For a brief moment, Maggie considers messaging everyone, but she sets her phone back down. Choosing to lean on herself, Maggie eases her nerves by skimming her preinterview notes, a list of essential details and conversational entry points:

Pamela Fawkes: the alcoholic mother who raised Ann in poverty

One million: the inheritance from Ann's absent father, which bought her a new life in Europe

Keith Whitaker: Ann's agent and dearest friend, who launched her career

Todd Langley: the love of Ann's life, a man with his own tragic past

As proven by previous interviews (as well as Keith's infuriating unwillingness to tell Maggie *anything* about her favorite author), Ann does not like to discuss her personal life—especially Todd. It is unconfirmed whether they ever reconnected after the accident that occurred in 1999. The topic remains a sore spot. This interview is the first time Ann will have broken her silence since those highly publicized and misrepresented events. It's a miracle (and, frankly, a mystery) she even agreed to *SBTS*'s request—but Ann's episode could spur a new era of high-profile guests and success for the podcast.

Needless to say, there's a lot riding on this interview.

To Maggie and the rest of the world, Ann's whole life feels like a half story, a myth. Everything Maggie knows—from Ann's tempestuous relationship with her mother to her fondness for Keith and her tragic romance with Todd—is in tiny fragments: rumors in tabloids, stilted interviews, fleeting footage from brief public appearances. Even Ann's travel essays and short stories—which kept her relevant all those years after *Chasing Shadows*, before the public gave up hope for a sophomore novel—leave much to the imagination.

But that's the point of the podcast.

This assignment—and the whole idea behind *Stories Behind the Stories*—is to unveil the person behind the work. Maggie isn't oblivious to the fact that better reporters, as well as fans, stalkers, and biographers, have already tried and failed to get the full Ann Fawkes story. The only difference for *SBTS* is timing. Keith died four years ago; Todd, two years ago. Two pillars of Ann's life—her longtime friend and her lover—are gone. Now that she has no one to protect, it's the perfect time for Ann to tell her story. Maggie said as much in her initial email to Ann's publicist, who was already amenable to scheduling promotional interviews due to an upcoming press tour for Ann's new short story collection releasing later this year.

Ann herself wrote back with terms:

Open topics: *Chasing Shadows*, travel articles, new story collection

Off limits: My personal life

Ann's terms were the antithesis of *SBTS*'s mission, but with Grant hovering over her shoulder, Maggie agreed. "For now, we'll take what we can get," he said.

The problem: Ann's writing *is* her personal life. Even her fiction is semiautobiographical, and her new collection—her only book-length publication since *Chasing Shadows*—is about her mother. Like it or not, everything Ann writes is tied to her personal life. She must've known that when she responded to Maggie's query.

And Maggie knew that when she agreed, anyway.

"We're in the door," Grant said once the email was sent. "Now it's up to you to convince Ann Fawkes to spill it all."

MAGGIE

San Juan Island, Washington State, USA
Saturday, January 6, 2024

Podcast: Stories Behind the Stories
    Episode #148: Ann Fawkes

Raw audio clip #3
    MAGGIE: *Test, test, test. Okay.*

Raw audio clip #4
    MAGGIE: *Can you introduce yourself?*
    ANN FAWKES: *My name is Ann Fawkes. I'm a travel essayist and* author of Chasing Shadows.
    MAGGIE: *Tell me about* Chasing Shadows.
    ANN: *What would you like to know?*
    MAGGIE: *Let's start with the stats.*
    ANN: *I'm really dating myself here, but it was released in 1987. It was a number one* New York Times *bestseller and NYT Notable Book, with a very popular movie. [Pause.] I sound rather vain.*

MAGGIE: *Not at all. It's impressive. [Pause.] At its heart, what do you think the novel is truly about?*

ANN: Chasing Shadows *is about a woman destroyed by love.*

MAGGIE: *[Chuckles faintly.]*

ANN: *Is that funny?*

MAGGIE: *Oh, I thought you were . . . that's an interesting description. Can you elaborate?*

ANN: *Have you not read it?*

MAGGIE: *I have. I'm just easing us in with a few simple sound bites.*

ANN: *Oh. Well, more literally, the book is about Jane, whose mother goes missing somewhere in Europe. In Jane's search to find her mother, she meets a handsome stranger who ends up betraying her.*

MAGGIE: *Spoiler alert.*

ANN: *Can a book as old as mine be spoiled?*

MAGGIE: *Fair enough. [Breath.] Some have speculated that the premise of* Chasing Shadows *was semiautobiographical. Is that true?*

ANN: *My mother didn't go missing.*

MAGGIE: *It's not a metaphor for a distant relationship?*

ANN: *All my relationships were distant. I lived halfway across the world.*

MAGGIE: *By design?*

ANN: *My personal life is off limits, remember?*

MAGGIE: *Apologies. I'm just trying to better understand the book.*

ANN: *It's fiction.*

MAGGIE: *I realize that, but—*

ANN: *Why don't we switch gears for now?*

MAGGIE: *Sure. [Papers shuffling.] For someone not on Facebook or Twitter, the news of your new story collection practically broke the internet. Why publish something now, thirty-seven years after the release of your first book?*

ANN: *That's personal.*

MAGGIE: *You can't expand on—*

ANN: *I'm happy to discuss the book, but the timing—it's complicated.*

MAGGIE: *The write-up in the* Post *speculated that, like* Chasing Shadows, *the new collection—called* Letters I Should Have Written—*is about your mother. Care to comment on—*

ANN: *I encourage readers to take the book at face value, without speculation.*

MAGGIE: *You have nothing to say about—*

ANN: *I think you're forgetting our agreement.*

MAGGIE: *Excuse me?*

ANN: *Our agreement: no personal questions.*

MAGGIE: *I'd hardly say these questions are—*

ANN: *They are.*

MAGGIE: *One might argue that all writing is personal.*

ANN: *Do you really want to argue? I was clear in my email.*

MAGGIE: *What would you like to talk about?*

[Pause.]

ANN: *You're right. Maybe this was a bad idea.*

MAGGIE: *I didn't mean it like that.*

ANN: *[Muffled.] I'm terminating the interview.*

MAGGIE: *Please, I apologize. I'm just looking for a deeper take on your writing.*

ANN: *I didn't invite you here for a deeper take.*

MAGGIE: *Then why* am *I here?*

ANN: *To pry, apparently.*

[Two voices at once.]

ANN: *[Louder.] Look, I know you came all this way, but I don't think I can continue. I'm sorry to waste your time.*

MAGGIE: *What if I turned off the recorder?*

[—]

"That doesn't change anything," Ann says, folding her arms over her chest. Her cobalt shawl billows behind her as she leads Maggie to the front door. "Please go."

As soon as Maggie steps onto the porch, Ann shuts her out. Shame burns across Maggie's face as she walks down the garden path toward her car. Frost crusts the gravel drive, sparkling in the morning light. The damp chill cuts through Maggie's North Face shell, her wool sweater, her skin, muscle, tissue—freezing her cells.

At least the cold might numb the pain of this massive failure.

Sliding into the driver's seat of her car, Maggie can already hear the disappointment in Grant's voice. She blew it. She absolutely *bombed*. It couldn't have gone worse if she'd tried. As soon as she sat down with Ann and hit record, all her interviewing skills went out the window. Not only was she starstruck, she was *mesmerized*. Here was a woman Maggie had idolized for years, finally sitting in front of her. She wanted to bombard her with questions, to learn every last juicy detail.

No wonder Ann felt uncomfortable. She could probably smell the desperation on Maggie's breath.

Seated behind the cracked windshield, Maggie grits her teeth. She should be turning the ignition, driving away, calling Grant. She should be *leaving*, as Ann asked.

But instead, Maggie feels a slight tug in her chest, a tether to Ann's home that's been pulling her here since she left Portland yesterday. A tether that's been tugging since she was a teenager in Colorado discovering Ann's novel for the first time. Whether aware of it or not, Maggie has been inexplicably tied to this stranger her whole life, all because of Keith.

No one can cut this cord. Regardless of her mother's warnings and Ann's dismissal, going home feels like the *last* thing Maggie should do. What she wants to do is bang on Ann's door and plead for a second chance.

She stares up the lavender-edged walkway, past the glistening doilies of spiderwebs strung up in the yard and illuminated by the sun. Her eyes rest heavily on Ann's front door. She can't turn back now. She can't not try. It's not just the job or Maggie's fangirl curiosity—some unexplainable voice inside is telling her she was *meant* to be here. The voice is soul level.

She gets out of the car.

She storms up the path.

This is so unlike timid, mild Maggie. It's as if her legs move independently of her reason. The tether is tightening now, spooling Maggie closer.

She rings the doorbell. She knocks. She calls out, "Ann, I can't just walk away. I think we were meant to talk."

A moment passes. Two. Ten. Silence fills the small porch space. Maggie's breath clouds around her face, and she folds her arms, shivering. Her phone buzzes in her purse, but she ignores it. She's considering sitting on the steps and waiting—however long it takes—when Ann's shape darkens one of the stained glass sidelight windows framing the door.

The knob turns.

"Why?" Ann asks.

Maggie's heart is suddenly in her throat. "Why . . . what?"

"Why do you think we were meant to talk?"

Maggie shifts her feet. She can't explain to Ann the ineffable soul urge inside her, telling her this interview was meant to happen. If she did, she'd sound like a crazy person.

"Because . . ." Maggie trails off.

When she first mentioned to Grant that her relation to Keith might help her connect with Ann, she promised herself that she wouldn't actually use it. It might've tipped Grant's scales, but knowing that she hadn't gotten this interview on merit alone had stung. She wanted to give herself a chance to prove her worth without the help of her relation, so she ultimately hadn't told Ann about it.

But now, standing in the cold on Ann's porch, Maggie knows Keith might be her only hope.

Ann tightens her shawl across her chest, crossing her arms against the chill. Slowly, she repeats, "Why do you think we were meant to talk?"

Maggie swallows audibly and forces herself to look—for the first time—straight into Ann's rum-gold eyes. "Because Keith Whitaker was my uncle. And I think he would've wanted us to talk."

MAGGIE

"Keith changes everything," Ann says, leading Maggie back into the living room.

Floor-to-ceiling windows form a wide crescent, exposing them to the blinding glare off the ocean beyond Ann's clifftop home. A philodendron hangs from one of the wood beams of the vaulted ceiling, a lush and tangled thing that reminds Maggie of Ann for a reason she can't quite name.

Clutching her notebook and purse, Maggie loiters by the gray-blue sectional.

"Tea?"

"Yes, please."

Ann floats into the conjoined kitchen. Beyond the windows, the soft brushstroke reflections of pine trees paint the ocean forest green. Above, seagulls tumble in the salt-white sky. Ann's shift in demeanor—from closed off to at ease—is as confounding as the pirouetting birds.

Ann returns with a tea tray, leading Maggie to a pair of cobalt wingback reading chairs opposite the kitchen. "My favorite seats in the house," Ann says, adding, "No recorder."

Maggie hesitates, then drops the gadget into her purse on the floor. She isn't in a position to argue, but the recorder's absence makes her fidget. She wipes her damp palms over the tops of her thighs, then crosses her legs and clasps her hands.

Ann smiles, pouring Maggie a cup of clove-colored tea from a floral pot. "Cream?"

"Please."

"Sugar?"

Maggie nods, watching Ann use a tiny pair of tongs to drop a cube into her cup.

Once the tea is prepared, she hands Maggie the matching cup and saucer and prepares her own in the same methodical fashion. If Ann is stalling, Maggie doesn't mind. She takes a long sip—it's chai, her favorite—and she's grateful as the spicy-creamy sweetness eases the corded muscles on either side of her spine.

Ann watches her with those gold, cunning eyes. With the sunlight streaming in, they appear almost amber. Maggie has seen plenty of photos of Ann from her younger days. She used to have copper-brown hair, but now that she's in her sixties, her hair is silver, a stunning moonglow. Wrinkles streaking out from her eyes and along her freckle-dusted cheeks suggest a wisdom that is beautiful and epic and storied. What makes Ann smile? What makes her squint in anger or appreciation? Maggie wants to know the influence of each one of those creases.

Ann leans back, settling into the wings of her chair. "So, you're a Whitaker."

Deep breath. "I didn't want my relation to Keith to sway you into doing this podcast."

"But you do now?"

"I . . ." Maggie trails off, diaphragm fluttering.

"That was a rude question," Ann admits. "I appreciate your honesty."

"Th . . . thanks." Where is this conversation headed? Without her recorder listening, it could go anywhere.

Ann folds her arms loosely. "I sort of lost track of all the nieces and nephews. Who's your relation?"

"Tracey and Bob."

Ann dunks a gingersnap in her tea, keeping eye contact as she bites down. The action is casual but seems calculatedly so. "Biological?"

Maggie flinches, a pinprick. The Whitakers have a trove of buried pain and secrets. As Keith's longtime client and friend, how many of those secrets was Ann privy to, before she and Keith grew apart?

Be careful, Tracey said.

"I'm sorry," Ann says, waving a hand through the air as if to erase the question. "I know they struggled with infertility, that's all."

Maggie shrugs it off, but in truth, she wouldn't know how to answer.

Her parentage is a question she's faced all her life: alone as a confused child, silently as an angry teen, and with resignation as an adult. It started when she was in elementary school. One night, she overheard her parents arguing. In fleece-footed pajamas, Maggie had padded halfway down the stairs, only to pause when she heard her name. "I refuse to allow Maggie's father to interfere," Tracey had said to Bob. Even as a child, Maggie's mind had snagged on the phrasing. *Maggie's father.*

As she got older, the memory of that night festered. She knew from her classmates that families came in all shapes, but this revelation seemed different. Was Bob not her father? And if not, was Tracey even her mother? Why hadn't they told her? Or had she heard wrong, entirely?

She tried to ask, once, but the words tangled in her throat. She knew what she heard, which meant that Tracey and Bob must've had a reason not to tell Maggie the truth. When she thought about it, the truth frightened her.

So Maggie had done her best to forget. She took the ache of suspicion, bottled it up, corked it, and stored it in a cool, dark place inside the growing cavern in her chest. Because not knowing was safe.

To this day, Maggie has never found the courage to ask her parents where she came from. It's the sad irony of her career as a journalist, as someone with a degree in finding answers. Maggie might understand the value of a true story, but she's still afraid of her *own* true story. It's pathetic.

But none of that matters now.

Maggie sits a little taller. "Aren't *I* supposed to be interviewing *you*?"

"I already told you, I can't do the interview."

"Then why did you let me back inside?"

"Keith."

Maggie grabs a cookie off the tray and takes a dry bite, waiting for Ann to go on.

She doesn't.

Maggie swallows, ginger scraping the entire length of her throat. She takes a long sip of tea to wash it all down. She begged Grant for this opportunity, convinced him that she was the right person for the job. If she fails now, he'll never trust her again. The thought of Grant; Brit; the executive producer, Joy; the host, Anita; and everyone else at the podcast *relying* on her to make this work causes the nerves in her fingers to short out. How is she supposed to convince Ann to do this interview?

Maggie tries, "Don't you think Keith would want you to humor me?"

Ann tips her head back and chuckles in amusement. "*Of course* he would. Keith was a saint. But there's something you should know about my relationship with him, Maggie: I never listened. I was always doing things against his better judgment, and he was always exasperated by me."

"So, this is par for the course," Maggie mutters, then pinches her lips together in horror at what she just let slip.

But Ann laughs even harder. "I suppose it is. I'm sure he's looking down on us from whatever new astral plane he's on, rolling his eyes."

"Then we're at an impasse."

"It appears so."

Maggie thinks back to that moment in the car, of storming up Ann's walkway and banging on the door. She didn't come all this way just to fail and let everyone at *SBTS* down—to let *herself* down. What would teenager Maggie think, watching this scene play out? She'd probably be furious if Maggie didn't at least *try* to engage.

When she was younger, she had *begged* Keith for Ann-related tidbits, had asked over and over for a signed book, a meeting, *anything*, but Keith had always protected Ann's privacy. Even Keith's daughter, Iris, and some of Maggie's other elder cousins—who had *met* Ann as kids—never had much to divulge. They hadn't even read Ann's book—a frustrating fact for teenage Maggie, who envied their underappreciated proximity to her favorite author. Even if they had been too young to recognize the significance of Ann's presence.

So today—*this moment*—is Maggie's only shot. If there's a chance to make this work, she has to seize it *now*.

It's up to you to convince Ann Fawkes to spill it all.

She takes a sip of tea, fortifying herself with the rousing heat of clove. "If you don't mind, may I ask, Why did you say yes to the podcast in the first place?"

"That's a good question." Ann frowns slightly in thought, glancing out the window. Seconds tick by, marked by the whooshing of the wind outside, the groaning gutters, and hissing pine-needled trees. The distant roar of the sea.

When Ann levels her gaze on Maggie again, even the blood in Maggie's veins stops moving. "Here's my offer: I'll tell you my whole story—nothing held back, everything—if you want to hear it."

Maggie sits taller. "You will?"

"But you can't record it."

MAGGIE

San Juan Island, Washington State, USA
Saturday, January 6, 2024

Maggie's first instinct is to balk. Grant would murder her if she listened to Ann's story and still came back with nothing. Not to mention the money she'd probably be on the hook for: travel expenses, lodging, salaried time spent *not* working. On a base level, Maggie can't afford it. Her student loan payments alone keep her living paycheck to paycheck.

But this is *Ann Fawkes*. Famous author. Lifelong idol. The opportunity to hear her unabridged life story is once in a lifetime, beyond her wildest dreams. So *of course* Maggie is tempted to say yes.

Maggie shakes her head. "If I can't record it, what's the point?"

"Well, why are *you* here, Maggie?"

"For the podcast. I fought for this interview, convinced my boss."

"I don't believe that's the only reason. What made you run back up my steps earlier?"

Maggie sighs, head spinning. "Honestly, I don't know. I just had a feeling that we were meant to talk."

"A *feeling*?"

Maggie recrosses her legs. "I know, it's stupid."

"I don't pretend to be enlightened or even very worldly, Maggie—at least not in the way most people seem to expect," Ann says, setting down her cup and saucer. "Frankly, I don't know much of anything. But there *is* one thing I'm certain about, and it's this: having a *feeling* about something is not stupid. In fact, I think it's the closest we get to divine intervention. I think we're born with an innate ability to *feel*, and from childhood we're trained not to listen, because it's illogical. But I'll tell you right now: all the most important decisions I've made in my life have been based on illogical feelings that I just couldn't ignore."

Ann spreads her hands, her bracelet tinkling faintly. "You asked why I agreed to the podcast. Well, it's time I told my story—the whole story. Everyone I love is gone; I have no one left to protect." Her eyes go distant for a moment, as if Ann is seeing someone in the room who isn't there. "I agreed to the podcast because I thought that maybe telling my story out loud would help me organize my thoughts. There's so much healing in the telling of things." Her eyebrows crease upward, an apologetic expression. "I'm sorry it took me until today to realize that I just *can't* be recorded. I know this is your job, but if you're being truthful about this *feeling* of yours, maybe you need to hear my story, Maggie—and maybe the rest of the world doesn't."

Maggie unclasps her fingers and leans forward, placing her hands on the arms of her chair. "This is ludicrous."

If she can't fulfill her job's requirements, she has no reason to hear the story . . .

. . . except her own burning curiosity.

Ann straightens her shawl. Her silver hair skitters off her shoulders like a river off rock. "Listen, I like you. You're clearly a smart girl. You seem to have integrity. I think this could be fun, but I understand if you want to go. It's entirely up to you."

Maggie frowns. It doesn't feel that way. *Nothing* is going the way Maggie wanted. Not her job or her bosses' lack of faith in her, not this interview or having to name-drop Keith, not the many mysteries of her life. It's entirely unfair.

Maggie takes a quick sip of tea, fully aware of Ann watching her, waiting for her answer. Temptation rises in her heart like the tide. If she can keep Ann talking, maybe she can eventually convince Ann to record some of her story for the podcast. It's a start, at least. It's better than admitting defeat right out the gate.

"All right," Maggie says, "we have a deal." It's a plunge into glacial water; Maggie shudders with adrenaline.

"Wonderful." Ann spreads her arms, grateful, inviting. "It's still your interview. Where should I start?"

Maggie isn't fooled. She's not sure *what* this is, but it's not an interview—not anymore.

She doesn't fall for it.

But she'll play along—play the long game.

Maggie pours Ann and herself more tea, letting the question hang in the air for a spell. Without her notes or the podcast guiding her, Maggie no longer has a road map. Where does anyone ever begin? Life isn't made up of starts and ends—it's a series of *and thens*. What's important, she decides, is where Ann *believes* the story should begin. Her definition of the beginning is far more important than the actual moment.

"Why don't you start at the beginning?" Maggie asks finally.

Ann is nodding, thinking. Her face shifts, an expression passing under her skin like a hand beneath a sheet. Her mouth tightens, her brows lift, her eyes crease—and then all the tension disappears, making way for a sort of resignation that, even without context, Maggie interprets as significant.

Like a vast prism of story and secrets, the many fragments of Ann's expression settle into a wistful smile: "It all began with one of those illogical feelings."

ANN

Venice, Italy
September 1984

It was past dark and drizzly when I arrived in Venice, my heart pattering with the rain. As I carried my suitcase out of the train station, a sense of uncertainty bloomed in my stomach. I had spent the entire summer traveling through France with my new inheritance, but this was the first time I felt homesick. Perhaps it was just my weariness after a long journey or the fact that I didn't know where my hotel was, or maybe it was because I was tired of having only myself to lean on.

I trudged into the increasing downpour, welcomed only by the wide cobblestone road. The ocean nudged the street, hissing with rain, sparkling in the low light. Boats bobbed on the soft waves. Even in the dreariness, Venice charmed me. Souvenir shops were closing for the day, and the shopkeepers huddled under awnings while they locked up. Tourist couples meandered beneath umbrellas, few and far between; I imagined most were in their hotel rooms, making love or watching the rain on their windowpanes with novels sprawled on their laps.

Romance. It penetrated my clothing like the rain, and seemingly everyone here felt it; we were all impervious to the bad weather and our sorry pasts because we were in *Venice*.

By the time I arrived at my hotel, I was soaked to the bone. But when the night manager showed me to my room, the last thing she said was *"Buona notte,"* and that's when I learned that Italian is the most beautiful language on the planet.

At sunrise the next morning, I carried my notebook to a café overlooking the gold-splashed canal. Writing calmed me—it always had—and overseas especially, it gave me something to do with my hands to look content when I was alone.

After ordering a cappuccino and pastry—*pain au chocolat* was a habit I had developed in France, along with smoking—I lit a cigarette and watched the shiny water taxis pass slowly by, thrumming in the wide channel beyond the buildings. Boaters shouted in mellifluous Italian. Pigeons scattered with thwacking wings. Moored boats bumped and bobbed.

I'd always dreamed of being a writer. As a child, I found solace in reading and making up stories; I invented alternate endings to my nightmares and amused myself with tales of bravery when I felt alone or scared, which for me had been too often.

I'd had a crush on Hemingway and F. Scott Fitzgerald and had written many mawkish short stories over the years. By some miracle or charity, I'd even had a couple published in small literary magazines. At twenty-five, I had cultivated a vision of myself: no longer living in American poverty but in European glamour. I imagined myself sitting in cafés like this, smoking cigarettes, writing novels, and partying with all sorts of lavish, artistic, eccentric individuals.

Of course, my summer of solo travel had not gone to plan. France was a wake-up call that I was not nearly as tough or experienced as I thought. In the span of four months, my young and hopeful heart had been broken twice: once by a one-night stand, and again by a man who I discovered had a fiancée. (I was not unlike my mother in that regard.)

Mostly, my summer had been lonely—but my notebook kept me company.

Now, I jotted down the Venetian details that captured my attention. The souvenir shopkeepers were reopening, dragging T-shirt displays out onto the street, propping their doors open, flirting with each other. It was the locals working their jobs and chatting with friends that helped me discover the dimension of a place. The drowsy in-between hours when one could see a city for what it truly was.

"Your coffee, madam," the waitress said, setting my breakfast down.

"Grat-zee," I said and stubbed out my cigarette.

She corrected my pronunciation with an amused smile. *"Grazie."*

I wrote down the word, practicing the syllables to myself—*grazie, graz-ie, graz-ieh*—as I turned my attention to breakfast. The pastry wasn't as flaky as those in France, but the coffee. The *coffee*. It wasn't bitter or harsh as I had known coffee to be; I tasted only the sweet feather pillow of the foam and the essence of nutty, bold espresso. It was exquisite, *transcendent*. The liquid traced a line of warmth from my breast to my navel.

I closed my eyes and breathed in the stony ocean air of the city. The breeze ruffled my hair, shirtsleeves, and collar. For the next hour, I watched Venice awaken. I scribbled observations as the light changed. Everything was built shrugged up against everything else—in the best possible way—as if the buildings *wanted* to get closer, closer, closer. A stray cat wandered among the café tables, well fed and soft looking; I scratched its ears, already feeling less alone. And for a while after my cappuccino, I simply counted the tourists coming round the bend, so many of them walking hand in hand, as if this city compelled them to be in love.

And as I soon discovered, maybe it did.

I was on my eighth day in Venice when my life changed forever.

I was having lunch by the ferry terminal on the northern edge of the city, overlooking the island of Murano. The sea on this end was choppy, little boats bobbing as they zigzagged to and from other ports.

A refreshing wind, whispering of autumn, cooled the summer sweat on my lip and ruffled the pages of my notebook.

I was studiously writing and rewriting the third chapter of a novel. Ever since my first morning at the café, my veins had coursed with inspiration—but I'd been grappling with the direction of the book. The words didn't match the vision I had in my head, so I'd spent all day in a stifling pattern of rereading and tweaking.

My rescue was the arrival of the pizza I'd ordered—hot and gigantic and covered in prosciutto. I was still caught in a creative state, so as I cut into my meal with a knife and fork, I mentally indexed the jumbled, bustling features of the port: the gulls, ticket sellers, water taxi drivers, hurried locals. Details I would write about later.

My attention snagged on a harried man of about my age, sad looking and laden with bags. He had to have just arrived: his brow had a sheen of perspiration, his cheeks were crimson with vexation, and a lock of dark hair had fallen between his glasses and his eyes. The street was crowded with people disembarking a vaporetto, bodies shoving up against him—he was bulky as a bull with all his luggage—and I sensed his frustration even from afar.

As he came nearer to the stand of outdoor café tables, one of the bags slung over his shoulder swung forward, throwing him off balance. He stumbled and bumped my waterside table, causing my wineglass to topple over the street's edge into the sea.

"Oh. Oh no. I am so, *so* sorry," the man said, his American accent sounding out of place (was that how *I* sounded too?).

"I give you a nine out of ten," I replied. "You didn't quite stick the landing."

He didn't seem to like my joke. "Your wine! How much was it? I can pay you back." He dropped his bags where he stood—much to the irritation of a woman trying to squeeze around him—and pulled out his wallet.

"That's not necessary, truly." I tried to meet his gaze, but he was still wrestling with his money.

He was tall and lean, but the way he carried himself—a slightly ungraceful, self-conscious hunch—suggested a pensive complexity. Nothing like the boys I'd known before. He reminded me of an old stone well; I had the urge to peer inside him to see if I could spot the still water far below.

But that was silly.

Still, the man begged to be rescued, and I could use some company. "Look, obviously you're having a rough day. Why don't you just sit? Have some pizza."

His dark eyebrows pinched. "Seriously?"

With him standing so close, I noticed that behind the glare of his glasses, his eyes were blue green. "I mean, unless you have somewhere to be?"

"I don't." His tone was hesitant; he probably thought I was weird for offering.

"It just seems like you could use a rest." I took a casual bite of pizza. Committing to the idea, I added, "To be honest, I'd love some English-speaking company."

This declaration seemed to light him up. He met my eyes, finally. I'm not sure what he saw in them, but then—with a great deal of fumbling and chair moving—he settled his bags under the table and collapsed across from me with a groan of relief. "It feels good to sit."

"I'm glad." I slid my notebook into my purse and shifted my bottle of sparkling water, making room.

"You sure I'm not imposing?"

"Do I look like I was waiting for anyone?"

He regarded me, and he had this expression that made me feel like he was taking in more than just my tangled hair and creased blouse. "You could be," he answered.

A little flattered, I assured him, "I'm not."

"I'm sorry about your wine."

"Don't worry about it, that was my second glass."

"Then I ought to catch up." He smiled, but not in his eyes. I wondered why not.

"You're American?" I asked, back to eating.

He nodded. "Colorado. You?"

My pulse jumped. "Same," I said. "Denver."

"The Springs. What are the chances?" He shook his head, amused. "How long are you in Venice?"

"I don't have a plan. I'm just traveling."

"Alone?"

Perhaps it seemed risky to travel solo. And maybe it was, but here, I felt safer than I ever did at home. There were times I was frightened or uncomfortable or lost, but never did I experience the kind of physical danger as I did when my mother was drunk or when a customer followed me out to my car after a waitressing shift. There was something comforting about the anonymity of traveling by myself—*being* by myself. I liked feeling self-sufficient, going where I wanted when I wanted and relying only on myself, the only person I could trust.

I tried to sound nonchalant when I said, "Why not?"

"That's . . . brave," he said. "I admire that."

The word made me wince.

My leaving home had been driven primarily by fear. Fear of the life of hardship unfolding before me. Fear of becoming my mother. Fear of being locked into that life forever. When I received my inheritance from the father I'd never met—a man who'd ruined my mother's life to save his reputation—all I had wanted to do was run far away and never look back.

Leaving had been a desperate act. I didn't consider myself brave at all.

Still, a small, shriveled part of me swelled with his compliment.

The waiter came and greeted my new lunch guest, who ordered a pizza exactly like mine, plus two glasses of wine. "Whatever she was drinking," he added sheepishly.

"You didn't have to do that," I said when the waiter had gone.

"I did, I did." He waved off the topic.

"So, what about you? What are your plans for Venice?"

Raking the hair off his forehead, he said, "I'm actually on my way to Greece to meet a friend."

I knew a bit about Greece; my mother had dreamed of visiting the islands ever since Jackie Kennedy went in 1961.

"But I've always wanted to see Italy, so I figured I'd come early and stay a week before I head down." He paused. "How long have you been here?"

"I was in France all summer, then came to Venice a week ago," I answered.

"Do you love it?"

"I do."

His gaze roamed the port. "It's beautiful so far. Beautiful down to the atom."

His words pinpointed an unnamable quality I'd sensed all week. Venice *was* beautiful—on a deeper level than just its bridges and stone walkways and vaporetti. It was beautiful in the spaces that *weren't*: the air above the canals, the sky carved out by rooftops, the wafting scent of espresso and ocean minerals. It was evocative and storied, beautiful in its essence.

He went on. "I know it doesn't seem like I'm enjoying it so far, but the wheel on my luggage broke—so much for *that* invention—and going anywhere has been a slog, so of course I took a wrong turn and got lost, and *all I want* is to find my hotel so I can dump my bags . . . and now it probably makes sense why I'm all sweaty and clumsy and rambling."

Charmed, I offered a small laugh. "It's fine," I said. "I've had my own similar moments."

"It's nice to feel understood," he said, and his sincerity penetrated me like a bullet through glass, shattering my smooth facade.

I took a bite of pizza, made skittish by the intimacy of conversation. He seemed to grow self-conscious, too—the strangeness of connecting with a perfect stranger—so we both took a beat by pretending to have serious interest in an approaching vaporetto. It sat low in the water, bogged down with pedestrians, the engine *thrgg*ing as the waves slapped the prow.

"How has that boat not sunk?" he asked.

I giggled. "I have no idea."

He kept staring at the ferry with those gentle eyes. He had a narrow face with an exquisitely straight nose and beautiful, full lips. His forehead was creased slightly, not with concentration or even present frustration, just a downcast quality that seemed to emanate from inside. His shoulders were square, tipped forward with a charming awkwardness that made me want to tuck myself into his arms. He had delicate, fidgety hands and tousled hair that begged to be pushed into place.

Talking to him, looking at him, I forgot all about the men who had broken my heart before. Like a wave slipping over footprint-laden sand, he erased the damage. My heart pattered anew. *God*, I was a hopeless romantic of the truest form. But it was hard to hate myself for that while sitting across from him.

He caught me staring, and my focus darted off, coy as a cat.

Thankfully, our new wines arrived, skirting us past the red-handed moment, and he lifted his glass in a toast. "To chance encounters."

"To chance encounters," I repeated.

We clinked.

"I'm sorry, talk about rude—we've been sitting here for ten minutes, and I haven't even asked your name," he said.

"Ann," I answered, hoping he'd chalk my blush up to the warm sun on my face and not the warmer feelings under my skin. "Ann Fawkes."

He smiled, and this time it made it into his eyes, just a little. "Nice to meet you, Ann Fawkes. I'm Todd Langley."

MAGGIE

San Juan Island, Washington State, USA
Saturday, January 6, 2024

"Are you all right? You're frowning."

Maggie blinks. "I've read everything about you, and . . . I've never heard this story."

Ann sighs, a soft sound that fills the quietness of her home. "I never told anyone about Venice because Venice was *ours*."

Maggie leans back, digesting this. In addition to her enthrallment, she mourns the audio she's forfeited . . . but recalling Ann's infamous interview from 2000—and knowing that, even with her secrecy, Ann couldn't prevent the public damage—Maggie can understand why Ann tried to keep her relationship with Todd to herself. The public eye can be cruel and invading.

Maggie used to resent Ann for being so aloof with her fans, but now she sees her with a newfound clarity. "Thank you for telling me this. The real story." She sits forward, ready for more. "When you met him—did you sense that you had just met the love of your life?"

The corner of Ann's mouth flinches. "I didn't know anything back then." She stands. "I'm sure you're getting tired. Why don't you come back tomorrow morning? Ten o'clock. I'll order breakfast."

"Oh—yes. Thank you." Maggie gathers her things, worrying she hit a nerve. It's probably hard *not* to hit a nerve when asking Ann about Todd.

Out on the porch in the bitter evening air, Ann touches Maggie's arm, slender fingers squeezing. "I'm trusting you to keep what I've told you confidential."

"Of course." And she means it, not only because if Maggie repeated anything, Ann could easily discredit her, but also because Maggie wouldn't *want* to share any of what she just heard without Ann's consent. Ann gave her a gift today, and though she's not entirely sure *why*, Maggie isn't about to give it away . . . no matter how much she wants to. No matter how disappointed Grant will be.

When Maggie plugs her phone in at her B&B—it died hours ago, having wasted its battery trying to connect with Canadian cell towers—it erupts with notifications. Five calls, two messages, and six texts are from Grant; three texts are from Brit; and one text is from Tracey.

Maggie opens the text from her mother first.

10:17 a.m.: Good luck today. Be safe.

The texts from Brit are from this afternoon, all in the vein of Please respond soon, Grant is developing a stress hernia.

Maggie opens his texts, which are a series of short bursts increasing in intensity.

9:55 a.m.: Text me before you go in?
10:10 a.m.: I hope you arrived on time.
12:05 p.m.: Any word? Call me.
12:15 p.m.: YOU SAID YOU'D SEND UPDATES
1:44 p.m.: CALL ME BACK
3:32 p.m.: You better not be screening my calls.

Jennifer Gold

Maggie sighs as she listens to his frantic voice mails. It's six fifteen now—she grabbed some takeout in town and scarfed it down in her car before returning to the B&B—and she's sure he's still fretting. She despises his micromanagement. Before he hired her at *SBTS*, Maggie had known Grant casually, and it's that unprofessional familiarity paired with his know-it-all self-importance that makes their working relationship so infuriating at times.

Maggie has spent her entire career at *SBTS* trying to convince him that she's capable and qualified and trustworthy. On good days, she reminds herself that his dubiousness isn't personal, that it comes from a deep care for the work itself—but on bad days, it's a blow to her confidence. She'd hoped that this project would finally turn that tide, but apparently not.

Of course, when he finds out that Ann refused to be recorded, he'll be *justified* in his distrust. He'll have a reason to continue nagging Maggie at every turn—with not just this assignment but future projects as well.

If he assigns her *anything* after this.

Maggie types a message to Brit. Remind me why we chose to work for Grant?

Brit responds instantly. You're alive!

I'm on an island. In the woods. Farther north than Victoria, BC. Does he really expect my cell service to work at all times?

He worries. I worry.

He's a control freak. You're just being a good friend.

True, but . . . it's Ann Fawkes! We're all dying to know how it went.

Maggie swallows—hard. Sure, she's irritated. But she's also terrified of Grant's fury when he finds out how the day went.

Brit sends another text: You haven't responded with happy emojis yet, so I'm guessing it didn't go great.

Maggie lies down on the bed, propped up on her elbows. It was actually amazing, Maggie types, it's just—

Her phone starts ringing, interrupting the text before she can send it. Grant.

A pang of fear knocks inside her like a piano-key hammer striking a tight string; her head rings, and her diaphragm trembles. Sitting up, she shakes out her hands before she answers.

"Hello?" Her voice is a mile off from normal, sounding high and strained. She clears her throat and tries again. "Hello?"

"I asked you to check in first thing." His voice is frighteningly level. "Check in first thing. That's all I asked. Was that too hard for you?"

"I, uh . . ." In a panic, Maggie toggles away from the call and texts Brit. WHY.

She responds immediately: I texted him that you were alive, that's it. He was worried.

Well, I'm dead now.

"Maggie." His voice makes her jump.

"I'm sorry, my service is bad on the island. My phone died halfway through the day."

"And before that?"

"I was talking to Ann."

"I asked you to—"

"You don't trust me." Maggie's tone is accusatory; she can't help it. "Why hire me if you don't—"

"Is that what you think?" He sounds genuinely surprised, his voice going soft. "You're still green, Maggie, and you're not the only one with bosses breathing down your neck. Joy and Anita were on me all day about this, wanting updates I didn't have."

The executive producer, Joy, is a hard-ass. Anita, the creator and host of the podcast, isn't so bad . . . but Joy has a way of drawing Anita into her whirlpool of worry. Most of the time, they're great to work with—but this is a big story to hand over to an assistant producer and editor like Maggie, and she can only imagine the angst swirling around the small studio.

No wonder Grant was calling all day. She shudders to think of how he must've had to cover for her silence. "I'm sorry," she says. "Truly. I'll try to be more communicative."

"Yeah, well . . ." He sighs again. "It must've gone well for you to only be getting out of there now."

Maggie opens her mouth but hesitates. Not only will today's lack of material disappoint him, but Joy and Anita will be livid. If Maggie doesn't lose her job outright, she definitely won't get the producer title she's been striving toward.

She bites her cheek. She could keep this from him—try to fix it—but what if she fails anyway? Better to be honest than risk later fallout.

Still, it isn't easy telling her boss that the interview she'd begged him to let her run failed spectacularly.

"It went great," she hedges. Technically true. Ann was utterly mesmerizing—the details, the insights, the opening up—it was as unexpected and breathtaking as the northern lights. "But Ann got cold feet."

"What do you mean? Did she not tell you—"

"She told me a lot," Maggie says. "She told me about her early travels and how she first met Todd."

"What's the catch?"

"None of it is on tape."

"*What?*"

"Don't freak out," Maggie says, but she might as well be telling water not to be wet. Her only option is to push forward and explain.

"Ann was really edgy during the initial recording, even when I lobbed her soft questions. Then she outright refused to be recorded. Said she changed her mind. Kicked me out of her house. I almost gave up and called you, but I went back and banged on her door. She agreed to tell me her story without any audio or notes. I . . . I figured . . ." She hiccups, trying to get ahold of herself. "If I could just *listen*, she might change her mind. I wanted to give her a chance to loosen up. My hope is that . . . maybe . . . she'll agree to be recorded later."

Maggie expects shouting and wrath.

Instead, the line is silent—which is far more frightening.

She continues. "You have to know how much I love this job, Grant. I'm determined to make this right. I *will* make this right."

Am I about to get fired? That's all she can think. The piano strings in her chest are now ringing nonstop, a crescendo of nerves.

"Grant?" she squeaks. "Say something, please."

"Well done," he says finally.

She puffs out a quick breath. "Huh?"

"Well done, Maggie. I'm impressed."

"I . . . I don't follow."

"Most people would've left," he says. "You problem solved. It's not ideal, but at least we still have a foot in the door. And with Ann Fawkes, as notoriously elusive as she is, that's big."

Maggie wipes her cheeks with her palms. "But . . . Joy and Anita."

"I'll tell them it went swimmingly, because that's the truth. If they hear about this, they'll try to take control, and it'll spook Ann from the project completely. Ann apparently likes you, so better to leave you to it. But, Maggie, I can only protect you for so long. You have to turn this around."

"I know." Despite the daunting task ahead, she's flooded with relief. "I will."

"Good," he says. "There's one more thing."

"Yes?"

"Find some damned Wi-Fi and answer my texts."

The next morning, Maggie awakens early to the blue glow of an overcast sky. It's impossible to fall back asleep—her mother's words ring out in the silent room: *She's not a very trustworthy person, dear.*

Tracey has never been shy about expressing her unflattering opinions of Ann, but Maggie always chalked it up to jealousy. Though Keith rarely spoke of his famous client, it was clear he had thought of Ann as a little sister—Maggie could see why Tracey, one of his actual sisters, might take it personally.

But what if there's more to Tracey's distrust? How well *does* Ann know the Whitakers?

Maggie reaches for her phone and finds a missed text from her dad, sent earlier this morning: Hey sweetie. Just checking in. Classic Bob: kind, direct, unassuming.

But it's also classic Tracey to try to reach Maggie through someone else, especially amid a fight. Did Mom ask you to text me? Maggie types.

While she waits for his reply, she toggles over to a second missed message from . . . Barbara, Keith's wife. Maggie hasn't heard from Barbara in months, but when she reads over the message, she doesn't have to guess that Tracey's behind it. Your mother told me about the interview. How's it going? I'm here if you need anything.

Here for what? Moral support? Is Barbara against this interview too? From what Maggie's heard, Barbara and Ann always got along.

Before she can reply to Barbara, Maggie's phone vibrates, and a text from her father slides across the screen. Nope. I texted you all on my own. Don't like how we left things.

Maggie smiles down at the tiny thumbnail photo of her and the man who raised her, eating ice-cream cones. Regardless of who her biological parents are, she's always been close with her father. Keith might've been the head of the Whitaker family, a charismatic focal point around which everyone revolved—fun loving, easygoing, sincere, eclipsing everything else with his charm—but Bob has always been her number one. Steady.

This is a big opportunity for me, Maggie texts. Will you and Mom please try to see that?

A moment passes, and then: I'll try. We are proud of you.

His words are a momentary balm on her heart—then she toggles back to the thread with Barbara. Long time no talk! The interview is going well, she says, then adds, I hope you're doing well.

Barbara's home was once the family hub, the place where Keith grilled on the barbecue all summer and hosted holidays in winter. After Keith's death, the family events stopped, as if no one wanted to gather in his absence, perhaps for fear of noticing the hole in their lives. Poor Barbara, all alone in that big house now.

Maggie never asked Barbara about her role in Keith and Ann's friendship, but of course she must've been friends with Ann, too—even just by proximity. But when Maggie was little, something happened between Keith and Ann to make it all go sideways, and though he remained her acquaintance until the end, Ann all but removed herself from Keith's life. What caused the falling-out? What if that story—the story of Ann's involvement in Maggie's family—is the key to getting Ann to open up and move forward with the podcast?

Maggie sends a second text to Barbara: How well did you know Ann?

Slipping out of bed, she retrieves her laptop and recorder. A relisten to the botched interview from yesterday might help her prepare for what topics to handle more gently today.

Her thumb finds the power switch, but the lever is already in the on position. Perhaps she forgot to power down the recorder after Ann asked her to put it away. Frowning, Maggie attaches the USB cord. As the upload begins, her laptop lags. The file seems much larger than it ought to be, but it's a new recorder—Brit ordered it for this occasion— so maybe the files are just higher quality?

Maggie opts to take a shower, blow-dry her hair, get dressed, and indulge in a coffee courtesy of the B&B owners downstairs. The upload has barely made any progress by the time she returns to her room.

"That can't be right," Maggie whispers to herself.

She cancels the upload and tries again, but again, the file seems too huge. She doesn't have time to troubleshoot. She needs to leave for Ann's soon.

Maggie unplugs the recorder and tries the playback option instead.

Raw audio clip #3
MAGGIE: *Test, test, test. Okay.*

Raw audio clip #4
MAGGIE: *Can you introduce yourself?*
ANN FAWKES: *My name is Ann Fawkes. I'm—*

Maggie skips toward the end. She expects to hear their terrible argument before Maggie shut off the recorder, but instead she gets a few seconds of rustling and—*dinging*? It sounds like her car when the door is open and the keys are in the ignition.

Perplexed, she rewinds farther.

Voices—many voices. And Mexican music. Dishes clanking. It sounds like a pocket dial. She realizes it *is* a pocket dial—a purse recording. She hears herself ordering dinner, paying, exiting the restaurant, the dinging of her door, then silence.

With the power button left on, the record button must've been bumped. That explains the massive file. How much space did she waste recording the inside of her purse?

Horror claims her breath. *When did it turn on?*

Maggie rewinds again, skipping through swaths of rustling and a humiliating stint of her poorly but enthusiastically singing along to the radio in her car. She stops when she hears Ann's voice, not as crisp as the initial interview, but muffled.

"Oh, fuck."

ANN: *My heart pattered anew. God, I was a hopeless romantic of the truest form.*

Maggie skips back.

ANN: *I was on my eighth day in Venice when my life changed forever.*

"No," Maggie whispers. "No, no, no."

Ann trusted Maggie with her story, and here Maggie is, listening to the playback of their confidential conversation. From her purse, the recorder picked up *everything*. The audio isn't good—muffled, staticky, far away—but it exists.

Maggie drops the recorder as if it were burning. It clatters on the desk, and the red light starts blinking. *Sheesh.* With quivering fingers, she moves the power switch off.

It's a crime to record in-person conversations without the consent of all parties, at least in Oregon. She's not sure about Washington's laws. Is it illegal if it's an accidental pocket dial? Regardless of the legality, she should delete it. *Obviously.* Except: What if Ann eventually agrees to record her story? Can the audio retroactively be consented to?

She listens to a few clips, savoring. The thought of losing this material makes her choke.

Guilt and temptation slither up Maggie's arms and down her back. Either option presents its own form of discomfort: one moral and one of missed opportunity.

Maggie's phone chimes. Grant: You promised updates.

She checks the time: nine thirty. It's too early for you to nag me. I'm going to start charging you a quarter for every unnecessary text.

The SASS this morning, he responds, adding a smiley face.

She sends a shrug emoji.

Shelving her awful conundrum for the time being, Maggie triple-checks the off switch on the recorder, then slides it into an outer compartment of her purse. She arrives at Ann's house ten minutes early, still fretting. As she texts Grant that she's arrived, her fingers are sweaty and slippery on the iPhone screen, leaving smudges.

Alone in the quiet of her car, Maggie grips the steering wheel, forcing herself to take three deep breaths. She's overly hot in her sweater, the edges of it irritating the skin at her neck and wrists. She glances into the rearview mirror, checking her makeup, smoothing her hair.

Maggie never looked too out of place with the Whitakers. In a family of Irish coloring, Maggie has the freckles and coffee-colored hair to fit in. But her bright, blue-green eyes, full mouth, and defined bone structure are all her own. *Unrelated.* They're features of another family, a map to her identity that she can't decode.

Staring into her own eyes in the mirror, she finds her anxious face unrecognizable.

That startles her.

Or maybe she's startled by the sudden tapping on her window.

Through the glass, the morning glare obscures the person's features. She grabs her purse, opens the car door, and steps out. The man's face is pulled into a scowl.

"Can I help you?" she asks, perplexed.

He's about her age, slight, and good looking—from the chisel of his cheekbones to his gently hooded brown eyes. His unzipped jacket reveals a T-shirt with a logo she doesn't recognize—maybe a local restaurant?

He gestures to Ann's house. "She doesn't take visitors, so don't even try."

"She invited me."

"Yeah, right. How would you feel if fanatics camped out in your driveway?"

"I'm not lying. I have an appointment." She moves toward Ann's footpath, but he blocks her way. "Seriously?" she asks, trying to step past him.

He matches her steps, left, right, left, right. "Seriously."

Maggie's irritation grows. "Who *are* you?"

"What's going on out here?" Ann stands on her porch, dressed in all black save for a knee-length, open-front scarlet wool sweater.

The man's dark eyebrows pinch together. "I was just asking her to leave."

"She's with the podcast I told you about." A doting smile. "You didn't think I'd be eating all those pastries alone, did you, Matt?"

"You know I'm not one to judge," he says, his voice smooth as syrup. He offers a quick *sorry* to Maggie before bounding down to the delivery van parked on the street; the decal on the door matches the logo on his shirt. A bakery.

Without Matt standing in her way, Maggie walks up the path to Ann's porch, offering a sheepish smile. "He thought I was loitering."

"Wouldn't be the first time he scared someone away."

"Pastry delivery and part-time security?"

"Something like that."

Matt returns with a big white box, taking Ann's porch steps two at a time. "Apologies again for the rude introduction."

Maggie waves her hand. "It's fine."

Ann leans forward, grasping the box and kissing Matt's cheek in the process. "Thank you, Mattie."

He smiles, dimples puckering, then jogs back down the path to the van.

"Do people really come to your house to pry?"

Ann ushers her into the house. "I really only ever get fan mail, but after the news dropped about my story collection, a man came to my house and wouldn't leave. It frightened me. I called Matt, he scared the guy away, and now Matt is a little . . . overcautious."

"It's nice of him to look out for you."

Ann shrugs, setting the big white box on the coffee table. "The bakery is the closest thing to real French patisserie I've found out here on the island. Matt's father owned it, and, well, I eat a lot of pastries, so Matt gives me the special treatment."

Maggie sinks to the couch, allowing her purse to slide off her shoulder and onto the floor. There *must* be more to that story, but she doesn't ask. Instead, she texts Grant one last update while Ann pours their coffee from a thermal carafe. She also notices a reply from Barbara: Way back when, we were all friends. But that was a long time ago. A vague nonanswer, with wistfulness written between the lines.

"Something important?"

Maggie shakes her head, flicking the vibrate button on her phone. "My boss."

"Do they know about our agreement?"

"He's hopeful you'll change your mind about recording the interview," she answers, adding, "as am I."

"My apologies for disappointing you." She has a peculiar look on her face: a half-creased, curious expression that Maggie can't read. Ann gestures at the plate of pastries. "Please, help yourself."

Maggie selects a plain croissant, using her coffee cup's saucer to catch any errant crumbs. Ann stirs some cream into her mug, then selects her own pastry: a chocolate croissant. She lifts it to her lips and takes an indulgent bite.

She chews, then says, "Don't be shy, there's no graceful way to eat these."

Maggie takes a messy, crumbly bite of her own. A butter-rich interior meets her taste buds. "Yum," she says. "Thank you."

It's a simple thing—eating pastries—and yet Maggie finds herself forgetting about Grant, the accidental recording, even Barbara. Because she's having breakfast with her favorite author. Because her inner fangirl is swooning. The excitement wipes her mind clean, and she's just there, in the moment, sitting on Ann's couch, trying to savor every crumb she can.

Ann stares out at the ocean beyond the windows, a gray-green silk sheet. The sky is pillowy as a duvet. Her expression grows nostalgic, melancholy, her eyes glassy and her mouth drawn down. "I believe in my story I had just met Todd."

ANN

I instantly loved the name. "Todd," I said, trying it out. "Todd."

"Will it do?" he asked with a chuckle.

"Ha, yes, sorry. I'm being weird." I balled my fists in my lap.

"No, no, you're perfectly pleasant."

"It reminds me of that kids' movie that came out a few years ago," I said. "*The Fox and the Hound*. I think the fox's name was Tod."

His mouth twisted, and I knew I'd made things weirder. A children's movie? What was I thinking? Either the reference was lost on him, or he thought I was childish for bringing it up.

Time stretched; then he burst out, "*Copper*—that was the hound's name! I was trying to remember. Copper like your hair."

I glanced down at my red-brown tresses.

He laughed. "*God*, I bawled my eyes out at that movie."

"You did?"

"It's so sad, don't you remember? Two friends who shouldn't be friends?"

"I always found it sweet," I said. "I *wish* I had a friend like that."

He glanced away—*yep, too weird*—but then gestured to the vaporetto, which was struggling against the choppy waves with a new crowd of passengers. "I was thinking about exploring Murano this afternoon. Care to join me? If you have nowhere to be, that is."

His invitation surprised me. Maybe he liked weird.

"No pressure," he went on. "It's just nice to have company, you know?"

"I'd love to," I said. "There's a glass museum there that I haven't seen yet."

"Then it's decided." He leaned back as his pizza was set down. When the waiter was gone, Todd appraised the uncut circle of dough and whispered conspiratorially, "Does everyone here eat with a knife and fork, instead of slices?"

"From what I've observed," I said, matching his tone. "I find it a little easier, anyway, when the crust is soft and thin like this."

He wielded his utensils. "Then you've saved me from looking stupid yet again, Ann Fawkes."

"It isn't an easy job, but someone has to do it." His face went blank, and I worried the joke was too harsh, but then he was laughing, and it was the nicest sound—lilting and melodic—and especially wonderful knowing that I had caused it.

"You're clever," he said.

I sipped my wine to conceal the gigantic grin on my face, but Todd was already preoccupied with his pizza. A lock of thick hair fell across his face, and his glasses slid down his nose ever so slightly as he sawed the dough.

Silence settled as we ate and drank and soaked up the warmth of the day. Summer was holding on for dear life, heat and light reflecting off the water.

If I didn't think too hard, it felt natural to sit across from Todd. His company was steady and amiable. We talked on and off, and though we were both clearly self-conscious about having lunch together when we didn't really know each other, the conversation and quiet fit together with no real forcing.

When we finished, Todd insisted on paying for the whole table, a point we argued for a good five minutes before I finally relented. After the waiter pointed Todd in the direction of his hotel—just one block from where we sat, a fact that gave us both a hearty laugh—I waited at the table for him to check in and leave his bags.

As I stared at the alleyway down which he'd turned, a sad panic rose inside me. What if he didn't come back? People, I had learned, were mostly ephemeral.

I lit a cigarette and sucked through it almost continuously; I was about to light another when Todd arrived with a camera bag slung over his shoulder.

"All set?" he asked.

I pocketed the unlit smoke, concealing my relief as we wandered over to the little terminal, bought tickets, and waited in line for the vaporetto.

On board, the plastic seats were hard and narrow. Todd wanted me to take the window so I could watch the water during our crossing. He sat with his hands on his knees and glanced over my shoulder at the view. The heat of his arm, hip, and leg made my skin tingle; when the boat shifted, our bodies would bump ever so briefly, igniting my senses.

Away from the shelter of land, the breeze grew wild, sea spray lifting into the air. Todd's hair ruffled and danced, and when he caught me looking, he ran a hand through it. My fingers curled as I imagined tracing the same path.

As we docked at Murano Colonna, he asked, "Do I look like Einstein now?"

"Not quite as manic," I answered.

"I'll take it."

We disembarked in a cluster of passengers, the crowd dispersing as we transferred from dock to solid ground. Todd veered right, using his long legs to get ahead of the more sluggish tourists. I jogged to keep up, delighting in how the day was unfolding.

Around a corner, we were greeted by a narrow walkway with restaurants and venetian glass galleries. Todd's pace slowed, and we walked shoulder to shoulder, soaking it in. Peach- and lemon-colored buildings with teal shutters and overflowing planter boxes rose above us. The street was bisected by a narrow canal, where moored boats tested their tethers. Occasionally, one of us would point out a particularly shiny water taxi or pause on an arching bridge to admire the street in the sum of all its parts.

After ten minutes of companionable quiet, I glanced up at Todd, wanting to hear his voice again. "So, what do you do back in Colorado?"

His whole body seemed to frown. "Oh, accounting, mostly," he said, too absently for the way his chest caved at the question. He didn't give me a chance to pry: "What about you?"

"I'm a waitress—*was* a waitress. At a gentleman's club. I quit before I came to Europe."

His nose wrinkled, and maybe he was judging me, but then he said, "Sounds harsh."

"It wasn't so bad. The money was good."

We passed under the humid awning of an outdoor café. A waiter invited us to sit, but we kept walking, squeezing past the clustered chairs.

"The job wasn't why I left the US," I continued. "My mom's an alcoholic. A mean one. And even when I moved out, it's not like I lived in the best part of town. I was just . . . stuck."

I dared a glance at his face, worried that I had said too much. Yet something compelled me to keep talking. "Then . . . well, I came into money. Unexpectedly. My father—I never met him—he died and left me a large sum. I found out that he'd been sending my mom money for years, money she pissed away." I thought of all the lean Christmases, the dreams of college I'd given up, the water shutoff notices taped to our door. "I didn't hesitate—just bought a one-way ticket to France and didn't look back. Probably not the wisest decision, but I figured I'd work on a novel." There was something safe about Todd. Comforting. I'd never confided in someone that way before; the words just tumbled out.

"Wow," Todd said after a moment. "I'm in awe."

I cringed inwardly, embarrassed by the lift his words gave me. My heart felt like a hot-air balloon, his kindness the fueling flame.

I changed the subject. "So . . . accounting?"

"For my parents' business," Todd said, that subtle grimace returning to his lips. "I'm sorry—it's not the most interesting thing. Can we talk about something else?"

I searched for a hint in his expression as to why he didn't want to talk about it. Were his eyes glassy, or was that the sun reflecting off his lenses? "What islands will you visit in Greece?"

"Mykonos, then Santorini. Maybe one more."

"My mother always dreamed of visiting Mykonos, but I don't know much about Greece," I admitted.

"Me neither," Todd said. "The trip was my buddy's idea."

Eventually, we came to a giant intersection of waterways. A huge metal bridge spanned the main canal; according to our map, the Museo del Vetro was just across. We paused at the bridge's apex, where we could see taxis puttering from all directions and boats tied up along the curved sidewalks. I leaned on the railing, and Todd leaned beside me, and there was a quiet contentedness that seemed to haze around us. I had never felt content with anyone before. I closed my eyes and breathed in the scent of stone and iron, happy.

When I opened my eyes again, I said, "It's so beautiful, isn't it?"

"It is," Todd said, but he wasn't beside me any longer.

I turned around and made eye contact with his lens; the camera clicked.

"Hey!" I said, but my heart pirouetted.

Todd lowered the camera from his face. "Don't you want to remember this day?"

I was quick to nod. "Do you want one of you?"

"Sure." He slipped the camera into my fingers.

We switched places, and I raised the camera to my face, admiring him through the viewfinder. He self-consciously adjusted his glasses and ran a hand through his hair, then stood tall, resting a hand on the rusty railing behind him. I began counting—*"One, two . . ."*—and he smiled a faux camera-smile, tight lips and vacant eyes. *"Three!"*

I pressed the button with a click. Then Todd was at my side again, taking the camera and sliding it back inside its case.

"Thank you," he said, eyes crinkling, and *there*. There was the smile I had *wanted* to capture. But it was too elusive, too fleeting. "Let's find the museum, hmm?"

When I explored the Louvre earlier that summer, I had gone alone. I told myself it was ideal, because I could linger at a piece as long or as little as I wanted. But at museums, I often got the urge to show a companion a detail in the paint or read an especially captivating plaque out loud. What good was art without someone to discuss it with you?

At the Museo del Vetro, Todd was all ears. Underneath massive, dustless chandeliers, we lingered over the prettiest perfume vials, pointed to our favorite beads, and waved at ourselves in historic mirrors. We stayed until closing.

"That was amazing," I said as we stepped out into the waning sunshine. "Thank you for inviting me to Murano."

"Thank *you* for the company."

Back near the large bridge, we paused at an outdoor restaurant for an aperitif and debated which modern glass sculpture had been the strangest. One drink turned into two, which turned into dinner, and we kept talking until the sunset sky faded to lavender and reflected in the canal.

I'd never met a man who didn't look distracted while I talked, who didn't glance at my chest, other women, or vehicles speeding by. When I sat across from Todd, he gave me all his attention. He didn't make me feel like the only person in the world—rather, he made me feel like the only person in the world worth listening to.

As I'd grown up convinced that I was nothing special, his sincerity meant *everything*.

After dinner, we wove along the charming streets and learned all the basic things we had in common: we were both only children, both fans of Fleetwood Mac, both loved the color blue. I wanted so badly to ask him if he had a girlfriend or if he'd ever been in love, but I didn't have the courage.

We ducked inside one of the many souvenir shops, ogling expensive vases and intricate figurines. I fell in love with a small glass horse the color of a tropical ocean. It had a funny ear, and the barrel of its body was filled with tiny air bubbles.

"Let me buy it for you," Todd said.

As the shopkeeper bundled it up in many layers of newspaper, I tried to stifle my overwhelming joy that Todd had bought me a gift.

On the vaporetto to Venice, I gave Todd the window seat and watched him watch the waves all the way back. The port was dark when we disembarked, and I fidgeted with the strap of my purse, not wanting the night to end. I would take him to my room if he wanted—I was naive enough to think that perhaps if we slept together, it wouldn't be so easy for him to leave.

"There's a great gelato place near my hotel." Slightly embarrassed by the insinuation carried in my words, I added, "Unless you really hate gelato?"

His forehead pinched—a strange response to my joke—but he said, "Gelato sounds great."

The walk was slow and hushed; I could hear him breathing. The air had cooled considerably, and we both seemed to instinctually move closer, our arms brushing every so often. We lingered on the occasional bridge, watching the water glisten below the intimate lights of apartments and restaurants that rose high above the liquid blackness. Sometimes a water taxi would cruise under us, humming through the calm.

There were couples everywhere: making out against railings, kissing wrists across dinner tables, holding hands as they meandered past us. I wanted to hold Todd's hand, but I didn't have the nerve. We'd spent the entire day together, but something about the darkness, the romance of the water, and the slippery sound of waves caressing hulls made me shy.

"Here it is," I said. From the back of the gelato line, we watched the tourists ahead of us point to flavors. "What's your favorite?"

Todd dipped his shoulders my way, speaking low. "What do you recommend?"

He was close enough that I could smell the soap on him—something like citrus or lemongrass. "Well, you're in Italy, so you have to try pistachio. Stracciatella is a classic too."

"What's that?"

"Cream with chocolate shavings. Simple, but good."

"Sounds like a winner to me."

"But you have to do two flavors. That's what I've heard. At least two, otherwise you're weird."

His chuckle was mostly breath. "Seriously?"

"An Italian woman told me that." I imitated her accent: "'Pick many flavor, because why not.'"

"'Because why not,'" he repeated. "Good advice."

I glanced at his lips, reveling in the way their mauve color bloomed into red where they parted, like the intense pigmentation of a flower at its center. "It's a good motto."

"Buona sera." The young man behind the counter waited expectantly.

I fumbled through our order in broken Italian, two cups with three flavors each: pistachio, stracciatella, and chocolate. I insisted on paying. "A thank-you for the pleasant day," I explained to Todd as we left.

Again, he smiled that smile that refused to reach his eyes. I began to wonder if something had happened in Colorado, some sort of heartbreak that made him so reserved despite the kindness and light clearly flickering inside him still. I wanted to ask but didn't.

We found a bench by the water and sat, picking at our gelato in silence.

"What do you think?" I asked, pointing with my wooden spoon. "Do you have a favorite?"

"Pistachio is good, but I have to say stracciatella," Todd said. "You?"

"Pistachio. I love the salt."

He nodded slowly, watching a water taxi buzz by. His demeanor had changed as the sun went down, growing subdued. I wasn't sure how to pull him out of it. Had I said or done something wrong?

Eventually we finished our cups, stood, and moseyed along the canal.

Hoping to reignite the connection we'd experienced earlier, I piped up. "Have you ever been somewhere tropical?"

He glanced down at me, questioning.

"I was just thinking about the glass horse you bought me. The teal color reminds me of a postcard."

"Oh yeah, it does."

"So . . . ?" I spread my hands in question.

"Hawaii," he answered.

"Was the water really that blue?"

"In some places." His gaze was distant. "Have you been anywhere tropical?"

I shook my head. "I want to, though. Maybe I'll do that next. Tahiti, perhaps."

"Tahiti?"

"Yeah, French Polynesia. South of Hawaii?"

"I know where it is." He bumped me with his shoulder, a playful nudge. I hoped this was a sign that he was warming up again. "I just mean, Why Tahiti?"

I shrugged. "Seems like a cool place, that's all." We turned down my side street. "If you could go anywhere, where would you go?"

"Tahiti."

I giggled. "Seriously."

"I'd visit Thailand."

"Thailand?"

"Yeah, it's south of China."

"I know where—" I cut myself off. "Very funny."

He bumped me with his shoulder again.

"What about Thailand appeals to you?" I asked.

"The temples," he said. "And there's a hospital for logging elephants and elephants whose feet have been blown up by land mines left over from the war. I'd want to see them."

"That's . . . really sad," I said.

"I heard about it on PBS and immediately wrote them a check."

His compassion made my heart squeeze.

We walked another half block, and then I halted. "Oh, that's my hotel," I said, pretending I hadn't realized our proximity until that moment.

"Oh."

I stared into his shadowy eyes. I wanted to ask him up, but I hedged. "I'm glad I met you, Todd Langley. This was a nice day."

"I agree."

"It's funny, had the wheel on your bag not broken, we might've never—"

"I can't do this, Ann."

"Do what?"

He touched my arm—in pity? Regret? "I'm not going upstairs with you. Maybe I'm being presumptuous, but it seems like that's where tonight is headed, and I just can't. Today has been great, but I think we should just leave it at that."

The sounds of the street—water lapping, boats motoring, people laughing—hushed. All I could hear was my own breathing, the rapid intake of my disappointment and hurt. "'Leave it at that'?" I asked, my throat thick.

He nodded, bent down, and kissed my cheek. "Please hear my sincerity when I say that it was a pleasure meeting you, Ann Fawkes."

If you sincerely enjoyed today, why cut it short? I wanted to ask, but I couldn't. My mouth was full of dust. My cheek burned where he'd kissed it.

I watched him go, his hunched shoulders bobbing down the street, the night making his outline turn silvery, then black. He crossed a bridge, then another, not looking back. Then he disappeared around a bend, and suddenly the night felt so cold, and tears pricked the corners of my eyes at the unbearable thought that I'd never see him again—and I didn't even know why.

ANN

In my hotel room, I pressed my lips together, my face hot.

I'd met Todd ten hours ago—*ten hours*. Logic told me that I shouldn't feel rejected, but I did. It was different from the rejections in France or the acute disappointments of my childhood—it was raw. I sank to the bed with a soft, involuntary wail.

This was stupid. I was being naive. This was just another heartbreak in an endless parade of heartbreaks. I didn't *know* him . . .

. . . and yet I couldn't ignore the sense that I was *supposed* to know him. I had never felt so at ease with another person. Content. Had I been wrong in thinking the magnetism was mutual?

Convinced that my frantic attraction was a sign of weakness, I was determined to climb above the ache, so I did the one thing that always helped me process my feelings: I wrote.

I spilled my heart upon those pages; the words tore and shredded. I uncorked a bottle of wine. I lit a cigarette, then another. I didn't edit; I didn't look back. Writing my emotions—abstract and nonsensical as they were—was the only way to pacify their urgency.

Thinking about Todd, and love, and disappointment also got me thinking about my mother. She'd been a quotation clerk on Wall Street before my father fired her to cover up their affair. How scary it must've been to raise a baby by herself.

Hardship made my mother irresponsible and mean spirited, but she wasn't a bad woman. She continually dated the wrong men, men who tore down her self-esteem. But at her core, she was an all-out romantic—always heartbroken over the world—and I think that's why she drank. I can't say I fault her for that. Loneliness could turn a person into a caged, hungry dog, growing wilder by the night.

Inside my own inebriated fog, I finally understood: alcohol put the dog to sleep.

As I wrote, I imagined my mother's life through a new lens and wove a story that was true and not true, her and not her, me and not me. I followed the story like a raft on a river, my emotions the undercurrent but the sights all new.

My creative urgency didn't last, though.

On the fifth day of my bender, I realized that as much as I liked the foggy productivity of being drunk in my hotel room, an abyss was opening up underneath me. I could hear my mother's voice in that abyss, calling me down, and I didn't want to join her. I set down my pen and drank three glasses of water. I spent my sixth and seventh days hungover and creatively blocked, staring at a blank notebook page as if I could *will* words onto it.

Doubt crept in, as melancholy as molding fruit. The rot led me to call my mother.

I'd checked in only twice that summer, and both instances, she had been hammered. Our conversations had been superficial and unfocused, like getting a whiff of the tar I'd spent my whole life stuck in. By leaving, I had freed my limbs of the sticky, awful life I'd had before.

But Mom was still the only person who'd understand the cloying sorrow that Todd had left behind.

I crept downstairs to the hotel lobby and convinced the night manager to let me use the phone. It was eleven in the morning in Colorado. When Mom answered, the sound of her hit me square in the chest. When she wasn't inebriated, she had a clear, feminine voice, like Glinda the Good Witch from *The Wizard of Oz*.

"Mom?"

"Annie?"

I was so far from home. So, so far.

"Is everything all right?" she asked.

A man's voice rumbled in the background, asking if she wanted rocks in her drink. She told him yes.

"Annie?" she prompted, sipping audibly, ice clanking.

"Hi, Mom," I said. "I'm in Italy."

"Is something wrong?"

We weren't close enough for me to just call. My heart fractured just a little, a delicate hairline crack. "No, nothing wrong."

"Really?" Another mumble from the man, a slight giggle from my mother.

"Mom, I think . . . I don't know what I think, actually. I met a man."

I explained Todd all in one big rush of breath: how we'd spent a day together, and how I'd felt such a strong connection to him, and how I realized—just on this phone call—that perhaps I ought to go to Greece to find him. Was that totally crazy?

"I'm being crazy, right?" The irony was not lost on me that I was asking my *mother*—she wasn't exactly an expert in relationships. But at least she was a dreamer.

There was a long pause before she said, "Greece, huh?"

I'd been so focused on Todd that I hadn't considered the Greece part of the conversation. I cringed, thinking she might be angry or hurt that her daughter was living the fantasy she'd spent so long aching for—to find love on an Aegean beach.

"Mykonos, actually."

"*Oh,*" she breathed wistfully. "Like Jackie."

"Is that where she went?" I asked, but of course I knew; I just didn't want to admit the full extent of my thoughtlessness. I waited, my teeth clenched. Instinctively, I held the phone away from my head, expecting a shout.

But my mother surprised me. "Annie, you must go to Greece. You *must.*"

"I—you're not angry?"

"*Angry?*" She sounded so surprised—but then again, her sober self might not have known the depth of her drunken cruelty. I heard her take another clanking sip and realized it must've been her first drink of the day. A screwdriver, probably.

"Hasn't Greece always been *your* dream?"

"A mother can live vicariously through her daughter, dear. Go to Greece. One of us ought to, and you're already so close."

A brief flash of empowerment darted through me like a hornet—and then a sting of doubt followed. "But . . . this isn't just about Greece. It's about Todd. Am I crazy for trying to track him down?"

I should note here, Maggie, that I had forgotten the magnitude of my mother's romanticism. I'd forgotten that she was even more senti-mental than I was, at least within the context of men and true love. So when she said what she said next, it bowled me over like a bus through an intersection—I didn't see it coming.

"Life is about risk, Annie, and there's no better risk than love."

My mother: she could be wise—when she wasn't a complete and utter mess.

I wiped the moisture from my eyes, stunned by the smack of her sentiment.

"Do it. Go to Greece. Track him down. Make the grand gesture. Then tell me all about it, all right? Take pictures."

"All right," I said, still uncertain, but I owed her this, at least. I owed her pictures of Mykonos.

She giggled again, and I heard kissing.

"I'll let you go," I said.

"Oh! While I have you: Can you send money? I'm behind on some payments."

"Payments for what?" Before I left, I had paid off her double-wide and car, and given her a sizable nest egg.

"Just little things. Phone, utilities."

The fracture in my heart filled with liquid heat. "I don't understand. How could you possibly be behind?"

"I spent it all."

"You—*what?*"

The night manager of the hotel—who had been reading on the couch in the tiny lobby—was watching me now. She probably sensed that the conversation had turned sour, even if some of the English was gibberish to her. I turned away, hunching over the receiver, trying not to make a scene. I felt like a dirty, low-life American—like I was sullying the elegance of this place.

Mom explained, "I gave Bill some funds so he could start his own car shop. But he's still getting things set up, so—"

Fuming, I growled into the phone: "I left you *fifty thousand dollars!*"

"Don't sound so smug," my mother hissed.

Just like that, all the connection I'd been craving drained out through my feet, leaving me brittle. "But how could you have spent it *all?*"

"*Excuse* me?" she said, and suddenly her voice was no longer Glinda the Good Witch—it was wicked. "All your money should've been mine. *All of it!* The sacrifices I made for you, the freedom I lost. Don't you dare scold me for asking for more of it, while you . . . you . . . *whore around* in Europe. While you steal *my* dream. Don't. You. Fucking. Dare."

There she was. The mother I knew so well.

"Dad sent you plenty over the years," I bit out. "This just proves that I was right! That even with that small fraction of *my* money, the money that he left *me*, you're too goddamn irresponsible to make any use of it."

"I'm irresponsible?" My mother barked out a single, cruel laugh. "Look where you are, Ann. Look around and tell me you're not a hypocrite."

My shoulders quivered with rage, with hurt. "You can't blame me for running away from my shithole of a life."

"You're right," my mother said, but her voice was slippery and mean. "I blame myself. I blame myself for raising such a little—"

I hung up. Or rather, I dropped the phone into the cradle.

My ears were ringing, my cheeks burned, and my eyes blurred with tears. I swiped a knuckle under my nose and slipped off the chair. Calmly, I thanked the night manager for letting me use the phone. Then I slunk back to my room.

The next morning, I packed my things.

I would wire my mother more money, but then that was it. She wouldn't get another dime from me, no matter how much she thought she deserved it. No matter how much she cursed or yelled. That morning, I promised myself that I would never go back to Colorado.

Instead, I was going to Greece.

I came up with a million excuses not to go—most of them relating to me seeming obsessive, stalkery, or immature—but despite my mother's wrath, she was right: life was about taking risks. And what else would I do? I had no home, no plan, nowhere else to be. Of all the people I wanted to talk to, to find comfort in, Todd was it. If I found him in Greece and he told me he never wanted to see me again, I would respect that. But first I had to try, because if I didn't, the endless wondering would eat me alive, and I would regret it for the rest of my life.

Those stakes were too high to ignore.

I don't know how else to explain it, other than to say: I just had a *feeling*. And remember what I said about feelings, Maggie? Going to Greece was no less than divine intervention.

ANN

My mother kept a magazine cutout of Jackie Kennedy and Petros the Pelican in Mykonos on her fridge. I didn't know what to expect beyond that, but by the time I arrived on the island—after missed trains and bumpy flights and lost baggage—all I hoped was that my room in Mykonos Town was better than the sketchy airport hotel in Athens.

My cab driver from port—chatty and proud, with not a lick of English—dropped me off at the very upper edge of Old Town. A steep, narrow sidewalk descended from the road into a cluster of white stucco buildings; a half mile down the slope, small boats bobbed in a quaint bay. In the intense sun, the ocean rippled silver-white, and the town shone bright against the dusty russet land. I was on Mars, and I'd just discovered a spectacular, alien paradise.

I raised the cheap camera I'd bought in Athens and snapped a photo of the otherworldly landscape, thinking of my mother. *She could have come.* Rather than blowing her money on a man, she could've traveled with her daughter and shared in the wonder. The realization was a lead ball resting in the pit of my stomach, the size of a pea but the weight of the moon. I had never thought to invite her along with me on my travels—but then again, my mother had had *years* of opportunities to change her circumstances and done nothing. What was the point of having a dream if she didn't seize it the first chance she got, like I had?

I tucked the camera back into my purse. A hot, dry wind swirled red dust around my ankles. Overlooking the town, I unfolded a map and tried to decipher the streets ahead, but Mykonos was a maze. Aside from the wide bayside square far below, the squiggly walkways were impossible to track—even on paper.

I shoved the map into my pocket, hefted my luggage, and started blindly down the hill, the steepness jolting my ankles. Beneath the intense sun, I grew damp under my arms and breasts. The path eventually angled into the labyrinthine streets by way of a narrow cobblestone alley. The pavers here were outlined with sealant, resembling a gray-and-white version of giraffe spots. Charmed, I kept trudging—then the alley opened up.

I halted.

The street before me was out of a storybook. Smooth, railless stair-cases led up to second-story balconies, where lush shrubbery spilled from planter boxes. Massive bougainvillea trees dazzled with magenta blooms, swaying in the Aegean breeze. Nearby, a black cat was coiled on a stoop, its eyes closed. From the freshly swept street to the clean walls to the sweet perfume of jasmine, none of it seemed real. Mykonos wasn't Mars—it was Eden.

I raised my camera and snapped another photo.

By the time I made it to the water, my blouse was drenched in sweat and my hair clung to the back of my neck. I had indulged many dead ends, and my shoulders ached from my heavy bag, but none of that mattered in light of the beauty all around me.

A domed Orthodox church—named Agios Nikolaos, according to my map—was at the square's center, casting a long shadow in the after-noon sunlight. A wide street followed the half moon of the small bay, where cerulean-hulled boats bobbed on crystalline water. Silver-blue schools of tiny fish shimmered like sequins on the fringes of the ocean's skirts. The air had a fresh mineral quality, like basalt.

A few buildings down, a pair of middle-aged men chatted at an outdoor café table, tall glasses filled with a milky-looking beverage on the rocks. They glanced my way, their gazes brief and barely interested. I was sure I stood out, with my clumsy bags and pit-stained shirt, but my anonymity was my armor. It always had been.

My hotel had, at one time, probably been someone's home. Inconspicuous, it had merely a small sign over the door in Greek lettering. The receptionist there greeted me as soon as I walked in.

"*Yassas.* Miss Ann?" She was a rotund older woman with thick eyebrows and a downcast mouth.

"That's me."

She led me up a steep, rather claustrophobic staircase. My room was tiny but very neat and smelled of citrus cleaner. Double doors—which led to a private balcony—were pinned open, and a warm breeze wafted in.

"Happy?" the woman asked, her Greek accent obscuring the word.

Had I ever been happy? I knew that wasn't what she was asking, but still, I couldn't bring myself to squeak out an affirmative. "Thank you," I said instead.

Alone in the privateness of my new, temporary home, I sank to the bed, then lay back. I closed my eyes, and little tears seeped out of their seams. It'd taken two days to get here, and I still didn't know if it'd been the right decision. Despite the beauty of Mykonos Town, I was still alone. I had no idea how I would find Todd in this place, but I wanted to know why he had left.

I wanted to know why people always left.

The next thing I knew, the room was dark, and I was ravenous.

The analog on the nightstand was set to 10:15 p.m. I doubted this quaint, sleepy town would have late-night dinner options, but I hoped I could at least find the Greek version of a 7-Eleven to satiate my need for food, any food, ASAP. I pulled a skirt over my hips, draped a shawl across my back, and hurried down the dark staircase, slipping out into the warm-breeze night.

The bay had been quiet even at midday, so I opted to start in the opposite direction. My stomach gurgled, a sound that seemed to echo down the long pathway ahead. Few people were out this late, mostly Greeks sitting on balconies and foreigners whispering in hushed tones. I tried stopping a duo of men to ask for directions, but they spoke only Spanish.

Nearing the western edge of town, though, I heard faint commotion: laughter, music, gleeful shouting. I followed the sound until the tangle of streets opened into a narrow waterfront walkway. The music grew louder, rattling and blasting in a crescendo of quick dance beats. To my surprise, I had happened upon a stretch of clubs. Low lights illuminated the immediate area outside various open doors, and different songs clashed. Clusters of people mingled on the street, gesturing and chatting in a jumble of languages.

My stomach gurgled.

A trio of blonde women in doll-size spandex outfits were walking toward me, chatting indistinguishably between giggles.

"Excuse me," I said, flagging them down.

They veered closer, fawn legs stumbling on stilt-high heels.

"Does anyone speak English?" I asked.

One with pixie hair stepped forward. "I speak."

"Do these clubs sell food? Or is there a convenience store nearby?"

She adjusted her miniskirt, tugging down the stretchy fabric where it had ridden up her thighs. "You look for food?" A German accent.

"Yes! Yes, food," I said.

"There's food inside, you come." She grabbed my hand; hers was hot and clammy, with a strong grip.

"Okay," I said, already being yanked along.

Once we were in step, she looped her arm through mine, her friends trailing. "I am Cindy," she said in my ear. Her breath smelled of licorice.

"Ann," I said. "Are you German?"

"*Ja!* Holiday from Germany." She held my arm tighter. "You are American." She whispered it like a dirty secret.

"I am," I said, equally conspiratorial. She was so drunk and I was so sober that I couldn't help but giggle. She giggled, too, and soon the four of us were all arm in arm, laughing like schoolgirls.

They took me to a loud club full of slick, dancing bodies. Cindy led me toward the bar, while the other two disappeared onto the dance floor. Leaning against the cool countertop, Cindy flagged down the bartender and ordered us each a glass of ouzo. It came out on the rocks, milky white in the dim lighting. I'd never tried ouzo. I sniffed, Cindy laughed, and we clinked glasses. The flavor was more botanical than I had thought, and it explained the licorice I'd smelled on Cindy's breath.

"You like?" Her hand grazed my lower back.

"It's good. Is there food here?" I glanced around, trying to spot anyone else eating, but the place was filled with dancers, the tables all pushed to the periphery.

"Yes, food." She smiled.

I wondered if it was a translation error, but then Cindy's lips were on my neck. Startled and a little ticklish, I pushed her away more roughly than I had intended. "I'm sorry," I said, touching her shoulder. "You startled me."

"I like you," she said, leaning in again, but I held her at arm's length.

"Oh, Cindy, I'm sorry." I glanced around, noticing only then that we were surrounded by same-sex couples.

Her eyebrows pinched. "You . . . men?"

I nodded.

A pout formed on her face, scrunching her lips, nose, forehead. She didn't wait for me to explain or apologize further; she stormed off.

My face grew hot with remorse; I should've been gentler in my rejection, but I'd been so caught off guard I hadn't really had time to think. I sighed, hoping Cindy wouldn't remember me in the morning.

I was still hungry, and tired, and travel worn. For the first time, it occurred to me that perhaps Todd had lied—perhaps he wasn't here at all. I threw back my ouzo, wanting to dull my edges. Couples were all around me, partying, kissing, laughing. I swayed a little to the beat, trying to soak up the giddy energy, but it wouldn't permeate. The bartender returned but didn't seem to understand my request for food, so with my stomach still gurgling, I paid for the drinks and left.

I decided to duck into a second club—I was hungry enough that I'd check every bar on the island if I had to. The crowd was thinner and the music not so loud, but there was still a party. More gay couples danced here, too, unabashed and blissfully drunk. The joyful vibe filled the place like helium.

I wove through the crowd, craning my neck to see if I could glimpse food on any of the tables that encircled the dance floor. When I reached the bar in the back of the room, I spotted a patron at the counter eating a plate of potato wedges.

"Oh, thank god." I slid onto the stool beside him. The ouzo had reached my blood by this point, and I forgot to be polite or ask what language he spoke. "Did you get those here?"

"Indeed I did," he said.

"Oh! An American." Relief flooded my veins—I don't know why. The ouzo had me all topsy turvy.

"Want some?" The man pushed his plate toward me.

"I'll order my own, thanks," I said, adding, "I'd eat all yours."

He beckoned the bartender. "Want a drink too?"

I shook my head.

After calling the order into the kitchen, the bartender delivered an empty rocks glass and a bottle of flat water; I drank two full cups, hoping my buzz would subside with hydration.

The man beside me leaned over. "So, what brings you here, ah—I'm sorry, what is your name?"

"Ann."

"Ann," he repeated. "You don't seem like the partying type."

I assessed his appearance, the curled russet hair and the soft collar of his polo. "Neither do you." He had a strong, wide jaw; thin lips; and earnest eyes—features that were at once commanding and kind.

He leaned in. "I'm not a homophobe, if that's why you're being vague."

I pivoted toward him, adjusting my seat so we could talk more directly. "That's good, but I'm straight. Is this island *known* for the gay bars? I had no idea."

"Apparently it is," he said, sipping his drink. "I hadn't the slightest idea either. Came here with a friend to let loose and—excuse the bluntness—hoping for a couple of one-night stands." He shrugged. "No such luck, here—unless *you're* interested?" His innocent grin made it clear he was being funny.

"Nice try," I said, shoving his arm.

My food was delivered and I dug in, not caring when the potatoes burned my tongue.

The man chuckled. "You weren't lying about being hungry."

"Nope," I said, mouth full.

"So why are you really here? You can chew first."

I swallowed. "The long story short is that I've been traveling all summer. Mostly France, then Italy, then here."

"Chasing down the rest of summer?"

I thought of all my summer heartbreaks. "Something like that."

He bobbed his head, seeming to understand that there was more to the story.

"I'm writing a book," I said, trying the words out loud. Funny how a four-word fact could be so empowering. It was the first time I had mentioned my writing as if I were really doing it.

"What's it about?"

"A woman," I said. "Travel, adventure, heartbreak."

"It's about you."

"Oh, god, no." I wiped my hand on a paper napkin. "Not me. Someone much braver."

"Bravery is overrated," he said, setting down his glass. "Fear is compelling."

I chuckled. "As someone who has spent a lot of time afraid, I have to disagree."

"You're here, though, aren't you?"

I didn't elaborate; the words that had already escaped were plenty. I had come here *because* I was afraid. Afraid of going through life without someone who made me feel safe or cherished. Afraid of living an angry life, like my mother. Afraid I'd never see Todd again. All those things were too personal to discuss with a stranger.

But he was only a stranger until I got to know him. "What's your name? I forgot to ask before."

"Keith," he said.

"And what do you do, Keith?"

"I edit books."

"You—oh."

"Don't worry, I won't ask to read yours," he said. "But can I offer a piece of advice?"

I spread my palms, inviting him to continue.

"Don't focus on the bravery," he said. "Focus on the fear."

Huh.

I finished my glass of water and slid off my stool. "It was really nice to meet you, Keith," I said, setting some money on the counter. "Thank you for the advice."

"I scared you off."

"No, not at all." I touched his arm to emphasize my sincerity. "Now that I've eaten, I'm exhausted. But maybe I'll see you around the island?"

"I hope so," Keith said. "I think my friend would like you."

MAGGIE

"I can't believe you traveled all the way to Greece to find a man you barely knew," Maggie says, struck by the audacity.

They're walking on the beach below Ann's home, a rocky, barnacled stretch with the bluff on one side and the tumultuous sea on the other.

Ann smiles, her ponytail thrashing behind her like a whip. "It was the stupidest, most important decision of my life."

Maggie wants to comment on Ann's mother, too, but what can she say without sounding naive or judgmental? She remains quiet, allowing the clap of the waves and the hiss of sand across the stones to erase her thoughts.

It's two in the afternoon, and Ann suggested they take a break to get some fresh air. While Ann was bundling up, Maggie was able to connect to Wi-Fi and update Grant. He was adamant she keep negotiating to resume recording, but when Ann reappeared, Maggie couldn't form the words. Pressuring Ann could make the whole deal crumble, and besides that, it feels almost brutal to push Ann after the vulnerability she's exhibited just in telling her story at all.

And perhaps a small, amoral part of Maggie simply wants to keep listening to the story about her favorite author, beloved uncle, and the lives they'd had before Maggie was born and before their falling-out. Barbara confirmed it: they had all been friends, way back when. What happened to tear them apart? Maggie might never find out if she pressures Ann to record too soon.

"I miss Keith," Maggie murmurs instead.

Ann's description of him was spot on. Keith possessed a mixture of confident and kind features that could make you feel safe and loved even as you were compelled to admit that it was *your* bike handle that scratched his car. How lucky Ann was to have sat down beside him in that bar and learned just how generous he could be.

"So do I," Ann says.

Maggie's throat narrows, and she gulps the rising sadness, changing the subject. "Your story is so . . . different from the public version."

A soft huff of a laugh. "I faced a lot of misrepresentation."

"That's horrible."

"It wasn't so bad," Ann says, her eyes trained on the ground, navigating the rocks and kelp. "Would I trade my fame to undo the years of hurt caused to the people closest to me? Of course. But few authors experience my level of popularity, the translations and special editions and film deal. I'm grateful for this life of privilege."

"What about Todd?" Maggie asks.

Ann's amber eyes lift to something in the far-off distance. A bird, perhaps. "What about him?"

"The press dug up his past pretty bad."

"You're getting ahead of the story, but yes."

"Did he think the spotlight was worth being with you?"

She's quiet for a while. "I'm not sure."

"Is the popularity why you stayed away? Why you lived overseas?"

Ann snorts a small, dismissive sound. "I'm an author, Maggie, not a movie star. My career—and by career, I mean that flash in the pan that followed me around forever—wasn't explosive enough to run from. I mean, don't get me wrong, people pried. They loved the idea of a jet-setting author. They loved the romance and adventure of the book, so of course that was also projected on me. But the book was peripheral to much of my life. I wasn't running from that."

"What were you running from?"

Her nose—red and dripping from the cold—scrunches. "I was running from who I thought I would become."

It's strange listening to Ann discuss the feelings Maggie harbored as a teenager when she read the book. Not just the glamour of romance and adventure but the melancholy angst and betrayal that ribboned under the surface of the main character's story. *Chasing Shadows* had a nostalgia about it—a nostalgia for things that hadn't happened. The book resonated because it spoke to that sense of delicate longing for times that never were, a wistfulness that all people experience at one time or another.

No wonder it touched so many readers. No wonder those readers (Maggie included) wanted to pry into Ann's life and know her better. They drank up the juiciest rumors because the truth wasn't as important as what the facade evoked.

To know that Ann was navigating such demons under the guise of this public caricature is a sad rewrite of the author Maggie imagined. It changes her recollection of adolescence: nagging Uncle Keith for a signed copy, overhearing Barbara's concern for Ann's well-being, even Tracey and Bob's disdain.

Who *was* Ann, to all of them? Who were they to her?

Maggie must have a strange look on her face, because Ann stops and says, "You're the one who wanted to see the woman behind the curtain."

Maggie stops too. "You're just rewriting some memories, that's all."

"Good memories?"

"Some."

"I'm sorry."

"Don't be."

Ann's expression is heartfelt. "Later in life, good memories are all we have."

Is that why Maggie has never found the courage to push her parents about where she came from? Aside from that one burning question, Maggie had a happy childhood—a doting father, a supportive mother, a close family. What if, in digging for her own answers, she unearths something she should've left buried? The irony is not lost on Maggie: she might be pursuing a career in truth seeking, she might *want* to know her family's secret history, but that doesn't mean she isn't terrified of what she'll uncover.

ANN

The next morning, I carried my notebook down to the western waterfront. The bars were shuttered. Cigarette butts littered the street, the only sign of last night's festivities. A single sleepy café was open. Tiny tables had been set up along the raised walkway; a high tide threatened to slosh over the cobblestones.

I sat with my back to the café. To my right was a curved stretch of blue-and-white stucco buildings built up against the sea; the waves splashed against their grimy foundations, while colorful laundry fluttered on balcony railings above. To my left was a rocky hill crowned by ancient-looking windmills, their wheel-spoke blades silhouetted against the bright backdrop of the sky. In front of me, the sea was dressed in the pastels of early morning.

I enjoyed the view for a while, then bent my head toward my notebook. I wrote with urgency. Keith's words the night before had permeated my creativity. Suddenly, the things in my story that hadn't been working, worked. The fresh perspective had opened a side door into new ideas.

The sun rose steadily, and more people came to occupy the café chairs. I finished one coffee, then two. The tide went out a little. Voices filled the street. Some were clearly hungover, but there was an easy pleasantness in the air. We were all glad to be here, in this beautiful place; we were all running from the dangers and doldrums of our real lives.

A shadow crossed my table, paused. "Fancy seeing you here."

Joy blossomed in my chest when I glanced up. "Keith."

"Working on your novel?"

Still high on the rush of writing freely, I wasn't embarrassed to admit, "I liked what you said last night, about fear."

"You took my advice?" He seemed pleased.

I nodded. A breeze flicked through the pages of my notebook, and I closed the front cover. "Want to sit?"

"I should get back to my friend," he said. "I just wanted to say hello."

"I'm glad you spotted me." For the first time all morning, I thought of Todd. Perhaps Keith could help me find him? "Before you go, I have to say: I wasn't entirely truthful last night, when you asked why I was here."

"Oh?"

"I'm looking for someone. I'm wondering if—"

Keith raised a finger, signaling for me to wait. "I know just the guy. Come to my table." He thought I was looking for a relationship, not a specific person.

I stood. "No, that's not what I—"

But Keith kept walking.

I tucked my notebook under my arm and followed him down the walkway, passing three tables until we got to his. A man was seated with his back to us, facing the windmills. Keith tapped him on the shoulder, and a flush came to my face as I grew flustered by Keith's misunderstanding . . . but before I could clarify, the words halted in the back of my throat. The man who turned and looked up at me was Todd.

Todd was the friend Keith had mentioned last night.

Maggie, I was gobsmacked. A part of me had assumed I'd never find him. But of course, he was your uncle Keith's best friend.

"Oh . . . *hello*." Todd set down his coffee cup and pushed up from the table as if he might hug me, but he didn't. Instead, he ran a hand through his unruly hair, front to back.

"Hi," I squeaked. I had the sudden urge to cry—a hot, itchy stinging in the corners of my eyes.

It was relief.

And overwhelming embarrassment.

I hadn't mentally prepared for this moment, the moment I'd have to fess up to stalking Todd after spending just one afternoon together. I clutched my notebook until the spiral binding cut into my palm. He looked good—really good. He wore a linen shirt that made him appear relaxed and breezy, and he'd already tanned from the intense Greek sun. He didn't look as weary as he had in Venice. In fact, he was squinting now, and thin little smile lines creased the sides of his face. If he was unhappy to see me, he hid it well.

"Did you follow me to Mykonos?"

"I . . . well . . . I, um," I stammered. *Here it comes,* I thought. *This is when he tells me that I'm a freak and he never wants to see me again.*

Keith cut in: "You know her?"

I considered throwing myself off the sidewalk and into the sea.

"Copper," he said softly, pointing at me.

The reference rendered me still.

"*This* is Venice?" Keith clarified. His face—pinched and creased with confusion—transformed into a big, unbelieving grin. "I can't believe it. Todd, this is the girl I told you about from last night."

"You told him about me?" I managed. It was gradually occurring to me just how creepy this could seem, my being there. How was Todd not startled, or angry?

"I can't believe I didn't realize the connection." Todd laughed in amusement. "Do you have plans today? We were going to check out the windmills and maybe go to the beach. Want to come?"

"That . . . sounds fun," I said. "Are you sure?"

"Of course! I'm going to pay for our drinks, I'll be right back." He disappeared inside the café and I watched him go, dumbfounded.

Gone was the melancholy man I'd met in Venice; in Greece, Todd's whole demeanor was heightened. Had he simply been tired when I met him? No, he'd full-on rejected me. *Leave it at that,* he'd said.

"You look perplexed," Keith commented. He was seated at the table, his legs stretched out in front of him, crossed at the ankles.

I sank into Todd's chair. "He *has* to be lying."

"About?"

"In Venice, he rejected me. How can he be glad to see me now?"

"He had a great time with you," Keith said.

"Then why . . ." I shook my head, burying my face in my palms. I had spent so many days expecting Todd to be furious or bothered or standoffish at the sight of me here—though I had hoped he'd be glad, I hadn't actually prepared myself for that outcome.

"He liked you. I know that because he told me."

"He did?"

"Yeah." Keith sat forward. "But Ann, there's something you need to know—" Keith broke off as Todd walked up.

"Ready to go?" he asked.

My heart skittered. "Absolutely."

The three of us stood and started down the pathway, Todd in the lead. I felt giddy. I had found him, and he was glad! I couldn't believe that I was about to spend another day with Todd, another day like the one I'd been thinking about for over a week. Whatever Keith had been about to say, I didn't care. It didn't matter. I was thrilled to be welcomed.

ANN

We spent the morning touring the windmills. At lunchtime, we sipped ouzo and ate gyros and told each other funny stories until Keith was wheezing with laughter and Todd and I had tears streaming down our faces. It turned out that we had similar senses of humor—we loved wit and irony and bad predicaments, but Keith could also drag us down into toilet humor and have us all snickering like teenagers.

It felt good to have company.

After lunch, we agreed to reconvene at two o'clock on a beach a little ways south—supposedly, it was the best beach on the island. Back in my room, I changed into a one-piece swimsuit I'd bought in France. It was red, with a flattering high-cut leg and a low V top. I slipped a gauzy white dress over it and traded my notebook for a shoulder bag that would fit a towel.

I arrived at the shore at two fifteen, having miscalculated how far it was from my hotel. The beach was full of naked sunbathers, and I unobtrusively scanned the faces for the two men I recognized. After about five minutes searching, I grew worried that the guys had stood me up—but then I saw them, far down the beach near a little rocky outcrop. They were clothed and snacking on olives and bread, and they grinned when I approached.

I spread my towel and plopped down beside them, reaching for an olive. "Did either of you know this was a nude beach?"

Todd shook his head, a slight pinkness coming to his tanned cheeks.

Keith's grin widened. "No clue, but it's *ace*."

Todd elbowed him. "Many of these women are gay, Keith. You have no chance."

"*Someone* has to be straight," Keith said. "And I'm determined to find her."

I rolled my eyes. "Are *you* getting naked then?"

"What? No way," Keith said.

Todd chuckled. "Come on, man. Remember when you were trying to convince me to come to Greece with you? What did you say?" He tipped his chin up, pretending to think. "Oh yeah, you said, 'We need to try new things. We need to let *loose*.'"

Keith shook his head. "I meant *you* need to try new things and let loose."

"Hypocrites," I mumbled, and Keith threw an olive at me.

"I don't see you getting naked."

I wrinkled my nose. "None of us want that."

They looked at me, eyes flicking to the thinness of my cover-up and the red swimsuit underneath. Neither of them responded, and I felt my face flush, both exhilarated and embarrassed.

Todd moved on. "*Anyway*, why don't I open this wine?"

"You do that," Keith said, standing. "I'm going to that restroom over there. Don't wait up."

When Keith was down the beach and out of earshot, Todd explained, "He just went through a breakup."

I leaned back on my elbows, wondering what kind of woman would break up with Keith. The men I'd been with were all so selfish and reckless; I never felt safe or understood around them. I'd thought all men were like that—until today. Todd and Keith were different. They were somehow charming *and* thoughtful, playful *and* serious. I got the sense that if a sudden disaster occurred—like, if one of the volcanic islands suddenly erupted—those two men would be reaching for my hand, helping me run. All the men I'd known before would've simply saved themselves.

After fishing a corkscrew from their bag, Todd offered the wine bottle to me first. I took a swig, then handed it to him. He drank slowly, his hair falling back. When I awoke that morning, I'd had no idea I'd be drinking wine on a nude beach with Todd. But here I was . . . and he seemed genuinely glad. What had changed? Was it Keith's presence? A good night's sleep? Vacation high?

"You're so tan," I said, breaking our amiable silence. "How did that happen?"

"I tan quick," he said. "Which reminds me, I should put on some sunscreen."

He removed his shirt, and my hungry gaze darted over his form, from his collarbones to the vertical line that bisected his abdominals. I glanced away, heart pounding in my ears, and stared out at the ocean. The sun was beyond bright, bounding off the pale-blue sea in a glittering, dazzling, blinding explosion. I heard the lingering hum of volcanoes in my thoughts and tried not to think about seeking safety in Todd's bare arms.

"Want some?" Todd held the sunscreen out toward me.

I'd never bothered with sunblock—I only ever wore tanning oil—but I'd heard the Greek summer sun was strong. I grasped the bottle without touching his fingers and laid it on my towel. Then I sat up and removed my dress. I pretended not to notice Todd watching me as I applied the sunscreen over my arms, shoulders, and modest cleavage; I pretended not to delight in his attention as I took my time with each leg, extending them out in front of me when I was finished. "Can you get my back?" I asked.

Todd looked around, perhaps to see if Keith had heard my request, but he was far down the beach now, talking to a topless woman, who was pointing and gesturing as if giving him directions.

"Sure," Todd said.

I pivoted so my back was to him; he rose up on his knees and squirted the sunblock into his palm. It took forever for him to touch me; by the time he did, my pulse was fluttering like a frightened bird. I reveled in the way he brushed my hair off my neck and slid his fingers under the straps at my shoulders. He took his time rubbing it in.

(My apologies, Maggie, for the overt sexual tension.)

"I think you're covered," he finally said. He shifted away, sitting on his towel once again, and took another long pull of wine.

"Thanks," I responded lightly, hoping he couldn't hear the fluster in my voice.

I lay on my belly, propped on my elbows, and reached for the wine. He handed it over, and I drank.

We relaxed in silence for a bit, enjoying the breeze, eating olives and bread. We were halfway through the bottle—the world fuzzing ever so slightly—when I decided to pipe up.

"Todd?"

"Yeah, Copper?"

I smiled a lopsided smile at that. "Are you angry that I followed you here? I half expected you to hate me for it—or be creeped out."

He snorted and turned to his side, resting his temple on his fist. "You're the least creepy person I've ever met."

I rolled onto my side, too, mirroring his position. "Okay, fine, but are you mad?"

"Of course not. I'm glad to see you." His eyes held mine for four heartbeats, five. It was the same gaze that had captured me in Venice— that steady, contented attention.

"But that's what I don't get," I said. "It seemed so final in Venice."

"Then why'd you come?"

I pursed my lips and looked down my nose at the sand. "I don't know."

He ducked his head, catching my vision with his own. I found brief calm in his lakelike irises.

"We had no closure," I said. "I thought . . . didn't you feel something?"

He looked out at the water, his eyes darkening with that same expression I'd seen before, a faraway pain—like spotting a storm on the horizon. "I felt terrible for leaving like that. And the truth is, I think you're really great."

"You do?" I leaned forward like a magnet, wishing he'd put his hands on me again.

"But . . ." His attention sank to my lips; he licked his own, then bit down. He sat up. "Ann, I don't want to give you the wrong impression. I can't be in a relationship right now."

I sat up, too, rejected all over again.

"It's just, well, I lost someone . . . and I can't . . ." He paused, swallowed. "I could really use a friend right now."

"Then why turn me away?"

He peered at me from under his eyebrows in a knowing look. "Maybe you don't sense an attraction here, but I . . ." I smiled, and he groaned. "It's hard for me to be around you unless we're both on the same page. Can we just be friends? Are you okay with that?"

"Of course," I said, but I was lying. I sensed he was lying too. What we had between us already felt *bigger* than a platonic relationship; I was determined to change his mind.

So later, when it blew up in my face, I had only myself to blame. I should've taken him seriously. I should've respected that something deeper was at play.

"Care for a swim?" I asked.

Todd shook his head, so I took off down the beach. As I slipped into the water, I knew he was watching. The ocean was salty and warm.

I paddled in the shallows for a while, then emerged when I saw Keith returning.

"Any luck?" I walked up, dripping wet.

"None," Keith said, eyeing me. Then he eyed Todd. "You two having fun?"

Todd rolled his eyes and lay back.

I flopped back down on my towel. "I saw you chatting with some woman," I said to Keith. "Still no naked sunbathing for you?"

Keith laughed. "Do you really want to see that?"

"I'm just saying," I egged.

Todd chimed in. "Yeah, you hypocrite, take it off."

"Do *you* really want to see that?" Keith repeated.

I took a swig of our waning wine. "Come on, your ass needs a tan."

He laughed, full and deep. "I see you two have been hitting the sauce."

"Okay, I'll strike a deal with you two," I said. "I'll tan my boobs if you tan your asses."

"You're bluffing," Keith said.

"What makes you say that?" I knew I had Todd's attention, stupid as it was to get it that way. But I was young and tipsy and finally having a good time. The dancers I'd known at the club in Denver had been so sex positive; though I was shy about my body, I craved a taste of that confidence. I wanted to do something daring—to be able to say, *Yeah, I've been to a nude beach. And yeah, I sunbathed topless.* Naively, I also wanted to tempt Todd.

"I know this gambit," Keith said, narrowing his eyes at me. "You wait until we take off our trunks, and then when it's your turn, you laugh your ass off."

"If you don't believe me, then I'll go first."

"You'll go first." Keith didn't sound convinced.

"If you shake my hand and agree to the deal, then, yeah, I'll go first."

"Deal," Keith said, just as Todd said, "No way."

I shrugged. "Suit yourself. Keith, you still in?"

He shook my hand.

I sat up. Though they were small, I liked my breasts well enough. I slid the straps of my swimsuit down and bunched the one-piece at my belly button, my skin tensing in the breeze. Forcing myself to be gutsy, I lay back with my arms behind my head. Casual. Smug. Todd was staring at the waves again, but Keith had met my eyes.

"You're ballsy, you know that?" He shimmied his shorts over his hips, and they dropped to the sand. I didn't look at his front when he lay down, but I did get a solid view of his extremely pale backside once he settled on his stomach.

I held up my hand as if to block the sun. "It's blinding!"

"Jesus Christ," Todd said, looking at Keith and then quickly looking away. "Why am I friends with you?"

"You don't have a choice, bud," Keith said.

Todd threw the sunscreen at him. "Put some sunblock on that thing before it bakes."

"Can you help me?" Keith teased.

Todd cuffed him on the back of the head, and all three of us laughed, good and loud and deep. Tipping my head back, I closed my eyes, and triumph filled my chest.

MAGGIE

"Did you ever think it was risky to befriend two strange men and spend so much time alone with them?" Maggie asks.

The weather outside is wet and blustery; when Maggie arrived this morning, Ann already had a fire going. Every so often, the house shudders with a pattering gust of wind and rain. From her wingback chair, Maggie can't even see the ocean; it's as if a gray curtain has been drawn all around the house, over the windows.

Ann's eyes narrow over the rim of her mug; she sips her coffee before answering. "For one, I was never truly *alone* with them, at least not early on. We were often in public places." She sets her mug down and dabs at her mouth with a napkin. "More importantly, they never gave me a reason to feel unsafe."

"Even topless?"

"Even topless."

Going to a nude beach in a foreign country with two men she'd collectively known for less than a day . . . Maggie isn't sure she could do something like that. It's a quality she admires about Ann—the way her search for connection often resulted in a great experience, a great story. No matter how fearful Ann *claims* she was, she still acted. "Were you always so trusting?"

Ann sits back, uncrossing her legs and recrossing them the other way. "I never would've described myself as trusting," she says. "But Keith and Todd were so obviously harmless."

Maggie nods. Keith was a warm sunbeam, through and through—first one in the pool, first one to suggest sundaes for dinner, first one to plan just one more camping trip before the summer ended.

"Did you ever meet Todd?" Ann asks it casually—Todd was Keith's best friend, after all—but her interest seems pointed.

"Yes," Maggie answers. "Once. Briefly, when I was a child."

Ann's expression is flat, save for an intense, sparkling focus in her amber eyes. "How did he seem to you?"

Maggie's memory of Todd—fuzzy and unfocused—is from a family barbecue when she was little. She had no idea who he was at the time, didn't know Ann existed. Maggie was sitting on the porch eating a Popsicle, her fingers sticky. A man showed up late and came through their back gate. Many adult eyes trained on him as he walked across the lawn. Keith was by the grill and dropped his tongs with a clatter when he saw him; they embraced heartily, clapping each other's backs.

"Maggie, come meet my friend Todd, here," Keith said.

She stood and walked over, still clutching her Popsicle. Up close, Maggie saw that Todd had the kind, creased eyes of a sad person.

He smiled, though, crouching down to her level. "Nice to meet you, Maggie."

It seemed strange, meeting some random man. He seemed nice enough, but she wanted to go back to the potluck table and nab a few chocolate chip cookies. Half her Popsicle had already melted down her hand.

Todd seemed to sense her impatience; he stood, his face dropping back into a frown.

Keith patted her shoulder, and she craned her neck up at her uncle; his red hair was still dripping wet from practicing cannonballs with her in the pool. "You can run along, Maggie."

She didn't need to be told twice. She darted off toward her father, who was standing by the food table. She'd never seen his fists balled like that before, the knobby whites of his knuckles showing, but when she threw her arms around his leg, Bob's hands relaxed, and he ruffled her wet hair. He handed her two cookies folded into a napkin, crouching down to her level to whisper, "Don't tell your mother," with a wink.

Todd didn't stay long. His hunched shoulders left the party just as timidly as they arrived. It wasn't until years later that Keith told her who the man was, that she had met Todd Langley, lover to her new favorite author, Ann Fawkes. She flexed those bragging rights on her friends at school, inflating the story far beyond what it actually was. The truth was that she didn't remember much of Todd at all. The most vivid thing about that afternoon, in her mind's eye, was not the semifamous stranger but the chewy cookies that her dad gave her.

Maggie answers Ann's question. "He seemed nice and kind of sad. But that's different. I was a child. I didn't have to watch out for myself like you did."

"The more you travel, the more you realize how kind most people are. I'm not saying I was the wisest twenty-five-year-old, but it never crossed my mind to worry."

"I've been wondering—I mean, I have to ask." Maggie sets down her mug. "Why didn't Keith ask you out himself? Was there ever any . . . interest . . . there?"

"Honestly, I wondered that myself, especially at the time," Ann says. "He seemed so keen on getting laid, I kept thinking, 'Why would he push me toward Todd?'"

"And?"

"He was nursing a broken heart on that trip—they both were. We all were."

"What about Barbara?"

Ann tips her head, seemingly surprised that Maggie doesn't know the story. "He and Barbara had a big fight and broke up, so Keith left for Greece, thinking he wanted a wild international guys' trip to get over her. But really, he just wanted her back. Shortly after he returned, they got engaged."

"I never knew that."

The family man version of Uncle Keith had been like a second father to her. His was the home she ran away to when she fought with her parents; he was the one who helped her sharpen her college admissions essays; and he was the one who taught her the perfect cannonball technique over the many summers she spent swimming in his pool. It's strange to realize that he was once a young professional, a matchmaker, a best friend, and a bachelor in Greece.

Maggie had thought they were close, but it's clear now that there were versions of Keith she never learned about. By the time Maggie was old enough to hear stories from Keith's young adulthood, her interest in Ann—a sore subject for him, by then—had eclipsed Maggie's interest in her beloved uncle. Maggie had needled Keith relentlessly for stories about Ann, and though he conceded with bland trivia—Ann's favorite gelato flavor, how she took her coffee—it was never enough. He had insisted that Ann's privacy outweighed Maggie's insatiable curiosity, but what if he'd been hurt by Maggie's lack of interest in *his* role in Ann's success? In *his* life story?

Did Maggie not know this story because Keith had kept it from her or because she never asked why *he* had been sitting in that bar in Greece? Was this a symptom of the distracted selfishness of youth, or had Maggie simply failed to take interest in Keith after she discovered his connection to a famous author, his former client and friend?

Whatever the answer, it's clear now that she missed out on truly getting to know her uncle.

Maggie stares out the window into the gray, a wedge of sorrow lodging itself between her ribs. It's prying bone from bone, making her side hurt. The longer Keith's gone, the more his absence seems to expand. Is it painful or cathartic for Ann to tell her story, to remember Keith and Todd in this way? Maggie hopes it's the latter.

"What happened next?" Maggie asks. "Were you able to change Todd's mind?"

Ann laughs. "Not in the true sense of the word—at least, not right away."

"But it's a long story."

"That it is, Maggie."

ANN

We had such fun together on Mykonos that the guys invited me on the second leg of their trip: Santorini. We took a dodgy cab ride from the port, cringing as the narrow road switchbacked up the razor edge of a five-hundred-foot-high cliff. Bumping and jostling shoulders with Keith on one side and Todd on the other, I peeked through nervous fingers as motorists whizzed round us on blind curves. At one particularly stomach-lurching hairpin, Todd gripped my knee, and a thrill jolted my heart. Perhaps I should've been more fearful of my impending death, but I was too busy reading into Todd's every move.

All three of us were wobbly when we arrived at a dusty dead-end street—supposedly not far from our hotel—but as soon as my feet hit dirt, I was no longer thinking about knee grabs or careening off precipitous ledges. From our vantage atop the island, red rock curved away, crusted with bright buildings that looked like square diamonds on a bronze tiara. Azure flags, fuchsia flowers, and hand-painted shop signs made colorful jewels. This high up, we could see *everything*—the jutting land, the placid sea, the faded lilac horizon.

We'd found rooms in a classic cave hotel, halfway between the two main towns of Fira and Oia. It was located in the middle of Santorini's crescent and faced the center of the caldera. Far below, a ferry glided over the submerged volcanic crater, tearing a white streak through the deep-blue fabric of the ocean.

"It's all right, I guess," Keith said.

Todd shoved him with his elbow.

"Eh, nothing special," I replied.

Keith winked at me.

Todd paid for the cab, and it sped off, gravel kicking up. "Ready?" he asked, grabbing my bag along with his own. I smiled to myself, tracking the lines of his shoulder muscles as he walked ahead, toward an inconspicuous blue-lettered sign announcing our hotel.

A narrow staircase led down into an open-air arrangement of balconies and walkways. We followed signs for the lobby, checked in, and were shown to our rooms. There were three levels built into the cliff—like a stadium—with a row of four rooms per level. Both our rooms were on the second level, Keith and Todd's all the way to the left and mine to the middle right. I could see their patio from my patio. I could see the whole world from my patio, from the potted aloe plant on the railing clear out to the glittering skyline.

The guys had gone into their cave, probably to argue over who got the only bed. It was just me, and the gusty wind, and the mineral-sweet scent of the Aegean. The breeze ruffled my blouse like hot breath, an indulgent exhale.

I raised my camera and snapped a photo for Mom.

Our days on Santorini were both idle and adventurous. We'd laze outside the guys' room (they dragged one of my patio chairs over to theirs so I could join them) or under umbrellas on a beach (clothed, though we still chuckled about Keith's pale ass). We ate a lot of fresh fish, olives, and fried feta; we drank ouzo and mastika and the occasional bottle of Assyrtiko wine. We toasted to anything worth celebrating: to Greece, to friendship, to sunsets, to cheese!

I rented us a pair of mopeds and let the guys drive, tagging along on the back of Todd's. I loved the excuse to wrap my arms around his waist, nestling my head between his strong shoulder blades and breathing in his citrus musk. We scooted all over the island, visiting red-sand beaches, getting lost among labyrinthine streets, and taking photos of blue-domed churches. We stroked thin donkeys' faces and fed stray cats off our plates. And after dark, we wandered and laughed and got drunk and talked about what fun this was.

We vowed to be friends forever.

When it came to my winning over Todd, Keith and I were downright conspiratorial. He seemed to believe that Todd and I were meant for each other too. He'd tie our shopping bags to the back of his moped so I *had* to ride with Todd. He'd sit so that Todd and I had to share a bench, scooch closer. He'd wander ahead—or disappear completely—to allow Todd and me to converse one on one.

If Todd noticed Keith's efforts, he didn't say anything. As the days sped by, we grew closer. It became easy to chat about nothing in particular, or laugh at an inside joke—*burro!*—or brush an eyelash from the other's cheek. He made me feel both understood and challenged, electrified and soothed. So I overlooked the boundary he'd built. In my mind, the ease and familiarity of our interactions proved his attraction.

But he was also a walnut—tough to crack. We talked about everything except the thing that made his eyes go dark sometimes, the thing that made his bottom lip twitch in a half grimace that he was quick to hide. *There's something you need to know,* Keith had warned. *I lost someone,* Todd had said.

I was afraid to ask.

I wanted things between us to deepen, but I was terrified that the secret lurking in his past would keep us apart. I had the sense that it was big, and maybe he didn't care for me enough to try to overcome it. But I also sensed that, day by day, we were becoming closer than *just friends*.

Did his hand linger on my waist?

Was that a relieved smile upon seeing me emerge from my room?

Did his eyes dart to my lips while I was talking?

These things did not seem chaste; the naturalness of them was not insignificant. I tried to offer my own signals, shy little hints that were meant to ask, *Are you sure you only want friendship?* A lingering hand on his shoulder, a long slow squeeze when I climbed on the back of his moped, a bright sunny smile just for him.

I spent many nights hoping he'd sneak the thirty feet from his patio to mine. I waited to hear a soft knock on my door—fantasizing about the taste of his lips—and was always devastated when he didn't show. Come morning, I would be determined to act coy and cold, but the moment he lifted his coffee cup in greeting, to beckon me over to their patio, all my frustration would melt and I'd gravitate toward him like a magnet, grateful simply to feel his pull.

Six days into our jaunt around the island, after a long afternoon exploring back roads with a bubbly Dutch couple we'd met at lunch, we decided to all meet in Oia for the sunset. Our new friends had found a spot not far from Oia Castle, a secret place that overlooked a trio of blue domes and provided a private sunset view.

An hour before twilight, I ducked into my hotel room to brush my teeth and freshen up. I swapped my tank top and shorts for a flowing dress I'd bought the day before. Though I'd abstained from makeup for most of the trip, I dug out some blush and mascara and dolled myself up.

The sun was sitting low in the clouds when we arrived in Oia. Keith had packed a few bottles of wine and some extra blankets, and Todd helped him carry the goods. The Dutch couple—I don't recall their names—led the way as the street transformed into a narrower residential pathway. Our guides slowed, walking side by side. Keith followed on their heels, with Todd and me in tandem behind.

Todd cleared his throat. "Is the dress new?"

My cheeks tightened, but I smothered the smile before it reached my mouth. "Yes, from that boutique yesterday."

He glanced at me. "It's nice."

"Thanks."

A pause. "I'm glad you came here with us. It's been fun."

Todd and Keith were heading to Crete next, just for a few days, before they returned to the States. Whatever happened with Todd—friendship, or more—the thought of him going back to Colorado while I stayed behind made my chest clench. I had no plans of living in America again—I couldn't bear the thought, really, of going back to the one place I would never flourish. But not seeing Todd every day . . . I couldn't bear that thought either.

"I'm glad you invited me along," I answered. "Truthfully, I never would've come to Greece if it hadn't been for you. And what a loss that would've been."

"Keith just dragged me here for beaches, women, and drinking." His mouth twisted, tiny wrinkles creasing his cheek. "We got so much more."

My heart did the opposite of a skip, a heavy *thud-thud*. "What's been your favorite part so far?"

His eyes lifted to the friends ahead of us, and his lips pursed. When he opened his mouth to speak, the Dutch husband interrupted from up ahead: "We are close."

We'd arrived at a freestanding stucco wall, set with decorative burgundy double doors that led to nothing. To the right of the doors, there was a small gap in the wall, and when our new friends stepped through, it looked as if they were disappearing into the sky. We were high up. A steep decline of white buildings and steps led down the cliff face toward the water far, far below. The ferries and pleasure boats were as tiny as grains of rice.

Keith—still carrying an armload of blankets and wine—squeezed through the gap and disappeared behind the others. "Come on, love-birds," he teased.

Todd's response was to frown, and my heart *did* skip, a sharp little disappointed pause.

"You go first," Todd said.

I moved past him and turned the corner, my right arm brushing the wall. The path was an easy decline past some stoops and houses, not at all precarious, as more buildings were built into the cliff. Their roofs reached my shoulder, and little alleys disappeared between structures, wedging us in, safe from falling.

Up ahead, we could plainly see the northernmost tip of Santorini. An old castle jutted up at the very end of the land, a promontory pep-pered with tiny, distant sunset watchers. Between there and here were lit-up homes, urban palm trees, stoic windmills, and—in our imme-diate foreground—three impeccable blue-domed churches. The literal postcard view.

The Dutch couple had made it down the path, near a half wall that separated the walkway from a convex stucco rooftop. The husband hoisted his wife first, then scrambled onto the curved surface. This was our spot. Keith handed them the blankets and wine, then climbed up. He offered me a hand, which I took, shimmying up the gritty surface. Once Todd handed me his own bundle of stuff, he clambered up. We all sat in a line facing the domes, our legs extended down the rounded surface of the roof.

Up here, it felt like we were the only people on the whole island.

The sky had donned its best pastels: periwinkle fading into peach. The shell-colored buildings of Oia took on a lavender cream coloring, illuminated by the gentle sunset. The crescent of Santorini stretched with stony arms, as if reaching to encircle the tiny islands in the middle of the caldera. Along the distant seam where sea met sky, the sun was an apricot orb surrounded by shades of ivory and melon. The fairy-tale colors, the warm breeze, the love bursting in my heart . . . I was inside a dream.

Keith poured wine into paper cups, emptying the first bottle. After raising our drinks to the sunset, we passed a second bottle around for refills. The wine was bright and dry, with citrus and mineral notes that went down smooth. Keith handed out blankets, with Todd and I sharing one.

As the sun slipped into the ocean and the sky darkened into plum and cobalt, the stars began to glitter. We chatted and laughed, and soon the Dutch couple were leaving. Keith, Todd, and I lingered, savoring the last little bit of light in the sky. The temperature had cooled, and the wind whipped off the water, chilling me. I felt Todd shift closer, resettling the blanket over our laps. There was one more bottle, which the three of us shared. My head swam, the wine warming me like a hot bath. Todd's cheeks were ruddy, and he had an easy smile on his face; Keith hummed softly.

"What is that?" Todd asked.

"Fleetwood Mac." Keith hummed louder.

I picked up the first verse of "Dreams," singing softly over his melody. At the chorus, all three of us broke into song. We finished the wine, and then we sang some more, until there was no remaining evidence of the sun ever having been in the sky.

Keith was the first to stand on unsteady legs. "Well, we can't drive now," he said. "Why don't we find a table at that restaurant near where we parked the mopeds?"

I didn't move from my place under the blanket. "I want to stay just a little bit longer," I said. Todd began to shift, and I put my hand on his thigh. "Keep me company?"

Todd glanced at Keith, who glanced at me.

With his eyes boring into mine, Keith said, "Meet me in fifteen? I'll order us some food."

"Fifteen," I agreed.

Keith waved as he walked away, heading back up the narrow path from which we had come.

Todd sighed. "It *is* nice up here."

"It's beautiful," I replied.

Lights illuminated small pockets of the vertical town in buttery auras. The silhouette of the castle was visible in the dark, still and stoic. The wind howled, ruffling our blanket.

Todd leaned back on his hands, looking up at the stars. He had darkness in his eyes again, a distant gaze. I wondered what he saw that haunted him so; I wondered how I could free him from it. As if it were a fantastical beast, I had no idea how to slay Todd's inner darkness—but I wanted to try. I wanted *him*. And back then, I was clueless enough to think that *I* could be the flame in his night.

I leaned against his chest, his arms propping both of us up. He sighed and pressed his face into my hair. Every part of my being tensed with longing. If I tilted my head up toward his, would he kiss me? I might've seemed overly confident when it came to seducing him, but in that moment on the rooftop, I was petrified. I didn't want my heart to be broken again; if Todd broke it, it might break beyond repair.

I turned my ear toward his collarbone and heard the rhythm of his heart. Over my own shoulder, I stared up at his jawline and the fan of his eyelashes against the backdrop of space. I whispered, "You never told me what your favorite part of the trip has been."

Without hesitating, he said, "You."

My blood whooshed and warmed in my veins.

He was still gazing at the view, but some of the darkness in his eyes dissipated. I knew he was drunk—we both were—but didn't that make us more honest?

"I have felt really lost these past few months, but with you and Keith . . ." I trailed off, wondering if my words were too vulnerable. But he was looking at me now, all his attention on me; his chest rose and fell with shallow breaths. I decided to finish my thought: "With you and Keith, I don't feel so alone."

His face was mere inches from mine—yet I still sensed a great chasm between us. "Copper, there's something you should know."

I didn't want to talk anymore, not with his breath—sweet smelling and sex-hot—on my cold cheeks. I craned my neck, closed my eyes, and closed the distance. For the briefest of moments, our lips brushed, and I saw stars and sunsets and love across my eyelids.

But then he pulled back.

Not just with his face, but with his whole body. He recoiled, chest twisting to break contact with my back. I toppled, drunk and humiliated, onto the grit of the rooftop. Shame and hurt blazed across my face.

"What are you doing?"

I clutched my own elbows, urging myself not to cry. "I thought—"

"You thought . . . *wrong*." He stood, and the blanket fell in a heap at his feet; he brushed the dust off his pants. "I thought we talked about this."

I felt stupid—so stupid—but I also felt duped. The attraction couldn't just be in my head. The way he'd smelled my hair, the way his breathing had shallowed. Had he paused against my lips before pulling away? How could I be his favorite part of the trip if he didn't want *this*?

"I'm confused." My voice sounded small and tattered.

There was an edge in his. "You're confused?"

"Yes, Todd," I said, gaining steam. "How can you not think there's a connection here?"

"It's not like that," he said. "I don't feel what you feel."

His words only angered me. He was lying. I stood up, the world tilting. In my inebriation, I felt off balance on that roof. "How can I be the only one who feels this . . . this *heat* between us?"

He stomped his foot. "Damn it, Ann. I told you what this was!"

"No, you told me what you *wanted* this to be. And then you gave me mixed signals!"

"What signals? I couldn't have been more clear."

"*What signals?* How about just now, for instance: snuggling up, smelling my hair. How about the fact that you *just said* that *I* was your favorite part of your trip? How about every morning having coffee together while Keith slept in? How about all the million little times I've caught you looking at me? All the times you've touched my arm, or my back, or my leg? That's not platonic, Todd. Not in the slightest. You're delusional if you think it is."

His jaw was clenched, eyes darting. I knew I'd penetrated a wall; my words had the weight of a wrecking ball.

"You're being immature," he mumbled.

"Immature?" My volume rose. "For what, *feeling*? Fuck you."

"Oh, now you're going to curse?"

"*Yeah*," I shouted. "Fuck you for not seeing what this is. Fuck you for trying to make me feel stupid for being honest with my emotions."

Our argument had roused a homeowner nearby, who yelled from his stoop in Greek. We didn't need to speak his language to understand that we were being a disturbance.

"Come on, Keith is waiting for us," Todd said, his voice low.

Drunk as I was, I didn't care if the whole neighborhood heard. "*No*," I shrieked. "We aren't done here. I can't ignore this anymore. I want to talk it out."

"You're reading into nothing."

More complaints in Greek didn't stop me from shouting, "*Nothing?*"

"Why are you doing this? We were having a good time."

"God, I'm *sorry*," I said sarcastically, "for thinking we'd be good together. I'm sorry for falling—"

"Don't."

"—in love with you." My voice cracked, and then tears were streaking down my face in quick, warm lines. Why was he angry with me? Why was he resisting? Our chemistry couldn't have just been in my head.

But he didn't come closer. He didn't wrap me in the embrace I craved. He didn't even apologize. All he said was, "I don't love you."

A pause spread between us like the spreading of space, slow and steady but also vast and empty, stretching and stretching until I couldn't stand being in my own skin anymore. My own beating heart was alien to me.

"I'm leaving," I finally managed, wiping at my face. I rushed past him along the roofline and slid down to the path.

"Ann, wait." Todd tripped on the heaped blanket at his feet. He grunted as he lost balance—top heavy in that drunken way—and tumbled off the roof.

Panic surged through me as I imagined him falling onto the ocean rocks far, far below. "Todd!" I screamed.

I ran to the alley behind the building. Beyond a flimsy gate, Todd was sitting upright on the ground, looking stunned. He'd toppled perhaps five feet; the house we'd been arguing on top of was nestled into the cliff face and framed by a steep pathway. His face was red and his eyes swam. I realized how drunk we really were, and maybe that was a good thing, because falling off that roof had probably hurt less in his state. I unlatched the gate and went to him, stopping a couple of feet away, hyperaware of the argument still simmering between us. His elbow was bleeding. He tested his wrist, twisting and flexing the joint and wincing.

"I think I sprained it," he said, looking up at me.

"Do you need a doctor?"

"Maybe tomorrow. It might be fine."

I crossed my arms over my body, resisting the urge to crouch down and hug him in my relief. "It's not broken?"

He touched each finger to his thumb, testing his dexterity. "No, I don't think so."

"Are you okay other than that?" I asked.

"Yeah."

"You didn't hit your head?"

"No."

"What year is it?"

"I didn't hit my head."

"What—"

"Nineteen eighty-four."

"Good. Let's go find Keith. We need to sober up."

We didn't tell Keith about our argument. I'm sure he sensed the tension between us—the way Todd angled his body away from me when we sat down—but Todd's wrist took precedence. We told Keith that Todd had slipped when we were getting down from the roof, hence the scrapes and possible sprain. Todd insisted on waiting until morning to visit a doctor.

So we ate, got sober, and drove home. Todd rode behind me. He did not wrap his arms around me but instead gripped the back lip of the seat, tucking his injured arm against his chest. We retired to our respective beds without talk.

I didn't entertain the fantasy of Todd coming to my room that night—this time, I was certain he wouldn't. Instead, I lay awake hoping that maybe Todd and I could go back to normal; maybe now that I knew for certain he wasn't interested, I could move on. But in the morning, when I emerged from my room and Todd was there on his patio sipping coffee, I knew. I knew I couldn't do it.

I had to leave.

I ducked into my room and packed my things. I waited until Todd went inside to shower, then pinned a note on their patio table with a rock. I don't remember exactly what I wrote, but it didn't say much. Just that I'd had fun, but it was time for me to go.

As I was dragging my suitcase up the narrow hotel stairs, Keith appeared.

"What did he say to you?" he asked.

"It doesn't matter," I said, yanking on my suitcase.

"Yes, it does."

I faced him, hands on hips. "Keith, why have you been throwing us together all week? You must've known he didn't want—" I bit my lip.

"He's . . . grieving." Keith stumbled on the word, perhaps in an effort to respect Todd's privacy. "This trip was about moving on. After Venice . . . I could tell he liked you. I was just trying to help."

I poked my suitcase with my toe.

"Just come back to our room, okay? Come with us to Crete. You'll see that—"

"What are the chances that Todd falls in love with me?" I asked with measured calm.

He didn't answer.

"That's what I thought."

"He *does* care for you, Ann. And so do I. Please?"

My heart was wet paper, disintegrating by the moment. "It's too humiliating."

He couldn't argue with the tears that blurred my eyes, so he grabbed my bag and carried it up the steep steps to the road. Wordlessly, he waited with me for my taxi, then gave me a long, fierce hug.

"You take care, all right?"

I nodded against his broad chest.

When we parted, he handed me a blue business card. "If you really want to be an author, get some work published. Short stories, travel articles. Then, when you finish your novel, call me."

MAGGIE

"Please tell me you convinced her to do some recording," Grant says.

It's nearing noon, and the weather's surge has died down. Maggie stepped outside to call Grant while Ann searches for something in her office—letters of some sort.

"Still nothing, but the conversations are going well."

"You can hear every juicy detail and it'll mean nothing to the podcast without permission to use it, Maggie."

Maggie winces. She still hasn't told anyone about the accidental recording, nor has she deleted it; she's holding out hope that Ann will ultimately change her mind, but she's growing doubtful. "I still have a few days left on the island to convince her."

"About that," Grant says. "Joy is really on my case about this today. Without any proven progress, the podcast can't continue to pay for your lodging."

"Joy actually said that?"

"Joy doesn't know about this mess we're in. *I'm* saying it."

Maggie shudders, hugging herself. She regrets not putting on her coat; though the rain has stopped, the wind is rough and carries a damp cold.

"If you're not getting material, are you really working?" Grant explains. "*SBTS* can't pay you to drink tea and chitchat for days on end—no matter how amazing Ann is. We'll have to involve Joy eventually, and when we do, I can't be responsible for that kind of financial loss." He pauses, then, as if his next words are cold molasses. "You're putting me in a difficult position."

It's not Maggie doing this, though. It's Ann. Her frustration rises like a wave, but it doesn't break. It rolls through her, followed by a trough of worry. Maggie can't afford to remain on San Juan Island. Without *SBTS* paying her travel expenses, she'll have to give up before she's had a chance to make it right.

A chilly breeze tousles her hair, and she shivers. "How many more nights can *SBTS* cover?"

"Tonight."

Quivering fingers lift to her mouth; she closes her eyes for two seconds, three. "That's it?"

"That's it."

"But you already reserved my room through the end of the week."

"I'm sorry, but unless you produce something this afternoon, I can't justify dumping funds into a dead project. That makes sense to you, doesn't it?"

Though Grant can't see her, Maggie can only nod. Her eyes pool with tears. The professional victory of nailing this story would be huge for Maggie. But more personally, Ann's stories, Ann's insights . . . these past few days have been a dream not even her teenage self could've imagined.

She can't lose this opportunity. She must give Grant *something* to warrant her staying here a few days longer. There's still time to turn this around, to convince Ann to make her story—her *full* story—public.

"Did you hear me, Maggie?" Grant asks.

She still has hope—she just needs time.

Maggie lowers her voice. "What if I told you I have a little material?" She hurries down Ann's garden path and climbs into her car, shutting the door. Her recorder rests in the cup holder, and she stares at it like it's cursed. "How much would be enough to hold Joy over?"

"At this point? Probably anything." Grant's voice drops, too, as he senses Maggie's hesitation. "Why? What do you have?"

"This new recorder that Brit bought . . ." Maggie breaks off, swallows.

"The special-edition H6? With the touchy buttons? Great sound, but *damn* if I haven't wasted *gigabytes'* worth of accidental—"

Maggie hears the intake of Grant's breath, his realization. Her own heart throbs in her throat. Maybe she could've bought herself more time some other way—but this is the only path she sees ahead of her that doesn't lead home, to defeat.

"Maggie . . . ," Grant says slowly. "Tell me you didn't pocket record Ann Fawkes."

"It was an accident," Maggie says quickly.

"Please tell me you deleted it."

"I . . ." She trails off.

"Oh my *god*, Maggie. I can't send our EP an unethical recording. You have to delete it—*immediately*."

"I know, I *know*." Maggie shakes her head back and forth, back and forth, as if she can erase this situation like an Etch A Sketch. "It's just . . . I was hoping she'd consent to the recording after I convinced her to retell her story on audio. The sound quality isn't ideal, but the material—"

"You can't be serious. Maggie, if Joy heard about this, she'd fire you. The only reason *I'm* not firing you is because you're our only shot at turning this disaster around."

Maggie tries to swallow, but she can't work her throat muscles around the swell of her pulse. She can't lose this job. She *can't*. This assignment was supposed to be her big break, not her undoing.

"Some of the recording is kosher," she says, one final Hail Mary.

"What?"

"The first part—the interview I completely botched—might be okay enough to spruce up and hand over to Joy, just to justify my existence here a little bit longer."

"I don't know . . ."

"Please, Grant. We still have a chance at getting this interview—the *full* interview. And if we do, it'll be big. You can't deny that."

He sighs. "Send it over. But by god, *do not* send me any unethical material. You hear me? My ass is on the line enough as it is. If this goes sideways, you're the only person getting fired."

Maggie wipes her tear-streaked face. Despite the cold car, she's sweating. "Okay," she says softly. "Okay. Thank you for this second chance."

"It's your *last* chance. I stuck my neck out for you, Maggie—I convinced everyone to give you a shot. And now, best-case scenario, you're facing years of behind-the-scenes bullshit work. Turn this around, or you lose your job."

He hangs up.

A single, agonized sob escapes her mouth.

The worst part: Grant is being reasonable. More than reasonable—*saintlike*. This offer is more than she deserves.

Maggie takes a minute to collect her emotions and allow the blotchy redness of her cheeks to dissipate. Then she gets out and trudges back up the path.

Ann is standing on the porch, waiting for her. "Everything all right?"

Maggie nods, hoping her torment isn't too plain on her face as she steps past Ann through the door, avoiding eye contact. Why is it that tears seem to flow freer with attention? Maggie girds herself, hoping Ann doesn't look too closely and trigger the faucet.

Through the massive windows in Ann's living room, fast-moving clouds smear across the horizon, revealing blue holes in the stormy sky. Maggie follows Ann into the kitchen, where two plates await them. Ann made sandwiches and tea. She gestures for Maggie to take a seat with her at the counter.

"Something's wrong," Ann observes.

A cloud obscures the sun, and the room dims.

"It's work." Maggie pokes at her sandwich. It's sourdough with what appears to be salmon, cream cheese, and cucumber. To keep her lip from wavering, Maggie takes a bite. She chews, swallows, wipes her mouth—and finally meets Ann's gaze full on. Rather than breaking down as she expected, the eye contact makes her stronger. Bolder. "Can I not record even a *little* of our conversation?"

"Absolutely not."

"What if I told you my job is on the line?"

"Why is that?"

"Isn't it obvious? They took a risk, giving me this assignment. They can't pay me to be here if I don't get any material." Maggie leans forward. "We don't have to record much—just something. Enough that—"

"I've made myself clear."

"Please," Maggie begs. "It doesn't have to be much."

Ann shakes her head, but Maggie spots a tiny crystal of fear forming in Ann's honeyed eyes.

Maggie straightens. "Why am I here?"

"You tell me. I was clear about this arrangement."

"But what's the point in telling me any of this? Why me? Why now? Why should I stay?"

Ann dabs her mouth with a napkin, though she hasn't eaten anything yet. "Don't you *want* to stay?"

"I do," Maggie admits. "It's an honor. But I don't want to lose my job. I can't afford to." She narrows her eyes. "There must be *some* reason why you're compelled to do this."

The corner of Ann's mouth quivers, just a little, just enough.

Maggie hit a nerve. She should keep prodding but doesn't want to push too hard, in case she's pressing not just a nerve, but a wound. "Just say you'll think about it, all right? We don't have to record everything."

Ann's nod is almost imperceptible, a tiny relinquishment.

But Maggie needs a verbal confirmation. "You'll think about it?"

"I'll think about it," Ann says finally.

It's a win—albeit a small one. But now a new question lingers, a question that Ann is clearly concerned about answering: Why is Maggie here? Deep in her gut, she knows the answer is more complicated than simply *Keith* or the healing power of *telling*.

But for now, Maggie won't push. Instead, she'll savor the small win of Ann agreeing to *think about it*. Because that's far greater than an outright *no*.

Maggie takes another bite of sandwich. It's good. She's hungry. "Should we continue?"

There's a shoebox sitting at the end of the counter. With a roll of her shoulders, Ann seems to gain some composure and slides the box closer.

ANN

In a fit of dark emotions, do you ever ruin some small, sentimental thing, only to regret it later? Rather than mail my mother the photos from Mykonos and Santorini, I threw the whole camera away. I was bitter and hurt and angry over many things at once. I never imagined I'd someday *want* to remember Greece, but oh, Maggie, how my mother would have cherished my captures. What I wouldn't give for those pictures now.

Shattered from the strike of Todd's rejection and frustrated with myself for having a porcelain heart, I traveled. That's the thing about travel—it makes your problems seem far away. I wanted to be a different person, a new person, a stranger. I slipped into anonymity hoping I could hide from my feelings—but they were my shadow.

I traveled through the Mediterranean for nine months before finally landing in Rome. I found an apartment in a charming neighborhood shrugged up against the Tiber River; the space was small but full of light, with a balcony and hardwood floors. I hadn't planned to linger for long, but Rome bewitched me.

It was summertime when I arrived. I used to joke that the fresh tomatoes and basil won me over. I befriended a restaurateur named Carmella who took me to all the best markets, showed me all the finest vendors, and spoiled me with decadent dishes. She was dating a barista at the time, who made us cappuccinos, and how could I not fall in love with a city so full of flavor?

Rome is also where I began my writing career.

I bought a Brother portable electric typewriter and poked out hundreds of thousands of words—not just in *Chasing Shadows* but following Keith's advice too. I wrote short stories and articles based on my travels and sold a good few to journals and magazines. I found a sense of purpose in my writing and began to build a name for myself. And all the while I worked on my novel.

Many consider *Chasing Shadows* to be semiautobiographical. I always found this speculation invasive and unrealistic: What art isn't personal? The book's plot was all fiction, but of course there was truth in its sentiment. It's harrowing, sorrowful, angry—but it's also brave, romantic, and big. This was the dichotomy of my emotional landscape after my mother insulted me and Todd rejected me. The book was a study in how to unravel love from disappointment.

Then, one day, *Chasing Shadows* was done. I typed out four hundred fresh pages and slid them into a box. Keith's blue business card was faded around the edges, worn and creased from months spent traveling with me across Europe. I hoped the address was the same.

I mailed the book off and waited.

Fretted, and waited.

Then waited some more.

I worried he'd forgotten me, or hated me, or hated the book. I was miserable with anticipation when the box finally returned. It looked as if it'd been through hell. Two corners were dented, and it had all manner of brown scuffs and foreign-looking stamps.

Inside was even worse. My manuscript's once-crisp pages were tattered and coffee stained, tattooed in red pen.

When I saw the state of my book, I grinned—no, I *beamed*.

Not only did Keith remember me, he had *edited* my book! This meant that he believed in the book—believed in *me*.

Included with the manuscript was a note:

> Ann,
> It's a delight to hear from you! Your novel is a work of art, and I believe it could go far. Do not be discouraged by the number of edits suggested here—I am thorough because I care.
> —Your Friend and Editor, Keith

While the novel had grown from a deeply personal place, I was not precious with it. It was a blackberry bush: scraggly, thorny, misshapen. I thought carefully about Keith's suggestions and where I wanted the story to go, seeking each sweet berry—an astute description, a strong sentence, a stellar word—and nurturing them to ripeness.

I worked tirelessly for three weeks—much to Carmella's chagrin, as she had then broken up with her barista boyfriend and wanted to go out almost every night after work. But I was almost there, I told her. It was almost perfect.

When I finished the edits, I wrote Keith a note to accompany the fresh draft:

> Keith,
> You flatter me. Thank you for the tough love. I think you'll like this new version.
> —Your Grateful Friend and Author, Ann
>
> P.S. How is Todd?

This time, the waiting was gratifying, like waiting for Carmella to make tiramisu. I spent my spare time working on a new short story. Then:

> *Ann,*
> *You are stellar. Here's your next round of edits.*
> *— Your Biggest Fan, Keith*

I'll admit, when I received that second box from Keith, I *did* go out with Carmella. It just goes to show how little I knew about novel writing, Maggie. I had thought I was done.

> *Keith,*
> *Send a bottle of wine next time, would you?*
> *— Your Exhausted Author, Ann*

By then, it was late November 1985. The river outside my window smelled sweet with rotting leaves. Carmella cooked eggplant dishes that tasted homey. I hadn't stayed in one place this long since I left Colorado; I realized I wanted to live permanently in Trastevere, Rome.

> *Ann,*
> *I've taped some wine-money to the last page. Don't skip ahead.*
> *— Sympathetic Keith*

In addition to letters, Keith and I also spoke on the phone, discussing the more contentious suggestions and editorial quagmires. Still, we liked the quaintness of attaching letters to the manuscript box—so we kept that up too.

Ann,

After our most recent call, I think we've hit a breakthrough. Can't wait for your next mailing.

   Also, some news: I left my job at the publishing company to start my own agency. I know I could've voiced this on the phone, but written proof makes it feel real. Everyone—including my wife (yes, wife!) Barbara— thinks I'm crazy. Be my first client?

   —Your (Hopefully) New Agent, Keith

   P.S. Todd asked about you. I told him you're a genius. He didn't seem surprised.

Nineteen eighty-six. I made my elderly landlord a cash offer on my apartment, and Carmella helped me with the visa paperwork that would allow me to stay in Rome longer term. I had found a home.

Keith,

I'm happy you and Barbara found your way back to each other. A new life, a new business: what a great way to start a new year. Send a contract—let's be official!

   —Your New Client, Ann

   P.S. ~~Tell Todd I miss~~ I hope Todd is well.

Ann,

We are official! Congratulations. I won't let you down.

   Also, I think we're almost done editing this beast.

   More good news: I'm going to be a father.

   —Daddy Keith

Keith,
Please don't call yourself "Daddy Keith."
    But congratulations.
    —Happy-for-You Ann

Ann,
Received the latest version—the book is perfect. Let's cast the line and see who bites.
    —Big Daddy Keith

MAGGIE

Months of correspondence are spread across Ann's kitchen counter; she kept every note, every draft. Ann's letters appear rushed, feverish, as if the words burst out of her. Keith's words are carefully constructed, as if they were *meant* to be saved in this way, captured on his own letterhead.

Maggie thumbs through the letters, hung up on the delicate swirl of her uncle's handwriting. She touches the imprint of Keith's signature. Her chest sags, heavy, as if filled with waterlogged soil. And yet a smile blooms across her face, warmed by the memory of him.

The Whitaker family has always been close. Keith was the eldest sibling, then Natalie and Tracey, twins. The family never spoke of the youngest sister, who died long before Maggie was born. She only ever heard whisperings on the anniversary of her death, a day that still sends her mom into a stupor.

The Whitakers considered family a priority: this value was a symptom of their loss, further fortified by their collective grief. There were Whitaker camping trips and ski trips, with neighborly visits in between. Maggie grew up surrounded by older cousins. Spouses like Barbara and Bob always seemed to be sucked into the Whitaker orbit; Maggie rarely heard about other relatives, let alone attended a function. Easters, Christmases, milestone birthdays—the Whitakers were their own solar system, and Keith was the sun.

When they lost him, everyone's usual orbits seemed to shrink, wobble, and collapse. Now that Maggie's grandparents and Keith are gone, and all the cousins are grown, it seems the family is floating out in space. And as the chasm widens, so does the question in her heart. How did Maggie—a meteor in the Whitaker galaxy—come crashing into this family?

"Are you all right?" Ann is watching her, her brows drawn together ever so slightly, as if she's trying to read Maggie's mind without Maggie knowing.

Maggie sets the letter on the counter. Nods.

When she was a sophomore in high school, Maggie attended her first unchaperoned party. Samantha Liu's mom had been working late and unaware of her popular daughter's habit of stealing cheap rum. When Maggie arrived with three of her Lit Club friends—all wearing their tightest pairs of skinny jeans—red Solo cups crowded every counter, side table, and shelf. Her classmates were smoking and laughing and making out in dark corners, and Maggie felt both thrilled and out of her depth.

Lit Club had just read *Chasing Shadows* for the first time, and Maggie wanted to be worldly like its main character, Jane. Jane smoked, drank, and had sex. And despite Jane feeling the same angst and melancholy that Maggie knew so well (for Maggie, a mere symptom of puberty), Jane was confident, and empowered, and bold. Maggie wanted to be just like Jane, so she picked up her first-ever Solo cup and choked through her first-ever cigarette, and two hours later, Maggie's head was spinning, and she burst out the front door to puke on the Liu residence's porch.

Her friend who'd driven her there was nowhere to be found. Maggie couldn't call her parents, for fear of their disappointment and wrath, and so Maggie called the only other person she could trust: Keith.

He picked her up fifteen minutes later, and she rode with her head between her knees all the way to his house. He parked in the driveway and shut off the car, their porch light shining through the windshield like a policeman's flashlight. Guilt burned across her face, but when Keith spoke, his tone was gentle.

"Adolescence is hard," he said. "You want to be independent, cool, and accepted by your peers. It's a rite of passage, I think, to try so hard to control what people think of us, all so we can learn who we really are." Keith held Maggie's bleary eyes, his gaze steadfast, anchoring her. "Did you feel like *you* tonight, Maggie?"

She shook her head, stirring up the spins and nausea still swirling through her system.

"Then this is a good lesson, don't you think?"

She became tearful, though she was not exactly sure why.

Keith drew her into a hug and kissed her hair. "Do you want to know a secret?" he whispered. "*Chasing Shadows* took a lot of editing. A lot." He pulled back but gripped her shoulders to stabilize her, ensure her attention. "We're all works in progress. Even Jane. Even Ann Fawkes. Even me. The important thing to remember is to learn from every experience."

Maggie stayed in Iris's old room that night and woke up the next morning thinking about *Chasing Shadows* and the betrayal Ann had captured on the page. It was the same sort of betrayal Maggie felt, a deep, bladelike cut slashing her heart each and every time she wondered where she came from: adoption, or infidelity, or a sperm donor, or one of those stories on the news, of a baby left in a dumpster or at a firehouse. Despite Keith's words being comforting, that night sharpened a pain in Maggie that she thought she had managed to dull.

A couple of years later, it was that same pain that made Maggie want to try a journalism course at the community college, and it's that same pain that slices through her now, sitting in Ann's kitchen.

"Are you sure you're all right?" Ann asks.

Maggie blinks from the letters to Ann's face. It's strange to think that this woman—whom Maggie has known for less than a week—possesses the same grief and enduring fondness for her uncle as she does. That both of them have their own collection of touching, embarrassing, and happy memories.

"I'm just surprised by Keith's impeccable penmanship," Maggie quips. "You're the writer, isn't *yours* supposed to be the neater script?"

At Maggie's joke, Ann's face transforms, brightening. "You forget that, despite being a golden retriever in a man's body, Keith had his shit together—far more than I did." She taps on a letter. "I always loved his handwriting—it was so methodical. It made me feel like he cared."

Maggie nods, remembering a similar feeling when she read the edits he made on her essays or the way he wrote such thoughtful cards on her birthday. She still has her high school graduation card from him.

Ann tilts her wrist to read her watch. It's evening now, the outside a deep indigo, glowing slightly in the remaining twilight. "I have more letters to dig out of the attic," she says. "Do you want to pause here?"

"Have you given more thought to recording—"

"Why don't we discuss it in the morning?"

Rather than heading back to the B&B to fret over her last night here, Maggie drives downtown and ducks into a dim, half-full bar. She takes a seat at a two-person table in the back, nestled against a wall. A waitress comes by with a happy hour menu and a plastic cup of water; Maggie orders a beer, and her first sip fizzes in her throat all wrong.

To distract from the soldier march of stress in her head, Maggie takes another three gulps and texts Grant an update: She's going to sleep on it.

Later, feeling a slight buzz, Maggie opens the Whitaker Family text thread on her phone. She doesn't allow herself to think or doubt, just type.

Remember the time Keith broke his clavicle at Breckenridge? she writes.

lol you mean the time he was being a sore loser? Iris replies.

Keith had challenged his daughter to a snowmobiling race and, when she was clearly in the lead, had tried to cut through a stand of trees and crashed.

He was constantly giving me frights, Barbara adds, and Maggie grins at her reply.

When the family group text had gone quiet, it was Barbara's message—Maybe another time—that had been left there at the bottom of the thread. It had been her last-ditch effort to plan a barbecue without her beloved husband, and she'd been met with noncommittal replies.

To revive this thread, even for a few minutes, feels like a small victory, sweet as rain after a drought. And to think a stupid memory about Keith's antics was the only thing standing between the family's silence and reconnection. And perhaps time too. Time to heal.

He was always young at heart, Maggie writes.

Aunt Natalie's son, Barrett, sends a link to "Forever Young" on YouTube.

You know, he broke the other clavicle when we were teens, Natalie says.

how?? Iris asks.

A typing bubble pops up from Tracey, and Maggie's heart skips. It disappears, then pops up again, pending, pending, and then: Sneaking out of Barbara's window the night before his high school graduation.

Iris sends a series of surprised, laughing, and horrified emojis.

Maggie sips her beer, watching the replies continue, the memories and jokes at Keith's expense, the love pouring out.

In a one-on-one text, Tracey sends Maggie an old photo of herself at twelve, on that same Breckenridge trip, clad in navy-blue snow pants and leaning against a snowmobile between Keith and Bob. You and your favorite guys, Tracey says.

It's the first thing she's received from her mom since their argument about Ann. Maggie takes a moment to dig through the Favorites folder on her phone and sends along a picture of herself and her parents making snow angels. Bob had been the one to drive Keith down the mountain to receive medical help, and when Keith was discharged, he'd taken this photo of Maggie and her parents on the snow-covered lawn outside the hospital.

Tracey replies with three heart emojis, and Maggie is staring at them when she's interrupted: "Ann's friend."

She lifts her head. "Ann's bodyguard."

"Pastry chef, actually." Matt smiles, revealing a set of straight teeth, save for one slightly out-of-place canine—a charming imperfection. "May I hold you captive for a moment?"

She pockets her phone and gestures to the seat opposite her. He sits, resting both elbows on the table and lacing his fingers together over his pint.

"Let me guess," Maggie says, "this is about Ann?"

His lips pinch. "I just wanted to say that Ann is very special."

"I agree," Maggie says slowly. "She's very talented and kind."

"No," Matt says. "See, that's exactly my concern. All you people—"

"'You people'?"

"Reporters, fans," Matt says, waving an irritated hand. "You don't see Ann as a person."

"Excuse me?"

His oaky eyes are hard-focused. "I know she's telling you her story . . . and you shouldn't take that for granted."

"What makes you think I am?"

"I've known Ann a long time," Matt says. "She's not as tough as she seems."

"So, you're her *emotional* bodyguard."

A smirk plays across his mouth. "I'm like a son to her."

Maggie finishes her beer. "Is that all you came over to say?" She stands, gathering her things, suddenly so tired from the emotions of the day that she could pass out.

Matt stands too. "Look, I don't know you—"

"That's true."

"—but I know Ann. And I love Ann. The people on this island . . . we're a tight-knit community. We look out for her. That's all I'm trying to do here. Keith and Todd . . . they're sensitive subjects."

Maggie isn't blind—of course Ann is hurting. Reliving her life like this must be hard for her to orate—even if it *is* therapeutic. Still, Maggie finds it difficult to believe that Ann is as fragile as Matt claims. "It's very sweet of you to be concerned, but if you knew anything about this, you'd know that the person most likely to be hurt at the end of all this isn't Ann—it's me."

Matt's concern, while endearing, is ill placed. Even in grief, Ann will remain unscathed in the telling. If anyone stands to get beat up by the truths Ann has been hiding—and Ann's unwillingness to be recorded—it's Maggie. If this doesn't work out, it's *Maggie* who stands to lose everything.

Matt frowns. "What did you say your name was?"

"Maggie." She moves past Matt, stepping up to the bar to pay her tab. The bartender takes her card.

Matt sidles next to her and spreads his hands. "Maggie . . . ?"

"Whitaker."

Matt's forehead creases, a pair of vertical lines forming between his eyebrows. He straightens and steps back ever so slightly, as if to look at her from a wider angle. "You're . . . related to Keith?"

Her phone is still buzzing in her pocket, a reminder of that relation and the love and grief and secrets attached to it. Poor Ann, to have been cast out from that connection. One of Keith's very best friends, left by the wayside. What had severed the ties between Ann and Uncle Keith?

Maggie signs her receipt and slides it back across the bar. "It's nice seeing you again, Matt. Thanks for your concern about Ann. It's . . . heartening to know that she still has people around who care about her." And with that, she exits the bar, leaving Matt and his odd sentiments behind.

ANN

"I have a surprise," Keith said as we walked side by side into the final bookstore on my book tour. "I added one more stop."

I halted, and my publicist, Kim—who had been walking behind us with a notebook in hand—stumbled to a stop behind Keith. "You're kidding," I said, not amused.

I hadn't enjoyed the tour—the last place I wanted to be was back in America, with its abrasive crowds and young, ugly cities. But my book had sold at auction. Three competing publishers had bid, driving up the size of my advance and garnering much anticipation. *Chasing Shadows* had received stellar early reviews from established authors and critics at trade journals, and suddenly my short stories and travel articles were getting into publications like the *New Yorker* and *Travel + Leisure*. Award buzz for *Chasing Shadows* was already humming.

The tour was inevitable.

My gratitude toward *Chasing Shadows'* success was the only thing that kept me going on the rigorous schedule. Five weeks after release, I'd visited eighteen bookstores and five radio studios in six major cities.

Today's afternoon event in Denver, Colorado, was supposed to be my final appearance.

For Keith to add a last-minute stop was just cruel.

Keith ushered me and Kim out of the bookstore's doorway, over to a display table filled only with copies of my book. "It's a small neighborhood venue with a lot of charm," he said. "I promise you'll love it."

"See, now I'm starting to think you're not kidding."

"I'm not kidding," Keith said.

"And when is this happening?" I asked.

"This evening," he said. "We'll do this appearance, have an early dinner, then drive to the last stop."

"You confirmed this?" I asked Kim. She was a rigid scheduler, and I knew she didn't like the unexpected.

"Why not?" she said with a shrug. "You'll sell more books." Clearly, the tour had worn her down too.

Seeing my horror, Keith added, "It'll be a mellow, intimate reading. No big deal."

No big deal had practically been Keith's catchphrase lately, and I was tired of hearing it. I hadn't been to the United States since I'd left three years ago, and it felt wrong to be here again.

In the fourteen months before my book's publication, my life in Italy had assumed a steady rhythm that was safe and content. In addition to my career—final edits, galley proofs, story writing, phone interviews—Carmella had helped me set up a business of sorts: translating menus for the clusters of trendy up-and-coming restaurants that were steadily moving into the area. Through free dinners and menu translations, I'd grown a sense of community and connection with the neighborhood.

I missed Trastevere dearly.

I missed my apartment. I missed my bookshelf, where, with pride, I had displayed the beautifully embossed prepublication hardback of *Chasing Shadows*. I missed my rickety balcony and backward water taps and the cats I often fed on the stoop. I missed drinking cappuccinos and having dinner with Carmella. I missed Rome. My home.

Though the booksellers I encountered on tour were friendly, the crowds overwhelmed me. The questions were prying, and there was no hiding behind microphones. Moreover, I felt like a fraud. Through brunches and schmoozy dinners, I couldn't wrap my head around why anyone would want to hear my words. I was shocked by my own accomplishments—so shocked, I believed I was undeserving.

But I was wrong to doubt myself, Maggie. I should've basked in that brief window of glory. I wish I had stood taller and thought, *Yes, I deserve this.* Because I had worked hard on that book, and so did Keith. I had gone through hell to write my main character Jane's emotions clear and true.

Homesickness, impostor syndrome, watery eyes and a raspy voice from sleep deprivation—for all these reasons and more, I wanted to flat-out refuse Keith's plan. But then the event manager of the bookstore found us forcefully whispering by the *Chasing Shadows* display, and her arrival defused the argument.

She introduced herself as Lisa and led us past the half-filled rows of audience chairs into a back room. While Keith unpacked a water bottle and my dog-eared reading copy of *Chasing Shadows*—which was worn and blank looking, long ago stripped of its shiny jacket, just as I felt—I asked Lisa if I could borrow a phone. She ushered me into a conjoined office and closed the door, leaving me to my privacy.

I leaned against the cluttered desk, staring down at the phone like it was a sick animal that might snap if I got too close.

A week ago, from my hotel in San Francisco, I'd dialed Mom's number and left a message with the time and location of my reading in Denver. I'd tried again last night, eschewing another voice mail when she didn't pick up. Nearing three years after Greece, I could count on one hand the number of times I'd spoken to my mother. Being in Denver had given me an uneasy sort of wistfulness I did not relish.

Still, I wanted my mother at this reading. The last time we'd spoken, she'd asked for more money; the least she could do was show her support in person. But I also wanted her to recognize that her daughter was better off, that the distance had ultimately been good for me—as if, in some way, my success could absolve me from leaving her behind.

I picked up the phone and dialed.

It rang, and rang, and each time it rang, my heart cracked a little wider. When I heard the voice mail tone, I hung up. I told myself she wasn't answering because she was on her way. Maybe she was already sitting in the audience.

When the time came, I followed Lisa out to the small podium. Eighty people had come, all crammed into sixty chairs, overflowing into the neighboring aisles of bookshelves. I searched the faces for one that resembled an older version of my own. Perhaps she'd hit traffic.

Throughout my reading, I periodically glanced toward the door, willing my mother to walk through. But then the reading was over, and still she had not come.

After the clapping died down, Lisa fielded audience questions for me to answer. *Chasing Shadows* was currently number one on the *New York Times* bestseller list, and despite the book being so new, many audience members had already read it. My voice sounded crisp but unrecognizable to my own ears through the microphone. I offered the same responses I'd been parroting for the past month. Vague answers to prying questions about Jane's absent mother, Jane's messy romantic life, Jane's terrible loneliness—trying to convince people that it was all fiction.

I could barely hear myself over the roaring disappointment in my head.

Finally, I was led to a nearby table to sign books. People lined up, clutching their to-be-signed books. I asked for names, spellings. My fingers began to cramp from scribbling my signature; the loops always flattened as a signing went on, my hand forgetting the shape of my own name, like saying a word so many times it loses meaning.

Without Mom there, all of it lost meaning. I didn't want to want her pride, but I did. So I clung to the last thread of hope that she would show. Every so often, my eyes flicked past the immediate reader to the line stretching behind them, out of view. Maybe I had missed a face. My heart clenched each time my gaze roved the queue of strangers with no recognition.

I kept signing. *And what's your name? How do you spell that? Thank you for coming.* The fancy pen Keith had bought me glided over the thick title pages, ink interrupting the textured off-white paper. There were a few *Chasing Shadows* phrases I cycled through: *Good luck in your chase*, and *Nurture your shadow*, and *Love is worth it.* Clever little things that related to the book and sounded inspiring but were, in fact, useless platitudes.

No wonder my mother hadn't shown up; her daughter was a hack.

As I greeted the next reader, I spotted Keith at the end of the line, about fifteen people back. He was talking to someone I couldn't see from my low vantage point at the table. I leaned, trying to see past the crowd, but I couldn't make out a face—just a flicker of auburn hair. Like mine.

The person in front of me cleared his throat. "Can you make it out to my wife? She couldn't come tonight."

I blinked, refocusing on his features. He wore a gray pinstripe work shirt with the name *Price* sewn in red cursive over his heart. "Sure," I said. "How do you spell your wife's name?"

I glanced at Keith again, my heart swelling. Had she come, after all? Had Keith seen her in the crowd and recognized her?

I blinked back to the man in front of me. "Can you spell it one more time?"

"P-a-m," he said, a slight frown pulling the corner of his mouth.

I pressed my lips together, embarrassed by my own lack of attention. "Pam? What a coincidence, that's my mother's name."

He merely shrugged.

Still resisting my urge to glance past the man to spot the woman-who-might-be-my-mother at the back of the line, I wrote his wife a special note in the book and handed it back to him. "I'm sorry I'm distracted—it's been a long tour."

"No problem." He smiled, then plodded away.

From my seat, bodies blocked my view considerably; there were still ten more readers. As I signed more books, Keith and possibly-my-mother inched closer. I worked faster, reeling them in with my pen. One book, then another. The line shifted, and a gap occurred. The person talking to Keith pivoted into view.

My heart screwed tight. The muscles in my pen hand twitched. It wasn't her. The woman with my mother's hair had a fresh face and a name tag on her blazer—a bookstore employee.

Mom had really not come.

I signed the rest of the books in haste, and then the event was over, and the red-haired employee was taking down the display of my books. Lisa and Kim came over to congratulate me on a successful visit. I don't recall what Keith said to them. I stared at the shelves of books surrounding us and imagined their collective weight on my chest, pressing down. I had the urge to write my frustration into my notebook—always scribbling my feelings away—and yet I was tempted to never write another word again. Because no matter how many words I wrote, my mother would never care to read them.

After a quick nap at my hotel, I climbed into the passenger side of Keith's rental car to drive to my surprise final event. My eyes were gritty and my mouth tasted stale; in an act of defiance, I hadn't even brushed my pillow hair.

"Where's Kim?" I asked, buckling my seat belt. My mood had not improved—in fact, I felt even more dejected—but at least the sleep had recovered some energy.

"I told her to take tonight off."

"What, my publicist can take the night off, but I can't?"

"We don't need her for this reading."

"We don't?"

"I told you: it's mellow." Keith handed me a small McDonald's bag. "Here, dinner."

"You sure know how to spoil a girl," I said, plucking out a fry. The salt awoke my hunger, and I crammed more fries into my mouth.

Weeks ago, in New York, had been the first time I'd seen Keith since Greece. I'd worried it would be awkward between us, but the book had long ago broken the thin layer of ice that had frozen between us after my departure from Santorini. He hadn't come along on the full tour; his visits coincided with other in-person client meetings—the brilliant but alcoholic debut author in San Francisco, the stony mystery writer in Boston, the odd essayist in Charlotte—but Denver was different. Like me, he had been raised in Colorado.

After devouring the burger, I asked, "Where are we headed?" He'd merged onto the highway, and it was clear we were leaving the city.

Keith confirmed my suspicion: "My childhood neighborhood. It has a charming bookstore. You'll love it."

In a slight panic, I asked, "You couldn't just *show* me this bookstore, rather than forcing me to read there?"

"Why miss an opportunity to sell books?"

"You sound like Kim," I said, crumpling my McDonald's bag. The greasy food was quickly turning sour in my stomach. "I'm not about to meet your whole family, am I?"

Keith chuckled. "No, I wouldn't spring that on you."

"Then—"

"No more questions. You'll see when we get there." He reached for the radio. Fleetwood Mac's "Dreams" came through the speakers, and we both hummed along. I could practically feel the Aegean breeze on my face, when the three of us had sung the same lyrics while gazing out over the caldera. The memory sat in the car as tangibly as a person in the back seat.

An hour later, we pulled into a parking space along a sleepy street lined with cute shops and quaint restaurants. Humid July air clung to my arms and thighs, the thick wind lazily wafting the hem of my dress. A chiseled mountain—or rather a hill, by Colorado's standards—loomed over the walkable main drag. We were in some suburb of the Springs, though I didn't recognize it. Too middle class for my childhood. I shouldered my bag and walked beside Keith down the clean sidewalk.

The bookstore was not far. A black awning with scalloped edges shaded the storefront, and a sandwich board boasted my name:

Ann Fawkes book signing TONIGHT!

The doorway was framed by bay windows. Behind the warped glass, old library ladders had been repurposed as display bookshelves, one on each side. High in the left window hung a delicate lantern painted like the sun, with yellow swirls and a serene burnt-orange face; the right window featured a moon lantern and many string lights. A small decal on the front door announced **Dreamer Bookstore**. A dream, indeed.

Keith turned the doorknob, and I forgot all my woes. Antique chandeliers provided buttery light by which to read, with plush chairs tucked into gaps and corners. The walls were adorned with beautiful murals: a book-shaped boat riding a tempestuous sea swell, a small girl reaching toward a star from atop a massive stack of hardbacks, a leafy jungle with vines spelling out words like *wonder* and *journey*. The bookshelves were not the standard cheap-looking uniform frames but sturdy repurposed wood in odd shapes and heights. The bookstore was a place of whimsy and adventure. A book lover's dream—the opposite of the major chains that had been the backbone of my tour.

I veered away from Keith, following a narrow aisle of literary fiction that led to the back of the store. A cluster of folding chairs had been set up in a half moon around a podium painted to resemble newsprint. People were already filtering in, chatting quietly in their seats. A modest display of *Chasing Shadows* had been set up on a side table, prominent but not flashy.

My spirits lifted. This was the first place at which I truly felt excited to read—and how could I not? It was all bookish charm.

"Ann," Keith said, waving for my attention at the far end of a row.

I backtracked, heading his way. "I hate to admit it, but you were right. This place is wonderful."

Keith smiled—not smug, but knowing. "I want you to meet the owner before we get started," he said, leading me toward the checkout desk.

When the man behind the counter turned around, the grease of my fast-food dinner clambered up my esophagus. I made a garbled noise, half gag and half gasp.

"Copper," Todd said. "I'm so glad you came."

ANN

I despised how easily the sight of Todd could electrocute my calm. It had been years—*years*—since I'd last seen him. How far had I traveled? How many men had shared my bed? Somehow time had no effect on my shame and desire. It all came rushing back in an instant.

Todd produced a bouquet of flowers from somewhere behind the front desk. "These are for you."

I took them, my senses still short-circuiting. Up close, Todd appeared better than ever: bigger muscles, brighter complexion, new frames for his glasses. He stood a little taller too. I glanced at Keith, my breath stolen by shock; he was grinning like an idiot.

I couldn't process it.

I swung my attention to something more palatable: the flowers. I leaned into the bouquet, the petals kissing my cheeks as I inhaled. The fragrance was a pleasant, sweet green. For a moment I felt safe with my head buried in the stems.

"Do you like them?"

I met Todd's eyes over the lilies and dahlias. Nodded.

"Surprised?" Keith asked me, still grinning.

Was this a joke? Or had he forgotten how things had ended in Greece? Perhaps Keith thought our correspondence and business partnership had erased the pain of Santorini, but it hadn't. Keith and I had formed new memories, but Todd—Todd and I were still on that rooftop, drunk and arguing.

I don't love you.

That was how I remembered Todd. The emotions of that night surged through me all over again, the distinct pitch of rejection after flying so high on infatuation. I thought I had grown in the three years since Greece, but standing before him now, I was still the naive girl he'd met in Venice, heart in her hand, destined for a letdown.

"I know this is . . . weird," Todd said. "But I'm ecstatic you could be here."

"Is this your bookstore?"

"Yes," Keith said at the same time Todd clarified, "My parents'."

I had to admit: "It's magical. The murals . . ."

"My father painted them. He was a children's book illustrator." *Was.*

"He illustrated all of Connie's books," Keith added.

"My mother," Todd said.

Realization clicked. *This* was his parents' business. A bookstore. Dreamer Bookstore. When we'd discussed employment in Venice, Todd had changed the subject. Had that been because his parents were no longer around? It broke my heart to think of them gone, their son carrying their legacy.

But Todd also broke my heart—smashed it to pieces.

I was sweating in my dress, wet rings forming under my arms. I grew claustrophobic, the beautifully painted walls closing in on me. "I . . . I can't read here," I whispered.

Keith touched my arm. "Of course you can."

I was shaking my head—or perhaps all of me was shaking. "I can't," I said. "I just . . ." I dropped the flowers on the counter and ran through the door, down the sidewalk, to the rental car. I bent over, dragging the hot evening air through my lungs. I thought I'd spent the past three years *healing*, but I'd merely been *forgetting*. Seeing Todd brought it all to the forefront again.

Keith stormed over. "What the hell was that?"

"That's what I'd like to know," I said, wheeling toward him. Out in the fresh, balmy air, the numbness of my shock now morphed into humming anger. My body was abuzz. "Why did you spring him on me like that?"

"It was a happy surprise!" Keith said. "I thought you'd be glad."

I threw my hands in the air, exasperated. "Why on *earth* would I be glad?"

"It's Todd!"

A pair of window-shoppers glanced our way, and I pinched my mouth closed, waiting for them to pass.

In a low voice, I asked, "Do you recall how Todd and I left things?"

"I thought that was water under the bridge."

"Did he tell you that?"

"No, but I—"

"Things are not *resolved* with Todd. I thought you knew better than to keep playing matchmaker. How did you get him to agree to this?"

"He asked if he could host you," Keith said, folding his arms. "He wanted to congratulate you. Celebrate you."

That angered me even more—that Todd thought he could use my book tour as a way to repent. But the anger was short lived. My eyes traveled the block to the bookshop, where Todd was standing out front, watching us with obvious concern etched on his faraway features. Though he was out of earshot, I worried he could infer the wobble in my voice when I uttered a weak, "Yeah, well . . . ," and dipped my chin. My heart was a sponge being squeezed of all its juices.

"What's wrong?" Keith asked, stepping closer. "I thought you remembered our time in Greece fondly?"

"I *do*," I said. "It's just"—my voice cracked, but I talked through it—"I thought I was over him, but apparently I'm not." Gaining steam, I added, "And my mother never came tonight—my own mother! And I'm tired, Keith. I just want to go home. I miss my stoop cats, and the markets, and my quiet life. I hate America. I hate being on *display*. I've been on edge for weeks, and—"

He drew me into his arms, cutting off my rant. "I'm sorry, I didn't realize. I didn't think of it that way."

I tucked my face into his chest and let a few tears fall before forcing myself back into composure. I released him, cleared my throat, and wiped my wet cheeks. Todd was still watching us from down the street. "I know it's wildly unprofessional, but I can't do a reading there."

"It's okay, he'll understand," Keith said. "But I'll have to go back to explain. Do you want to wait in the car?"

"Yes, please." It occurred to me that Keith had not seen his best friend in a long time; he hadn't been home since Christmas. "Will you have another chance to visit with him?"

"Tomorrow," he said, handing me the car keys. "I'll be right back."

A big sigh rolled through me. I climbed into the passenger seat and turned the ignition, dialing up the air conditioning. In the side mirror, I watched Keith return to the bookstore. He clapped a hand on Todd's back. As he spoke, Todd's face sank, but I couldn't tell whether it was disappointment or simply a trick of shadow. Next, they hugged, and then Todd retreated back into his shop and Keith returned to the car.

"Was he . . . ?"

Keith buckled his seat belt and put the car in drive. "Understanding."

"Thanks."

"He's a good man, Ann."

"That's the worst part."

We drove the rest of the way in silence. Outside my hotel, Keith hugged me one more time, squeezing me until my muscles ached.

"Thank you for . . . all of it," I said lamely.

Keith's eyes crinkled. "I'm really proud of you, Ann. I hope you know the magnitude of what you've accomplished."

"I couldn't have done any of this without you," I told him, and I meant it. He'd been the one to suggest I write short stories and articles to get my name into the world. He'd been the one to edit my novel and sell it and advocate for good publicity. He'd single-handedly launched my career. And though my mother wasn't around to be proud, Keith was—and that meant the world to me.

"I'm very glad we met," he said.

"I've made you a lot of money."

He chuckled. "Yes, but I'm also glad about the friendship."

"Me too."

And with that, my book tour was over.

My flight to Rome was a red-eye the following night, and I slept that last day away, feeling lonely and sorry for myself, wondering why I wasn't happy in the center of all that success.

I could have visited my mother before I left, Maggie. I had the time. But I didn't. Why should I show up for her when she couldn't show up for me? That was my logic. I was too preoccupied by my run-in with Todd and too angry with my mother to do the right thing.

I don't have many regrets in my life, but not visiting her before I returned to Rome is one of them, because it would've been the last time I saw her.

But of course, life isn't about knowing things ahead of time.

MAGGIE

San Juan Island, Washington State, USA
Tuesday, January 9, 2024

Maggie wishes she could know things ahead of time—or at least know how this assignment ends. It's Tuesday morning, and she has a lot on her mind—volumes' worth, straining her shoulders, pulling her neck muscles taut.

Her conversation with Matt last night made seeing him this morning—delivering a small coffee cake for Ann and Maggie to share—rather uncomfortable. He'd fixed her with a weighted stare before he hugged Ann goodbye.

Then there's Grant. When she checked in with him this morning, he said he could stall Joy a little longer—but from here on out, all expenses are out of Maggie's tiny pocket. With her entry-level salary and steep student loan payments, just two more nights on the island will obliterate her personal budget. Then she'll be forced to give up and potentially face unemployment for her professional failure.

And finally: Tracey. Maggie hasn't heard anything from her since last night, though the Whitaker Family thread has continued to buzz with chitchat—a small buoy in Maggie's sea of stress and doubt. But when things get quiet, Maggie can't help but hear her mother's warning, like a storm brewing in the distance, a static rumbling in the background of everything else. *Be careful.*

It's all too much.

Ann pauses, seeming to sense Maggie's distracted state.

Maggie pushes her thoughts aside and leans forward. "But you didn't know," Maggie says of Ann's mother. "You can't blame yourself for acting as you did if you didn't know."

"Regret doesn't work like that, dear."

ANN

One year after my novel released—after the hubbub of the tour and the NYT Notable Book honor—I received a letter with handwriting I didn't recognize.

I was carrying a basket of tomatoes, herbs, fresh cheese, and a cantaloupe, returning to my apartment from the market. It was summer, the streets muggy, and I was eager to duck into the shade of my home, strip down, and lie in front of a fan with a glass of chilled wine. I'd started writing a new novel, one that saw false starts and was really quite the problem child, but I'd been thinking about the story all morning and had planned to work on it as the afternoon heat rose.

But the letter.

I set my groceries on the counter along with the stack of other mail and kicked off my dusty sandals. I swiped a fingernail under the envelope's adherence and slipped the letter out. A photograph fell from the folded paper and glided toward the floor, ultimately sliding under my oven. I followed its escape, letter in hand—then paused. I looked down at the letter—really *looked*—and there at the end of a long cursive paragraph was the name *Todd Langley*.

Not possible, I thought.

I read from the beginning.

> Dear Ann,
>
> I've thought about writing you many times but kept talking myself out of it — that is, until just now, upon finishing your book. I hate to admit that I avoided reading it this long. I can't say why, except perhaps because I knew that it would be as lovely as you are, and I've spent a lot of time trying to forget your loveliness.
>
> But I've read it now. And I was blown away. And I thought perhaps I ought to tell you that I think you deserve all the success in the world. Of course, Keith has kept me up to date, always with an air of pride and — to my annoyance — smugness. You were right to stay in Rome; Keith is insufferable.
>
> All jokes aside, I'm sorry I sprung myself on you when you visited Colorado. I truly was glad to see you in my bookstore, but Keith and I were naive to think you would take well to a surprise like that. I'm sorry I didn't look at the situation from your side. I hope this letter is not unwelcome.
>
> Speaking of letters: Keith said that you are fond of letter writing, but please don't feel any obligation to reply. I merely wanted to offer my belated but sincere congratulations. You are sensational, Ann Fawkes. At the very least, I'm proud to be able to say, "I knew her when."
>
> —Best wishes, Todd Langley

My pulse was an ocean in my ears. I read the letter again, warmed by his praise, heated to see the word *lovely* written in his handwriting. Had anyone ever called me lovely? I couldn't recall, but now that Todd had said it, no one could ever use that word again, not with the same meaning. I traced the indentation of his pen on the page, then touched my bottom lip.

I would be lying if I said I hadn't thought about Todd in the year since my tour. I couldn't blame myself for my anger and shock that night, but a part of me regretted how I'd treated him. Had I misplaced some of my frustration with my mother on Todd? That night might've had a much happier ending had I done the reading as Keith planned.

And what if I had turned my back on something important? After Greece, I hadn't expected to ever see Todd again, but the tides of life kept bringing us back together—perhaps it was time to swim with the current.

Paramount to all those swirling thoughts: his letter made me happy.

I turned the envelope over in my hand, reading his Colorado address. Then I dropped to my knees, forearms, reaching for the picture under the oven. I knew what it was before I retrieved it: the photo he had taken in Venice.

In it, a young me stared into the camera with light in her eyes. Her mouth was parted in surprise, eyebrows arched high. A lock of hair streamed across her face. She was wayward, and sun kissed, and full of wonder. I realized that I'd never seen myself appear so free. I realized that my expression was a look of genuine love. Mere hours into our meeting, it was a look meant only for Todd.

Painfully as it ended in Greece, he'd brought out that romantic side of me. Why had I spent so much time hating this girl? At least she had dared to love.

And Todd had kept the photo all these years.

I raced to my desk, eager to respond, but when pen met paper, none of the words seemed right. I couldn't put them into any sort of order.

~~Todd,~~
~~My goodness, is it wonderful to hear from you!~~

~~Todd,~~
~~Do you really think I'm lovely?~~

~~Todd,~~
~~I thought I had moved on from you, but~~

Too cheerful, too desperate, too clingy. Each failed attempt was the wrong sort of camera filter: saturated, sepia, black and white.

I stood and returned to the kitchen, where the photo still rested on the counter. I opened a bottle of Frascati and sliced the cantaloupe I'd just purchased. Nibbling the sweetness down to the rind, I stared at the photo. It was rendered with accurate color, as if I could reach through and touch the railing of that Venetian bridge. Unfiltered. Honest.

That's what I had to do with my response to Todd.

Taking the bottle of wine with me, I sat in front of the fan and tried again.

> Todd,
> I would be lying if I said I was not happy to read your letter, not because of the praise (you're too kind), but because I've missed you. I apologize for my behavior in Colorado—it was quite a shock to see you and I didn't handle it well. Truth be told, I often think back on our time in Greece. I'm grateful it happened, even if I regret how it ended (did your wrist heal all right?).
>
> I'm sorry about Keith's smugness; there's not much I can do about that.

> *Thank you for the photo — it's nice to see myself all*
> *shiny and new. What a fun day we had in Venice.*
> *—Ann*

I waited and waited for his response.

The first week, I spent a great deal of time translating menus and taking long walks along the river. The next week, I called Keith to "check in on sales" and tiptoed around the subject of Todd before chickening out and hanging up. I then cleaned my whole apartment and went out on the town with Carmella and two of her cousins, who were visiting from Sicily.

Eighteen days after I mailed the letter, I dug into the back of my closet, searching through a box of knickknacks from my early travels. I found it wrapped in its original newspaper: the glass horse Todd had bought for me. Unfolding the wrapping revealed its glinting, translucent delicacy—the thin and still-intact legs, the crooked ear, the animated mane flicked up as if by wind. That evening, I set it on my bookshelf next to the hardback of *Chasing Shadows*.

Twenty-two days after I mailed the letter, I was certain he wasn't going to write back. I must've said something wrong, something awkward. Or perhaps the international postage system had lost my letter? Of course, that was the day—the day I grew despondent—that I finally received his reply.

> *Ann,*
> *Thank you for writing back. The wrist was merely a sprain,*
> *but that was the least of my concerns in the days after you*
> *left Santorini. I'm sorry for the hurt I caused you. I was*
> *hurting too. I know that doesn't excuse my unkind words,*
> *but perhaps it helps you understand them.*

I thought back to that night in Santorini.

I had been so wrapped up in my own feelings. I'd overlooked Keith's cut-short caution; I hadn't taken Todd's confession—*I lost someone*—seriously. Todd hadn't broken my heart—*I* had. I had pushed him too hard, and therefore he'd pushed me away completely.

But now, it seemed, he was back.

> Let's not live in the past. Tell me: How are you now?
> Aside from the booming career, I'd love to hear more about
> Ann. How is Rome? Keith said your address has stayed the
> same for a while, so I assume you love it.
> —Todd

> P.S. Apologies for my delayed response—I am
> buried in endless home renovations and lost track of time
> and mail.

A silken breeze came through the window, billowing my curtains. It streamed across my face, through my hair. The muscles in my neck uncoiled. I smiled to myself. Todd wanted to talk—to *me*. Not only had he written me a letter, but he'd written a second. An apology. A bid to move on, move forward, and reconnect.

I plunked down at my desk, pushed my new novel aside, and penned a response.

> Todd,
> Rome is a dream. The food, the architecture, the energy . . .
> it all conspires to seduce me. I've fallen hard for this city—

My pen paused above the paper. I remembered Todd's attentive expression—the one that had captured my heart in Venice and made me feel like I mattered. His letter was the paper embodiment of that expression. It compelled me to be honest.

145

—but truth be told, it can be lonely at times. I have friends and local acquaintances, a community of market vendors and butchers and baristas whom I know by name. I've even gone on the occasional date—but I find meaningful companionship difficult.

Steady romantic relationships seemed too risky. I hadn't even been intimate with a man since before my book tour.

Rome is a dream, but sometimes I feel like none of it is real. My life here is an uncomplicated stasis. Growing up, I never had security; here, I have so much stability that I find myself yearning for more. Sometimes I wonder if I've walled myself off from something truly great. Does greatness always require risk?

By then, my pen was moving of its own volition.

What do I have, outside my career? The answer to that question frightens me. The stories and articles keep me relevant, but to what end? The book tour was a good distraction, but now I feel an immense pressure to write another knockout. *Chasing Shadows* took so much from me—I wonder if I have anything left.

This is all probably more than you wanted to know, but there you have it. That's how Ann is doing. Ann is as complicated as ever.

How is Todd?

—Ann

P.S. For the record, I'm sorry about Greece too.

P.P.S. I recently rediscovered that glass horse you bought me. I still haven't seen water that blue, but it's a wish of mine to someday find the same shade of teal.

His next letter came swiftly.

Ann,

I am touched that you'd share your feelings with such openness. I won't pretend to have answers for you, but I do hope our correspondence is a balm to the occasional sting of loneliness. I still maintain that you are the bravest person I know.

How is Todd? I'm still figuring that out.

Two years before I met you, my heart had been shattered by a tragedy from which I don't believe I will ever fully recover: my parents, wife, and newborn daughter died in a hospital fire.

A small sound of anguish escaped my lips, like a bird escaping a cage. Instinctively, I cupped a hand over my mouth as I read further.

The only thing I have left of any of them is my childhood home and the bookstore. The trauma of that loss still grips me much of the time. The man you met in Venice was lost, heartbroken, and selfish. And—in the interest of honoring your honesty with mine—my attraction toward you was too much to bear.

Since Greece, I have tried to heal. I've attended therapy in earnest, which has helped me process my grief. I still have a long way to go, but I'm improving, and the progress gives me purpose.

Perhaps this is too much for a mere letter, but all this is to say: I understand what you mean when you say you feel like you've walled yourself off from something great. I recognize that inclination because that's what I've been doing for the past six years.

We're all works in progress, aren't we? I hope you consider me a friend you can turn to when you're feeling uncertain.

As for companionship: put yourself out there. You deserve to feel cherished.

—Todd

P.S. I once heard that Tahiti has blue water like that.

I sank to my mattress, clutching his letter to my chest.

His entire family had *died*. The word had been penned in an off-kilter, slightly shaky cursive—a reflection of how hard it must've been for Todd to write it. I'd spent much of my life mourning the family I never had—I couldn't imagine possessing my dream family only to have them torn away.

I had been careless in Greece. I hadn't known the whole story, hadn't listened when he said he needed friendship. After that letter, I vowed never to push Todd like that again.

MAGGIE

Todd's letters are strewn across the coffee table. Maggie finds herself getting choked up, her throat tightening with a sudden wet ache; she can't imagine how gutting this must be for Ann, to recount these memories in such detail.

"Is something wrong?" Ann touches Maggie's shoulder.

Maggie looks up, and Ann appears a little blurry, wearing her white blouse and black jeans. "I'm just . . . moved," Maggie admits.

Ann doesn't smile, not really—her lips press together, turning neither upward nor downward. She seems slightly surprised. "Why don't I brew more tea?" Ann leans forward out of the plush cushions of the couch.

A shaky sigh slips past Maggie's lips. She's moved, and she's also surprised. The tragedy wasn't just Todd's, but he omitted those details from his letter. While Ann is in the kitchen, Maggie rereads his words, musing on the evasive truth.

The incongruous details of Ann's story only add to Maggie's other stressors. She brought the recorder into Ann's home again today—hopeful after their conversation yesterday—but recording never came up.

The letters were already on the coffee table, taunting Maggie with their humanity. Their honesty.

Maggie's glance dips to her purse on the floor and the recorder inside. Like a screwdriver, guilt twists Maggie's sternum, loosening her resolve.

Ann returns from the kitchen with the teapot and cups on a tray. Over the past few days, Maggie has come to admire the mauve, flowered porcelain set. Without asking, Ann prepares Maggie's tea exactly to her liking.

"Before we continue," Maggie says, and her voice comes out squeaky and tense. "We need to discuss our arrangement."

The small sugar tongs in Ann's hand hover over her mug in a near-imperceptible pause; then she drops a cube into her tea. She doesn't look up when she says, "I'm sorry."

The answer is plain. Mere days ago, Maggie had wondered at the many causes of the creases on Ann's face. Now, Maggie is one of them: a frown. Ann still doesn't look up from her task, and Maggie realizes there's a thread she hasn't yet pulled, one that's been dangling between them this whole time.

"What are you hiding from me?" Maggie asks.

Ann's amber eyes flick up, finally. "What do you mean?" A throwaway question.

"Over our time together, the thing I've admired most about you is your openness." Maggie swallows. "Now, I realize you've been hiding behind half truths."

"No, I haven't," Ann says, firm.

"Then explain to me why I'm here."

Ann leans into the couch, as if not even her spine can hold up her words. "I'm sorry."

Maggie's time has run out. She has no option left, no way forward, but to practice the honesty Ann has spoken so highly of, the honesty that Ann herself can't—or won't—practice now. She bends, reaching into her purse, and holds up the recorder, her finger hovering over the power button: the pin in the final grenade.

She flips the switch.

Ann's muffled, staticky words blare through the tiny speaker. She sounds tinny and far away, but there's no doubt it's her. Her words echo throughout the living room. Something about Italy, something about Todd.

Pure shock ripples through Ann's usually stoic features, and Maggie pauses the recording.

"What was that?" Ann's voice is resonant, harsh.

"Honesty," Maggie says.

MAGGIE

"You recorded me. In secret." Her amber eyes are pure fire.

Maggie can only pray that this desperate gamble can douse the flames and set everything right.

"At first, I was just as horrified. It's a new recorder, and my sound engineer didn't warn me about the touchy buttons." Maggie drops the recorder into her purse with the power switch still on; she shakes the bag and then retrieves the recorder, heart in her throat. To her great relief, the light starts blinking. She shows Ann, then turns it off. "When you asked me to put the recorder away, I forgot to power it down. The button was bumped, like a pocket dial."

Ann waves a dismissive hand. "Why should I believe this story?"

"Why should I believe yours?" A pause. "Trust."

"How can I trust someone who threatens me?"

"I'm not threatening you. I'm being honest with you." Maggie hands Ann the recorder. "This is the only copy of that conversation in existence. Delete it."

Ann brushes a neat, unpainted fingernail over the record button. "I don't understand."

"It's a gesture." Maggie smiles, hoping Ann can see her sincerity. "I don't know why you're doing this, but I'm not here for merely a job, not anymore. I'm here for *you*—because I admire you. I respect you. This is proof." She points at the recorder, still cradled in Ann's fingers. "If you respect me, you'll reconsider recording. Because the fact is, while I'm here for more than just the job, I can't stay here without it."

Ann's angular face appears unreadable—almost blank, if it weren't for the slight tension in her upper lip and the tightening along her lower lashes. A whisper of an expression, faint as breath.

"You're bold, you know that?" Ann says finally. "You're sharp too. Perceptive. You wear your heart on your face; you're probably terrible at poker."

Maggie's brows crinkle together, waiting.

"My point is, I like you." Ann sets the recorder on the middle couch cushion—an offering—and gestures between them. "I like this."

Wind gusts against the bay windows, the sun slipping behind a mass of chaotic, lavender-gray cumulus clouds. With the dimming light, Ann's eyes darken into a deep whiskey.

"I have a new agreement in mind," Ann continues. "I will discuss recording with Grant. I have a few concerns and stipulations to iron out, if we're going to record this the way I've been telling it to you."

"Wow, I—"

Ann holds up a hand. "In exchange, I need you to talk to Tracey."

"What does Mom have to do with the podcast?"

"Before I can continue, you need to have an honest conversation with her about the past."

Maggie's heart stumbles. Thoughts strobe through her mind: her parents' warning, that first conversation when Ann inquired about her biological parentage, the details Todd omitted from his letters.

"What do you know?" Maggie whispers.

"This isn't about what I know. This is about *you*. I suspect your mother wasn't pleased about you speaking with me." Her lips twist.

"I won't continue until she's said her piece. That's my deal, take it or leave it."

Maggie holds Ann's gaze, willing her to say more, searching for a clue to her motive. But all she sees is Ann, practically innocent in the clearness of her expression.

Maggie touches the recorder still resting on the couch between them. "I thought you'd be angrier."

"I know what it's like to feel desperate. And I know what it's like to beg for forgiveness." Ann leans forward and clasps her hands over Maggie's. "Talk to Tracey, and I'll talk to Grant. Deal?"

Maggie nods and nods, resisting the quiver in her lip, realizing that this is it: her honesty won. "Deal."

Ann sits straight, smoothing her blouse. "Great. In the meantime, let's have lunch, and I'll tell you more about Todd—off the record. How does that sound?"

It sounds like a waste, without the podcast details ironed out, but Maggie isn't ready to face her parents or even Grant just yet. Her body is loose with the deflation of adrenaline, a small thorn of paranoia still spiking her senses. *Talk to Tracey.* About what?

While Ann retrieves more letters from the box, Maggie takes a hasty sip of tea.

Maggie had once thought that Ann had no one left to protect, that she could tell her story—the full story—without concern. But maybe that's not true at all. Maybe Ann *is* still protecting someone.

ANN

There's a delightful discomfort in awaiting a letter, a sweet angst, an achy anticipation. In my opinion, letters supersede all other forms of communication. Everything is instant now, Maggie—and with that privilege comes carelessness. A rapid-fire text, a hasty or drunken email. Pocket dials. When you write a letter, address an envelope, and buy a stamp, the labor lends itself to candor. There's no point in putting in all that time and effort for flimsy sentiments.

Todd and I applied that care to our letters for the next two years. Sure, we had landlines, but nothing could replace the intimacy in folded pages and licked stamps. We shared preferences, pains, inside jokes. I told him about my pseudochildhood, and he sent me copies of his parents' children's books. He challenged my impostor syndrome, and I encouraged him through renovation headaches and business taxes. But mostly, through our friendly confessionals, we made each other feel less alone.

During that time, I dallied with a string of men—free spirited, rowdy, fun—and Todd dated a woman named Ellen. Our platonic correspondence empowered us to pursue romantic companionship with less expectation. I was floating along; each letter was a buoy that kept me bobbing at the surface of a sea whose depth scared the shit out of me.

Meanwhile, despite Keith's nudging, progress on my sophomore book was slow. My mind was stifled by crushing expectation, made worse by the growing success of *Chasing Shadows*. When it was optioned for film the first time, Todd and Keith mailed congratulatory notes and arranged for flowers to be delivered to my apartment, and Carmella took me dancing—and while I twirled to the music, all I kept thinking was that someway, somehow, I was destined to let everyone down.

Then, in August 1990, my mother died of liver cancer, and my successes, the letters, the life overseas—all of it paled compared to my grief.

I was thirty-one, and we had long since grown apart. We hadn't seen each other in the flesh since I left the States—not even for holidays—and I'd stopped calling after she failed to show up to my reading in Denver.

The day before she died, Mom called me from her hospital bed to tell me what was going on. Her fairy godmother voice had become worn and raspy. She didn't have the energy to explain much beyond the basics, despite there being years piled up between us. I did my best not to keep her on the phone all night.

Not twenty-four hours later, I was slipping my passport into my purse when I received the news that she was gone.

My aunt had been the one to call. "Cancel your ticket," she said, then hung up.

My bag slipped from my shoulder, and I sank into my desk chair, still clutching the phone.

There was so much my mother hadn't told me until her final call, so much I had missed. She'd gotten married. She'd gotten *sober*. She'd started chemo. And she hadn't bothered to tell her own daughter until it was too late.

Mom had spent so much of my childhood lamenting that I had held her back—that I was at fault for her shortcomings—and maybe that was true. Because as soon as I skipped town, Mom had cleaned up her life. And then cancer stole it away.

My eyes burned, and I finally released the phone into its cradle. My plan had been to hold my mother's hand, to say all the things I wanted to say in person. Now, I never would.

The last time she'd asked for money was the fall after my book tour. Had she not attended my reading because she was sick? Had she asked for money to cover treatment? Why hadn't she told me any of this? Had I known, I would have forgiven her for her absence rather than spitefully refusing her request. Had I known, I would've sent her every last dime.

My aunt didn't invite me to the memorial.

ANN

Rome, Italy
November 1990

When I finally wrote Todd about my mother, nearly three months had passed since my last letter, and he'd sent two in the meantime.

> Todd,
> I'm sorry for not writing. My mother died at the end of August and I've had trouble focusing since then. It's like I'm suspended in a cloud—numb and chilled—with guilt and sorrow storming inside me. I know you are familiar with grief, so I probably don't need to explain any further.
>   I hope you are well.
>   —Ann

Rather than wallow in my grief, I filled my time translating neighborhood menus and helping restaurateurs and waiters improve their English. Through these meetups, I strengthened my fluency in Italian and deepened my roots in Rome. I filled every minute I could with company. The less time I spent alone with my thoughts, the better.

Trastevere was getting trendier by the day—boutiques and eateries of all sorts had opened to accept the influx of tourists exploring beyond the Colosseum and Pantheon. Food tours frequently brought big groups into restaurants, and Carmella's was a regular host. The place was often booked up on the weekends, but Carmella kept a small table for me on Friday nights, where she spoiled me with off-menu items and kitchen experiments.

I'd recently started dating one of my tutoring clients, a Roman named Luca. He was five years my junior, sweet and a little timid but very sexy. We sipped cappuccinos and shared cigarettes, and he proudly showed me more of his city. It was still very new. We hadn't slept together yet, but we'd kissed and touched, and for once I liked taking things slow.

Mid-November came, bringing with it a stretch of clear-skied, chilly weather. Leaves were tossed by the crisp wind, corralled into the nooks of narrow cobblestone streets, collecting in rafts on the river. My grief was beginning to scab over; I wasn't so raw or weepy anymore.

It was a particularly cold Friday evening when I found myself tucked into my usual seat at Carmella's. She never gave me a menu, so I was people watching out the fog-frosted window, delighting in the sweetness of first dates, of newly grasped hands and awkward, too-big gestures. Luca and I didn't hold hands like a couple I spotted outside; we didn't try each other's food like the pair sitting in an opposite corner of Carmella's. I liked his sharp haircut and quick Italian words; I liked when we didn't speak at all. But did he make me feel cherished and understood, as I saw hinted in the actions of other couples? As I so craved in a romantic relationship?

I sipped my sparkling water, wondering if something was missing.

"Hello, my friend!" Carmella had come to my corner, her white chef's outfit tarnished by the tiniest splatters of orange. Her melted-chocolate eyes held mine, full of warmth and welcome. "How are you?"

"*Sto bene,*" I said, "*e tu?*" My Italian was slow, but quite good, and I liked conversing with my friend in her native tongue.

She switched to Italian. "I'm well. Wine?"

"Of *course*, thank you."

"I recommend the Pèppoli tonight. It's a Chianti Classico that will go well with this new dish I'm trying."

"Sounds fabulous."

She disappeared into the kitchen. A waiter (and occasional bar-hopping buddy) named Paolo delivered the bottle and poured me a generous glass. Shortly thereafter, he brought a plate of *crostini neri*.

I sipped the wine—mild, but pleasant—and nibbled on the appetizer, back to people watching.

Halfway through my crostini, there was a bit of a ruckus at the door. An American man with a suitcase couldn't be seated because the restaurant was full. I couldn't see his face past the heads of diners between myself and the door, but I heard the man clarify that he did not want a table. He needed directions. The host didn't speak English well enough to help piece together the misunderstanding. I considered standing up to help, but then another waiter approached the front, crowding the situation.

I continued eating and sipping and listening to the commotion.

"*Dove . . . dove si trova . . .*" Even in broken Italian, the fumbling American voice sounded . . . *familiar*?

I stood halfway out of my seat to catch a glimpse, unbelieving. My heart thundered, and an adrenaline-like bolt of astonishment and elation struck me. It crackled through my veins and lit up my insides.

"Todd!" I squealed, catching his attention—along with that of the waiters and irritated diners in the immediate vicinity.

"*Copper.*" He sounded breathless and relieved.

My napkin fell from my lap as I stood all the way up. He dropped his suitcase, and I rushed toward him, halting just in front of him.

Instead of knocking him back with a hug—which is what I wanted to do—I grasped his shoulders and kissed his rough cheeks, once on either side. The European greeting was a little less embarrassing than my desire to body-slam him. I became shy. I had laid myself bare on the pages I mailed him, but seeing him in the flesh exposed me in a different way. Here, I could stare past his lenses into those stormy blue-green eyes.

"Copper," he said again, smiling with his soft mouth. His hand lingered on my shoulder, then fell.

He looked different—older, I realized. His face had thinned, not unattractively so, and he had the slightest peppering of silver hairs at his temples. He wasn't much older than me, but grief had aged him, and it made me wonder what differences he saw on my face. Regardless, he looked good. His personal growth had changed the posture of those usually sunken shoulders; he stood taller. I felt suddenly squirmy under his gaze. To think I'd been sending vulnerable and embarrassing letters to this beautiful man for the past two years made my blood sizzle.

"What are you doing here?" The chill coming in from the doorway puckered my skin.

"Looking for you, of course," he said, low.

I led him out of the way of an incoming foursome. "I have a table."

In Italian, I asked Paolo to take Todd's suitcase into the back so it wouldn't be in the way in the tight restaurant. Paolo shot me a gossipy look, then hefted Todd's bag and disappeared toward the kitchen.

"Do you know them here?" Todd asked when we were settled at my table.

"*Todd.* This is Carmella's! My friend's restaurant."

He wiped a tired hand over his face, chuckling in amusement. "No way. I asked for directions at your friend's place? How lucky is that?" He looked around the intimate restaurant, taking it all in. Carmella's was a cozy spot—romantic. After roving the room, his attention settled back on me. "Your Italian is very good."

I waved a hand, clearing the compliment away. I couldn't believe he was sitting across from me. Here. In Carmella's. In Rome. I beamed. "What are you *doing* here, Todd?"

"I already said, I'm here to see you."

Paolo came by with a second set of dishes and lifted my wine bottle to fill Todd's new glass; I ignored his half smirk and raised eyebrows.

"But *why*?" I pressed.

Todd's expression darkened, lips pulling into a frown. "Your mother," he said. "I know you have friends here, but I thought you might want some company. Someone who . . . understands."

My body gushed with warmth. I grasped his hand, overcome by the gesture. For three seconds, four, everything felt right: the city, the restaurant, the man, and our skin touching, practically electric. Is that how the couples I'd been watching felt? I blushed, self-consciousness flaring, and returned my hand to my lap.

"A man is here," Carmella said as she approached the table. She held a single plate of squat, round *mezze maniche* noodles coated in a sweet-smelling sauce.

"Carmella, this is my dear friend Todd."

She knew very well who Todd was and what he meant to me, but thankfully, she played it cool. "Pleased to meet you." Before he could respond, she added, "You look hungry. I'll fix another plate."

"*Grazie*," Todd said, mispronouncing the thanks as I had so many years before.

Carmella was endeared. "Ah, look at you speak Italian. *Bene.* You keep my Ann company, and I will be back."

When she was gone, I didn't pick up my fork; with Todd sitting here, I felt so full I feared I wouldn't be able to eat. "You came all the way here for me?"

"It was all I could think to do."

"Thank you," I said, "truly."

"It's nothing."

"It's *everything*." No one had ever gone to that sort of trouble on my behalf.

Carmella returned with Todd's dinner, pinning me with a scandalized glance before she left. I tried not to imagine the gossip happening in the kitchen.

I asked Todd, "Are you just getting in? You've probably been traveling for twenty hours."

Todd spread a napkin over his lap and picked up his fork. "Twenty-four," he said. "But the look on your face is worth it." He took a bite of the pasta, eyes fluttering closed in ecstasy.

"What's the look on my face?" I asked.

He opened his eyes again, chewing. He swallowed and wiped the corner of his mouth. "Surprise. Happiness."

"Both true," I said, finally taking a bite of my own dish. It was some sort of pumpkin-and-tomato sauce, perfectly balanced with pepper and Romano.

"Your friend is a great chef," Todd said, practically halfway through his food already. "Will she deliver seconds? This is a small plate."

"Slow down," I said. "In Italy, we *savor* our food."

"I've been traveling for an entire day, Ann. I've sustained myself on peanuts and weird airport food."

I sipped my wine. "Fine, continue gorging."

Todd gave me a devilish smile before finishing his pasta.

I poked at my plate, my belly still full of fluttering songbirds. "I just realized something," I said, dropping my fork. "The first time we met, you were just arriving in Italy, and I shared my table. It's happened again!"

He chuckled. "My god, you're right."

"You're like a drifter," I said. "Do you *ever* get your own table, or do you just sit down wherever?"

"Hey, now, you invited me to sit—both times."

"I'm terribly lonely," I said, "remember?"

He didn't laugh at my self-deprecation. Instead, his lips spread into an affectionate smile and he topped off my wine.

"Do you at least have a functional wheelie bag this time?" I asked.

"I'm not an *actual* drifter." He ran a hand through his luscious hair. "Discounting my current state of dishevelment, of course."

"That reminds me, where are you staying?"

His chin dipped. "Truth be told, I didn't get a hotel. I bought the ticket rather impulsively and figured I'd find one later."

"You can stay with me, drifter that you are. I have a shower and everything."

"Oh, I don't want to put you out—"

"You could never do that."

We stayed late at Carmella's, talking face to face for the first time in forever. We polished off two bottles of Pèppoli, and after closing, Carmella brought out tiramisu and Todd peppered her with questions about her restaurant, food, and Rome. After that, Todd and I strolled along the river toward my apartment, the rattle of his luggage echoing through the sleepy streets. The scent of the river clung to us, earthy like mud and decaying leaves and ancient stone. My face was hot from the wine, but the nighttime air made me shiver.

"I feel like I'm dreaming," I admitted. We had warmed up to each other by then, and I had my arm slung through his.

"You're just saying that."

"Are you kidding? You and Keith are the closest thing I have to family now—this is a *reunion*."

"What about Carmella?"

"Carmella is a dear friend, but she doesn't understand my pensiveness. We aren't share-all-my-thoughts close like you and me."

"Kind of you to spare her from all your thoughts," Todd quipped. I elbowed him.

"There's no one else you're close to? Not even a boyfriend?"

I glanced at him, wondering if his question was mere curiosity or something more weighted. "I'm seeing a man. Luca. It's new."

He cleared his throat. "Oh?"

"We're taking things slow," I added. "He doesn't even call me his girlfriend. So, no, now that my mother is gone and her sister hates me, you and Keith are it."

I sensed he had another question, but he didn't speak.

"How is Ellen?" I asked, eager to change the subject. He'd mentioned her a few times in his letters; she was a friend of Keith's sister Natalie.

"That ended a while ago," Todd said.

"I'm sorry."

He waved his hand, dismissing the sentiment. "It's all right. There was always something missing."

I wanted to ask him *what* was missing. But Todd and I had found a good balance in being friends, and it didn't feel right to pry. After what had happened in Greece, I was determined not to make that mistake again.

I led him up to my apartment, unlocked the door, and welcomed him inside. The studio had an open layout, yet even with the tall windows and high ceiling, his presence seemed to fill every corner.

I felt stripped naked as his eyes roved the room, tactile as fingers on skin as he observed the intimate fixtures of my life: my desk, with fresh manuscript pages plain to see; my bookshelf, with its meaningful trinkets and indulgent display of *Chasing Shadows*; my dirty laundry on the lone reading chair, underwear mixed with T-shirts and crumpled dresses; and my bed, such a suggestive piece of furniture, its duvet parted from the headboard to reveal the flower-patterned sheets beneath.

By seeing my home, Todd was seeing another facet of who I was. The confessions in my letters felt somehow more revealing with him physically here.

Another problem: I didn't have a guest room. I didn't even have a proper couch—just a love seat, too short for lying down. Where would he sleep? I hadn't thought this through at all.

But he didn't complain or question our sleeping arrangements; he simply said, "What a great place."

"I'd give you a tour, but this is it." The kitchen and small dining table were to the right; my desk ahead, near the balcony doorway; and my bed to the left, framed by the bathroom and closet doors.

"I love it."

"So do I," I admitted.

Todd approached the glass horse on my bookshelf and touched its crooked ear with a finger.

I unwound my scarf from my neck and draped it over the back of the laundry chair. "I'm assuming you're desperate for a shower?"

"Are you saying that I smell?" He lifted his arm and faked a sniff.

I pushed his shoulder. "No—but I always hate that germy airport feeling on my skin. Don't you?"

I set him up with a fresh towel, warned him about the backward temperatures on the knobs, and left him alone to shower. Meanwhile, I dug through my closet for an extra pillow and some blankets so one of us could sleep on the floor.

I was checking my hair in the reflection of my balcony window when I heard a knock on my front door. With a squeak of the handles, Todd's water shut off, and the towel whooshed as he dried off.

I opened the front door to find Luca standing there, a bouquet of lilies in hand. He stepped forward, but I barred his entrance. "Luca." We kissed cheeks. "What are you doing here?"

"I cannot stand it any longer, I want you." He cupped my cheek and kissed me deeply, holding me flush against his body with his other arm. He tasted of wine. "I know you want me too."

"Luca," I said, pushing his chest slightly. "This isn't a good—"

"Ann?" Todd called from the other room.

Luca's face contorted, and he released me.

"I didn't know where to put the towel, so I just—" Todd came up behind me. "Oh, sorry to interrupt."

"Who is this man?" Luca asked softly, his eyes reddening.

I told the truth. "A friend."

"He doesn't look like a friend," he said in Italian. "He looks like a lover. You'll sleep with this man but not me?"

I knew in that moment that I wouldn't be able to convince Luca otherwise. Todd was an attractive American man in my apartment, late at night. He was shirtless, hair wet, shower-fresh.

"Can you trust me when I tell you he's a friend and not a lover?" I asked in Italian.

"No," Luca said. "How could I?"

"This isn't what it looks like," Todd said, clearly wanting to help but not helping at all.

It would've been easier had Luca gotten angry. Anger I could handle. Anger made the breaking easier.

But he didn't get angry. He handed me the flowers and—his eyes growing wetter by the moment—said, "*Arrivederci, mia bella.*"

I watched him hurry down the hallway toward the stairs, remembering my time in France, when I had learned that my boyfriend was engaged to another woman. How awful and hurt and stupid I'd felt. I hated to think that I'd made Luca feel that way—but I knew I had.

The realization was excruciating.

But there was no way for me to fix it now—and maybe I didn't want to.

"Ann," Todd said. "I'm so sorry. Do you want me to go after him and try to explain?" He stood close, the heat of the shower still clinging to his skin.

I shook my head and closed the door. "He wouldn't believe you," I said. "It's okay, truly."

"You don't seem okay." He guided me to the foot of the bed. We sat. "It's just a misunderstanding, it's fixable."

I looked at him, then looked away. "No, it's fine."

"You seem to have cared for him."

"I did—*I do*. But like you said about Ellen, something was missing," I said. "Whether now or later, we would've broken up. Better to have it happen before we were both more invested."

I knew he understood. He rubbed my back in steady vertical streaks. "I'm sorry."

"I know. It's all right." I met his eyes, resisting the urge to glance at his lips. If I wasn't careful, I would fall into the same trap as I had in Greece. *Friendship*—Todd wanted only friendship from me.

I patted his leg and stood, trying to shake off my emotional weight. I didn't want to ruin things between us a second time. "You must be exhausted. I'll sleep on the floor, and you can take the bed for tonight."

"No way. You just went through a breakup—not five minutes ago—and it's my fault. If anyone deserves the floor, it's me."

I knew I couldn't argue with him, so I simply handed him the bundle of blankets I'd gathered. He arranged himself on the floor while I washed my face and changed into a slip. When I reemerged from the bathroom, Todd was lying on his back at the foot of the bed, cushioned from the hardwood by a small area rug. I felt bad for him down there but knew it was futile to try to convince him to take the bed. I turned off the light, slipped under my duvet, and stared at the ceiling.

Should I have gone after Luca? Or had it been right to let him go? I wondered if my doubts about him had been warranted or imagined. Significant or self-sabotage. Perhaps I was just like my mother: plagued by romanticism yet incapable of cultivating a healthy outlook on love. Was I broken?

Tears beaded on my cheeks and slid toward my ears, wetting the pillow. Grief pressed down on my chest. I sniffled.

My mother had loved me. She hadn't excelled at showing it, but she had. And look how *that* had ended: I hadn't even been there for her when she was dying of cancer. My mother was gone, and our relationship would always be unresolved—and it was my fault.

My grief was complicated, Maggie. Sometimes I wished it could only be one thing—sadness—but it wasn't. It was resentment and heartbreak and self-hatred too.

A faint draft from my window cooled the wetness on my cheeks.

A sigh emanated up from the floor, reminding me that for once, someone was there—and he was there because he cared. My grief suddenly didn't seem so vast. And what a gift that was. What an unimaginable gift.

"Thank you for coming," I whispered to the ceiling.

"You're welcome." His voice sounded so deep and strong, filling my whole apartment with his steadiness.

Minutes went by. He shifted positions with a soft groan.

"Are you comfortable?" I asked.

"I'm perfectly fine," Todd answered.

More time unspooled. After a while, his blankets again whispered his discomfort.

"Todd?"

"Yeah?"

It was a risk to ask, but I took it. "Why don't we just share the bed?"

"What?"

"You're uncomfortable," I said. "And there's plenty of space. I don't mind, really."

A long pause followed. I could tell he was weighing the idea.

"All right."

He stood and got into bed, the duvet wafting as he settled. Two feet of mattress remained between us. I folded my arms over my chest.

"Better?" I asked.

"Yeah," he admitted.

I turned my head away and looked out the window. Flecks of dust dotted the outside of the pane, and the edges of the glass were blurred where the trim had been shoddily painted. Silver light streamed in, and the curtains framing the window glowed, dancing ever so slightly from the draft. Sadness billowed in my chest; my throat tightened.

As Todd's breath slowed beside me, I cried again—as quietly as I could. I cried for the men I'd been with, the pain they'd caused, the way I'd walled myself off from heartbreak until I felt lonely and dissatisfied. I missed my mom. I missed feeling like love was right around the corner. I had once been so hopeful, but I'd killed my optimism bit by bit, beating it until it lay down and stayed down. I thought I could evade the hurt, but what was left was a hole. Even Todd's letters hadn't completely filled my need.

I wiped my face and, in a moment of weakness, scooched closer to Todd's warmth. I closed the gap from twenty-four inches to twelve to six, and when he didn't seem to awaken, I moved until merely a body-heated inch parted us. Always inching closer, never reaching what I wanted.

But then Todd woke up—or maybe he'd always been awake—and he turned toward me, sensing my tears. He stroked his thumb over my face, wiping away the moisture, smoothing my hair.

And then he did exactly the thing I wanted, the thing I'd been craving for so long: he drew me to his bare chest and held me while I cried.

ANN

Rome, Italy
November 1990

Late morning, I awoke in Todd's arms.

He was still asleep, and I remained perfectly still, not wanting it to end. I was tucked into the concavity of his chest, my face nestled into his collarbone, with one of his arms beneath my neck and the other draped over my waist. My cheeks were puffy from crying. I worried what he'd think when he woke up—*Will he still see me as brave, after last night's display of weakness? Will he regret holding me like this?*—but for the time being, I simply breathed in the natural freshness of his skin.

Outside, I heard the distant city awakening. Taxis, motorbikes, voices. The windowpanes—glowing with pale light—muffled the sounds. I rarely slept in, trading nightlife for the morning market on most days, but now I wondered why I ever got out of bed.

Of course, most days, Todd wasn't in my bed.

He shifted, his lashes fanning as his eyes squeezed tighter against the morning light. I reveled in the pale blush of his lips and the graceful Cupid's bow that shaped them. I wondered what he tasted like. I imagined his lips brushing against mine, and then I forced myself to stare at the ceiling, slapping my own proverbial wrist.

Had I learned absolutely nothing from Greece? He was here to comfort me, nothing more. I valued his friendship too much to risk ruining it all over again.

As I lay there scolding myself, his hand began to slide over the silk of my slip. It moved from my hip to my soft lower belly to my other hip. It made the same trip in reverse and then lifted straight up, as if he realized the path he had just blazed.

Todd cleared his throat. "Um, sorry."

The arm under my neck twisted, and we untangled ourselves from each other. The sheets on my proper side of the bed were cold. Rather than linger, I swung my legs over the edge, feet meeting chilly hardwood.

"It's all right," I said, my cheeks ablaze. With my back to him, I readjusted the top of my slip, then stood. "I'm going to shower."

I hurried straight into the bathroom and closed the door, panting a little. My stomach still tingled from where his hand had trailed. I stepped under the too-hot water, attempting to burn away my desire. Six years. It'd been *six years* since I made a fool of myself in Greece. Todd and I had grown a lot since then. We had shared so much: our thoughts and dreams and secrets and beliefs. Things were good between us—*easy.*

But clearly things were simpler with five thousand miles between us, when I couldn't admire the swell of his upper lip or his citrus-musk scent. Though I cared deeply for Todd, the fact was, we simply worked better as friends. I had to stop getting so flustered in his presence, respect his wishes, and let platonic love be enough.

When I reemerged from the bathroom in a thick robe, the apartment was empty. Had he left? A sinkhole opened up in my chest. I'd ruined it again.

But then I noticed the door to my balcony was cracked; the steam from the bathroom swirled like enchanted mist toward the opening. I peeked through and immediately felt full again. Todd had donned a sweater and was leaning against the railing. Two coffees steamed on the ledge.

When he saw me, he smiled. "I helped myself to some coffee, I hope you don't mind."

"Not at all," I said, sidling up beside him. A crisp breeze chilled my wet hair, but my robe kept most of the cold off my skin. My fingers slid around the curve of the second mug, and the chocolaty, earthy scent filled my nostrils.

Todd turned to me. "I'm sorry I . . ." He trailed off and started again. "I, uh . . . I'm sorry I was latched on to you this morning."

"I'm the one who invited you into bed."

"It *was* more comfortable than the floor."

"Yeah, but the crying . . ." I rubbed my puffy eyes, too embarrassed to look at him. "That was too much."

"Don't *ever* apologize for hurting."

"It was nice to be . . . held . . . for once."

"For once?"

I didn't need to repeat myself. He knew that being held and being held by someone who *understood* were two very different things.

"Well, I'm sorry if I made it weird." He glanced away.

He thought *he* had been the awkward one? Had I given him the wrong impression by exiting the bed so abruptly?

"I liked waking up that way." I took a long, slow sip of coffee before daring a glance in his direction.

His eyes were on me, clear and bright and serious in the morning sunlight. "I liked it too," Todd said softly.

I wondered what he meant, but I was afraid to ask directly. I wouldn't allow myself to read into his words. "Oh . . . good."

"Ann." His tone—flat and earnest—urged me to acknowledge something, but I was a ball of rubber-banded uncertainty; my emotions were too taut to risk stretching any further. I didn't want to mess up as I had in Greece. I didn't want to lose Todd all over again.

"Ann," he repeated, tender this time.

"Yes?"

He reached for my face and traced a thumb along my bottom lip. I didn't dare move, for fear that if I did, he'd pull away. But then he bent down and kissed me, and I was overcome. His lips were not as I had imagined, not pillowy or gentle; they were assertive. He devoured me with desire, drawing me closer as my limbs turned to liquid.

Too soon, Todd's hold slackened, and he released me. Apprehension clouded my craving for more. I was sure he regretted what we'd just done. Yet when his eyes found mine, they were searching, as if he were trying to read my face. He appeared almost embarrassed by the kiss.

He was worried about *me*, I realized. *My* reaction. For all my self-doubt and restraint, there was no misreading his expression. He wanted this, but he wasn't sure if I did too. His concern was endearing. As if *I* would be angry, the one who had already made plenty of hopeless attempts to do what he had just done.

After a few seconds studying my face, he frowned and stepped back. "Ann, I'm *so* sorry—I shouldn't have assumed—"

I moved into his personal space, pressing my body against his, and placed a hand on his chest.

"Are you—?"

"Yes," I interrupted.

"Ann—"

"Yes."

"I just—"

I kissed him, like a pinch to confirm I wasn't dreaming. When I pulled back and saw a smile twist onto his face, I knew the dream was real.

I grasped his hand and led him back inside my apartment. The air was still thick from shower steam; it made me feel like we were worlds away from any place we'd been before, a jungle of bursting blooms and lushness.

I wanted him. I'd wanted him since the moment I met him.

After a few languid moments kissing at the foot of my bed, I reached for the hem of his sweater. He paused, releasing a slow breath, and grasped my face in his hands. "This isn't just sex for me, Ann," he said firmly.

"I know," I said, but I hadn't, not until he said it. "Me too." That I did know.

I slid backward, out of his hold, and shrugged out of my robe. He stopped trying to speak, to tell me what this meant. I wanted him to show me what it meant.

He hovered above me, his arms braced on the pillow beside my head, sheltering and strong. My pulse was as loud as Niagara in my ears. The anticipation stole my breath.

I apologize if this is embarrassing to hear, Maggie. Will you allow an old woman to indulge in a memory?

I know I don't need to describe the mechanics of it. He took a lot of time for me, I remember, which was so unlike other men. He might not have kissed me on the mouth the way I expected, but elsewhere, his lips were everything I'd imagined. Plush and featherlight. He lingered until waterfalls of warmth gushed through me. I had been holding myself back from Todd for years, trying to respect his space—then, with him that morning, all that effort broke open like a dam.

When we were face to face again, I don't think I'd ever felt so *seen*. Understood. Cherished.

Empowered.

I felt like *myself* with Todd. My most confident, beautiful self. And there with me, he was his most beautiful self too. The connection we'd established in our letters made it all the clearer. Though it was not the first time I'd had sex, it was the first time I ever made love.

Afterward, he left the bed to clean up, and I lay there fearing that when he reemerged, the darkness would've returned to his eyes. I had not forgotten the closed-off expression I'd seen in Greece that could pass over his face like a storm cloud. He'd explained it all in his letters: a personal history so tragic I wondered if Todd would ever open himself up again. Would he regret opening up to me, both in writing and—today—in body?

Would I ever get to love him like that again?

He came out of the bathroom buck naked and whistling but halted when he saw me. "You okay, Copper?"

I must've had a strange look on my face, because he sat beside me and brushed a strand of hair from my cheek. "Should we not have . . . ?"

"No, that was great. I just . . ." I searched for a trace of darkness in his eyes.

He seemed to know what I meant. "I've wanted to be with you since, well, forever."

"I don't want you to regret . . ."

"Ann, I love you," Todd said.

"You—what?"

"I love you."

"You love me?" I sucked in a quick breath—helium.

"Yes."

It should've been obvious, Maggie. He'd come to Rome, for god's sake. The ultimate grand gesture. But I'd spent years denying myself this possibility. So when he said it, it just didn't make sense. "As a friend?"

"No." He drew me into a kiss. "Not like a friend."

"Say it again?" I asked.

He met my eyes. "I love you."

"I love you too," I squeaked. "Are you sure?"

He laughed. "I'm sure."

"What changed your mind?"

The corner of his mouth twitched, then pulled into a deeper smile. "Nothing," he said. "I always loved you. I just got tired of denying it."

I wanted to ask why he had denied it so long, but grief wasn't linear. It didn't have a timeline. So I simply basked in the glow of knowing Todd Langley loved me *now*. "I'm really glad you're here," I said.

"Me too."

I could've stayed in bed with him all day, but he assured me we'd have plenty of time to explore each other later—for the afternoon, he wanted to explore Rome. I acquiesced, because I found it very hard to say no to this new version of Todd, the one that loved Ann.

We started along the river, stopping briefly at a to-go pizza place, where crisp rectangles were folded in half and handed to us in gritty brown paper. After eating, we walked the Ponte Sisto. I'd seen many couples cross the bridge holding hands but had never done so myself, not in all my time in Rome. When I admitted this to Todd, he laced his fingers with mine and squeezed tightly. We took our time, pausing every so often to touch the smooth marble railing and watch the Tiber flowing below us.

I remembered the couples I'd watched through the window at Carmella's, the locked fingers and dreamy glances. I knew now what I had suspected: something had been missing from my relationships before. Now, all the romance of the world was within my reach.

We visited the Pantheon next, then drank macchiatos at a nearby café. Todd told me funny, blackmail-worthy stories about his and Keith's shenanigans as best friends. On the table, our hands met, and he stroked my knuckles with his thumb, listening intently to my own travel stories: the time I accidentally ordered two pints of beer for breakfast in Spain, the time I boarded a train to Germany instead of Italy, and the time I inadvertently broke into the ancient Agora of Athens. We laughed and shared a pastry, and everything felt normal even though we hadn't done this together before.

At Trevi Fountain, we sat on the wall and watched tourists pose for pictures. I hadn't spent much time at Trevi—I tended to avoid touristy spots—but that day, I was mesmerized by the wild and docile chariot horses and Oceanus's triumphant stance.

Before we left, Todd insisted we throw coins. The clear pool glittered with thousands of them. The story went that a coin tossed with the right hand over the left shoulder into the fountain would ensure a return to Rome.

"But I *live* in Rome," I said, chuckling. "Of course I'll return—I'm already here."

"But if you ever leave, you'll know it won't be permanent."

His comment reminded me of the terrible reality of our situation, something I hadn't considered since he arrived at Carmella's the night before: that I lived here, and Todd lived in Colorado.

"Come on," Todd said. "Let's do the tourist thing."

I forced the worry from my mind. "All right."

We sat side by side on the edge of the fountain, and Todd handed me a coin. We counted backward from three, flinging them over our shoulders with a plunk. The coins were an unspoken promise; someday, we'd be here again, together. It gave me hope that Todd and I would last.

We could figure out the distance.

Todd stood and offered his hand. I grasped it, and he pulled me straight into his arms, kissing me in a dramatic dip. I laughed against his mouth as he brought me upright.

"There's a stellar gelato place nearby," I said. "Interested?"

"Do they have stracciatella?"

"It would be a travesty if they didn't."

Todd pecked my cheek. "Let's go."

Hand in hand, we retraced our steps toward the Pantheon. Quick clouds brushed over the sun, dimming the sky intermittently. Light splayed in an odd patchwork across ancient marble and new stone, spotlights that brightened gold and faded into blue gray as we walked.

Beside me, Todd sighed and wrapped an arm around my waist, hooking a finger through the belt loop at my opposite hip. "What a stunning city. It must be nice to just wander around all day, not a care in the world."

I prickled, craning my neck to study his expression, to see if he was kidding. He was staring ahead at the piazza we were approaching. Pigeons fluttered around as market vendors packed away their goods for the day.

"I have cares," I said.

"Of course," Todd said. "I just mean, it must be nice not to work. To simply enjoy Rome all the time."

"I work . . ."

Todd unhooked his finger from my belt and glanced down at me. "Oh, I didn't mean to make it sound like your writing isn't work—"

"You make it sound like I'm here lollygagging my life away." I didn't want to argue, but I didn't want Todd to think of me as a carefree rich girl, either. That stung.

"Aren't you?" When he saw me frown, he added quickly, "I'm not trying to offend you, I'm just saying it must be nice."

"I'm grateful for what I have here, Todd, but it's not all cake and roses. I have expectations from Keith and my publisher. I tutor the neighborhood in English. I have a full life. I—"

"Whoa, hey," Todd said, patting the air. "Never mind, okay?"

"No, I want to understand your opinion of me," I pressed. "You think I'm entitled?"

He stopped and turned to me, his mouth twisted up in hesitation. "I think you're privileged," he said carefully. "You have to admit that the payout from your father was—"

"I'm incredibly lucky," I cut in. His words were thorny on my heart. "But I'm not an airhead trust fund baby. You know my past. Don't insinuate that I don't recognize and appreciate what I have, what I've *accomplished*."

"Ann," Todd said, touching my arm. His fingers were firm and warm—soothing. "I think you're the most amazing woman in the world. The things you've overcome, the things you've achieved . . . you're strong, talented, courageous. I guess I'm just saying I'm jealous of this." He swept a hand toward the beauty of the city, a spotlight of sun on the street ahead of us. "I wish I could travel more. Maybe go back to school. Do something bigger with my life. But I have the bookstore— my parents' dream, their legacy—and I'm limited by that. I'm envious of the freedom you have." Cautiously, he added, "And I hope you don't waste this gift simply floating along."

We stared at each other for a beat.

I reached into my purse and pulled out a cigarette. After a long inhale, I whispered, "Okay." His words were sinking in through my pores, making me reevaluate these past few years. What *had* I done with my money, beyond traveling and squirreling it away? Had I enjoyed my time, or had I wasted it?

"I'm sorry." Todd kissed my head again. "I didn't mean to hurt your feelings."

"It's fine."

"No, this was meant to be a nice day, and I said the wrong thing."

"It's fine," I repeated.

"It's *not* fine. You should live your life how you want—I shouldn't criticize that." He nudged me with his shoulder. "Look at us, our first fight."

I sighed a weak laugh. "Yeah."

"We shouldn't argue on a day like today. Forget what I said, all right?"

I nodded, but I couldn't simply forget what he had said. His words bothered me because they struck a chord; they rang true. Though it rattled my pride, Todd was right: I should do something meaningful with my time and wealth. How could I give back? "I'm just glad you care enough to have an opinion," I said.

"Of course I do." He wrapped his arm around me once more. "Come. Where is this gelato place?"

"Oh." I looked around. "We passed it." I grasped his hand and led him down a side street, backtracking.

After ordering, we carried our cups to the piazza and sat on a stoop, warming to each other again. Pretty soon, we were sharing bites and kissing the sweetness off each other's lips.

I thought about the last time we had gotten gelato together, six years ago in Venice. How different today was by comparison, full of love and surprise and depth. Full of care and *real* conversations. When I said as much, Todd hugged me close.

"I was an idiot back then," he said.

"You were," I agreed.

"Maybe I still am."

"Maybe," I said, and he laughed.

As we meandered home, we dipped into antique shops and leather-goods stores. It was sprinkling rain when we reached the Ponte Sisto, and we jogged the rest of the way to my apartment, laughing as we went.

For dinner, we snacked on *prosciutto e melone* and sipped wine. We chatted until the world outside was inky black and the lights inside glowed liquid gold. I basked in the warmth, blushing under Todd's steadfast gaze. That night, the city didn't exist beyond *us*.

When we turned out the lights, Todd guided me toward the bed. His mouth was wine sweet, and his hands splayed over my skin, firm and sure. We tasted and lingered and took all the time in the world, because that night, it felt as though the world was finally ours.

MAGGIE

The answers Jane sought were demons in a dark room. Perhaps it was bet-ter to leave the lights off. Perhaps it was better to lock the door behind her.
—Excerpt from Chasing Shadows, *by Ann Fawkes*

San Juan Island, Washington State, USA
Tuesday, January 9, 2024

Maggie leans against the hood of her car, watching the sun set and the sea become more turbulent. She left Ann's house twenty minutes ago and drove to Westside Preserve, a rocky outcrop along the island's main circumferential road. The location is private, cleansing.

They covered a lot of ground in Ann's story this afternoon—ground that should've been recorded, but Ann's story was the perfect distraction from their deal: Maggie talks to Tracey, and Ann talks to Grant.

Between reading letters and listening, during the tea breaks and pee breaks, Maggie has racked her mind all day as to what to say to her parents. What *is* there to say? It's a conversation she's been avoiding for practically her whole life—because it's painful, frightening, *uprooting*. The anguish of not knowing her family's truth has always seemed like the better choice. But now, Maggie has no choice. Either have *an honest conversation with Tracey about the past* or forfeit the podcast.

It's 3:30 p.m. in Colorado. Maggie circles the car and climbs into the driver's seat. Enclosed within the cab, she inhales the lingering scent of kelp salt, and the windless air is suddenly unbearably still. She counts herself down—*three, two, one*—and selects the top favorite in her phone: her parents' landline. The line crackles. She hits speakerphone and sets her cell on the dash.

"Hello, sweetheart." The innocence of her father's voice jars her.

"Hi, Dad."

"What's wrong?"

Maggie has to laugh. "What do you mean, 'What's wrong?'"

"I raised you," he says, and it breaks Maggie a little, because this call is an affront to that fact.

"Nothing's wrong," she hedges, "just a long day."

"I'm sorry to hear that."

"Is Mom there? I need to talk to her."

"Sure, let me go find her." Maggie hears footsteps as Bob continues. "It was a nice thing you did, reviving the Whitaker thread. Your mother has been texting all day. Her whole mood is lighter. She even made lunch plans with Natalie and Barbara this Friday."

"That's nice, Dad, I'm glad."

Maggie saw the ongoing chatter in the group text this morning; she'd had to silence her notifications before going into Ann's. At the time, it'd heartened her to *have* to mute her phone—to know that it was a false silence and not a lack of connection—but now . . . now she's afraid the fragile camaraderie will be broken. What if the family doesn't survive the secret she's about to ask her parents to unearth?

"Here she is," he says, but there's a note of reluctance in his words, as if he knows what Maggie is about to do.

"Actually . . . can you both stay on the line?" Tracey might be the one who holds a grudge against Ann, and Ann might've specified that Maggie talk to Tracey, but Bob deserves to stay. Though Ann initiated this call, *Maggie's* reason for this conversation involves both her parents.

"You're on speakerphone," her dad says.

"Hi, dear," Tracey says, sounding just as reluctant. Maggie can imagine the glances her parents are exchanging.

Maggie swallows, trying to build up the emotional fortitude to stumble through the next sentence. "Ann asked me to call you."

"What did she tell you?" Tracey bites out.

"She said we couldn't continue the interview until I talked to you."

"About?" Bob asks.

"She wasn't specific, but I think you know."

Bob pipes up, "I—" but Tracey cuts him off: "We don't."

Maggie grips the steering wheel to steady herself. "Mom, my job is on the line over this."

"That witch," Tracey says. "How dare she threaten—"

"No," Maggie interrupts. "No, she's not threatening me. I think she's holding back. And I think you know why."

"Maggie, I have no idea what lies Ann has—"

"I overheard you two talking one night." Maggie squeezes the wheel and closes her eyes, as if the car is crashing into the tumultuous sea. "Mom said 'Maggie's father,' as if Dad wasn't . . . *isn't* . . ." Maggie wrenches one hand free of the wheel to cradle her own face. "For so long, I thought it was better to pretend I didn't hear it. But I deserve the truth. I'm not asking you this because of Ann"—and she's not, Maggie realizes; Ann was the catalyst, but this conversation is a long time coming—"I'm doing this for the little girl who lay awake countless nights, crying and *wondering* and . . . and . . ."

"Oh, sweetheart," her father says.

"We ought to have this conversation in person," her mother adds.

Maggie drops her hands to her lap, balling her fists. "You've had my whole life to have this conversation." Her voice is steel. "No more waiting."

Tracey sighs, a slight quiver trailing out the end of her breath. Resolving herself. "You heard correctly that night."

The truth is a punch underwater, flowing over Maggie with a radiating force.

"Your biological father is Todd."

The fact lands on Maggie's consciousness like a leaf on a pool. It doesn't sink in. "That doesn't make sense," Maggie says, her voice muffled. "Todd *Langley?*"

Tracey's voice is anguished as she confirms, "Yes."

"How?" The word is a strangled sound as the news morphs from leaf to anvil, dragging her under, displacing everything she thought she knew.

"Bob and I tried for so long to have a child of our own, and then with Todd, well, we stepped in. We wanted you so badly, and we love you so much, and it seemed only right to keep this secret from you because—"

"Because abandonment would be too hard a pill to swallow?" *How is this possible?*

"Todd didn't abandon you," Tracey says. "He needed . . . help. After he lost . . . he couldn't handle responsibility. He wasn't ready."

Maggie knows all about Todd's tragic loss and how it overlapped with the Whitakers'—she came across it accidentally, via Wikipedia, when she was a teenager.

Because no one ever told her.

It was an awful way to find out something about her own family. Sobbing in the computer lab at school. Realizing *that's* why Tracey cried on the same day every year.

Anger bubbles up from her core. "So, I was an accident, and because he lost a child before, he just . . . gave me up? That doesn't make any sense."

Bob's voice is gentle when he says, "Grief never makes sense."

Maggie reaches up to cradle her face and finds it slick with tears. "He didn't want me? What about the woman he—"

"*We* wanted you," Tracey says, her tone fierce and comforting. "You were wanted. You were loved. You *are* loved."

"If Todd is my father, who is my mother?" She's unable to ask the real question, unable to even *think* it outright.

"Not Ann," Tracey says, her voice impossibly low.

Maggie flinches. "How do you know?"

"I *know.*"

"But—"

"Not. Ann," Tracey repeats.

If not Ann, then who? Maggie can't force the words out. If not the love of Todd's life, then Maggie's mother must be some random woman—and for some reason, the implied insignificance of half her DNA *hurts.*

After a long pause, Tracey says, "I'm sorry we're having this conversation over the phone. It's not how I intended—"

"Did you *ever* intend to tell me?" Maggie snaps. "Did anyone ever intend to tell me how messed up this family is?"

"Ann shouldn't have—"

"*Ann,*" Maggie enunciates, "is the only person who has been honest with me."

"Sweetheart," Bob says, "will you be all right tonight?"

How could her parents have kept this from her? Was it an act of protection, to keep Maggie's abandonment from her? Or something else? Something to do with Ann and Keith's falling-out?

Does Ann know who Maggie truly is? Or was this stipulation made on a hunch?

"I can't handle another moment of this," Maggie says. "I'm hanging up."

"Maggie, we love—" Tracey's voice cuts out as Maggie ends the call.

She drops her head to the steering wheel, allowing herself a few minutes to shudder and cry and then, collecting herself, texts Ann—per Ann's request—to confirm: I called Tracey.

Ann responds shortly thereafter: I'll email Grant. How'd it go?

Maggie sets her phone facedown on the passenger seat and starts the car.

Sitting on her bed at the B&B, Maggie oscillates between numbness and the acute sting of emotion, slippery and without shape but deadly as a jellyfish. It's not *one* feeling but many, tentacles of anger, curiosity, betrayal, and a deep-burning pain. She feels stupid. She's disbelieving. Todd *gave her up*. The whole family lied to her.

It seems that the more Maggie learns, the less she knows.

Maggie's phone blips with a text; she flips it over and reads the cracked screen. Missed calls from family members clog her notifications—but the new text is a simple Check your email from Grant. Maggie toggles over to her in-box.

Dear Grant,

I know you are aware of my agreement with Maggie to have an open dialogue off the record. After a compelling bid from Maggie—

She pauses. Since when is admitting a crime a "compelling bid"?

—it has come to my attention that my unwillingness to be recorded has threatened Maggie's long-term career with *SBTS*. My behavior has been unfair to your time and the efforts of your employee. Therefore, I have decided to renegotiate the terms of my original agreement and resume the interview-recording process.

That said, I have some concerns and stipulations. After thirty years of battling the media's skewed interpretation of my life, I have grown wary of misrepresentation. Please call me tomorrow at ten so we may hash out the details over the phone.

Best,

Ann Fawkes

The email should feel like a victory—her job is safe, the assignment is back on track—but instead, her mind is crowded with questions. She rubs her tear-gritty face, as if she can massage away the stress. But it doesn't work like that. Tomorrow, she's going to have to listen to Ann's story . . . knowing full well that Ann's story is the prologue to her own.

MAGGIE

"Hungry?" Ann asks.

It's the first word out of her mouth since she blew up Maggie's life—or at least since she convinced Maggie to blow up her *own* life. A cinnamon loaf rests on the counter, the whole house smelling of sweet spice.

As if on autopilot, Maggie slides onto a barstool, her phone buzzing in her pocket for the thousandth time. When she arose today, freshly missed calls—Tracey, Bob, Barbara, Aunt Natalie, even her cousin Iris—crowded her screen. Desperate texts have been filtering through since the wee hours of the morning, when she was still kidding herself, thinking there was time to fall asleep and not dream about Todd.

"I love this bread with cream cheese, but I also have butter," Ann continues. "And I think Matt threw some frosting in the bag, if that's more your speed."

From the messages Maggie has read, it's clear her family wants to apologize. But are they sorry for lying her whole life or sorry things got messy?

"Maggie?" Ann prompts, slicing through the bread with a huge serrated knife.

"Oh. Um. Butter."

Ann saws the loaf, sliding the big knife back and forth. Maggie sways as the slices fall, the bread billowing cinnamon steam. Where will Ann's story lead now?

Ann pauses midslice, her bright eyes penetrating before dropping back down to her task. "You're edgy this morning," Ann observes. "Did it not go well?"

Maggie gives her head a small shake, trying to dislodge the nagging question of her birth mother from her brain. "We argued."

Ann sets down the knife. "I'm sorry to hear that."

Maggie studies Ann's face and is startled by how blank it is—no furrowing or frowning. "Why did you have me call her? Why make that the deal?"

"I wanted Tracey to have a chance to say her piece."

"About?"

Ann shrugs, her expression vacant. "About why she hates me so much."

"You don't know?"

Ann goes back to slicing bread. "My relationship with the Whitakers is . . . complicated."

Does Ann know that Maggie is her longtime lover's daughter or not?

"I didn't want to cause friction between you and your mom, that's all. I wanted to give you two a chance to air that out, so we can continue without complication."

Maggie doesn't believe that. Ann must know about Todd, she *has* to . . .

. . . but on the off chance she doesn't, Maggie isn't about to risk the podcast by detonating that bomb.

"Tracey doesn't like that I'm here. That's about all she said."

Ann stares at her for two seconds, three, before retrieving a block of cream cheese and a butter dish from the fridge. If Ann doesn't believe Maggie, she's clearly not about to say so.

She begins preparing their bread slices with the desired toppings. "I bet you five dollars that Grant will call early."

Grateful for the shift in subject, Maggie shakes her head. "No way, I'm not taking that bet. The opposing odds are terrible."

"Oh, fine." Ann hands her a cup of coffee and slides a bread plate toward her across the bar counter. They carry their breakfasts to the couch. Ann eats unhurriedly, amiably. Maggie's stomach is too filled with questions to feel hungry. She has the sinking sense that there are many stones yet unturned.

At five till, the phone rings.

"See? Terrible opposing odds," Maggie says.

Ann smirks, straightens, selects speakerphone, and sets the phone on the coffee table. "Grant, hi." Her voice sounds entirely different from the soft-toned woman Maggie has grown accustomed to. Her vowels are harsh, her consonants too loud. Defensive.

"Miss Fawkes, thank you for getting on the horn this morning."

The horn? Maggie stifles a laugh. She's *never* heard him use that term. Grant sounds different too—his voice a lower register, a little more clipped. Is Maggie the least nervous person on this call?

She meets Ann's eyes, uncertain if she should make her presence known to Grant. Ann returns her gaze, mouth pressed thin. Maggie has heard a lot about Ann's life by now, a lot of personal, intimate details . . . but this is the first time she's seen Ann look truly vulnerable. Which is funny, because as far as Grant is concerned, Ann holds all the cards. Maggie opts to stay quiet, not wanting to insert herself in the conversation—and not interested in picking sides.

"I understand Maggie's job is on the line," Ann begins.

"Well, I wouldn't put it—"

"I'm prepared to start recording again, but I have three require-ments," Ann continues. "Number one: I want to listen to the final episode before it airs."

"Absolutely, we do that for all our subjects."

"Two: I want the right to make corrections and, if it comes to it, refuse the final product before it's aired."

"Miss Fawkes—"

"It's Ann."

"Ann, with due respect, that's a little—"

"Three," Ann says, leaning toward the phone. "Maggie will be the *only* person in the room during my recordings, and she will edit the audio *on her own* before bringing it to the rest of your team."

Maggie's eyes shoot over to Ann, shock tingling up her spine.

Grant clears his throat. "Miss Fawkes—Ann—we pride ourselves in journalistic integrity at *SBTS*, and your requests are . . ." He coughs. "We can't give you full authority."

"All I want is to be represented honestly."

"That's our goal too. I'm sorry the media has misrepresented you in the past, but I'm concerned about Maggie being the only one to hear the raw recordings."

"Why?"

"Well, her personal connection to you through Keith, for one," Grant says. "Who's to say that Maggie doesn't have her own spin?"

His words prod at her ego, but of course, he's right—and Maggie shares his concern. How can she be objective, knowing what she knows?

Grant continues. "This is just an extreme example, of course. I'm not trying to sound suspicious. But we have a process for these things."

"How can I agree to a podcast about my life—my *personal* life— when they ask me to relinquish control over how I'm portrayed?" Ann asks. "Too many times, I have signed away my rights and had my words clipped and edited and spliced back together so that I come across as a different person entirely. I will not allow it again."

Maggie hunches, ashamed of not deleting the accidental recording as soon as it happened. *I know what it's like to beg for forgiveness.* That's what Ann had said yesterday; her compassion is astounding.

"I'm horrified by your suggestion that we would splice your words dishonestly."

"So am I," Ann responds, "but the truth of the matter is that it *has* happened. I'm not trying to censor you or lie to your listeners. I'm try-ing to protect myself." Ann's hair has fallen across her face, obscuring her feline cheekbones. She looks small, sitting on the other end of the couch, and yet she's larger than life. Her vulnerability is her strength.

Grant sighs. "How's this: I'll agree to your first two stipulations—pending approval from my boss, and with the understanding that *both* parties need to be happy with the final product. If you suggest changes we aren't comfortable with and we can't come to an agreement, we won't air the story."

"That's perfectly fair."

"However, *someone* else needs to listen to the raw recordings. We won't publish them. We won't disclose them. But for the sake of integr-ity, we *need* other producers involved. What if we had the other person sign some sort of confidentiality agreement?"

Steepling her fingers, Ann peers at Maggie from underneath arched eyebrows. "What do you think, Maggie. Does that sound fair?"

Adrenaline hits Maggie in the chest like a fist.

"Maggie, you're on the line?" Grant's voice has talons. He doesn't like to be caught off guard—or look like a fool.

"I'm here," Maggie says, regretting not announcing herself earlier. She scoots closer to the phone. "I'm fine with whatever you two decide."

"Maggie, do you have someone in mind whom you trust to listen to the raw recordings?" Ann asks pointedly.

Ann has suddenly put Maggie in an impossibly uncomfortable position with her boss. She considers the other members of the podcast team, weighing her options. She knows she ought to suggest Grant—he would be the *correct* response—but instead, she answers honestly. "I'd like Brit to hear the recordings—we're a good team in the editing room." She lifts her gaze to Ann, explaining, "Brit is a sound engineer, but we worked together in college. She has a good eye for story. And she's the only one at *SBTS* who hasn't read your book, so she'll have less bias."

"You're also friends," Grant says, clearly unhappy with the suggestion.

"You and I are friends, too, Grant—or at least I thought we were." She regrets the words as soon as they're out, but this week has left her tactless.

Grant doesn't answer.

Maggie has made quite a mess over the past few days, but she's also gotten further with Ann than anyone else on the team could have hoped. And now that she has her chance to right this ship—to prove her worth—she's not about to let Grant get in her way and take over.

Ann breaks the silence. "If Maggie wants Brit, I'm comfortable with that."

"Maggie, I'd like to remind you that I am lead on this episode." A warning.

Then again, Grant was the one to give Maggie this chance in the first place. A calculated risk on Grant's part, but a risk, nonetheless. Cowed, Maggie drops her gaze to her hands. "I trust Grant too."

Ann leans forward and mutes their end of the phone, so Grant can't hear them talk. "Is that how you really feel?"

Unaware that Ann and Maggie are muted, Grant says, "I appreciate that, Maggie, thank you."

"This is awkward," Maggie admits to Ann. "You're putting me in an awkward position."

"How do you think *I* feel?"

Maggie sighs. "I would prefer to work with Brit," she says. "But I don't think Grant will go for it. He can be . . . controlling, and I know he feels out of the loop with me here instead of him." Maggie touches Ann's arm. "But he's an excellent producer. I trust him with your words."

"Ann? Maggie? Are you still there?" Grant asks.

Ann is nodding. "All right." She unmutes her phone and says, "Grant, I'd like Maggie and Brit to do the first pass, the first whittled-down edit, and then you may get involved. I want confidentiality agreements from all three of you."

"I—"

"That's my offer."

For a moment, the phone is silent, save for the sounds of Grant's breathing and the slight crackle of winter island wind and quivering cell towers. Finally, he says, "I'll take it."

Ann smiles, straightens, brightening from within. "Splendid. Maggie and I will resume recording today. Is there anything else?"

"No, I'm all set. We'll get the contracts prepared and send them over this afternoon. Thank you for your flexibility."

"Thank *you*." Ann reaches for the phone, ready to end the call. "Bye now—"

"Wait," Grant says. "I'd like to speak with Maggie—privately."

Ann looks up, worry on her face. Maggie is heartened by her concern, but it doesn't buoy her feelings. She's about to be chewed out—she can hear it in Grant's taut words.

Breaking eye contact with Ann, Maggie grabs the phone and slips out the kitchen's side door, onto the back porch. The weather is cold and blustering.

"All right, it's just me," Maggie says.

"Brit? *Brit?* I love the girl, but *fuck*, Maggie, what were you thinking?"

"I was being honest." Maggie glances over her shoulder, through the window. Ann is washing a serving platter in the sink; a teapot rests on the stove, already steaming. "Ann was *staring* at me, I couldn't lie."

"She's not a mind reader," Grant says. "And besides, why wouldn't you *honestly* think of me?"

Because you would take over.

Because your micromanaging shouldn't be rewarded.

Because Brit truly is a better story editor than you.

Maggie doesn't voice the angry answers swirling in her head.

Grant sighs, a forceful breath that seems to go on forever. "Do you understand what an absolute shit show this is, Maggie? Do you understand the level of—"

"Todd Langley is my father," Maggie says, a whisper that feels like a shout, the way it erupts from her throat. She glances back again, but Ann isn't visible anymore—she must've gone into another room.

"Todd is—*what did you just say?*"

"My biological father," Maggie says, realizing that—of all people—Grant is the first person she's told. "I found out last night."

"Ann said so?"

"*No,*" Maggie says. "God, no. My mother"—she trips on the word—"Tracey told me."

His voice has lost its scolding staccato when he says, "Do you . . . I'm sorry to ask, but . . . do you know who your mother is?"

"Not Ann, according to Tracey."

"Do you think Ann knows about Todd?"

"I'm not sure."

"You can't mention this," Grant says. "Maggie, the podcast is *finally* back on track. You can't tell Ann about Todd—it would change everything about these interviews. It might skew the way she tells her story."

A cold wind ruffles Maggie's hair. "I know."

"All the more reason why I should be involved in the first edit," Grant says. "*Damn* it!"

Maggie balls her fists, bracing against the cold and the conversation. She's a stalk of grass blown free from a beach, her roots grasping at nothing. The sand that once kept her sturdy has eroded away. "I know my relation to Ann complicates things. I know this isn't ideal—"

"—not ideal, it's worse than—"

"—but you need to trust me. You need to trust that I care about this project too. I care about its integrity. I care about the story. I care about Ann. I'm determined to stay on track. I need you to allow me the space to do that."

"I've been very forgiving here, Maggie."

"You have."

"You can't tell Ann about Todd."

"I won't."

"Good. And Maggie?"

"Yes?"

"I'm sorry."

She frowns. "About what?"

"It must be hard for you . . . this news."

"Oh. Yes, it is. Thanks."

"But you understand why you shouldn't mention it, right?"

"You're not the only one who values this job, Grant." She hangs up before he can hear her voice break.

Maggie stands on the porch another couple of minutes, letting the wind pulse against her. She sniffles and wipes her eyes, hoping her face isn't too red, too revealing. When she slips back inside, the warmth of Ann's home envelops her. She closes the door, then sets Ann's phone on the kitchen counter. Ann appears from the hallway, her own face a little blotchy.

"I hope he didn't scold you too harshly," Ann says. "But I think that went well?"

"You didn't make it easy on me."

"I'm sorry."

"Should we get to it?" Maggie asks, not ready at all. Not prepared to hear about Todd—her *father*—in any capacity . . . but especially not as Ann's lover.

Ann nods. "Should we carry on from where I left off? Fill in the earlier bits later?"

"That makes sense."

"All right," Ann says. "Get your recorder."

ANN

Todd and I didn't discuss maintaining a long-distance relationship so much as we simply sank into one—and miraculously, it worked, at least for a while. Todd took vacations to Italy, or we met in some other city—London for Christmas, Montreal for Todd's birthday—and in between the bright spots of our international meetings, we wrote letters and racked up long-distance phone bills, and the longing became a part of our love. The longing made the moments of connection so much sweeter.

Believe it or not, Maggie, we did this for two and a half years.

We were, of course, distracted by our own pursuits.

Dreamer Bookstore was doing better than ever, so Todd had extended the open hours, adding evening book clubs and author events to an already packed schedule.

I dove headfirst into getting my English-teaching credentials so I could legitimize my tutoring business. The program was a welcome distraction from my crushing self-doubt over my second novel, which had morphed into a terribly mawkish melodrama. Adding salt to the wound of my sophomore slump, *Chasing Shadows* was in its second movie-option process after the first fell through, so Keith and the film people were calling constantly.

Todd and I were so busy that months slipped past practically undetected. Each visit was a lighthouse flash across the ocean of my life.

Then came April 1993. I was invited to New York to meet with our executive producer and screenwriter and sign the papers that would make my book a movie. I asked Todd to meet me there, and of course Keith was delighted to have a reunion in his city.

The meeting was a big deal. I'll never forget walking into the room and having everyone turn toward me as if *I* were the big shot. They asked me to sit at the head of the table, and someone passed over a plate of cookies. I was out of breath, dizzy, as if I'd just climbed a mountain and now stood higher than the clouds. Everyone else seemed comfortable at these heights—confident, even—but I kept thinking, *Do they know how far I've come? That the elevation makes me queasy?*

I felt like they were all just humoring me. *Chasing Shadows* wasn't *mine* anymore: it belonged to the readers, the audience, and these executives. The script was superb. I didn't have more to say. I just wanted to ride the elevator back down to the ground floor, where I could breathe again.

After the meeting, Keith and I exited the skyscraper into the honking, shouting chaos of Midtown. He was wearing a suit that accentuated the broadness of his chest and the extra ten pounds he'd gained since Iris was born. I loved how *the same* he looked. The curly russet hair and all those freckles. He still had that Santorini glint in his eye, all these years later.

"You didn't hear a word she said in there, did you?" he asked.

I shook my head.

"You okay?"

"I think so, yeah. It's just . . . crazy."

"It is."

"You did this, Keith. You made this happen."

"You're terrible at being successful, you know that? It's your story, Ann. This is all you."

"But you sold it."

"Fine." He winked. "Call it a tie?"

"Deal." I checked my watch, my mind swiveling toward another thrill: seeing Todd. I was giddy. I felt so unbelievably happy about how the three of us had ended up. Would we all be meeting in New York like this, had I not followed Todd to Greece?

"My god, you're smitten," Keith said, reading my face. "You just signed the biggest deal of your life and you're checking your watch, thinking about a *man*."

"Don't make me sound unfeminist. I was thinking about all of it."

Keith squinted in amusement and ran a hand through his hair. "When does he land?"

"Three."

"We're having dinner tonight, to celebrate. Just me and you and Todd. Yeah?"

It was eleven, and I was trying to think of how to waste the afternoon before Todd landed and I could meet him at the hotel. "Celebrate?"

"The *movie*! Jesus, Ann."

"The movie stresses me. Let's celebrate our reunion."

"Whatever you say." Keith kissed my cheek. "Six o'clock."

I nodded once and gave him a little wave, and we parted ways. Keith had more meetings; I decided to visit the Met. I spent a long while in the air-conditioned halls of Renaissance paintings, awed by the art and where my life had taken me.

When I left the museum, the unseasonal warmth of the day embraced me. My heels—which I'd chosen for the meeting—were taller than I was accustomed to, and I stepped carefully over the cobble-stones as I walked through Central Park. I relished the fresh air that sifted through the elms, my flared blue midlength skirt billowing in the breeze. Heading for the subway, I turned right on Eighty-Sixth. I wanted to freshen up at the hotel before Todd arrived.

Distracted with thoughts of the movie and Todd, I had just reached Park Street and was stepping—teetering, really—off the curb into the crosswalk when a sudden steely force slammed into my hip. I was knocked—hard—onto the ground, and my elbow broke my fall. The breath whooshed from my lungs, and the squeal of tires echoed through the block.

Street grit dug into my arms and calves. My hip ached immensely, but it was my right arm that screamed with acute pain. Dazed, I shifted off the pavement onto my back, right there in the middle of the sidewalk. I cradled my elbow and stared up at the blue sky, watching wispy smog-gray clouds float far beyond the organic fluttering of tree leaves and the harsh edges of apartment buildings. I noticed the butter yellow of a taxi in my periphery, and it finally clicked that the cab had hit me.

The driver was getting out, apologizing profusely in accented English. A woman walking nearby had a Motorola in her purse and called the police. A man in a janitor's jumpsuit helped me sit up, asking if I was dizzy. Another passerby urged me to test the range of motion in my elbow.

Far more clear headed after the initial shock had worn off, I told the panicking driver to leave. Perhaps six people had gathered—all were against the idea of letting him go—but I didn't want him to get fired for *my* mistake. *It was my heels,* I told the witnesses. *I stepped off the curb early. I wasn't paying attention.* Mostly, I just wanted to get on with my day; I wanted to meet Todd at the hotel and go to dinner.

But one of the witnesses—a self-proclaimed journalist—recognized me as Ann Fawkes, and this started a strange sequence of me signing scraps of paper with my left hand for everyone in the general vicinity. The janitor was asking me very pointed questions about the character development in *Chasing Shadows* when the police arrived, and the cops seemed just as perplexed by the fanfare as I was. Soon, I was whisked away to the hospital, where I learned I had gotten off easy for this kind of accident: a bruised hip and a sprained elbow. I'd need to wear a sling and brace for the next few weeks.

By the time I was free to leave, it was past six. Impatience crawled like fire ants across my skin, making me squirm. I caught a cab (the irony not lost on me) directly to the restaurant. My limbs were heavy from the day's events, but it was my heart that weighed the most. It was two hours past my agreed rendezvous time with Todd at the hotel, and either he thought I had stood him up or he was worried sick, both of which I hated to imagine.

I must've looked a wreck when I stepped through the door of the steak house. I still had pavement smears on my legs. My hair—loosed from its ponytail—was tangled, and my skirt was dirtied along the hem and bum. I wore an arm sling and was terribly wobbly from my too-high heels and tired ankles as I followed the hostess toward the back of the restaurant.

All the air in my lungs pushed out in a rush when I saw them— both of them—fidgeting at a small circular table. Keith spotted me first. Todd had his back to me, but when Keith rose out of his seat, Todd's head swiveled. His hair was longer, shiny and unkempt as always; he looked weary from his flight, or worry, or both.

"Ann," he said, standing. He drew me close, tucking me into the hollow of his collarbone, kissing my hair. "We were so worried."

Keith pulled a chair out for me, and I sank into it with relief. I took a long drink from the untouched water glass in front of me, the ice stinging my teeth. "By the time I had a chance to call your office, it was after five," I told Keith.

Todd scooted his chair close and lightly touched the brace on my arm. "What happened?"

I explained it quickly, downing half of someone's wine in the process. The waitress delivered another glass and filled it from the open bottle on the table.

"That's it, I'm getting a mobile phone," Keith said.

"For the next time I'm hit by a car?"

Keith nodded.

Todd said, "At least you're okay."

"You look terrible, though," Keith added.

Todd shot him a dark look, but I giggled and smoothed my hair. "I'm sorry I worried you."

Todd leaned in and kissed my neck, squeezing my knee under the table. "For the record, I think you look great."

Keith made a garbled sound of disgust. "I'm not used to you two being so . . ." He waggled his finger between us. *"Together."* This was the first time the three of us had been in the same room since Todd and I had started long-distance dating.

"You were practically throwing me at Todd in Greece," I countered.

"I didn't consider the PDA."

Todd smirked, then planted his arm on the back of my chair so his hand could gently cup the nape of my neck. There was a genuine crease in his eyes, his relief plain. Despite my aches and pains, desire surged through me like a spring river. I hadn't seen Todd since the New Year.

Keith seemed to sense the palpable sexual tension. "Let's talk about books!"

I rolled my eyes as Todd asked, "What about them?"

"Ann needs to write another one."

"I thought you were working on something?" Todd asked me.

"It's garbage," I said. "Hot garbage. Banana peels, coffee grounds, old diapers."

Keith waved his hand to clear my words from the air. "It can't be that bad."

"It's bad." I hoped Keith couldn't hear my anxiety. "Besides, I've been preoccupied with my latest article for *Condé Nast*."

"Your publisher—"

"I'm not under contract. As my agent, you—"

"Remember when we saw Keith's butt in Greece?" Todd interjected.

Keith and I quit bickering and looked at him. Three entire seconds passed before we all burst into laughter.

"Still thinking about it, bud?" Keith asked.

"Just trying to defuse the shop talk," Todd said. "This is a *reunion*. Let's talk about reunion stuff."

"Such as . . . ?" I asked.

Todd brushed the hair from his face, and another pulse of desire thrummed through me. "I don't know, memories. Nostalgia. Funny stories."

Keith raised his palms. "Okay, okay. Just can we please not talk about my butt? This is a nice restaurant."

"It was a nice butt," I said, and we all laughed again.

Todd launched into retelling the time his moped stalled after turning the wrong way down a one-way street, eliciting angry honks from locals whizzing past. That story led into the next moped misadventure, when Keith had mistaken someone else's parked bike for his own, straddled the seat, and promptly gotten hit in the back of the head with the owner's purse as she rushed to defend her ride.

As we reminisced, I lost myself in the bright, oceanic blue green of Todd's eyes, magnified by his glasses. Whenever we came together after a long time apart, I always noticed details I'd forgotten—the exact angle of his straight nose, the freckle just under his ear—my memory a shadow of the real thing. His cheeks were flushed from the warm restaurant, the wine—and maybe from seeing me again?

Keith was telling another story, and Todd was laughing, and suddenly I felt so unbelievably glad to be in this restaurant with these two. Aside from Carmella, they were the realest, truest companions of my life.

When the waitress returned, Keith ordered the bruschetta appetizer—pronouncing it with the soft *sh* of someone who hadn't been to Italy yet.

"It's *broo-sketta*," I enunciated. "You would know that by now if you ever came to visit."

"As soon as Iris is a little older, we will."

"How much older?"

"Hey, when *you're* flying eight hours with a kid, you can set the timeline." Keith wiped his mouth with his napkin. "That reminds me—and I know it's a long way off, but—what are your plans for Christmas? Barbara and I decided to invite my whole family upstate. We'd love for you both to come."

After so many Christmas letdowns as a child, I'd let go of all holiday expectations. Even visiting London with Todd last year had been modest—delightful, but modest. Christmas with the Whitakers sounded wonderful and overwhelming. Keith and Todd had been friends since they were kids, so the family already knew Todd. I'd be a stranger. And yet this was my chance to indulge in a *real* celebration. Intimidated as I was, it sounded perfect.

"I would love to," I said, glancing at Todd.

His eyes had gone distant; he set down his fork. "I don't know . . ."

With a soft, earnest voice, Keith urged, "They'd love to see you again, bud."

I put my hand on Todd's arm. "I've never had a big holiday before."

"You haven't?" Keith asked.

"Growing up, it was always just me and my mom, and sometimes one of her boyfriends." A twist of sorrow made my sternum ache. I loved the prospect of starting a new tradition—or being a new part of an old one. "Your family won't mind having a stranger there?"

"They'll adore you," Keith assured. "And they already love Todd."

"They're pretty great," Todd admitted. "But it's only April. Can we think about it?"

I studied his face, trying to make sense of his reluctance.

"Of course," Keith said gently. "We have plenty of time."

ANN

That night, I nestled into Todd's embrace, enjoying his delicious warmth against my skin. Unfamiliar lights and sounds filtered in from the wooden blinds covering our hotel window. I ran a hand through his sparse chest hair and kissed the soft flesh where his collarbone met his shoulder.

"I missed this," I whispered. It'd been months since our last visit, and I was basking in the glow of this lighthouse blip of brilliance.

Todd's entire body stiffened, but then he pulled me closer. "I was so worried about you today."

"Maybe Keith was right about getting a mobile phone."

Todd sighed. "I don't like being apart so much. This long-distance thing—"

"It's hard for me too."

Tonight wasn't the first time this had come up. He wanted to live closer, or together. And I wanted that, too, of course, but I had a sickly suspicion that Todd wanted me to move back to Colorado. That he wanted *me* to make that sacrifice. The thought of leaving Italy—my *home*—made me wilt.

With each passing visit, I worried that Todd and I were approaching an impasse. I would not leave Rome—I couldn't. I had a happy life there—one I had carefully cultivated for the past eight years. He hadn't asked point blank yet, but I knew it was coming. I dreaded the day that I would have to tell him no and instead ask whether he would leave Colorado. I feared his answer. I feared the futility of our future together. It was easier to float along, stealing sweet moments together whenever possible. I didn't love long distance, but what was the alternative?

I changed the subject: "Why don't you want to see Keith's family for Christmas?"

"It's so far into the future," he said, rolling away from me. His feet hit the floor, and he padded toward the bathroom. "Do we have to discuss it now?"

I propped myself up on my elbows, staring at the open doorway. "I just want to know what the hesitation is."

After a minute, Todd reappeared, illuminated by the harsh bathroom light. He flipped the switch and returned to bed in darkness. "Keith and I have been best friends since high school." He settled the sheets over us again. "There's a lot of history there."

The tragedy. Keith's family had shepherded Todd through the worst event of his life.

I thought he would go on, but he didn't. My gaze traced the dim outline of his straight nose in the dark. I wanted to know what she'd looked like, learn her name, but whenever the topic came up, I sensed the monumental anguish in Todd's heart, and it didn't feel right to prod him with questions. Though he hadn't explained much about his wife over the years, I knew Todd had loved her deeply.

Did he love me that way?

I sometimes worried I was second best to the woman who had carried his child. A memory of a person is always superior to what stands before you—my mother had taught me that. And he'd built a whole life with her—a history, a home, a child. I was a nomad by comparison, a passerby in the life of Todd Langley.

"I was so worried today, Ann." His voice was raw in a way that told me he, too, had been thinking of her. "I was afraid you—" A soft suck of breath strangled his words, but they still hit me with a force. "I don't want to sound controlling, but I worry. I hate being so far apart."

Long distance was hard for me, but was it torture for Todd? I couldn't bring myself to ask. Instead, I wondered, "When was the last time you saw Keith's family?"

Todd exhaled in a long, measured way. "Moving forward was the hardest thing I've ever done," he said. "It was our hometown, and the fire occurred in our small local hospital. The news spread fast, and I couldn't escape it. Everywhere I went, I received pity from strangers, when all I wanted was to heal in solitude. Keith and his family were the only people I could rely on during that time. It's hard to be around them since then. There's so much pain in our shared memories."

"What if it's time to reconnect? It could be . . . therapeutic?"

"Maybe you're right." He hugged me to his chest and kissed me. "Distance doesn't help anything, does it?"

I thought of Rome even as I conceded. "No," I whispered, "it doesn't."

MAGGIE

Todd's daughter, that child he lost, was Maggie's half sister. It hadn't occurred to Maggie until now, and it doesn't counteract her anger toward him, but . . . her heart clenches. She's uncertain *how* she should feel about Todd. Every instinct is a contradiction: rage and pity, blame and sympathy.

She blinks, trying to quell the tears forming in her eyes. Ann is still talking, but when Maggie wipes her cheek, Ann stops.

"Are you all right?" she asks.

What Todd did to Maggie is inexcusable. He'd *abandoned* her. And yet she recalls the shock and sorrow she experienced when she first read the details of the tragedy online—her fury that no one had told her its impact, on not Todd but the Whitakers. In Ann's version, a connective detail has been left out.

Does Ann know the other half of the story?

Ann's eyes—penetrating, firm, but compassionate—don't offer any answers.

"We can take a break?" Ann asks.

Maggie wipes her cheeks again and shakes her head. "I'm fine. Go on."

ANN

On my last day in New York, I met Keith for breakfast at a nearby diner for some overdue shop talk. I arrived first and was seated by the window, which meant I could see the strife on Keith's face as he approached from half a block away. His strides were quick and purposeful; his cheeks were flushed with agitation. He yanked the door open, glances like missiles hitting table after table until he spotted me.

I steadied my coffee as he jostled into the chair across from mine and slapped a tabloid down.

"What's this?" I asked, picking up the newspaper.

"Page Six."

A waitress brought Keith a coffee while I flipped to the source of his vexation. The spread was cluttered with photos and headlines, a visual cacophony. "You're going to have to narrow it down," I said.

He tapped his finger on a grainy horizontal photo of a woman lying on the sidewalk. Because her knees were bent up, her skirt was hiked, revealing a scandalous amount of thigh. The headline read: **Famous author hit by cab!**

That was *my* thigh. I bent forward, reading, unbelieving. It seemed so unlikely that I would end up in a tabloid. I was a *writer*, not an actress. The write-up mentioned a "hit-and-run" and—

I met Keith's eyes. "What the fuck."

Someone had spotted me, Keith, and Todd exiting the steak house. *Could this mystery man be a real-life Frank?* Seeing my photo in a tabloid was a shock, but it was the fixation on Todd and the reference to my book—in which Frank *betrayed* Jane—that made my mouth go dry. A recent interview had completely rearranged my sentiments about my "new relationship" and the delay of my next book, putting the blame unfairly on Todd—now, this.

"Is Todd's privacy at risk?" I asked, knowing he'd feel violated just by the speculation.

"Probably not." Keith sipped his coffee. "But we need to sell another project."

"What does a new novel have to do with tabloids?"

"If people don't get another Ann Fawkes story, they'll write their own."

"That seems a little melodramatic, don't you think?"

He reached into his briefcase and pulled out another rag, dated back to January 1991. He flipped to a dog-eared page and swiveled the headline in my direction.

It was about my mother.

It said that she died of cancer. That I had refused to pay her medical bills, and I hadn't even gone to her funeral. All true, but without context, *cruel*. Each word sizzled on my heart like a brand.

"I didn't show you this one because I knew you were grieving."

"It's not true," I whispered.

"I know."

"My aunt. Or one of my mother's broke friends . . ." They had probably sold the story after I wrote my mother's obit. It'd garnered national attention because of my name, *her* name. Fawkes.

The waitress interrupted to take our orders. Neither of us had looked at the menu, so we both ordered cheese omelets.

Keith laid a hand on my arm. "There are more of these. I know they seem objectively harmless, but do you really want *this*"—Keith tapped the tabloid again—"to be your legacy?"

I released a long, slow breath. "What do other authors do?"

"Other authors haven't written a bestselling NYT Notable Book with a cult following."

"I can write more articles, short fiction."

"That's not going to cut it anymore."

"I can't write another novel—I can't do it." A sob escaped my lips, and I clamped my hand over my mouth to stifle any more noise. I didn't want to make a scene. "*Chasing Shadows* is all I had in me."

"Ann, you're a brilliant writer—"

"Do you know how vulnerable, how *violated* I felt on my book tour? *Chasing Shadows* might've been fiction, but it was personal, and my readers could tell. That's what made the book *good*. But I can't do that to myself again. It'll destroy me." It was the truth I'd been avoiding with Keith for months.

Todd came through the door, then, his hair pleasantly tousled and his face textured with dark stubble. "I got hungry, so I decided to crash your meeting—" Todd cut himself off when he saw my panic. "Is everything okay?"

I could barely look at him; instead, I fixated on the act of unfolding and refolding a paper napkin and wiping my face. Keith handed him the tabloid, and Todd sank into the seat beside me, reading. I dared a glance. His full mouth had pressed until his lips went thin and pale; his brows pinched low over the bridge of his nose. His eyes darted quickly over the words. I saw how violated Todd felt—it was plain as a headline on his face.

And it was my fault.

"Why do they give a damn who *I* am?" Todd asked, looking between us.

My fingers shook as I crumpled my napkin.

Keith frowned. "It'll probably blow over."

Though the article hadn't mentioned his name, this was the second time Todd's identity and relationship to me had garnered speculation. After learning of his public pain after the tragedy . . . I could see how this attention would feel too close for comfort.

I raised my eyes to Keith's. "I'll get you ten thousand words and a synopsis as soon as I can."

"By December."

"December it is." I grasped Todd's hand under the table. If a new book would shelter us a little—divert focus from my personal life before my movie thrust me back into an unwanted spotlight—then it was worth the effort.

"You're a pro," Keith said. "It'll be a piece of cake."

ANN

At the airport, Keith and Todd wished me a safe flight and told me they loved me. But when Keith stepped back to give me and Todd a moment of privacy, Todd's kiss wasn't the firm, indulgent press it usually was. His movements were quick, barely a peck.

He was still annoyed by the tabloid, but I think the goodbye itself was what bothered him. He wanted to be getting on a plane *together*. He wanted to be heading *home* together.

And I wanted that too. Just not to Colorado—not the one place where I'd see my mother around every corner.

"Think about Christmas, all right?" I asked, curling my fingers through his hair one last time.

He glanced back at Keith, who was standing by the doors with his hands in his pockets. "Listen, Ann, there's something I didn't mention before, about my family—"

"Shh." I didn't want to open another difficult conversation; I just wanted to savor him before I got on the plane. "I love you."

He studied me, blinked, then said, "I love you too."

Mine was a long journey home, filled with delays and layovers. By the end of it, my skin and hair were oily, throat dry and scratchy. I dumped my bags on the floor of my unlit apartment, then slipped off my shoes and filled a glass of water in the kitchen, downing it in three big gulps that did little to soothe. I kept the lights off, afraid that if I illuminated the dark space, I'd see its emptiness more plainly.

For the first time since I'd moved to Rome, the apartment felt foreign. The teal glass horse sparkled on my bookshelf beside the first edition of *Chasing Shadows*, but the rest of my things—the bed, the desk, the empty vegetable basket on the counter—were interchangeable, like a stage set.

Was this place a home, without someone to share it with? While I cherished my simple, independent life, my heart had grown cavernous and hollow from the ever-present lonesomeness of living so far from the man I loved.

I approached my landline, calculating the time difference between Rome and New York—or was Todd back in Colorado by now? His flight had been twelve hours after mine. I'd lost track of the time between us.

When I reached the phone, there was already a message waiting. I hit play and pressed my fingers over my mouth. Static rustled the speakers; then Todd's voice came through crisp and clear.

Ann, it's Todd. You're probably on a plane now, but I couldn't wait to hear your voice, even if it was just your recording. I'm back at the hotel, packing and checking out. Sweetheart, I'm sorry about how we left things at the airport. I'm sorry I didn't grab you and kiss you like I meant it. I hate our goodbyes, don't you? I hate being apart. I hate this distance between us. Change is scary—because this is so good, isn't it? this thing we have going on between us?—but you can't blame me for wanting to be closer. I want all of you, Copper.

Anyway, I know I'm rambling. I guess I called to tell you that I miss you already, and I think maybe we should go upstate with Keith this winter. I haven't had a real Christmas in a long time, and I'm ready to have a real one with you.

In the meantime, I hope you get some writing done; I hope I'm not the reason you've been struggling to write something new.

Okay, I need to leave for the airport. I love you.

I played the message again, just to continue listening to his voice.

MAGGIE

Back at the B&B, Maggie collapses onto the bed with a long, ragged exhale. Her phone died hours ago, entirely spent from all the missed texts and calls from family; after the day she's had, she's grateful to finally be alone and unreachable—but then a soft knock sounds on her door. She ignores it. Probably the innkeeper with fresh towels, or some other nonurgent service.

Maggie rubs her sandy eyes, sighing again.

Another knock, this time more persistent.

Again, Maggie ignores it. She's not sure she could heave her tired body off the bed; her muscles ache from the monumental emotions of the past twenty-four hours.

This time the knock is forceful—downright impatient. "I saw your car parked out front, Maggie, I know you're in there."

Maggie sits upright, not quite believing the muffled voice she just heard. When she unlocks the door, she finds Brit in the quaint hallway, a grocery bag in hand.

Resting a hand on her hip, Brit says, "I can't believe you told Grant before you told me."

"What are you doing here?"

Brit scratches the back of her neck, ruffling her hot-pink pixie hairdo. "You're my friend."

Maggie smiles at the unspoken explanation: that when you care about someone, you show up.

"Besides," Brit says, pushing past Maggie into the room, "Chunky Monkey solves all."

Twenty minutes later, they're nestled against the headboard eating ice cream out of coffee mugs, cackling with laughter at Grant's expense. Apparently, after he got off the phone with Maggie and Ann this morning, he spiraled into a tizzy fit. Maggie isn't proud of the delight it gives her to imagine her boss spilling coffee on himself midtirade, but it's been a long day, and it feels good to laugh.

After they've caught their breath, Brit sets her mug aside, and Maggie knows what's coming. "Do you want to talk about it?"

Maggie has been compartmentalizing the news of Todd all day; now, it wells in her eyes like a spring—but she doesn't let it spill. "I'm still . . ."

"Processing," Brit finishes for her, nodding. "I get it."

Maggie grasps her friend's hand. "Thank you for coming."

This must be how Ann felt that first time that Todd flew to Rome for her; Maggie's chest is warm with surprise and gratitude and relief. A brief respite in the midst of upheaval.

"When do you have to go back?" Maggie asks.

"Already sick of me?" Brit elbows her. "I'm on the first boat tomorrow morning. But don't worry, you can keep the leftover Chunky Monkey."

"Thank goodness."

"I would stay longer, but you have your interviews, and there's a lot to do at the office now that your episode is back on track. Next time, warn me before you undermine our boss and drop a career-altering project in my lap?"

"Will do," Maggie says. "I still can't believe you came all this way."

Brit shrugs. "The drive is only, like, five hours—when you do it right."

Maggie sticks her tongue out, and they descend into giggles.

Maybe Maggie should spill her guts to Brit while her friend is here—she'll have to work through her emotions at some point—but for tonight, she allows herself some levity. Of all the people in her life, Brit is the only person whose company is uncomplicated—and that's exactly what Maggie needs right now.

ANN

Mohonk Mountain House, New Paltz, New York, USA
December 1993

The New York I'd seen in spring—all short sleeves and steaming exhaust—had donned a gown of frost. Skyscrapers glimmered like glass ornaments, delicate and silver as tinsel. As I snuggled between Todd and Iris in the back seat of Keith and Barbara's 4Runner, a world of gray flew past my vision. The heat was on blast, whirring in the silent cab as the miles multiplied.

Todd and I had barely spoken since the Whitakers picked us up at the airport. I hadn't even had a chance to run my fingers through his new haircut. Like the air off the East River, our reunion had been colder than I anticipated. We hadn't addressed the long-distance issue since April, and now all those unresolved feelings were stirring again. I didn't know what to say to him.

Consequently, the 4Runner was full of brief glances and separate thoughts. Barbara was looking at a map; Keith was checking his side mirrors; Iris was galloping a toy horse along her windowsill. Manhattan slid away, a steely silhouette against a backdrop of slate clouds. The landscape grew more rural, bare trees shivering under more and more snow the farther north we traveled.

"So . . . ," Keith said, "how's the book going?"

Todd, Barbara, and I groaned.

"What?" he asked. "We weren't talking about anything else."

"Keith, dear, can't you save the shop talk until *after* the festivities?" Barbara asked in her dripping-honey southern accent.

"I'm going to side with your wife on this one," I said, and Keith squinted at me in the rearview.

Barbara reached back from the passenger seat and patted my calf. "Let her breathe, Keith. Women like to be wooed, after all."

"What are you suggesting, she'll hand over a book if I bring her chocolates and flowers?"

"Maybe," Barbara and I said at once.

The men laughed.

Iris blinked up from her horse. "Mama?"

"Oh!" Barbara raised her hands, remembering something. "Hot chocolate, anyone?" She passed back three thermoses and a bag of marshmallows.

While I added marshmallows to Iris's thermos and rescrewed the cap, Todd reached for the bag of marshmallows on my lap and tossed a handful into his mouth. He sipped his hot chocolate, offering a small smile over the rim of his mug, all crinkled eyes and cheeks. It was similar to the smile he had given when he peered over the edge of his wineglass at Carmella's—and finally I felt the frost between us melting. His hand came to rest on my thigh, and he squeezed twice. I turned and kissed his shoulder, breathing in the scent I'd missed so much.

"I *do* have some pages for you, actually," I said to Keith.

He glanced back. "Don't tease me."

I held up my hand, as if under oath. "You can read the first *twenty-five* thousand words when we get to the hotel."

His expression was not unlike a child's upon learning he could have ice cream for dinner. "Stop," he said. "That's a cruel joke."

"It's not," I said. "I got some writing done this summer and edited it through the fall, just for you."

"Is this the project you referred to as 'hot garbage'?" Keith asked. "Which, by the way, is *not* something you should admit to your agent, no matter how much it stinks."

Iris giggled, wrinkling her nose. "Ewwww."

"It's a new project, actually," I said, nudging Iris's arm.

"Daddy, are you going to work all Christmas?" Iris asked.

The question made my chest clench. Perhaps if I could sell another book, Keith wouldn't have to hustle as hard. My sense of duty had driven me to take this new project seriously, and I was jittery about handing it over. It was a love story, a travel story—derivative of *Chasing Shadows*. But it was a start.

"No, dear," Keith answered his daughter. "I won't work the whole time."

Todd clapped his hands once, as if closing the book of that conversation. "With that out of the way, Barbara, I'd love to hear more about this new project you've been working on."

While Barbara spoke about her interior design business, Todd's arm draped across my shoulders, his middle finger drawing idle circles on my arm.

But something had changed between us; I felt it in the firmness of his fingers. His touch didn't exude familiarity or lust—it felt like he was desperately trying to hold on. How could I convince him that I was *right here*, no matter the miles or inches between us?

I told myself I was sensing distance only because we hadn't been alone yet, that once we had a chance to reconnect in private, we'd be stronger than ever.

But even those self-assurances felt forced.

We soon found ourselves driving through a rural, prairie-like land of fences, barns, and trees, all sugarcoated with snow. Keith hung a left onto Mohonk Road and transitioned into four-wheel drive. Quilted with patches of fallen leaves and frost, the sparse forest outside glittered with ice and sunlight. Glimpses of untouched undergrowth made me feel as though we were in a fairy tale.

This impression was intensified when we pulled up to the hotel itself, which had towers and arches, like a true castle. A lengthy, narrow building, the Mohonk Mountain House overlooked a valley on one side and a frozen lake on the other. Inside, the house had an 1800s charm—dark woods, faded plum-and-emerald carpeting, and stained glass window panels that resembled silver fish scales. Christmas garlands and satin ribbons of cream and gold wrapped every exposed beam and railing.

While Barbara and Todd checked in, I stood off to the side with Keith and Iris, perusing the welcome brochure, which included a long list of activities, from cookie decorating to guided snowshoe walks around the lake.

Keith nudged my arm. "How are you feeling?"

"Nervous," I admitted. I wanted so desperately to make a good impression. Not only was this Keith's family—in a way, they were Todd's family too. "And tired," I added. My bladder was vaguely full, I was stiff and stale from the long car ride, and I craved a moment of quiet to regroup before meeting everyone.

"I know it might be awkward, but they'll warm up to you, I promise."

My remaining ounce of confidence shrank. Awkward? If Keith was admitting it, then perhaps my anxiety was more warranted than I'd hoped.

Just then, Todd and Barbara returned with our room keys.

Todd glanced between Keith and me, clearly catching a whiff of my heightened discomfort, but he simply said, "Third floor."

We shuffled over to the elevator, and I hit the up button about five times. When it *finally* arrived, we were halted by a high, cheerful voice. My pulse quickened. Iris ran toward the voice. Keith and Barbara hurried close behind—he raised his arms while she squealed with joy. Todd pivoted, his hand on my waist, and I allowed him to gently guide me away—but not before watching the double doors of my escape slide closed with a flat *ding*.

"My goodness, is this a lovely place, Keith," a brunette was saying. "I'm so glad you suggested this over the usual Whitaker to-do." She kissed his cheek before wrapping her arms around Barbara in a warm, welcoming hug. When the women parted, the brunette held on to Barbara's hands with both of hers. "How was your drive? Wasn't the scenery *breathtaking*? Like being in a snow globe. Oh, Barbara, it has been too long, hasn't it? I love what you've done with your hair."

Filled to the brim with sudden nerves, I looped my arm through Todd's, using his shoulder as a half shield as we approached. His eyes had gone a little tight around the edges, the darkness creeping into his expression like fog along the edges of a lake. I waited for it to obscure him completely, but when the brunette swung her gaze in our direction, a quick grin lit up his face and the fog cleared.

"Natalie," he said, opening his arms. He stepped out of my hold and into hers. The two of them rocked like a metronome for a few beats, then parted.

"Todd, just as handsome as ever," Natalie said.

Keith nudged me forward. "This is my sister Natalie," he said to me. "And Natalie, this is—"

"Ann Fawkes." Her greeting embrace—while appropriately brief—was sweet smelling, her silk blouse smooth under my fingers, her hair feather soft on my cheek. When she pulled back, I could see her resemblance to Keith, a darker version of his features, with the same freckles, kind eyes, and strong mouth.

"It's *such* a pleasure to meet you." Natalie's hand lingered on my arm. "I loved your book—and not just because my brother worked on it. We've been following your fascinating life for years—it's a thrill to meet you in person!"

I smiled. "Thank you, that's too kind."

"And *gosh*, do you and Todd make a handsome couple. Todd's an honorary Whitaker, as I'm sure you know, and it's *delightful* to see him smiling like that." She wiggled her fingers at him, a ruby-crusted tennis bracelet jangling on her wrist. "Come, everyone's in the common room."

With no choice but to follow Natalie away from the elevators, I grasped Todd's arm again to steady myself against the coming onslaught of introductions. I hoped the rest of the family was as sweet as Natalie, but Keith's words—*I know it might be awkward*—chanted through my head.

Around the corner, a large room was filled with plush chairs and multiple themed Christmas trees—one cluttered with blue and white orbs, another decorated with carved wooden forest animals, and so on. A fireplace brought warmth to the expansive space, while a wall of floor-to-ceiling windows opposite the entrance offered a frigid view of the frozen lake and landscape. An attendant was serving tea and cookies at a table near the doorway, and people were gathered all round: a pair of men playing chess, a family of four by the fire, an elderly couple reading (one of them asleep in her chair).

Was this how regular families experienced the holidays? Tinsel and cookies and warm fires? Once, my mother's boyfriend had found a scraggly pine growing by the highway and cut that down as our tree. We had gaudy plastic ornaments that all looked the same and stale-tasting candy canes my mother collected in her purse from work. It was always just me and mom and maybe one of her friends or a date. A stocking with gum, a toothbrush, some chocolates. Small gifts in big boxes—the whole holiday empty but overdressed.

Thinking of my mother and the holidays made my heart ache with an odd, sad sort of regret. She hadn't *wanted* to disappoint me. She would've loved the themed trees here, the heavy glass ornaments, the scent of cookie frosting. She would've cherished a Christmas trip like this.

Mom wasn't here, though.

But a new family *was*.

As Natalie led us through the common room, I felt so out of place my skin itched. I often got the sense that the first impression I made was a letdown. Because of my book, fans built me up in their heads as this eloquent, impressive author—but most of the time, I was reserved and inarticulate. I wished I could edit myself as heavily as I edited my writing. I worried I wouldn't measure up to their expectations and their pleasantries would grow more forced as they realized I was not nearly the woman they thought I would be.

Natalie halted when she reached a family settled into a cluster of couches by the window. "Look who's here," she announced. Thankfully, Keith and Barbara's presence buffered my arrival; they shared a flurry of hugs and greetings while I waited with Todd off to the side.

(I apologize in advance, Maggie, if it's uncomfortable for me to talk about your family in detail. I hope you'll keep in mind that these were my personal interpretations—yes?)

From knowing Keith so long, I was familiar with their names, but Todd kindly whispered who was who. Keith's parents, Hugh and Una, were easy to spot, as their age gave them away. I had already met Natalie, which meant the slightly rounder version of her must be Natalie's twin sister, Tracey. She was married to Bob, a stocky bald man clutching a newspaper. Natalie's husband, Jackson—tall with chestnut hair—had stood to greet Keith, slapping his back with enthusiasm. The kids—Iris, along with Natalie and Jackson's twins, Beatrice and Barrett—had already run off to play in front of the fireplace.

Just as it had gone with Natalie in front of the elevators, everyone greeted Todd next, commenting on how long it'd been, how good he looked, how happy he seemed.

Natalie threw an arm around my shoulders and walked me forward, presenting me to the group. "Everyone, this is Ann Fawkes. Can you believe a *famous author* is joining us for Christmas?"

Trying not to outwardly cringe at the "famous author" label—the *pressure* that put on me, the *otherness*—I offered a little wave. "Thank you so much for including me in your holiday. It's wonderful to finally meet everyone, Keith is such an important person in my life." Barbara clasped her hands sweetly while Keith leaned in to kiss my temple. Todd rubbed my back a little, and for a moment I was completely bowled over by the attention and joy and warm physical touch.

"Did Keith tell you to say that?" Jackson asked, and everyone laughed.

So far so good.

"Sit, sit," Natalie said, tugging me onto the couch between her and her twin. Tracey shifted over to make room.

Todd took a seat on the couch opposite, lined up with Keith, Jackson, and Bob. He held my gaze in that steady, familiar way, signaling that he was there for me and I would be just fine.

"So, tell us about yourself, Ann," Natalie said, shifting her knees toward me. "Keith has told us absolutely nothing—he's a terrible gossip."

"That isn't a bad thing," Tracey said, defending her brother.

Natalie rolled her eyes, then touched my arm. "Tell us about Rome! Jackson and I went to France for our honeymoon, but I think Italy should be our next big trip—once the twins are older, of course."

"Rome is . . . enchanting," I said.

"You're quite the jet-setter, so it must be particularly great for you to stay there so long," Jackson said.

"We've read your articles in *Condé Nast Traveler*," Una added, patting Hugh's hand.

I pressed my lips into a smile while my nails scraped the insides of my palms. All their eyes were on me, watching, waiting for me to be charming.

"Do you think you'll ever settle down?" Barbara asked.

I was about to tell her that I *was* settled, but Natalie cut in. "She's clearly too cool for diapers and PTAs."

Though I didn't see myself in the role she described, the assumption smarted a little. Did I not seem cut out for that sort of life? I wanted to glance at Todd to gauge his response, but I feared what I might see.

"What the *best* place you've been, Ann? Your all-time favorite?" Natalie asked.

The answer came easily. "Venice."

Todd's lips curved into a soft smile.

Natalie clasped her hands and bounced on the couch cushion. "Oh, I've *always* wanted to see Venice."

"What about you?" I asked Natalie. "What's your favorite destination?"

I expected an immediate answer, but instead, she sat back against the couch and thought. Tracey studied me, and I pretended not to notice.

"Maui," Natalie said finally, appearing very pleased with her choice, if a little wistful.

The others did not appear so happy. Una stiffened, Jackson shifted in his seat, and Keith and Todd both looked away. *What's uncomfortable about Hawaii?*

I tried a neutral follow-up question. "When did you go?"

More shifty gazes—except Natalie, who visibly brightened. "Years and years ago," she said. "Before the twins. We all went—including Penny."

You probably see where this is going, Maggie, but I'd never heard of Penny.

"*Natalie,*" Tracey hissed. "Why did you have to say that?"

"*What?*" Natalie fixed Tracey with a harsh glare—and then, like the snap of fingers, her intensity disappeared, and she addressed me again.

"Some of my happiest memories are from Maui. The beaches, the sea turtles, the blue water."

The rest of the family didn't appear so nostalgic. Una was covering her mouth and staring out the window; Hugh and Bob were suddenly very interested in their newspaper pages; Tracey was downright prickly; and, on the other side of the couch, Barbara took great interest in a nonexistent thread on her sleeve. I met Keith's eyes, and he glanced away. Todd stared at his hands.

Jackson was the only one to acknowledge Natalie's choice. "Maui was special," he said to me. "Natalie and I had just started dating, and it was my first time meeting her family. She invited me on this trip, and I thought, *I don't even know these people yet. Do I really want to go on a whole vacation with them?*" He chuckled. "I was crazy about her, so I agreed. It was so much fun. Everyone was so welcoming."

Una reengaged. "That was where you asked Hugh for permission to marry Natalie."

Jackson nodded slowly, remembering. "It was way too early for marriage, but I was having a beer with Mr. Whitaker, overlooking the waves, and I figured I'd just go for it. Take the first step, at least."

"I didn't know that," Keith said, patting Jackson on the back. "Well done."

Natalie was beaming. "See? Happy memories."

But everyone was edgy after that, strange and pensive and distracted. We exchanged shallow pleasantries for another ten minutes, and then Natalie swiveled toward me. "Ann, you must be exhausted! Don't let us keep you."

"I *would* like to settle a bit," I admitted.

"I agree, I'm beat," Todd said, standing.

I rose from the couch. "So nice to meet you all, thanks again for having us," I said politely.

The family nodded, waved, or uttered quiet *you too*s.

When Todd and I were finally in the elevator, I collapsed against him, snuggling into his chest.

"Tired?" he asked, wrapping his arms around my waist to hold me up.

"Exhausted," I said. "I hope I made a good impression."

"Keith's family is easygoing. They don't have any expectations."

"Of course they do," I said. "I'm the 'famous author,' remember?"

He squeezed me closer, crushing my ribs against his in the most delicious way. "They loved you."

"*Natalie* loved me. The rest I'm not sure. Is Tracey always so quiet?"

"She can be," Todd said, but I sensed that there was more to her story than Todd was willing to divulge.

And speaking of stories: "Who's Penny?" I asked, pulling back to see Todd's face.

He blanched, letting go of me completely. The elevator doors slid open. Stepping into the hallway, Todd fished our room key out of his pocket.

We walked in silence, my question hovering in the air between us like a wasp. It dipped and darted, but Todd evaded. He located our room and opened the door. Our luggage had been placed just inside the door on racks, and I set my purse on top of my suitcase.

"Todd," I said gently. "Who is Penny?"

He walked farther into the room, pausing by a pair of chairs posed next to a large window that overlooked the lake. "Keith's youngest sister. She died."

I brought my palm to my chest. "He never mentioned her."

"Yeah, well . . ." The usually strong, straight lines of his shoulders had rolled forward. "It's a sad memory for everyone."

I had thought Keith, Todd, and I were close, but now I felt like a stranger invited to someone else's dinner table. I wanted to ask more but thought better of it.

"I'm going to unwind with a shower," I said instead. "Care to join me?"

Todd turned, but his eyes remained distant, as if he were still staring out the window. "Nah, you go ahead. I'm going to unpack a little."

I walked over and kissed his cheek. His hand didn't come to my waist, nor did he bend down to receive my kiss. The result was me on my tiptoes, kissing a wall—wondering if he'd ever let me all the way in.

ANN

Mohonk Mountain House, New Paltz, New York, USA
December 1993

I awoke to early-morning sunlight illuminating our window. Todd's arm was draped over my waist, still heavy with sleep. I slid out from under his hold and used the bathroom, then located my cigarettes and shrugged into a complimentary robe. I shuffled past the **No Smoking** sign on the wall and opened the door to our private balcony.

The cold hit me like an Amtrak, pressing a gasp out of my lungs. The temperature must've been in the teens. I pulled the robe tighter around my body, then lit my cigarette and puffed through it as quickly as I could before stubbing it out in the crust of ice on the railing. When I returned inside, Todd was stirring. The warmth of the room flushed my skin; I abandoned the robe on a chair and slid under the warm duvet. Todd pulled me to him, spooning me close.

"That's a bad habit," he mumbled into my hair.

"Smoking?"

"No, standing outside in the cold."

I sighed. "You're probably right."

"Of course I am."

"I've been living in Europe too long."

"I agree," he said with emphasis. I waited for him to push that topic further, but he only nuzzled closer. "You're an ice cube."

"You're a furnace."

He put a single finger on my bare hip. *"Tssss."*

I giggled, and he pressed his body flush to mine, sliding his hand under my sleep shirt.

"I missed you," he said.

"I missed you too."

The hand on my breast squeezed.

"Todd?"

He was already undressing himself, me. The room was silent save for the soft kisses he planted on my neck. His breath warmed my hair. One of his arms wrapped around my chest while the other traveled down my body to spin magic between my legs.

"I didn't think this trip through, Copper," he mumbled, but I was only half listening. My mind was floating out in space, tethered only to his movements. "I realized this morning that I won't have you to myself hardly at all."

We joined together, slow and intense. I felt secure and liberated in his arms. Held fast against him, I rocketed through the stars.

"I hate when we're apart," he whispered, the last word elongated by the groan of his release.

We didn't move for a few minutes afterward, enjoying our togetherness. But then necessity outweighed comfort, and we cleaned ourselves up in the bathroom before tumbling back into bed. Todd lay with his arms behind his head, and I curled naked against his strong body. It felt, finally, like we were *us* again. Close.

"You seem better this morning." I kissed the nearest patch of skin: his inner bicep.

He shifted, ticklish. "What do you mean?"

"Last night . . ." I paused. "You seemed off."

"Seeing everyone is a big deal for me," he said. "I think it's a big deal for them too." He turned to face me. "But I know last night was overwhelming for you. I'll try to be more supportive."

I gazed beyond him, at the snow floating past the window. "It's hard being the newcomer."

"You've never had a holiday like this."

His statement poked at a soft place between my ribs, a squishy emotion I couldn't name.

"They liked you," he went on. "I know it was difficult to tell, but they did. I think they were just as nervous about you as you were about them."

"What? No," I said. "Not possible."

"You're very accomplished, Ann," Todd said. "No matter how awkward you feel about that, it's intimidating to other people."

I kissed his bicep again, then dared a glance at his face. He was smiling. "Thanks," I said meekly.

He brushed my hair away from my face and kissed my mouth, his lips melding with mine. "Don't mention it."

Two hours later, I found myself seated at a long, plastic-lined arts and crafts table with the women and kids from Keith's family. The men were off on an outdoor snowshoeing trek, of which I wasn't jealous. After the instant earache and icy burn on my cheeks that morning, decorating ornaments—with the inevitable gluey fingers, glitter everywhere, comparing each other's skills—seemed far preferable to the tundra. It would at least be a good icebreaker.

So there I was.

Pipe cleaners, sequins, paint, and more were scattered before us. Barrett and I had decided to create monster ornaments, decorating our orbs with green sequins, paper triangle spikes, blue paint, pipe cleaner teeth, and googly eyes. Iris and Barbara were painting nature scenes on theirs—Iris with a tawny smudge meant to be a deer, and Barbara with an incredibly detailed goldfinch. I couldn't see what the others were up to, but as expected, it was messy, sticky—*fun*.

I might've felt silly—a thirty-four-year-old meticulously adding glitter glue around googly eyes—but I was too swept up in the moment. I had loved crafts as a kid but rarely ever had more than a marker and paper to play with—let alone company. Looking around the table, I cherished the quiet concentration of the kids, the equally focused adults. There's something vulnerable about being creative in the presence of other people. They can see how hard you're trying and all your mistakes. But we were in this together, passing supplies and giggling and chatting without eye contact as we traced lines and secured pipe cleaners. Bonding.

"Well, look at those," Natalie said of our monsters. "How scary."

"*No*," Barrett corrected his mother. "They aren't scary monsters, they're friendly."

"Of course!" Natalie said, earnest. "I was looking at him upside down—let me see. Oh, yes, you're right, very friendly. What's his name?"

"Josh," Barrett said.

"Josh is the name of his class guinea pig," Natalie stage-whispered to the adults. "Let's see yours, Ann."

I angled my monster in her direction; her laugh was lilting and genuine. "What about you?" I asked.

She held up her ornament, a study in red: crimson sequins, cherry-colored glitter, swirling maroon paint, and scarlet ribbon. "I went the abstract route."

"Oh, look at *that*," Barbara said. "It's like the sky in *Starry Night*, but red."

Tracey held up her own ornament, a similar design but in gray and white. "We had the same idea."

"I love it," I said.

Tracey offered a brief, pressed-lipped smile.

"They'll look so pretty together on the tree," Una said.

"The tree?" I asked.

"All the guests put their ornaments on that tree over there." Natalie pointed to a tree strung up with simple lights, already half decorated in ornaments as eclectic as ours.

My chest warmed as if it'd been filled with chamomile tea, a honey-eyed sensation that spread into my extremities.

"The only thing missing from this perfect family day is Penny," Natalie said softly.

Tracey frowned. "You always get like this around the holidays. Do you have to keep bringing her up?"

"Do you have to keep pretending she never existed?" Natalie bit back.

Una raised her hands. "Please, you two."

"At least we have Ann," Barbara offered. "I think she's a fine addition to the family, don't you? We're having fun, aren't we?"

The comment would've made me giddy if it weren't for the thick tension between the Whitaker twins.

"Ann can't replace Penny," Tracey said slowly. "Todd might think so, but she can't."

My mouth twisted in confusion.

"Todd isn't *replacing* Penny," Una said. "You're not a replacement, dear," she added, touching my hand, which was frozen on the table among the craft supplies.

Me, *replacing* Penny. If that was a concern, then that meant Penny was once *something* to Todd. Despite the hot room, my blood turned to slush in my veins.

"Nobody said she was replacing Penny," Natalie continued, glaring at her sister. "Why can't Todd move on, *hmm*? Without you judging and carrying on?"

The whites of Tracey's eyes had turned a pale, fibrous pink. Tears hung heavy on her lower lash line but didn't fall. "*Someone* has to stand up for her."

"No," Natalie said softly. "Penny is gone, and she's been gone for years. Todd can miss Penny and still fall in love again—we all can. Why the sudden vitriol? Why—" Natalie kept speaking, but my slush-blood had rushed into my ears, and I couldn't hear her anymore. I experienced the room as if through packed snow: muffled.

Todd can miss Penny.

He can love again.

Realization iced over my mind like a hard frost. My diaphragm clenched so hard I thought, for a moment, I was having a heart attack. I had to suck in air. Todd's tragic story—his wife and child—his friendship with Keith and his closeness with this family . . . Was *Penny* Todd's wife? Was Keith's youngest sister the woman Todd had loved and lost? I had never asked her name, never voiced any of my many questions about his past. After Greece, I had tried so hard to respect his grief, but what if by not prodding, I had sent another signal: that he couldn't come to me with the details of his loss? But it's not like we hadn't discussed it at all—so how could Todd leave out such a monumental detail? The detail that connected everyone together—everyone but me.

I felt like a fool.

Natalie was finishing her speech. ". . . but there's room in this family for new faces too."

Her sentiment was ephemeral, flimsy in the storm of this news.

"Is Penny . . ." I trailed off, clearing my throat. "*Penny* is the woman Todd lost in the fire?"

The entire table—all four women, all three children—swiveled their heads toward me. There was a moment that stretched like gum, drawing thin and stringy the longer it was pulled apart. I tried to meet Natalie's eyes for confirmation, but even she evaded my gaze. I looked to Una, but she was fiddling with a piece of ribbon. This time, only Tracey was willing to hold my stare.

The whites of her eyes were red now, her forehead pinched so harshly that her brows almost touched above the bridge of her nose. Her lip quivered, and then—as if her body was a pressure cooker—she exploded. She threw her arms in the air, and her tears were finally shaken loose.

"*She didn't even know*," Tracey screeched, startling the kids. She pointed at me, seething. "She didn't. Fucking. Know."

A father at a neighboring craft table glared, making a show of covering his boy's ears.

"*Language*," Barbara scolded.

Tracey continued, clearly not caring about her volume. "If Todd really cared about this . . . this *famous author* . . . he would've told her! Having her here is an insult to our family."

People were openly staring now. Una placed a hand on Tracey's shoulder. "Calm yourself," she said. "You're embarrassing us."

"Oh, I'm *embarrassing*?" Tracey asked, louder now. "*I'm* embarrassing? Fine, then I'll *leave*." She pushed away from the table, rattling the undecorated glass orbs and bowls of supplies. A tube of glitter tipped over with a puff of shimmering dust.

Tracey stomped out of the common room, her footsteps audible long after she was out of sight. Una slumped in her chair. Natalie had finally dared to look at me, eyes sympathetic, as if she could cradle me with that gaze. My own face was slick and snotty. Shock and betrayal made my mouth tremble. I balled my fists in my lap.

"He didn't tell you he was married to Penny?" Natalie ventured.

"He didn't," I confirmed.

"But he told you about the fire?"

I sniffled. "If you'll excuse me . . ." I stood and somehow managed to stumble my way to the elevators. I was rapidly pressing the up button when Barbara found me.

"Ann," she said sweetly. "Are you all right, dear?"

"No," I whimpered and tumbled through the elevator doors as soon as they parted.

Barbara didn't follow; she watched me as the doors slid closed again, her warm expression unflinching, as if she could melt the hurt I felt just in that single glance.

She couldn't.

MAGGIE

The recorder rests on the table between them, and Maggie leans forward, hitting the pause button.

Ann's eyes are glassy. She glances down, smoothing her herringbone sweater, a tear sliding down the bridge of her nose. She swipes it away with a finger. "Thank you," she says, gesturing at the recorder. "I've never told this story in full, and it's . . . well . . ."

"It's fine. Do you need a moment?"

What Maggie really means is, *I need a moment.*

When Maggie first read about Todd and Penny online—*Aunt Penny, her own family!*—she'd been a moth in a rainstorm: dazed, disoriented, dodging water droplets. Realization had knocked her to the ground, practically drowned her. She knows exactly how Ann felt at Mohonk—the betrayal, the shock, the fury.

But this is what the Whitakers *do*: they try to bury truths that are impossible to hide. Truths that later sprout up like weeds.

It's clear why they didn't want Maggie talking to Ann—Ann knows too much. She *must*. Maggie has no idea how far the lies go, but judging by how her story has unraveled the family so far, she suspects Ann knows them all.

So it makes sense, now, why Ann would want Maggie to talk to Tracey before continuing with the story. Ann was giving Tracey a chance to tell Maggie the truth. Is her father the only piece of the puzzle Tracey knows? Or did Tracey blow her chance to open up to Maggie completely?

Maggie meets Ann's tearful eyes. "I didn't know there *was* another Whitaker sister until Natalie told me," she says. "I was eleven years old when I learned her name." She wonders if Ann finds comfort in not being the only person kept in the dark; Maggie does. "Natalie was the only one who'd talk about her, while the rest of the family . . ."

"Silence."

Maggie nods. "For how 'close' the Whitaker family is, they're terrible at sharing their emotions." She plucks a tissue from a box on the bookshelf and hands it to Ann.

Ann presses it beneath each eye only once, then crumples it in her fingers. "Did Natalie tell you about Penny's marriage to Todd?"

Maggie's heart clenches tight, making her extremities tingle. "No, she left that out—as everyone seems to. I found out about them on the internet when I was a teen. The 'personal life' section of your Wikipedia article refers to Keith and Todd as brothers-in-law, referencing a news article about the fire. I pieced it together from there."

Ann touches her fingers to her mouth, shaking her head.

"Pretty shitty, right? I never met Penny, of course, but it still stung."

Ann unfolds the tissue, blows her nose, and appears a little sheepish balling it up again.

Maggie wishes she could talk to Ann about Todd being her father, but she can hear Grant's words in the back of her mind, telling her to keep her mouth shut. Bottle it up. Maggie might not be a biological Whitaker, but she's no stranger to keeping her biggest emotions underground. Still, she despises keeping secrets from Ann; Maggie is a hypocrite in the truest form.

"How did you reconcile with all the secrets Todd kept from you?" Maggie asks. *How do I reconcile with them?* she wonders.

Ann blanches. "Well, if that isn't a whopper of a question." Her nervous chuckle echoes through the room, and she again smooths her sweater, which was already smooth. "Reconciliation is, I think, too strong a word for what we did," she finally says. "Todd and I got very good at moving forward, even when it hurt, even when we were dragging mountains behind us."

"That doesn't sound healthy."

"It wasn't," Ann agrees. "It took us a long, long time to independently sort through our own baggage. It's what we should've done all along. To see each other for our true selves—flaws and all, no ego—*that* is true love. I loved Todd since the moment I met him, but it wasn't *true* until we got over ourselves and took responsibility for our own shit. No secrets."

No secrets. Was Maggie a secret that Todd eventually divulged to Ann?

Maggie is bobbing on a tempestuous sea; to ask would be to admit her relation and abandon the lifeboat. *This isn't my story,* she tells herself.

Maggie leans into the cradle of her chair, folding her hands together.

It doesn't feel right to mention Todd.

But it doesn't feel right to hold her tongue either.

"Should I continue?" Ann seems to have collected herself; her eyes and forehead are neutral again, yet her mouth wavers, revealing a flicker of remaining emotion. "We still have a lot of ground to cover."

Maggie reaches for the recorder, her ears rushing with the sound of wind, ocean, and the threat of jumping overboard. "Yes, let's continue."

ANN

Alone in our room, I sank to the floor at the foot of the bed, leaning back against the hard frame.

Penny.

Penny.

Penny.

Her name pulsed in my temple. An avalanche of new information had buried me, and now I sat in the quiet aftermath, quivering and claustrophobic.

I was betrayed. Embarrassed. Angry.

But more than anything, I was confused. Why would he leave out such an important detail? Not only had he lost his wife and child in a fire, but his wife had been Keith's sister. He should've warned me before we came to Mohonk, protected me from the inevitable perception: to the Whitakers, I *was* a replacement. And I would never measure up. How could I?

Yet I was torn. I couldn't tell Todd how to grieve; nor could I force him to open up about something so traumatic and personal. A better person—a less jealous, less desperate person—might have been more understanding. But after nine years of knowing him, it hurt that Todd still didn't trust me—or love me—enough to let me in.

Maybe Tracey was right: if Todd really cared about me, he wouldn't've hid behind a half truth. I might've been keeping Todd at a physical distance, but he had kept me at an emotional distance, and that was so much worse.

And Keith—was that what he'd meant yesterday, about my presence being awkward? Had he assumed I knew? Or had they *both* withheld this from me? I thought we'd been thick as thieves, but really, they'd kept me out of everything.

As I sat on the floor in the hotel room, with the old heater ticking and snow falling outside the window, intense rejection spread across my skin like frostbite. That's when the in-room phone rang.

"I ditched the kids," Natalie said when I answered. "You, me, and Barbara are going to the spa."

"Oh, I don't know . . . ," I said, spinning the phone cord around my finger.

"The appointments are booked and nonrefundable, so you have no choice but to feel better."

My mouth twisted into the tiniest smile. "What time?"

"We'll meet you there in thirty minutes."

"All right."

The line was silent for a few seconds, long enough to know what was coming next. "Ann, I'm so sorry."

"It's fine. It's not your fault."

"Tracey's outburst was inexcusable, but . . . well, she's had a harder time than the rest of us. It wasn't about you." She sighed. "Todd has always been reserved, but I'm angry that Keith didn't . . . that they . . ."

"It's fine," I repeated, because what else could I say? It was kind of Natalie to sympathize with me. It was kind of her to include me, and apologize, and try to make it right. Her kindness was a hand breaking through the snow. A form of rescue.

She cleared her throat. "Spa. Half hour."

"See you then."

During facials and massages, Natalie and Barbara talked through the incident with me, offering solidarity and support. Two hours later, I exited the spa with heavy muscles, oily skin, and a cottony headache—still embarrassed and confused and tense in my stomach but less alone in my pain. The guys were just returning from their hike, and Todd barely checked in with me before retiring to our room to shower. Then it was dinnertime, and afterward, a nightcap with Keith, Natalie, Jackson, and Hugh, telling empty stories for laughs. "Tell them about the time you accidentally broke into the Agora!" Todd said to me, his breath smelling of lemon and whiskey.

By the time we retired, Todd was sloshed from hot toddies and promptly crashed. As I tucked myself in bed beside him, I couldn't bear the thought of confronting him. To fight with Todd over Christmas, only to immediately leave for Rome, sounded awful.

So I let the Penny issue slide.

From the outside, everything remained the same. Natalie, Barbara, and Una must've agreed among themselves not to bring it up. Tracey ignored me. The kids' attention spans were too fleeting to fixate on the incident. And I plastered a holiday-cheer smile on my face.

The deception, however, was a rot that spoiled me from the inside. My muscles were mealy, my heart brown. Did Todd not trust me, or did he simply not see me as a true partner?

I'd been learning Todd's story for years, uncovering layers like a miner cutting through rock, in search of that tender vein of understanding, that glittering gold thread of intimacy. In all the many letters we'd sent, pouring our hearts out onto those pages, it amazed me how much he'd actually held back. I had seized every opportunity to open up to him and thought he'd done the same—but I was wrong.

The day after Christmas, as we were all heading to lunch, Keith stopped me in the hall. He led me into a narrow, carpeted stairwell and paused on the landing between floors, where we had some privacy. "Natalie told me what happened. Actually, she *yelled* it at me."

I frowned. The incident at the craft table was days past.

Keith continued, "That's why I asked, when we were checking in. I thought you knew. I assumed Todd told you."

So Keith *hadn't* kept me in the dark on purpose. It was a small relief but didn't take away the sting of Todd's betrayal. "Yeah, well, he didn't."

"Have you talked to him about it?"

"What's there to say?" I asked. "What could I possibly say? She was his *wife*, Keith. I can't yell at him for not talking about his dead wife."

Keith flinched, and I realized my mistake.

I touched his arm. "I'm sorry for the blunt phrasing," I said. "But you see my predicament, don't you? Todd has been so withholding—"

"Which is why—"

"—I shouldn't pressure him. Clearly he's still hurting." The last time I had tried to pressure Todd was in Greece, and I had ended up heartbroken and alone.

"Clearly *you* are hurting," Keith said, touching my cheek. It was a sweet gesture, a comforting one. It was the kind of gesture that was so simple and well meaning that it had the power to completely unravel me.

Tears tingled in my eyes. "I don't want to scare him off."

"I know you care about him," Keith said. "So do I. But he's not a wild animal, he's a man. And if he's hurting you, you need to tell him so he can make it right." Keith gripped my shoulders and looked into my eyes. "You deserve to have your voice heard, Ann. Todd loves you—I can tell because I've seen him fall in love before. But if you want a trusting, *lasting* relationship, my advice is to be honest with him about how his actions have affected you."

I swiped a tear from my jaw. "You had to have known Todd wouldn't . . ." I bit my lip. *"Keith."*

The set of his jaw faltered, the red-brown stubble on his chin rippling with his frown.

He released my shoulders and cleared his throat. "As you might've guessed, in my family, we don't talk about Penny."

I waited as a million expressions passed over Keith's features: the nostalgic furrow of his brow, the squint of a smile by his eyes, the wrinkle of pain at his nose, the pinch of restraint at his mouth. His hand met the wall beside me, and he traced the floral wallpaper with a finger.

"I remember dunking her Barbies in the toilet. I remember walking her to school and threatening her first-grade boyfriend. I remember thinking that no man would ever be good enough for my baby sister . . . and then I met Todd." He sighed. "We became fast friends—inseparable. His parents were busy with the bookshop, so he spent a lot of time at our house.

"Penny loved Todd from the get-go, even as a kid, but he was a few years older and didn't notice her until college. God, I was there when he saw her on campus, the first day of her freshman year. She had grown up a lot over the summer, and Todd hadn't seen her in over a year. She spotted us and started walking our way, and he said to me, 'Damn, do you know her?' And I shoved him so hard he fell on his ass on the lawn." Keith exhaled a chuckle. "'*You* know her,' I said. When she reached us, I could tell she was still smitten as ever. And I knew right then it was all over."

Keith was flicking at the seam in the wallpaper now, not looking at me. "When Penny got pregnant, they'd been terrified to tell me—*me*, of all people. But all I could think was that if it had to be someone, thank god it was Todd." Keith's eyes were reddening, a sheen blurring the color of his irises. "Those were the happiest days, and then—" His voice cracked.

I rubbed his arm, and his mouth pulled into a wan smile.

"My parents' approach to the tragedy was to pretend it didn't happen. But doing that is to pretend Penny was never here . . ." He coughed. "I think we all got into the habit of pretending. It's just easier that way. Even Natalie usually doesn't bring her up.

"But you see, I grew up with Penny. I didn't choose her, I just loved her because she was family. We all knew Penny for twenty years before she died. But Todd . . ." His voice thickened. "Todd *chose* Penny. And he barely had any time with her at all."

My face burned. I didn't know what to say.

"We don't talk about Penny because it hurts, but we also don't talk about her out of respect for Todd." Keith ran a hand through his hair, pushing it away from his red-splotched face. "His parents had come to visit them in the hospital, and he'd gone to the cafeteria to get his mom some orange juice. When the alarm sounded, he thought it was a fire drill. He was ushered outside, into the parking lot. Then the firetrucks arrived, and he . . . he saw the roof collapse. I think he's always wondered what would've happened had he gone back upstairs instead of following the nurses into the parking lot. Wondered if he could've . . . *done* something."

My hand rose to cup my throat. It wasn't grief that had kept Todd from telling me the truth—it was guilt.

"Losing Penny is one of the greatest heartbreaks of my life," Keith said. "But Ann, when I think of losing my parents along with Barbara *and* Iris . . . the loves of my life . . ." His face pulled into a stricken, horrified frown. "I can't fathom it."

"Keith . . ." I drew him into a hug.

We held each other for a minute; then he wiped his face and pulled away.

"I should've told you, or made sure he . . ." He shook his head. "I just wanted to respect the privacy of his grief. Because his grief was—*is*—very different than mine."

I nodded in understanding, and with the motion, more tears fell from my face.

Keith's brow furrowed. "But he *should've* told you—long before this trip."

How could I be angry with Todd over keeping this secret? It didn't seem right to press him where he hurt most. Yet I *was* angry. And I was hurt too.

Keith smiled lopsidedly. "When I met you, I knew immediately that Todd would love you."

I grimaced.

"It's true," he said. "You're so much like her. Funny, smart, unique. It sounds weird, but I knew by the sound of your voice that Todd would adore you. Something about your humble inflection and the sense that you're much more cunning than you let on . . . I knew Todd would fall hard." He smeared a tear off my cheek. "But I see what his secret has done to you. You haven't been yourself all week, and I know Todd has noticed, but I think he's afraid to ask. Which is why I think *you* need to talk to *him*."

I shook my head. "I can't—my complaints are nothing compared to . . ." I shook my head again.

"There's something my therapist said that I think you'll benefit from," Keith said. "'Another person's broken wrist doesn't mean yours is any less sprained.'" He paused. "Your pain is valid, Ann. If it bothers you, go talk to him. Trust me."

I stared into Keith's eyes, which had cleared of tears. His earnest stare rendered me all the weaker. "Keith . . . you're my best friend. Did you know that?"

"You can do better," he said, pulling me into one last hug. "Come on, I'm starving."

MAGGIE

San Juan Island, Washington State, USA
Thursday, January 11, 2024

"Oh, Keith."

Ann grasps Maggie's hand, eyes crinkling. "He was the best, wasn't he?"

"He really was."

Best friends. They had been *best friends. What happened between you two?* Maggie wants to ask. But she can't. Not yet, at least.

Instead, Maggie says, "Even so many years after his death, I still find myself regularly asking myself, 'What would Keith say?'"

"Me too." Ann releases Maggie's hand, her gaze going distant. "He always had the best advice, didn't he?"

Maggie nods, and for a moment, they sit with his memory, silent. Two women who never met before this week, invariably linked by a great man whom they both cherished so much.

ANN

Hearing the whole story had shifted my understanding of Todd's sorrow, and I didn't want to ruin our last day.

When Todd and I returned to our room for our final night at Mohonk, I couldn't bring myself to confront him—even after Keith's insistence. It was our last night together before I went back to Rome and he returned to Colorado. We wouldn't see each other again until spring at the earliest, and I didn't want to fight.

Instead, we made love.

I hid my tears afterward, crying into the pillow while he drifted off. I wondered if I would ever truly know Todd or if he'd always hide a piece of himself from me.

I wondered if he'd ever love me as much as he loved Penny.

I fell asleep wondering, and the next morning, we packed in silence. Then it was a flurry of goodbyes in the lobby, hugs all around. I had grown to admire Una and Hugh; Natalie and Jackson and their kids; Bob, with his silent newspaper reading; and even Tracey's fierce family loyalty.

Maggie, I don't know what exactly you know about Penny, but Keith later explained that Tracey had been very close with her younger sister. She was deeply affected by the loss—more than anyone else in the family. While they had all tried to move on, she had *held* on. I could see why she disliked me, the *replacement*. She had disliked the idea of me before she even met me, but that afternoon, I decided not to take her attitude personally.

Natalie was the last to give me a big, tight hug. "You are a delight," she said into my ear. "Please visit. We'd love to have you. We live not far from Todd."

"Thank you for welcoming me."

Her private smile said it all: she considered me a part of the family. It was the greatest Christmas gift I ever received.

As we piled into Keith's car and drove off, waving at the Whitakers, I had never been so sad to leave the United States. Despite the tensions, I would miss them when I returned to Rome. I was glad to have a family worth missing.

At the airport, Keith and Todd hugged first, a strong, clapping embrace. As they held each other in temporary parking, I saw them in a new way. Here were two men who had grown up together, fallen in love alongside one another, and endured grief together. Here were two men who loved each other. I envied their bond.

When Keith hugged me next, the warmth of him penetrated through our thick coats. His whisper was summer against my cheek. "Take care, my dear Ann." The comfort of his friendship melted the winter around us.

"Thank you," I whispered.

Of course, it was hardest to say goodbye to Todd—and not just because I'd miss him. I had left Rome ready to discuss moving in together—but now, after learning what he'd kept from me, I wasn't so sure. My feelings were tangled like fishing line, grimy and cutting, getting tighter the more I tried to struggle free. I had so many thoughts running through my mind that I was rendered silent. He kissed my forehead and told me he loved me, and I breathed in his citrus-musk scent and held him tightly, reciprocating his words with melancholy in my heart.

ANN

Just after the new year, Keith called. "I read your pages," he said by way of hello.

To say I was nervous about this call is an understatement. News of the *Chasing Shadows* movie was abuzz, and I was getting calls for interviews and "insider information" about casting rumors, the screenplay, and other things I had nothing to do with. The attention had compounded the pressure to produce something new.

I reached for my cigarettes and cracked the window by my desk. My eyes tracked the street below, where a woman was walking a small dog. "And?" I asked, when Keith had paused too long.

"Well . . ."

My stomach tumbled. "You hate it."

"I don't hate it," he replied slowly. "But I don't think it works."

"So you hate it."

"It needs . . . editing."

I could handle editing. "*Chasing Shadows* was a slog in the beginning."

"It was, but this would be . . ." He sighed. "I think it would be easier to start something new."

His words hit me like a shove, like the smack of pavement. "What?"

"I'm sorry, I hate telling you this."

"But why?"

"You want me to tell you what's wrong with the book?"

"Yes, I want to know."

His chair creaked as he presumably leaned back from his desk. "How about I send you notes?"

"It's really that bad?" I asked, stubbing out my cigarette. An all-body shiver shook my shoulders, and I closed the window. "So bad you won't tell me your thoughts over the phone?"

"It lacks structure, Ann. And tension. And a story. It's cloying and slow." A pause. "It doesn't have the energy that *Chasing Shadows* did. I can tell your heart isn't in it."

He had a point.

My heart *wasn't* in it—not like the first book, which was practically an emotional tidal wave of urgency. I *had* to write *Chasing Shadows*; it was a survival tactic. The new book had been the opposite of urgent: forced, stagnant. The truth was, I wasn't sure I could re-create the magic of *Chasing Shadows*. Worse: I wasn't sure I *wanted* to—that period of my life had been heartrending, and I didn't want to go there again, not even to write another bestseller.

What if my talent was rooted in strife? Writing had been a coping mechanism for so long—I was horrified to think that my art could be beautiful only when life was ugly.

(Maggie, don't ever buy into the myth that art must come from pain—the sad-artist trope is a dangerous one, and simply untrue. Unfortunately, at the time, I believed it.)

"Do you have other ideas?" Keith asked.

I knew what he wanted. I'd never confronted Todd about Penny, and he wanted me to dig into my current confusion and frustration. A novel could again be my way of processing pent-up emotions.

But I wouldn't. I *couldn't*. "I'll send more ideas," I told Keith, "but I can't write my woes like I did before."

"It could be therapeutic—"

"No." I'd seen Todd's horror when the tabloid included him in my aura of gossip. I couldn't use our relationship as inspiration for another book—one emotionally autobiographical rumor mill was enough. "Anything I write, from now on, has to be a separate thing. I can't stand the spotlight. I won't do that to myself, and I won't do that to Todd."

"I'm just trying to be helpful and jump-start your creativity a bit. But of course, you're right." He sounded tired, stressed.

My throat constricted, and my ears grew hot. "I'm sorry I'm failing you."

"Oh, Ann—sweetheart, no. You could never fail me. It's hard to be both your agent and your friend. I'm being a bad friend by suggesting these things."

"No, I understand." I rose out of my chair. "I'll send you a whole host of ideas, and we can talk more, okay?"

"Yes, perfect."

"Great."

A week later, I was in the midst of a fitful, late-night bout of writing when my phone rang.

"Hello?"

"*God*, I missed your voice," Todd said.

The bookstore's winter programming had been hectic since the new year, and we hadn't talked much, having been unable to align given the time difference. The ache of missing him—bone deep, like growing pains—had returned. I found the ache comforting somehow, like we were back to normal.

I pushed away from my desk and lay on the bed. "I missed yours," I replied. "It's nice to hear from you."

"Keith told me about the pages."

"Of course he did."

"He also told me that you refused to write about . . . personal stuff." A pause. "I wanted to thank you," he said. "I know it's bad for your career, but . . ."

"It's nothing," I said. "How are you?"

"Actually, I've been wondering . . ." He trailed off and started again. "The thing is . . ."

While he struggled with his words, I tried to measure the hesitation in his voice. Our romantic relationship had been built by phone calls, and I had grown accustomed to deciphering his lilts and pauses. That evening, I heard the pliable, weighted tone he used when he disagreed with me or was about to say something he knew would sting.

I sat up and held my breath.

"Flights are getting expensive," Todd finally said. "I don't think I can come to Italy anytime soon."

Disappointment was an anchor; I sank. "Oh. I could visit you?"

He blew out a breath. "Sure, yeah, but . . . do the visits feel like enough?"

"What are you saying, Todd?" It was late, I was tired, and I'd been struggling with words for hours—I wanted him to simply *say it*, whatever it was. I knew from his tone I wouldn't like it, but the waiting was unbearable.

"Is long distance as hard for you as it is for me?"

Was this that old familiar argument, or was this the end of us?

Short on air, I repeated myself in a whisper: "What are you saying?"

"Do you love me?" he asked.

"*Of course* I love you." My voice became reedy. "Todd, honey, please just say whatever it is you need to say."

"It's just . . . I'm wondering if you're set on Rome."

"'Set on Rome'?"

"Would you ever want to settle down?"

"I've been living in Rome for the better part of nine years, I *am* settled."

"I mean here."

The prospect strangled me. "Settle in Colorado."

"Is that a no?" When I didn't answer, he said, "I'm asking you to move in with me—here." I could hear the smile in his voice. "I want you to live with me."

For a moment, his words brought relief—but it didn't last. This was the conversation I'd *thought* I was ready to have, before our trip to Mohonk changed everything. Deep inside my cavernous heart, a nocturnal, instinctual part of me was thinking, *The distance is safe.* While I despised being away from him, the distance grew longing. Without distance, would Todd still long for me? Because every time I was fully *present*—Venice, Greece, New York—Todd gave me a reason to pull back.

Besides, I was happy here—Rome was not an insignificant thing to give up. I had my apartment, my markets, my neighborhood. I had Carmella and the cats I fed on the stoop. I had earned my international teaching certification and hadn't even put it to use yet.

I loved Todd, but could I really give up my life here for him?

I sagged forward, my shoulders crumpling toward my knees. "I would love to live with you," I said, "but I can't see myself in Colorado. Never again."

"Why not?"

There were too many ghosts in Colorado, too many bad memories. I had traveled a long time to find a sense of safety, comfort, and belonging—I couldn't give that up.

"Italy is home," I said simply. "It's the *only* place I've felt at home."

"What about with me?"

The way he threw that in my face made me blanch. It wasn't a fair question. "That's not what I meant," I said. "I love you. Why can't you move here?"

"I have a business," Todd said. "A house."

"You're saying I don't have a life here?"

"I'm saying that I have roots."

"Roots you wouldn't want to give up for me?"

"That's not fair."

"But it's fair to ask the same of me? To assume that I don't have roots in Italy?"

"You've never had roots, Ann," Todd said, so quietly I wondered for a moment if I was imagining his venomous words. But then he continued. "I'm asking you to finally plant yourself—with me."

"Is that how you see me?" I cleared my throat, willing it steady. "Just gallivanting overseas, not a care in the world?"

"I know you like it there, but what have you built for yourself in Italy, truly? A tiny apartment, a couple restaurant friends. That isn't a community, that's a long holiday. You're a tourist." His tone was gentle, but only because he knew how the words would strike.

My cheeks blazed hot. "That isn't true."

"Not all of us have the privilege of endless funds to wander the world in search of purpose. Those of us in the real world don't have that luxury. In the real world, we have to build our lives from the ground up."

"You're blaming my money?" I asked. "I thought you knew me better—"

"I don't want to argue."

"Then why are you criticizing my happiness?"

"*Are* you happy, though? I've seen your apartment."

"What does *that* mean?"

"You're half-packed, Ann. Sure, you have knickknacks on your bookshelves and food on the counter, but it's sparse. It looks like you could leave at any moment."

I surveyed my clean desk, my half-empty bookshelves, a single used mug on my kitchen counter. Was he right? Was living in Rome its own form of running? The uncluttered nature of my apartment didn't seem intentional one way or the other. "I live simply," I mumbled.

"No, you live such that you can run. That's not permanent."

I raised my voice, enunciating every word. "I've lived in Italy almost *nine years*. How is that impermanent?" I heaved a breath. "I love you, Todd, but I also love my life here. Can't you see how unfair it is to make me choose?"

"What's the real issue, Ann? A few months ago, you would've come—I'm sure of it."

Like the filament in a lightbulb, something inside me snapped. And somehow, in the dimness and without the glare, I suddenly saw so much clearer.

"Why didn't you tell me you were married to Penny?" I asked.

"What?" It came out as a strangled cough.

"Penny," I said tightly. "Your wife was Keith's *sister*, and you never fucking told me."

His stilted voice exposed his surprise. "Where's this coming from?"

"Tracey," I said. "Natalie. Keith. They all thought I knew. You never told me."

He didn't respond.

"How long have we known each other, Todd?" I went on. "How many opportunities did you have to tell me the *entire* truth? You left out such a massive detail. How could you keep that from me? *Why* did you keep that from me?"

"I wanted to tell you. At the airport, last April."

My laugh was mocking. "But you didn't."

"You cut me off."

"You could've gone on. You could've had the balls to—"

"Don't lecture me about opportunities," Todd hissed, "when you decided to confront me about this over the phone, a million miles away."

"I was *humiliated*," I said. "And hurt. That *hurt*, hearing about her from near strangers."

"You could've asked," he said, but the words were half-hearted. He knew this was not my responsibility, not entirely.

"I assumed you were telling me the *full* truth to begin with—which apparently was a mistake." Maybe it was my fault he didn't feel comfortable enough to open up to me. But he *had* told me half the story—why he'd left out the most important detail didn't make sense to me.

"I'm guessing Keith didn't get this heat from you?" He was no longer caught off guard; he was angry.

"Keith and I aren't *lovers*," I shouted. "We aren't talking about uprooting our lives to *move in together*."

I looked out the window, to where the tree branches were rattling against each other. A single, skeletal leaf—dead but still clinging—quivered in the breeze, silver as a coin.

"Do you even trust me, Todd?" I asked. "Because every few months I feel like I'm meeting you all over again. How can we ever expect to make things work—to have *intimacy*—when you're not willing to open up to me?" I thought about Venice, and Greece, and New York—all the times Todd could've opened up but didn't. "Will you ever love me as much as you loved her?"

"*Jesus*, Ann, what kind of question is that?"

"You're asking me to move halfway across the world for you," I said. "You're asking me to give up my entire way of life. But you haven't been honest with me. You haven't been open with me. How can you ask so much when you offer so little?"

"*So little?*" Todd fumed. "My grief aside, when have I ever held you at arm's length? We've written letters, I've spent thousands of dollars flying to Rome for you, I've neglected my business for you. What more can I do to prove to you that I love you?"

I was shaking so hard the phone rattled against my jaw. I squeezed the comforter with my other hand, trying to steady myself against the words I knew were coming next.

"If you can't see that," Todd said slowly, "if you can't appreciate all that I *have* done, then maybe this isn't working."

Every part of my being was screaming to speak in that moment, but my tongue didn't work. My jaw wouldn't cooperate.

"Maybe we should take a break from *whatever* this is," Todd said. "To figure out what we both want."

Suddenly, the distance between us felt massive. The things that divided us were rocky and treacherous. I couldn't see a path around them. I couldn't see how Todd and I could work—not now, not when he wanted a quiet suburban life in Colorado and I wanted anything but. We were standing on opposite sides of a ravine, wondering if the trek was truly worth the risks and the miles in the end.

I didn't have words for this feeling; I was out of breath from the climbing I'd already endured.

Todd waited a long time, and then the phone line clicked, and he was gone.

ANN

Over a year passed in which I spent very little time in the home I had fought so hard to defend on the phone with Todd. He lingered in every corner of Trastevere: a shadow on the Ponte Sisto, an empty seat across from mine at Carmella's, a spare pillow on my bed. I was hurting, so I did what I always did when I hurt: I ran.

I took every travel-article assignment offered to me. I visited pyramids and mosques, lochs and ruins. The Taj Mahal and the Great Wall. I have photos of myself on three different continents, places I don't quite remember. In the photos, I look thin and worn.

You're a tourist, Todd had said. He was right.

It's just that I wanted so badly to rewrite my story without Todd's name showing up on so many of my inner pages.

MAGGIE

Maggie can relate.

It's something she and Ann have in common. Open one of them up, and Todd is scrawled across the inside in permanent ink. It's comforting to Maggie to know she's not the only person who has been rewritten by Todd Langley.

"It's late," Maggie observes.

Beyond Ann's windows, the clouds and the ocean are equal shades of dim, ethereal gray blue. The skeletal trees and bluff grasses are mere shapes in the odd twilight, like block prints stamped in black ink; they bleed around the edges, shadows expanding. Inside, the honey yellow of the kitchen's overhead lights is a different season altogether.

"Stay," Ann says, not a command but an urging. "We have a lot of catching up to do, and I know Grant is breathing down your neck. I can order takeout, if you're hungry."

"All right." Maggie switches off the recorder and follows Ann into the kitchen.

Ann opens a drawer and digs through a stack of colorful takeout menus.

"It wasn't over for you and Todd, right?"

Ann pauses, her fingers brushing the edge of a menu—but she doesn't look up. "Todd and I were never truly *over*." She lifts a simple trifold, mint green, with faded letters. "How about Greek food?"

"Not Italian?" Maggie jokes.

Ann waves a hand through the air. "Carmella ruined me for any Italian food other than hers. It's why I visit every year. But this Greek place . . ." She smiles warmly, wrinkles forming around her eyes. "The owner is from Crete. The food is very good."

"Sounds great."

Ann dials the number listed on the front of the brochure. She utters a greeting in Greek, and there's muffled joy on the other end. While she relays a few dishes, Maggie watches her, the thin bones of her wrists, the wispy ends of her hair, the way the overhead light illuminates freckles that had once been darkened by the Greek summer sunshine. Here is a thoughtful, successful woman. A woman who has experienced pain and heartbreak and disappointment for much of her life. A woman who has seen the world. A woman Maggie once envied so hard she could barely stand it.

She doesn't envy Ann now—but she does admire her, respect her.

Maggie lifts her gaze to the windows again, but the world outside has grown dark. All Maggie sees is her own reflection, watery and unclear. She has no idea who she is or where she came from. She fears what is beyond the windows, the nocturnal secrets of her life barred only by thin panels of glass.

"Should be here in thirty minutes," Ann says.

"Thank you." Maggie smiles at Ann, this woman who has already changed Maggie's life irreversibly, with so much story yet to be told. "Do you want to record more while we wait?"

ANN

"Can you pass the suntan lotion?"

Dimitri stepped closer, his bare feet slapping the deck. A floppy hat covered my face, shielding my eyes from the harsh sun; when a shadow crossed my vision, I peeked out from under the braided brim, the holes in the weave splaying little sun dapples across my chest. My eyes traveled up Dimitri's body, unabashedly lingering on his strong legs, hard abdominals, and bare chest. Tan skin everywhere, most of it fuzzed with black hair.

"Need help?" he asked through a half grin. The boat bobbed under his feet, but he had his sea legs; he didn't hold the railing.

I set my hat on the folded towel nearby and turned over. "Sure. Get my back?"

I was tanning on the bow netting of his catamaran, my new favorite pastime. Underneath me, the Aegean was crystal clear, sloshing against the double hulls. I spotted the dark, jagged outline of coral thirty feet below, and a school of electric-blue fish turned this way and that, showing off their colors.

Dimitri's rough hands delicately pulled on the strings of my bikini and spread the lotion across my back. Todd had done this same thing for me on Mykonos eleven years before; each swipe of Dimitri's slick hand wiped away another memory of Todd's traveling the same path.

Dimitri was nothing like Todd. Boisterous, confident, and broad chested, he was every woman's Mediterranean fantasy. Even his accent was charming, a mix of Greek and the British English intonation of someone with family in the UK. I liked his dichotomy. He was a fiercely loyal family man who cried when he spoke of his nieces and nephews. But he also held his liquor, smoked cigars, and wanted sex every hour of the day.

Plus, he had a boat.

(This fling might've been terribly immature, but when I lost Todd, I lost some of my dignity too. I thought recklessness was the path to forgetting.)

When I had befriended his cousin Chloe in a London pub, I thought she was joking when she invited me down to Crete for the summer to party on Dimitri's tour boat. Since I'd suffered a year of anguish over Todd—and the *Chasing Shadows* movie had been officially delayed for budgetary reasons—getting lost in the Aegean with strangers sounded like the perfect distraction.

It wasn't like I hadn't done that before.

And this time, I knew to keep my infatuation in check. Light and lustful and casual.

What I didn't expect was to stay. But there I was, three months later, still tanning on Dimitri's boat.

When Dimitri finished slathering me in sunblock, he rolled onto his back beside me. The netting dipped exaggeratedly under his weight, and gravity slid me closer to his body. I caught a whiff of the sea salt that creased his skin from our earlier swim.

"Chloe and Katerina arrive tonight," he said with a relaxed grunt.

Settling my cheek on the back of my hand, I said, "Can't wait."

It was late August, nearing the end of tourist season. Chloe had spent the past month island-hopping with her older sister, Katerina. More of Dimitri's relatives were coming to Crete for the occasion, before Chloe returned to university in England.

"Nikolai and Bella will be big," Dimitri said of Katerina's children. He spoke of them all the time.

"Kids grow so fast," I said. "They're like weeds."

He frowned. "I don't like missing it."

"What?"

"Their childhood."

I patted his barrel chest. "They love you, though."

"It's the boat."

"It's more than the boat," I said with a laugh. "You're great with them."

"I want my own," he said.

"Children?"

"Yes." He rolled onto his side, facing me. His pectorals pressed together, and his arms bulged. He was so beautifully *tan* compared to the washed-out brightness of the white deck, the pale water, the dusty hills of the island in the distance, and the white sky.

Practically dozing, I asked, "When?" I did not yet understand the weight of what he was telling me.

"Soon," he said.

"Don't you need to find a woman first?"

"Are you not a woman?" he asked.

I cracked one eye open to find him staring at me. I lifted my head.

"How would you like to wed, Ann?"

I thought he was joking; I really did. We'd known each other for only a few months. It seemed ridiculous, me lying there beside him on his boat, with red rope marks crisscrossing my skin. Our time together seemed like a textbook fling to me. How could we be on such wildly different pages? It was as if we weren't even reading the same book; mine was in English, and his in Greek.

And yet, for a brief moment, I allowed myself the fantasy of saying yes.

I imagined being welcomed into a huge, devoted family. I imagined a big wedding, honeymooning on Dimitri's boat, sailing to Spain. I imagined getting pregnant, bearing his children, a boy first and then a girl. I could write between nap times and cooking, start a garden and fumble through domesticity. Dimitri would offer gentle encouragement, patience, and fierce love.

It was a pleasant fantasy, but I saw it from a third-person perspective, like watching a movie. The wife looked like me, but I didn't truly recognize her. I'd experienced this hesitation before, with Luca—something about us didn't fit.

I rolled onto my side and looked into Dimitri's black-brown eyes. I studied the untamable curls of thick hair at his temple, pushed back and held in place by the grit of dried salt water. I wanted to kiss him one last time, but I knew that if I did, he'd get the wrong idea.

"I think you would make a fine husband," I said, "but I would make a terrible wife."

Dimitri was passionate, but he wasn't a fool. He knew that what I'd just said was *no*.

The net wobbled under his weight as he stepped across the knotted ropes and onto the deck. Without a word, he walked toward the stern and out of sight, leaving me where I lay.

Is this what I've become? I wondered, watching the fish dance below me. *A disappointment in someone else's story?* I had been naive to think that I could move through life like this—noncommittal, disengaged—without someone getting hurt.

Dimitri was a turning point for me; I owed him that.

When I returned home in the late summer of 1995, I applied—finally—for a volunteer teaching program. It was about time I showed up and did something of meaning. Back at Trevi Fountain, on that first day Todd and I slept together, Todd had been right to criticize my idle lifestyle. Teaching, I soon found, gave me purpose. It was not fragile and fickle, like my creative writing. It was not static success. It was equal parts challenge and reward.

For the next three years, the volunteer teaching program took me across the globe. In the off months, Keith and Carmella became my blips of joy. I went on day trips to Tuscany and Milan with Carmella, vacations to France and Portugal with Keith and sometimes Barbara and Iris too.

And for a while, I had purpose.

And some days, I even forgot to miss Todd.

ANN

In September 1998, I was just returning to Lima from volunteer teaching in Sacred Valley, Peru. I hadn't been in touch with anyone for six months—my lodging had been remote—so I'd asked Carmella to forward any important-looking mail to my hotel to meet my arrival. Sprawled on the cool duvet of my hotel bed with a large stack of missed correspondence, I dialed Keith.

"She's alive," he answered. He sounded older—or perhaps just tired. It was nine thirty in the evening in New York.

"Keith? It's Ann." I pinned the phone between my ear and shoulder so I could thumb through envelopes.

"I know it's Ann. Who else would call me from a wacky foreign number at this time of night?"

I chuckled. "Telemarketers?"

"I'm glad you didn't die in the jungle."

"Almost did," I said, "from a fever back in Cuzco."

"Yet there you are."

I glanced around the dim room. "Here I am."

Despite the humbling and transformative work of teaching, I remained a walking contradiction: both travel obsessed and dissatisfied as a nomad. No matter how far I traveled, no matter how many strangers I met and laughed with and got to know, I missed the certain contentedness that only a close friend could offer.

"So . . . ," Keith prompted. "What's new in Ann Land?"

"I have so many stories to tell you." The kids in Sacred Valley had been earnest, kind, inspiring. This country and its history were astounding. I wanted to share everything with Keith. "I don't know where to begin."

"I want to hear *everything*, of course . . ."

"But?"

"But maybe we should discuss business first."

I snorted. "Sheesh, Keith. What about *friendship* first? It's been months since we last talked. I missed you."

"No, you didn't."

"I *did*."

I could hear the smile in his voice when he said, "Me too. We were worried about you."

"We?" I'd managed to quit smoking, but thinking about Todd was an addiction I'd yet to kick. I missed knowing he was there for me.

"Me, the family," Keith clarified.

Right. "And how are Barbara and Iris?"

"They're great. Barbara just landed her biggest client yet, and Iris is playing the lead in her school play."

"Iris decided to audition?" I asked, elated.

"She was inspired by that theater we visited with you in Lisbon."

I beamed at the faded hotel wallpaper, my joy bright enough to illuminate the lonesome room. "What is it like, being surrounded by strong, successful women?"

"Exhausting." Keith laughed. "And humbling."

His words were champagne bubbles in my chest.

"But totally worth it," he added. "I'm in awe."

I smiled against the phone. "And what about you? How is work?"

"Well, that brings us to the business part of this conversation, doesn't it?"

I sighed, exaggerating my exasperation. "Fine, fine."

"Your short story, 'Ashes.'"

I didn't need to hear more. "Absolutely not."

In addition to my regular travel articles, I'd continued to write the occasional short story. For whatever reason, they were just . . . easier than novels; I didn't have to open an artery to write them—just mere veins. But one in particular—"Ashes"—had been so well received, my last three conversations with Keith had pivoted to the topic of adapting it into a full-length sophomore book.

Which I would not do.

"What if I told you there was an offer on the table?"

"Keith. You know how I feel about this."

The story was a nod toward Todd, of course. All my best work seemed to come from that place of longing deep inside me. *Chasing Shadows* had been that way. Now this. The short stories had been a compromise—something for Keith, my publisher, my fans, the film—but this one skirted too close to home. That's probably why it had become so popular.

"Wait until I tell you how many zeros—"

"I said no."

"Seriously? Any other author would be thrilled by the opportunities thrown at you. Do you really want to waste this?"

I didn't want to disappoint him, but here we were. "You knew when I handed it over that I was uncertain about its publication."

"You're joking. This is a cruel joke."

"Don't pretend you're surprised. Did you really think I'd want to expand on an idea I didn't want to publish in the first place?"

"Ann, I've talked this up to *everyone*. Deepa, Vicky, the entire team. Why not? Why can't we move forward?"

I pushed my hair away from my face and pinched the bridge of my nose. "You know why."

"This is about Todd, isn't it?"

"Of *course* it is," I said, surprised to find myself suddenly shrill.

"You haven't spoken to him in forever."

The wounds had healed over, yet every once in a while, the tight scar tissue across my heart ached, reminding me of him—taking me immediately back. "I can't betray his trust like that—no matter how long it's been," I said. "The story is about a fire, for god's sake. Didn't the parallels make *you* uncomfortable?"

"This deal is worth the discomfort."

"Perhaps Todd wouldn't mind a cut of your percentage, then?"

"I just mean all stories come from a place of truth," he said.

"I should've never written it."

"Todd can't fault you for drawing inspiration from real life."

"He's your best friend. You *know* a full-length book would bother him. I'm sure the story already has."

Keith's frustrated groan told me I was right. "Did you at least get his letters?"

The scar tissue on my heart pulled tight. "Letters?"

"I'll take that as a no."

"Carmella has been collecting my mail. I only just received . . ." I rifled through the stack in front of me, truly *looking* for the first time. Sure enough, a handful of letters had come all the way from Colorado via Rome. "I . . . I have them right here. I had no idea." The first one displayed a postmark of six months ago. "Oh my god."

"I recognized the parallels," Keith said while I stared down at the letters with my chest aching. "But it's not like anyone else will. No one knows who Todd is."

I tore my attention away from the envelopes and sat up. "'Real-life Frank,' that's what reporters have called him—more than once, now," I said. "It wouldn't take much to dig up the old newspapers reporting the tragedy, find his name, make a connection." I shook my head. "I'm sorry, but I was clear about this from the get-go. You knew where I stood."

Keith's sigh rattled the phone speaker like a gust of storm wind. "I knew. But I hoped I could—"

"Change my mind?" I chuckled, not unkindly. "What were we saying earlier about strong women?"

"I believe I said it's exhausting." He huffed a laugh, and the tension between us diffused.

I traced the outline of one of Todd's letters with my finger. The edges were wrinkled and worn soft from travel, not unlike me. "How is he?"

"Todd? He's fine. He's . . . well, you ought to read what he wrote."

I swallowed and—though Keith couldn't see me—nodded.

"Just think about the deal?"

"I already have."

"All right, okay." When he spoke again, his strong business voice had returned. "One more thing: the movie."

"I remember." The premiere was set for next year, and the studio wanted me to be involved in the press tour. They were waiting on my teaching schedule to book a strategy meeting. "I don't know where I'll be, yet."

"You're going to keep traveling?"

"Why wouldn't I?"

I heard the sandpapery sound of him scratching his stubble.

"I can practically *feel* the opinion coming," I prompted.

"Look, Ann, I've tried to be patient, I really have."

"About?"

"The teaching."

"Volunteering?"

"I know you think you're doing a good thing." A pause. "But this is just another form of running away from your problems."

I flinched. "Teaching brings me *purpose*."

"No, teaching is a distraction."

"So, let me get this straight," I said. "When it's family vacations and travel articles—things that benefit you and your stake in my career—it's fine for me to travel. But when it's my own thing, as teaching has been—"

"Ann," Keith cut in. "I've known you—what, fourteen years?—and you do this every time. You travel to forget. And sure, I'm grateful for the time we've spent together and the relevance your articles have helped you maintain. And I know that with teaching, you're doing something that benefits others—but face it: just as the stamps on your passport won't patch up your heart, those kids aren't your therapy."

"How dare you," I said, outrage blooming in my body like the plume of a bomb. "This work is rewarding. *Meaningful.*"

"You're trying to fix other people instead of yourself."

"I—" It was more of a wrathful sound than a word. I opened and closed my mouth, starting and giving up on every snarling thought that came to mind. "Where is this coming from?"

"Frankly, it's long overdue. As soon as things get real, you run. That's what you do—what you've always done."

"This is about the novel, isn't it? You're angry I haven't produced something new for you to sell."

"That's not true."

"I'm just a walking dollar sign to you, aren't I?" Angry, flaming words, meant to scorch.

"After all these years, if that's what you think . . ." I'd never heard his voice so tight and terrifyingly measured. "You know what? Stay in Peru as long as you want. Stay far away and waste your mind and heart and talent hiding from your problems. Waste away, for all I care. But from now on, leave me out of it. Don't fucking call me."

He hung up. Just . . . *click*.

I slumped.

I hadn't meant what I said, of course. Hadn't meant to accuse or harm. But I'd felt so *good* about teaching. Virtuous and purposeful. His criticism had enraged me—no, it'd *wounded* me. So I had wounded back.

I released the corded phone into its base with a clatter and wiped my cheeks with my fingers, pressing my palms into my eyes to blot out the threat of tears.

I sighed, deep and heavy, and stood up.

Paced.

Fretted.

I knew I should apologize.

I picked up the phone and dialed Keith's number. It rang and rang until I reached the machine, a cute recording of Iris suggesting I leave a message. I hung up and tried again with the same result: *You've reached the Whitakers* . . . The third time, someone picked up but immediately severed the connection.

I sank to the bed again, overwhelmed by the silence of my hotel room, the strange city sounds a muted din beyond my closed curtains. Alone—I was so *alone*. And it was by design. My fault.

Who else can I call?

My mind went straight to Mom. I hadn't wanted to call her in a long, long time, but within the agonizing aloneness, the grief of that urge stung behind my eyes. Eight years after my mother's death and I was still terrified of becoming her; she had spent her whole life falling in love and landing flat on her face. After Todd, I thought I was destined to do the same—and yet I craved her advice now. I craved her candy-coated voice and her sober optimism. Because the truth of the matter was that I was just like her. Weak and afraid and cruel in anger. Hopelessly romantic and also simply hopeless.

I tried to think of someone else I could call. Usually, lately, when I was upset, I dialed Keith—a sour irony, now. I could talk to Carmella, but she wouldn't understand my strife over Keith's accusation.

I ran cold hands over my hot cheeks. When I opened my eyes again, my attention sank to the letters.

Todd's letters.

Todd.

I knew his number by heart, and though my hands shook, my fingers flew over the buttons on the phone base. As the phone rang, my shakes grew worse. I hit the speaker button and sat back, waiting. The phone seemed to ring forever.

"Hello?"

His voice took me back to that moment four years before, when he had said it was over. He sounded the same. I *felt* the same. With Todd, time wasn't linear. Time didn't heal. Time was inconsequential—it could slow down to a moment, or speed through years, but he was constant.

You travel to forget. Buried under the rubble of my anger: a kernel of truth in Keith's words.

"Hello?" Todd asked again. "Helloooo?" His line whooshed and creaked as if he were about to hang up.

"Wait," I finally managed.

"Ann?"

I gripped the bedside table at the sound of my name on his lips. How could he disarm me with only my own name? It was an unfair superpower.

"Are you there?"

"Yeah, sorry, I—I didn't expect you to answer."

I hoped I heard a smile in his voice when he said, "Well, I did."

Such a simple statement, as if we hadn't just gone *years* without speaking.

279

"Keith's being a real shithead," I blurted.

He huffed a laugh, and I heard what I thought were sheets crinkling.

"I'm sorry, did I wake you?"

"No, no. I was reading." The echo of his voice changed, perhaps from walking into another room. "So Keith's being a shithead."

"He thinks I should return to Italy."

"Where are you now?"

"Lima."

"Ah. And you don't want to leave?"

"I . . ." I trailed off. I didn't know what I wanted. My argument with Keith had unearthed all my uncertainty. "I've been volunteer teaching, and it's *so* rewarding. You wouldn't believe the kids, Todd. They're amazing. Smart and warm and eager to learn."

"But Keith wants another book," Todd said.

"We got into a huge argument. Just now. I tried to call back, but he's not picking up."

"So you want me to try him?"

"No, I . . ."

He waited.

"I just wanted someone to talk to, I guess."

"Oh." A bright, buttery vowel.

"Is that okay?"

"Of course that's okay," Todd said. "That's always okay."

The inside of my nose stung, and I blinked, trying to keep the emotion from my voice when I said, "He accused me of running. From my problems."

"Are you?"

I tucked my knees up close to my body and rested my chin on them, my back pressed into the headboard. Teaching *was* a crutch—a way to feel needed without commitment. *You're a tourist,* Todd had once told me. Maybe it was time to listen to what he and Keith were saying.

"I guess so," I admitted.

"I hate it when Keith's right."

That made me chuckle. "It's the *worst*, isn't it?"

"The absolute worst," Todd said emphatically.

We both paused—an amiable silence. I noticed the hum of the city outside my window again, but with Todd on the other end of the phone, the sounds didn't seem so empty or foreign. I didn't feel so alone.

"You sent letters," I said.

"Indeed."

"I had Carmella forward my mail to this hotel. I only just received them. I've been teaching in a pretty remote area."

"Regardless of what Keith says, I bet you're great at teaching."

"It's been amazing, but . . ." I considered Keith's words with an open mind, facing the truth of them. "It's not what I'm meant to do, I don't think."

"You miss Rome."

"I do."

"I bet the stoop cats miss you," Todd said. "Carmella skimps on all her portions."

A dismissive *pah* escaped my lips. "Gluttonous American sensibilities."

"You know I'm right. Remember that pumpkin pasta she made?"

"I could've bathed in that."

"Right, but how big was the portion?"

"That's one example."

"What about the melon soup, or that pesto—"

"Fine, you have a point." I stretched my legs out, crossing them at my ankles. It might as well have been the old days, talking to Todd like this. My heart swelled like a book in the rain, my feelings pulpy and delicate.

"So . . . ," Todd drawled, "did you see Machu Picchu?"

"I did."

"Was it—"

"Why did you write to me, Todd?" I interrupted. "I'm sorry, I just—I'm surprised."

"You haven't read them." Not a question.

I retrieved one of the letters from the stack, smoothing its bent corners. "Not yet."

"Right." He paused a beat. "Well, I read 'Ashes.'"

A pang in my sternum.

"It hit close to home."

"I shouldn't have published it."

"At first I was mad," he continued. "But it was so beautiful, so . . . tender. I forgot what an incredible writer you are. It reminded me of the first time I wrote to you, after I read *Chasing Shadows*, and then that made me miss you, and . . ."

My heart fractured like a dam pressed by the weight of too much water. A tiny *oh* escaped my lips, a liquidy breath of emotion. "I've missed you too," I squeaked.

Todd blew out a breath, and then—

—and then I heard a woman's voice, sleepy and melodic. She was calling from the other room: "Todd, are you coming back to bed?"

And just like that, the dam of my heart burst.

I cleared my throat, but my words still came out unsteady. "I should let you go," I said, but I was thinking I should've let him go a long time ago.

The next morning, I awoke to ringing. I'd fallen asleep with one of Todd's letters pressed to my face. I flung myself upright and scrambled for the phone, my heart in my throat.

"Hello?"

"I'm ready to make up, are you?" Keith.

"Thank *god*. Yes. Keith, I shouldn't have said . . . what I said. I'm so sorry."

"I'm sorry too. I was frustrated."

"You were *right*," I insisted. "You were so right."

"Well, I'm one to talk."

"What do you mean?" I stood, stretched, wandered over to the window. The cityscape beyond my curtains flared bright with sunshine.

"I ran away to Greece when Barbara and I broke up. It's how you and I met, remember? All three of us were running from our problems."

"I forgot about that."

"You were a little distracted."

I smiled at the memory—*smiled*. Me and Todd—it had seemed so fraught at the time, but so many years later, I felt only fondness for my former self.

He continued. "When I went to Greece to try to get over Barbara, I almost lost everything. I'd hate to see you do the same."

The sentence was out before I could think. "But I have nothing to lose."

The phone line crackled in the pause that followed, crackled through my bones like an electric current. It *hurt*, this truth, deep in my marrow.

"Well, that's simply not true," Keith said. "You have your career. You have me. You have Carmella. And you have Todd, apparently."

"He told you I called him."

"Of course he did."

"He also told you what I, um, heard?"

"Did you think he'd be celibate?"

"I had hoped."

Keith snorted. "You two are a soap opera."

I wished he could see me roll my eyes. "Thank you for the tough love."

"I'm sorry I was more *tough* than *love* last night."

"No," I said, growing emotional again. "I needed that." I closed my eyes. "I just . . . I don't know what to *do* with myself. I don't know who I'm supposed to be."

"You're Ann fucking Fawkes, that's who you are," Keith said. "Internationally bestselling author, honorary Roman, and friend. All things you're currently thousands of miles away from."

I fixed my vision on my suitcase. "So, what, I just go home?"

"That's a start."

"And then?"

"And then you write another knockout. Not for me, or the money, or your fans—but for yourself."

"Okay," I said, nodding. "Okay."

"Good." Keith's chair creaked as if he were leaning back in his seat. "You really should read Todd's letters."

I wandered over to the bed and plucked a letter off the pile, which had been strewn about the duvet from my restless sleep.

"I'll call you when I'm back in Rome." I wrinkled my nose in a scrunched sort of smile. "It's nice to hear your voice—even when it's saying tough things."

"Yours, too—even when it's saying stubborn things."

I laughed.

"Take care, my friend," Keith added. "I love you."

"I love you too. Send my best to Barbara. And tape Iris's play for me."

We hung up, and I knelt on the bed, the mail scattered before me. I didn't know what I'd hoped for when I called Todd last night, but hearing the woman's voice on the line—it stung. I wasn't sure I could stomach his letters—letters I'd missed while I'd been running all over the globe. Running from *him*.

There were nine in all. I sorted them by date, then slid my nail under the weak adhesive of the first envelope. The letter was a single page of Todd's neat, careful writing—and not at all what I was expecting.

Ann,

There are four years and a thousand emotions between us,
but: I miss writing to you. I miss getting my thoughts out
on paper and having someone on the other end to comment
and crack jokes and lend support. I guess what I'm really
saying is that I miss our friendship.

Keith said you've been teaching in a remote location in
Peru, so I know it's unlikely you'll receive this letter anytime
soon. When you do, I hope it's not unwelcome.

Todd

The next came four weeks later:

Ann,

I thought you would like to know that I adopted a shop
cat. I remember you saying once that the stoop cats gave
you purpose, and I thought, hey, why not find one of my
own? She's an orange-and-white rescue named Creamsicle
(my staff calls her Creamy).

What I didn't know when I adopted her: she has "stomach issues" and eats this terribly expensive prescription food.
She takes about a million medications and hides in the stacks
when it's time for me to administer them. I had no idea what I
was getting into. I can practically hear you laughing as I write
this—that smug little cackle you do when you're amused by
my stupidity.

Still: I wouldn't trade her for the world.

Todd

I laughed, but it wasn't a cackle. It was delight. We had used to send
each other letters like this—letters about nothing in particular. Todd

had been such a comfort last night, and his letters were a comfort too. I'd forgotten what a gift his friendship could be.

> *Ann,*
> *So I adopted a friend for Creamy. His name is Edwin, which I find to be an extremely formal and hilarious name for a cat. Thankfully, he's fat and low maintenance. The staff have a bet on how many cats I end up adopting. Since there's no male alternative to cat-lady (because of sexism, I guess?), they're calling me cat-man, which sounds more like a superhero than an insult.*
>
> *In any case, I want to rescind all jokes I made about you and your stoop cats; I now realize that they are a joy. I hope that wherever you are, you have a few felines keeping you company.*
> *Todd*

Letter after letter about the cats, the bookshop, his life. I couldn't believe he'd written so many one-sided conversations. I wondered why he'd felt the urge, when he had a woman to share his bed.

He had missed me. Maybe not the way I wanted him to miss me, but nonetheless, he *had* missed me.

MAGGIE

"Who was she?" Maggie asks.

Seemingly perplexed by the sudden question, Ann says, "Her name was Alison. That's all I know."

Maggie pauses the voice recorder. The clock reads 9:37 p.m., the Greek takeout boxes have been scraped clean, and Ann's mascara is smudged under her eyes. Maggie probably looks even more bedraggled. It has been a long day, yet it seems far from over.

"That's truly all you know?"

"Why the sudden interest?"

Maggie shifts in her seat, strung out, stretched, drawn taut and about to snap. Her conscience tells her to keep her mouth shut about her father, to continue with the podcast. What pep talk would Grant offer, if he were here?

It doesn't matter, because he's not.

And who's to say he'd be able to convince Maggie to remain quiet, anyhow?

Her silence feels heavy, like a giant boulder resting on her ribs, hindering her breath, threatening to crack bone and crush her. She no longer remembers the logic of her silence. Journalistic integrity, maybe? Nothing about her experience with Ann rings of integrity. This whole week has been filled with bad morals, secrets, and unsaid things left to fester. There is no way Maggie can remove herself from this story. It's not possible. Todd's blood is her blood, and there's no separating herself from that.

"Maggie, what are you getting at?"

Suddenly, nothing seems as important as finding out where she came from. And Maggie *deserves* to know, no matter what her parents or Grant have to say. The words inside her become inevitable. They build like a hurricane, wind and rain and pressure all swirling around a calm eye of resolve. The full force of the storm surges through her. She braces for the impact of gale-force revelation.

"Todd is my father," she says aloud.

The wind screams. The rain is a hundred thousand pinpricks on her skin. She can barely hear over the storm—or is that just the blood rushing in her ears?

In front of her, Ann doesn't move.

"Is that woman, Alison—is she my mother?"

Ann's forehead creases, and then she frowns with her whole face, her mouth, eyelids, and brows crumpling. "I—" She shakes her head. For a moment she looks as though she'll say more, but then she presses her lips together and runs a hand over her face. She stares out the window—or perhaps *at* the window, the glossy reflection of the two of them sitting on the couch. Abruptly, she stands and closes the curtains; the sharp ringing of the grommets scraping against the curtain bar pierces Maggie's ears.

With the curtains closed, Ann remains where she is, facing the seam of fabric.

A deep and devastating ache pulses through Maggie. She's never experienced such an acute sense of *wanting* in her entire life. "Did you already know?" Maggie quietly asks. "Is that why you wanted me to talk to Tracey?"

"I wanted to give her a chance to say her piece."

Ann passes a hand over her lips, then turns around. Her expression is once again neutral, and she meets Maggie's gaze with her orange, cat-like eyes. Maggie searches for truth in those eyes. A hint. Anything. *If Ann is my mother,* Maggie reasons, *would she act this way? Cold and silent and withholding?* And if Ann isn't her mother, then perhaps Maggie came from this other woman in the story—but every time Maggie tries to piece it all together, the precarious structure of her thoughts tumbles.

"I know this is unprofessional." If Ann isn't going to speak, Maggie will fill the silence herself. "I know I'm putting you on the spot. But my parents told me about Todd only two days ago, and—and—and I thought I could do this assignment without bringing my own shit into the mix, but you were such a huge part of my family once. I want to learn who my mother is. Tracey said it wasn't you, but *someone* has to know. Todd is dead, and you're the only person who has been straight with me."

Ann returns to the couch, placing a comforting hand on Maggie's knee. "I'm so sorry your family has put you through this." She scoots closer, drawing Maggie into her arms.

With that single act of compassion, Maggie fractures, deep cracks spreading through her heart like a slow shatter. She crumples freely into Ann's embrace. The weave of Ann's sweater is itchy against her cheek, but Ann is warm and surprisingly soft for how thin she appears. Maggie squeezes her eyes shut tight, until she sees bursts of tingling color.

For a moment, she is calmed, but no matter how comforting Ann's embrace is, Maggie's mind revs like a car in neutral. It hums and burns, but it can't go anywhere because, aside from Todd, Maggie knows nothing—and she's sick of being kept in the dark about her own existence. She won't accept it any longer.

She pulls back. "Tell me what you know."

Ann's arms fall to her sides. "I'm sorry, dear, I don't know."

"You're lying."

"I'm not."

Maggie can see the restraint on Ann's face. The slight pucker of her bottom lip, the tension in her jaw.

"Why don't you lie down?" Ann asks. "You can rest in my guest room."

"No. If this conversation is over, then I should go." Maggie stands, looking around for her purse. She passes the back of her hand over her face to wipe the frustration off.

"The roads are probably icy. You shouldn't drive while you're this upset," Ann says. "I have a perfectly good guest roo—"

Maggie lifts her hand, halting Ann's words. "I'm fine."

"You're *not* fine. And you shouldn't be alone—"

"Oh, what do you know?" Maggie bites out.

"I know a lot about crying alone, actually," Ann says pointedly. "Please. Just stay here. Rest a bit. The sheets are clean."

"You have to understand how hard it is for me to be here right now."

"I can conceptualize," Ann says gently. "But I still think you should stay. When you wake up, we can keep working."

"I don't know if I can continue . . ."

"Sleep on it, dear." Ann's voice is full of compassion, yet her expression is stern, unmoving.

Maggie sighs.

"Come now. It's down the hall."

Maggie doesn't sleep, though Ann's guest room is cozy enough. Once she's tucked into the Tide-scented sheets, an intense loss quivers through her bones, a homesickness for a life she's never known. Maggie had a privileged childhood, a loving family and supportive guardians. It's not that she doesn't cherish Tracey and Bob—it's the secrecy that plagues her.

It's knowing that people aren't telling the truth.

It's knowing that her story has been *kept* from her—intentionally.

And if it has been kept from her, then she must come from some kind of shame. Something the Whitakers, Ann—whoever knows—doesn't want to talk about. Is Maggie's existence *that* terrible?

The unfairness of it is loud. The hurt is even louder. The noise keeps her awake.

As the night fades and trees outside the window begin to stand out against a deep-blue sky, Maggie detects Ann rousing. She hears the creak of her door and footsteps on carpet, then slippers on kitchen tile, a soft rubber smacking. She hears the rattle of coffee beans in a grinder, the hiss of a kettle. Tired and unstrung, Maggie could stay in this room forever, but the longer she waits, the harder it will be to emerge, so she rolls out of bed, slides back into her jeans, and treads down the hall.

Ann is curled on the couch with a throw draped over her lap, a candle flickering on the glass coffee table. She's wearing an old T-shirt, and her hair is braided down one shoulder. Meeting Maggie's eyes, Ann points to the prepared coffee press. Maggie pours herself a cup and joins Ann on the couch.

Minutes pass. A quarter of an hour. The two of them sit in silence, sipping, breathing.

Ann clears her throat but doesn't look at Maggie when she says, "Did you sleep?"

"No."

"Me neither."

Maggie fixes Ann with a hard stare. "Are you going to keep me in the dark, like everyone else?"

"There's nothing for me to say on the matter."

Ann's words sound less like *I don't know anything* and more like *It's not my place*. Either way, it's clear that Ann has decided to remain silent.

"Then we should keep recording." Maggie has no idea how she'll string together this shit show of a podcast, but she can at least get the damn thing recorded.

"All right." The voice recorder remains where they left it, resting beside the candle in the middle of the sparse table. Ann leans forward and turns it back on. "I believe I left off when I returned to Italy."

ANN

Carmella kissed my cheeks and handed over the keys to my apartment, along with a warm container that seeped a heavenly comfort-food scent. The small portion reminded me of my conversation with Todd in Lima, but I kept that opinion to myself. "Thank you for watching things while I was away, Carmella. You're a good friend."

Her brows darted together. *"Stai bene?"* She was concerned about me.

I sank into her embrace. *"Stanca,"* I explained. Tired.

My apartment was the same as it had been, though it smelled faintly of Carmella's candy-sweet perfume. She had left some fresh vegetables on the counter and a few blocks of my favorite cheeses in the fridge. A new letter rested on the counter.

> *Ann,*
> *You called me last night from Lima. I'm sure you could tell that you caught me off guard. After you didn't respond to my letters, I figured you didn't want to hear from me*

anymore, so I was surprised — and glad — to hear you on the phone.

I know you overheard a woman on my end. Her name is Alison. I hope my moving on doesn't stop you from reaching out again. I have no idea when you'll return to Rome, but when you get this, know that your letters have always been a thing I look forward to.

(Hopefully) your friend and continued pen pal,
Todd

My throat cinched, as if my heart—attached to my esophagus by a thread—had turned to lead and sunk, pulling the drawstring tight.

I set the letter on my desk and dug into Carmella's steaming to-go box, delighted to find *spaghetti alla carbonara* waiting for me. Not nearly enough of it, of course, but Carmella knew my favorites: she'd added extra *guanciale* and cooked the jowl bacon until it was crisp and caramelized. I hunkered into the cheese and carbohydrates, even as my mind spun like a scratched record, skipping over the same half thoughts.

It took me a week to finally muster up the emotional fortitude to write Todd back. I knew I could call him, but there was something therapeutic about putting pen to paper. More than that, however, I liked writing letters because that was our thing.

Todd,
Despite this strange and winding road we've traveled, there is nothing — nothing — that could come between me and my gratitude for knowing you in all the shades and capacities I have known you over the years. I won't lie and tell you that hearing her voice wasn't painful for me; but not so painful as the prospect of losing you. These many months

of silence have reminded me how deeply I cherished our periodic letters. So of course I'll be your pen pal. Always.
   In friendship,
   Ann

There is nothing more courageous in this world than loving someone—in friendship, in romance, in family. When I sent that letter, I felt brave, Maggie. I was accepting his friendship as all I'd ever get, and while I mourned the prospect of more, my words felt right. Carmella, Keith, Todd—they were my people. And I wasn't ready to lose a third of my family simply because he had found someone else to share his bed.

That letter began another string of correspondence with Todd. He did not mention Alison again, nor did I mention the men I dated. We mostly talked about our day-to-day, the people we encountered and the things that made us smile. And, of course, the adventures of Creamy, Edwin, and the Stoop Cats (our official fake band name).

I have to admit that being Todd's friend was far easier than being his lover.

ANN

I settled back into my idle life in Rome, focusing on writing more short stories in the months leading up to the *Chasing Shadows* film premiere. I had turned forty that past February and reasoned that my age demanded some semblance of professionalism. And, on the side, I worked on the "knockout" Keith had encouraged me to write. A novel just for me.

The rest of my time was spent with Carmella and her friends in the restaurant scene. A flirtation developed between me and one of the food-tour guides who frequented Carmella's with his tourist groups. Bertie was barely thirty, boisterous, and his confidence was contagious.

One evening in September, I ran into Bertie after a tour. We got to talking and shared a cigarette (my first in *forever*), hyperaware of each other's mouths. We passed the filter between our lips until we decided it would be more efficient to simply kiss. Unlike the men before him, nothing about Bertie felt desperate or agonizing. Whatever happened, happened—and if that kiss was as far as it would go, at least it was a good kiss.

A few days later, I was on my way out to meet friends when I ran into my postman. Another letter had come from Todd, and I sat on my stoop beside an orange tabby that was sunning himself in the mid-day sunshine. I wore an ankle-length button-down dress, and when I extended my legs, my shins poked out from under the fabric, the sun reaching down to warm them.

I was expecting Todd's letter to be lighthearted and superficial, as was our pattern lately.

I was expecting to read Todd's letter and be on my way.

Instead, I got this:

> Ann,
> A few letters back you mentioned that the fifteen-year anniversary of our meeting was coming up. How would you like to be together in Tahiti on the day? I think it's time we followed through on that teal-water daydream.
> Todd

I glanced around the street, unsure of what to make of the letter. All around, people were milling about, eating street pizza, holding hands, laughing. They were all so breezy. I'd gotten a taste of that feeling with Bertie, but now it seemed far away. The tectonic plates inside me were shifting again, creating new peaks and valleys.

Todd's letter posed a question—and not just a practical, logistic one. It posed a question about who I wanted to be.

I reread his words. I suspected Todd's intention was to be spon-taneous and romantic, but I was so tired of the touch-and-go, the give-and-take.

So tired.

In past years, I might've melted from a letter like that, but on that warm day, I grew angry. First: Why hadn't Todd sent this letter years ago? Second: Why was he sending it now, and what of Alison?

I couldn't discern his tone from syntax alone, but I felt imposed upon. I wondered at the assumptions attached to his words. Did he truly expect me to come running after all this time? Was it cocky of him to think I would? Or did he see this as a hopeful gamble?

Frustration bloomed like a fresh bruise, deepening the longer I stared at Todd's handwriting. I was sick of feeling purple and blue.

I pushed up from the stoop in a huff—disturbing the cat—and tromped upstairs to my apartment. I picked up the phone and dialed.

He didn't pick up on the first call, so I rang again.

When he answered, I waved the letter as if he could see it. "Why did you send this?"

"Ann, it's five in the morning here." He sounded groggy with sleep.

"I don't care," I said, lighting a cigarette from the half pack Bertie had given me. I stepped out onto my balcony and sucked in a massive breath, holding the filter between my lips while I smoothed the letter on the banister. "Why did you send this?"

"You got my letter."

"Todd."

"I sent it because I meant it."

"What about—"

"That ended a while ago. It was sex and no substance."

I flinched at the word *sex*, then shook my head, furious at my own weakness for him.

"Look, Ann. You're *it*, okay? You're the only one I want to—"

"Don't do that." My fist clenched. "Don't say that unless you're serious, Todd, because I can't fucking take the heartache." After all that travel, I hadn't bested my romanticism—it'd been in hibernation. Now, it lumbered through my chest, awake and ravenous.

"You hurt me, Todd." I wasn't sure which time I meant—all of it, I supposed. Venice, Greece, New York—even Lima, with Alison's voice on the line, hope stolen.

"I know I hurt you." He sighed. "This apology is long overdue. I should've been truthful with you—from the beginning. It wasn't fair of me to keep secrets. I was selfish, and evasive, and you deserved better. I'm sorry.

"Look," Todd continued, "I've tried to move past us. I really have. But the harder I try, the more certain I am that it's impossible to forget you. What else can explain the fact that *five years* after our breakup, I still can't stop thinking about what could have been? *Fifteen years* after our first meeting, I still crave your company? That must mean something. I know I fucked up, but I'm not ready to give up. That's why I sent that letter. The real question is whether or not you feel the same way."

For a long time I had no words.

He was at fault for his secrets, but hadn't I been too careful with him? Hadn't I had the chance to confront him, push him, stand up for myself? It didn't excuse his behavior, but I knew I could've been a stronger partner. My fear of losing him had clouded my honesty, and that hurt both of us.

God, what stupid games we'd played. With each other, and with ourselves. I had grown so accustomed to chasing him that when finally he was ready to turn around and embrace me, I evaded. I wanted to correct the imbalance by pulling back, just a little, just enough, to feel like I had some control.

But that's the thing about love. There is no control.

"It's easier to be your friend," I finally admitted. It was easier to chat and laugh and pretend the stakes weren't higher than that—like surfing a three-foot wave as opposed to a tsunami.

"It *is* easier," he whispered. "But doesn't it hurt more?"

I imagined myself falling from a surfboard onto rocks versus falling into the deep. I imagined the thrill of riding a big wave as opposed to a small one. Then I stopped imagining and asked, "Why Tahiti?"

"I figured you hadn't gone there yet. And the glass horse—"

"I remember."

"I'm not messing around, Copper," Todd said, his voice like warm honey. "Will you see the blue water with me?"

"I . . ." I trailed off, stubbing out my cigarette. "I have to think about it."

"Take all the time you need."

We hung up, and I stared at the wrinkled letter on the banister, the corner of it pinned under my ashtray. The wind rustled the nearby trees, a shower of leaves falling like a thousand what-ifs. What if we were never meant to be? What if we were? What if I stayed home and gave myself the chance to move on? What if I regretted *not* going to Tahiti for the rest of my existence?

If I had even a chance at being happy, it would be with Todd. No one else.

ANN

When I arrived in Papeete, Tahiti, the warm air pressed against me, heavy and sweet. The hiss of car engines and bugs was a constant din beyond the glass walls of the airport, punctuated by strange birdcalls. Outside, the early-morning sky was cloudy; dark swaths of purple rain clouds were interspersed with fast-moving streaks of white and sunrise pink. Plumeria perfume wafted from the taxi stand, and I breathed deeply, anticipation fluttering in my heart like a million vibrant winged insects. Beyond the steel and concrete of the city, the jungle-textured, mountainous wild loomed.

I was Dorothy stepping into Oz. The rest of my life was about to start—a life of color. A life with Todd.

We had booked a suite at the Pearl Beach Resort, which was poised on the edge of Matavai Bay, just east of the city. It was a spacious, clean place, with fountains and big-leafed flora filling the gaps between long hallways and wide staircases. There was a swimming pool, an open-air restaurant, and a black sand beach. The bay was a dark turquoise, shaded gray by the moody clouds overhead. In three days, we would take a ferry to the neighboring island to snorkel in a true teal lagoon.

But for the night, I had the suite to myself; Todd's flight wouldn't arrive until tomorrow morning.

So I unpacked.

Wandered the beach.

Swam in the pool.

Read.

Ate dinner and turned in early.

I awoke at four, having slept nearly ten hours. I walked onto the balcony and watched the sky gradually bloom with light. The tropical breeze was velvet on my skin. White birds swung out of treetops that swayed just beyond my top-floor view. Everything was awake. Everything was lush and pulsing and *alive*.

I felt alive.

I felt lush, and pulsing.

At five, I found a table with a red umbrella shrugged up against the beach on a planked patio. The hotel staff were still setting up, but they brought me bad coffee and heavenly fruit. I lit a nervous cigarette and watched the surf kissing the sand.

Todd would arrive soon. Any minute.

I watched the shape of the beach change as the tide shifted. An hour passed. The sky darkened and opened up, rain pattering on my umbrella. In the distance, beams of sunlight streaked the sky. The rain departed as quickly as it had come, leaving behind the fresh scent of wet soil and hibiscus. I closed my eyes as the breeze caressed my neck.

The breaking of my heart that morning was a gradual thing, like the eroding of a cliff.

It started with the surf, then the rain, then my checking the time. People emerged from their rooms, filled up the restaurant. The waitress asked me about eggs, toast. I barely knew what was happening. I wouldn't allow myself to worry. My heart would squeeze, and I'd tell myself gently: *Don't fret.* Perhaps his flight had been delayed; perhaps he couldn't catch a cab right away; perhaps the cab had gotten lost.

Perhaps: *He's not coming.*

By ten thirty, waves of realization had battered the sandy bluff of my heart; I was the sum of a million fragmented, pulverized parts, drawn into the sea. By eleven, I wondered if I could ever reassemble myself into the solid land I once had been—or if I would remain as strewn and tiny as sand, from that morning into eternity.

I waited through the afternoon. Storm clouds continued to collide with the mountains, and rain pummeled the palms, the umbrellas, my balcony. In our room, I shivered with anger and worry. Either he had stood me up, or something terrible had happened. My mind circled through all possible scenarios, from Todd's plane nose-diving into the Pacific to him organizing this trip with the sole intention of abandoning me as some sort of cruel revenge.

I fell asleep fretting and awoke to the phone ringing. I clambered for it, knocking the base off the side table. I held the receiver to my ear, saying, "Hello? Hello?"

"Ann," Todd said, and a surge of relief thrummed through my core.

"Where are you?"

"Colorado."

"What happened? Was there an emergency?"

A pause. "No emergency."

I was glass shattering against rock. "But I . . . I came all this way."

"Ann, there's something I need to tell you," he began.

"Well, what is it? The bookstore? Keith?"

"Just listen, all right?" His voice was strained. "Before I contacted you about Tahiti, I . . . slept with someone. It was only one time. She's an old friend, and we got drunk, and—" He sighed, rattling the receiver. "The day before my flight . . . she called to tell me she was pregnant."

I closed my eyes against the battery of emotions that smacked me all at once:

Jealousy and betrayal.

Bitterness and sorrow.

Anger and anguish.

"You had already departed, so I couldn't reach you. But I had to talk to her—be there for her—so I missed my flight. Today . . ." His voice grew watery. "She just called, and she . . . she miscarried."

Deep in the tissues of my organs, a dull and numbing hurt bloomed. I didn't dare move. If it was relief that I felt, it was horrible and guilt ridden.

"This news has gutted me. It took me right back to—" He stopped and cleared his throat. "I'm so sorry, Ann. I didn't mean to keep you waiting, I—"

"I came here for you," I said. "Tahiti was *your* idea, not mine. I was doing fine before you invited me here, but now—" I choked back a sob. "Don't you see what you're doing to me? You're giving me whiplash. You're—"

"What was I supposed to do?" he said, his voice all breath and force.

"Not get a girl pregnant!" The situation made me seethe, bleed, *ache*.

"That's not fair," Todd said. "How could I possibly have control over—"

"I'll tell you what's not fair, Todd: flying halfway across the world for a man who didn't come. Loving a man for the better part of fifteen years and never knowing where I stand. Either love me and be here with me, or don't."

"Ann, I *want* to be there with you."

"But you're not."

What I meant was: I was a fool.

I was a fool for having hope when time and time again, the world proved that Ann Fawkes was meant to be alone.

"Copper . . ."

"I can't do this," I said. "I can't sit here—*alone*—and listen to excuses. I just can't."

I hung up.

Fuck him. That's what I was thinking. As I cradled my head in my hands in that big suite in Tahiti, a small part of me cringed to think that I had shut him out, but I had grown so accustomed to looking out for Ann. It was safer to push him away.

So that's what I did.

ANN

I never saw the teal water Todd promised. The next morning, I returned to the airport and boarded a flight back to Rome. Not four weeks later, Keith and I met in LA for my movie premiere.

When I arrived at our hotel, Keith was waiting in the lobby and spread his arms when he saw me. "You've been in the air longer than you've been on the ground, lately." He was aware of what happened between me and Todd, though I'd tried not to involve Keith in our dramas.

I hugged him. "It sure feels like it."

"You ready to see your movie?"

"I really am."

After so many delays, it was surreal watching my story and characters rendered on the big screen. The actors were superb, and while some scenes had been dropped and new ones added, the director succeeded in portraying the heart of my book. I knew it would be a hit, and I was glad—not necessarily on behalf of my own career but on behalf of all the people who believed in the story. I was glad for the studio, the producers, the actors. I was glad for my publicist, editor, and Keith. I was glad for my fans.

After the credits rolled, I was invited to an after-party but declined. Shy and tired and overwhelmed, I opted to walk back to the hotel—and, well, you know what happens next, Maggie. Everyone knows. I don't care to detail the brouhaha that occurred outside the theater, because it's on camera. You can see it on YouTube. You've seen it, haven't you?

MAGGIE

"Yes," Maggie answers. "I've seen it."

Maggie isn't surprised that Ann would rather not go into detail. In the video, Ann exits the theater via a side door, around the corner from the commotion of the red carpet. Clad in a glittery navy dress and high heels, Ann stops short when she sees a figure cross the street and approach her. The footage is grainy from the contrast of bright lights and the dark evening. The audio is muffled; subtitles appear.

ANN: *Todd, what are you doing here?*
TODD: *I came to explain.*
ANN: *Don't touch me.*
TODD: *Can we just talk? Can you hear me out?*

A second man approaches.

MAN: *Hey, this guy bothering you?*
TODD: *No, no, I just—*
MAN: *I didn't ask you.*

ANN: *It's fine, truly.*
TODD: *Just be on your way.*
MAN: *Don't tell me what to—*

The film shows Todd turn back to Ann and touch her arm again. He doesn't grab her; it's more of a tap, as if to get her attention. The other man—who is short and stocky—puffs up.

MAN: *Hey, get your hand off her!*

The other man inserts himself between Ann's and Todd's blurry figures. The camera jostles, as if the operator is jogging across the street for a closer shot. Ann teeters and steps on the hem of her dress. Todd catches her arm so she doesn't fall backward, but the other man clearly misinterprets the contact.

TODD: *Whoa, whoa—*

The second man cocks his elbow and hits Todd square in the mouth.

ANN: *[Screams.]*

Chaotic sounds—shouts, shrieks, grunts, and smacks of fists on flesh—flood the audio. The camera tries to track the scene but gets bumped and topples.

ANN

By midnight, I was sitting on the bed in my hotel room clutching a tiny bottle of vodka from the minibar. Two other bottles rested on the carpet, empty. I had a few bruises on my arm from falling onto the pavement when the fight broke out. My ankles were sore from walking in bad shoes; I rolled them this way and that, watching my bare, unpainted toenails swivel. I didn't know where Todd was or what had happened after Keith found me and whisked me away. Police had come. I'd spotted blood on Todd's lip. The cab that took Keith and me back to the hotel had smelled of incense. Keith had offered to stay with me for a while, but I wanted to be alone, so he'd retreated down the hall.

Tonight was supposed to be triumphant. *My* movie premiere. The movie based on my words, my emotions, my characters. I wondered what Jane would've done in a situation like that, a fight breaking out all around. She probably would've socked Frank in the face. She probably would've taken off her heels and joined the melee.

That was the point of Jane. She stood up for herself even when she was afraid. Jane was the woman Todd thought I was—the woman I should have been.

I hadn't spoken to Todd since Tahiti. Back home, Carmella had helped me talk through my feelings. She was a good listener, but her solution was always to rebound. Throw yourself into the arms of the next man. Visit a club, kiss a stranger. Call Bertie.

I didn't want to call Bertie, though. Just like with Luca, or Dimitri, I couldn't see a future with him—nor any man I met out on the town. Carmella didn't get that. She had laughed and changed the subject. If I couldn't be like Jane, I should've been more like Carmella—free spirited and lighthearted—but that wasn't me. I wanted all or none, just like my mom. Did that make me a romantic or a masochist?

Around one, a soft knock startled me out of my thoughts. My gaze flicked from the ugly carpet to the door. I stood. There was no need to check the peephole; I knew who it was. I just didn't know if I wanted to let him in.

Did I want to hear him out? Did I want *him*?

I hadn't made up my mind when I reached for the doorknob, nor when I saw him standing on my threshold, but the moment didn't feel like an ending. Todd had dried blood on his lip and a red-edged cotton ball taped to his temple. His hair was sticking out on all sides, and the collar of his shirt was flipped up. He hung his head, peering at me from under perfect eyelashes.

"Thank you," he murmured.

"For what?"

"For opening the door." And the way he looked at me—it was the same way he'd looked at me all that time ago, in Venice. It was a look that could move mountains and reverse rivers and pause lightning, if only that might compel me to forgive him. "Can I come in?"

Jane would've told him it was too late.

Jane would've told him to get lost.

But I wasn't Jane. I was Ann—soft, romantic Ann. Was that so wrong?

I stepped aside. When he walked past, I could smell the city night on him. Pavement and car exhaust. I closed us in, and there we were, alone in my room, standing ten feet apart.

A soliloquy waited on my tongue like a legion lined up for battle. There was so much to express: fury, frustration, fear. I shot my first question like an arrow: "Why did you come tonight, Todd?"

"Tradition," he said.

"What?"

"Well, you see, I ruined your book tour, so naturally I had to keep with tradition and ruin your movie premiere too."

"That's not funny."

He ran a hand over the back of his neck. "Sorry. You're right."

"What's the real reason?"

He took three steps forward, then one timid step back. "I wanted to make a big, romantic gesture."

"Then you failed miserably."

"Trust me, I know. I'm so sorry, Ann."

I folded my arms. "You should be."

He had the courtesy to appear sheepish.

"Don't you get it?" I asked, stepping into his personal space, hoping he could feel the wrath emanating off my skin. A bit of Jane, after all. "You showing up here . . . that was performative, not romantic. I never needed a big gesture—I needed you to be reliable."

"You were so happy when I showed up in Rome all those years ago."

"You hadn't just stood me up," I countered. "And it wasn't the miles, it was the fact that you were *there for me*."

"That's what I was trying to do tonight."

I laughed. "Well, it couldn't have gone worse."

"Believe me, I know," he said. "I came to apologize and support you, not make a scene."

"Is that why you're here now?"

"I'm here now because I can't stay away. I can't . . . *do this*"—he waved his hands, expressing some inexplicable idea—"do *life* without you. I felt it when I wrote to you while you were in Lima, I meant it when I invited you to Tahiti, I've always . . ." He reached into his pocket, retrieving an unsealed letter. He held it out to me. "I came here to give you this."

Warily, I plucked the letter from his fingers.

"I wrote it while you were in Lima, before . . . well, just read it."

> *Ann,*
>
> *I have not forgotten the pattern of freckles across your nose, nor the sound of your laugh. I have not forgotten the way your hair gets mussed by your pillow, nor that soft sigh you make as you're drifting off to sleep. I have not forgotten the lopsided frown you make when you're uncertain. I'm gutted to realize that I may never see your mouth again. I would've never stopped trying to make you smile had I known that would be the case.*
>
> *I've always said that you're the bravest, most independent, enamoring, inspiring person I know. The sum of all these things is maddening.*
>
> *Todd*

I rested my fingertips on my lips as I reread the adjectives he'd chosen, hanging on his words as if I were suspended in the weightlessness of space. What kept me returning to Todd? I have ruminated on that question for years, Maggie, and finally landed on this: he always made me see the good in myself. And for a girl who'd never heard her parents say they were proud, that was a gift.

I looked up. "Why didn't you send it?"

A shrug. "I didn't think you'd want to read it."

"That's stupid," I said, staring down at the letter again.

He had the levity to chuckle. "Well, obviously I changed my mind about giving it to you." He stepped forward, and I met his eyes. "The main reason I came here tonight is because you're Copper, and I'm Tod, and—"

I surged forward and kissed him.

I don't know what came over me, only that I was sick of the back-and-forth. Sick of not getting what I wanted. Sick of airports, planes, phones, and misunderstandings. Sick of fighting *against* what I wanted instead of *for* it.

In a way, that was my Jane moment after all. I took what I wanted.

The kiss surprised us both, but his arms were quick to accept me, and his mouth opened to devour mine. We stumbled toward the bed. He unzipped my dress, and it pooled around my ankles. I yanked his shirt over his head, and he unbuttoned his pants. Naked, we tumbled onto the duvet and crashed together with a blend of passion and anger and sorrow and all the many *sorry*s we'd never spoken aloud. We crashed together as only a wave and a beach could, mingling like the rush and froth of the tide. Todd was rearranging the pieces of me once more—but this time, I was thinking to myself: *Yes. Flow over me like the sea. I am sand—I am meant for this.* What is a beach without the tide, anyhow?

When it was over, I lay flat on my back, staring at the ceiling. In the silence, I heard the ocean roaring in my ears—or perhaps it was my blood. My heart stung as if it'd been doused in salt water. Todd lay beside me in the same position, not touching me. I was caught between the fury of reality and the comfort of a dream.

But I had to wake up. I had to know: "The woman who . . . Do you care for her?"

Todd rolled onto his side to face me. "It was a one-night thing. A mistake."

"Todd . . ." I trailed off.

"I know. It's awful."

"Does Keith know?"

"Not the details."

I sat up, stood, dragging the sheet with me, wrapping it around myself. I walked to the window and peered through the thin gap between the curtains. I didn't know if children were in my future—I was forty, after all, and uncertain about my fertility—but thinking that another woman had not only been naked with Todd but gotten pregnant with his child . . . it bothered me. It bothered me, in part, because maybe that was something *I* wanted with Todd. I couldn't see a future with other men, but when I pictured Todd and me together, our future was as clear in my mind as sunshine on a cloudless day.

He came up beside me. "I'm sorry I left you there alone."

I nodded stiffly, staring at the late-night brake lights darting on the street below.

"The only question is, Can you forgive me?" He dropped to his knees, then. I found it strange, looking down at him; I wasn't used to seeing his face from that angle. "Can you forgive me? Could you still love me? Because I wasn't kidding when I said that you're *it* for me."

I took stock of it all. He hadn't cheated on me. He hadn't even lied to me. I was still upset over Tahiti, but I began to wonder if this was something Todd and I could move past. We had been so close to going the distance—it seemed a shame to let an accident steal that away from us.

How many years had I already spent laughing with him, being vulnerable with him, sharing my life with him? I thought back to my book tour in Colorado; he hadn't seen me in *years*, and yet he'd wanted to support my career. I thought back to our long correspondence and the news of my mother's death; he'd flown to me at the drop of a hat, to comfort me in my grief. Even Mohonk was, at first, a sacrifice he'd made for me; he had known how much I'd cherish a family Christmas and tried to set aside his own heartache to enjoy it with me. Even tonight— it had been the wrong sort of gesture, but it was still a gesture. An effort.

Through ups and downs, secrets and misunderstandings, time and distance, letters and visits, Todd had always been there for me. When it came down to it, I couldn't imagine any scenario in which I stopped loving him. I'd loved him for the better part of fifteen years. If I hadn't stopped by then, maybe I never would. Like the curtains in that hotel room, my optimism hadn't drawn completely closed. There was still a gap, and hope streamed in.

I looked down at him, then, and smoothed his hair, my fingers lingering by his ear. "I will never *not* love you," I whispered.

He made a soft little sound, halfway between a gasp and a moan. Alleviation. He hugged my legs, kissed my stomach. "I'm sorry, Copper. For all of it."

I grasped his shoulder, urging him up. He rose above me, drew me against his chest, and held me close. "You're the only one I love," Todd said. "You're the only one on the planet."

MAGGIE

"Is this okay?" Ann asks, and for a moment Maggie thinks her question is still part of her story. "Maggie?"

"Oh, hmm? Is what okay?"

Ann leans forward and clasps her hands. "Hearing about Todd like this."

Maggie swallows a prickly lump in her throat. "Don't censor the story for me."

Ann frowns in an odd, tense sort of way. "Just making sure."

ANN

By the window, Todd held me for a long time. Cars continued to slow and accelerate below; red brakes and white beams blinked in the light-polluted city night. We rocked there by the curtains, seeing out, watching and not watching the world continue on, wishing we could hit pause forever.

When goose bumps washed over my bare skin, we returned to bed. I nestled my back against Todd's chest, and his arms encircled me; he bent his knees until they were flush with the backs of mine. He pressed his mouth into the tender spot between my earlobe and collarbone, and I sighed.

But I didn't sleep. I didn't want to slip into nothingness while he was holding me like that. We'd been apart enough for me to know when to cherish our togetherness. And unlike in years past, when I found an odd sort of pleasure in the torturous longing of long distance—this time, I dreaded our inevitable parting.

"Do you think," Todd said slowly, "that you could ever forgive me?"

My eyebrows creased. "Honestly, I'm not sure there's anything to forgive."

"There's plenty," he countered.

I considered all the things he'd done to protect his grief and guilt—the evasiveness, the secrets. How were they any different from my own shortcomings?

He had kept me at an emotional distance, but I had kept him at a physical one. The truth was, opening up to Todd was easier when he was thousands of miles away; I couldn't witness him screw up if he was in another country. And I expected him to screw up. I expected everyone I loved to screw up, just as my parents had. The problem with expecting people to hurt you is that you're constantly looking for a reason to be proven right, and you forget all the instances you're proven wrong.

"I don't want to think about it," I said. By then, we both had so much to be sorry about—as far as I was concerned, we were even. "I only want to think about how good your arms feel around me."

He grazed my skin with his lips and squeezed me closer.

"When did you know you loved me?" Todd asked after a while.

"Venice," I said without hesitation.

"Venice?"

"You sound surprised."

"Not Greece? Or when I came to Rome?"

"It's Venice and you know it."

He chuckled. "Well, when exactly? What *moment?*"

"Why?"

I felt his smile form against my neck. "I want to know if your answer is the same as mine."

I shifted, trading our puzzle-piece position for one where I faced him, with the heat of his breath on my face and his bare chest against mine. "You loved me in Venice?"

"Of course I did."

I looked into his eyes. "I knew it when you took my picture," I answered. "I was so . . . *content* just being with you on that bridge."

He kissed me firmly.

"What about you?"

"It was the moment you asked me to sit down."

"What? No," I said, pushing his chest with my hand.

"I remember seeing you and thinking, *Wow, look at her.* The way the sunlight hit your hair and your skin glistened with just a touch of sweat."

"That's *lust* at first sight."

"I wasn't done." He nudged my nose with his. "You seemed so bold to invite me to your table. Both generous and brave. Alluring and self-assured. It captivated me, flustered me. When you asked me to sit, I felt blessed."

I didn't recognize the woman he described. I had been anxious and self-conscious. I had been desperately lonely and profoundly glum. Asking him to sit had been an act of survival. But I didn't correct his words. Instead, I took his bottom lip and bit down ever so gently, the way I knew he liked. I bit down until he groaned.

"You like that answer?" he whispered against my mouth.

I nodded. It explained so much about that day. If he had felt that way about me almost immediately . . . "No wonder you pushed me away," I said. How could he grieve Penny and fall in love with a stranger?

He cupped my cheek. "I'm so glad you followed me to Greece," he said. "So, so glad."

We dozed through the blackest hours of the morning, then woke early and placed an order for room service. As the sun rose, so did my worry. I was set to take the red-eye that evening. Then I would be back in Rome, and Todd would be back in Colorado, and . . .

"Everything okay?" Todd appraised me from the desk, where he was pouring coffee and unwrapping our breakfast. "You look tense."

I nodded, but it was half-hearted.

"Come on," he said, carrying the food tray to the bed.

I met his sea-storm eyes. He wasn't wearing his glasses, and it felt like the partition between us was down. "I fly out tonight."

He blinked away and sipped his coffee.

"Where do we go from here?"

"I don't know. I want to figure this out."

"Me too."

"I'm not sure my feelings have changed."

I didn't know exactly what he meant, and I was afraid to ask. Long distance had been an emotional crutch, but that didn't change the fact that Rome was home. Here we were again, facing the same blockade. I felt like I was pressing my palms into a wall, searching for a secret lever, a hidden knob, a trapdoor.

"I want to find a good compromise," Todd said, "but I'm out of ideas."

My mind fumbled along the wall, searching.

A knock came, startling us both. Todd stood and unlatched the door.

Keith was in the hall. His gaze swept from Todd to me, still nestled in bed with the breakfast tray. He rolled his eyes. "*Jesus*, I can't keep up with you two." He pushed past Todd into the room, and Todd allowed the door to click shut.

I could tell Keith was trying to keep the amusement from his face, but he was failing, and the result was a twitch at the upturned corners of his mouth. "My apologies if I interrupted . . . whatever." Keith chuckled to himself. "A long time ago, I made a pact with myself to never get in the middle of you two, so just . . . don't explain, okay?"

I sat a bit straighter. "What are you doing here?"

Keith circled the bed and plucked a strip of bacon from my plate. "After that hellish conclusion to your premiere, I came to check on you—though apparently that was unnecessary." He sank into the desk chair and ate the bacon in two bites.

"That's thoughtful," I said. "Thank you."

Keith smirked.

"Coffee?" Todd poured Keith a mugful, then sat at the foot of the bed, by my feet.

"Remember morning coffee on Santorini?" I asked, taking a sip of my own.

"That *view*," Keith said. "I'll never forget it."

"I was always the first one to get up," Todd said. "Right as the sun was rising. I'd watch the shadows on the water fade."

We all sat with the vision, remembering.

"Look at us, back to reminiscing," Keith said. "I expected to find Ann a puddle of emotion this morning."

Before I could respond, the hotel phone rang.

Reading my mind, Keith stood and answered it for me. "Hello? Oh, yes, hi, Rosa. This is Keith."

My stomach turned, and I looked at Todd, frowning. Why was the studio publicist calling?

"Are you sure you—all right. *Wow*—I—" Keith's face morphed and sank in a mix of disheartenment and anger. "You're kidding." His jaw ticked. "Shit. *Shit*. Okay." He met my eyes briefly, then turned away, hunching over the receiver with his back to me. "Well, what do you—all right, yeah. Of course. Thanks for calling." He slid the phone into the cradle.

Todd stood and placed a hand on Keith's shoulder. "What did she say?"

Panic rose in my chest. Rosa never called me directly. And if Keith was this shaken, well, something was wrong. My voice wavered when I prompted, "Did the fight . . . ?"

Keith's face was red when he faced us again. He glanced between Todd and me. Whatever it was, it involved us both.

I set my plate down on the bedside table and leaned forward. "*Keith*," I said, so sharply that Todd jumped.

With one more darting glance at me, Keith's eyes finally settled on Todd. "They know your name," he said slowly. "You're no longer the 'real-life Frank.' You're Todd Langley . . . and they found the local news articles."

Todd crumpled like paper—forehead, shoulders, back. He lowered himself to the bed again, elbows on knees, cradling his head in his hands. The physicality of his devastation was alarming.

This was the exact outcome I had feared all those years ago, the outcome I had tried to prevent.

"A tabloid found the old headlines, and they"—Keith broke off, restarted—"they drew the connection back to 'Ashes.'"

The news was too terrible for *I-told-you-so*s.

"Apparently Todd was recognized last night," Keith explained, "and a press contact of Rosa's clued her in this morning. A gossip column is going to run a sob story about Todd"—Keith faltered—"and myself. About Penny."

"Why?" I asked, indignant. "Why is *that* necessary?"

Keith shrugged helplessly. "The premiere, the fight, my sad shared past with Todd, your short story—the way it's all connected is juicy."

"But it'll blow over," I said, lifting onto my knees. I rubbed Todd's back. "It'll blow over, and it'll be fine."

Todd was shaking his head. "No, Ann, it won't be fine. They'll dredge up all of it, everything I tried so hard to get over and forget."

"They'll get bored quickly," I said.

"There are gossip publications on the web too," Keith said. "Stories stay online forever."

Todd met Keith's eyes. "This is going to hurt the bookstore."

"It can't," I said in denial. "Tell him, Keith. Tell him this can't possibly affect the bookstore."

Keith ran a hand across his clean-shaven face. "It might."

Todd reached for the phone. "I need to check in. Lorna should be opening soon—it's still early there."

He dialed Dreamer Bookstore, clutching the phone with enough intensity to make his fingers turn white. Keith and I shared a sympathetic glance; then Todd was speaking.

"Lorna, hi, it's Todd." His voice took on an authoritative register, but that didn't mask the concern that wobbled the edges of his words. "Listen, something happened here that might bring . . . everything back into the news for a while. A tabloid—" A pause. "What's that now?" His voice lost its professional resonance. "You're kidding. What did you say?" Another pause. "Good, good. Thank you. All right. Yes, please tell—yes, just say 'No comment.'"

When Todd hung up, he grimaced. "A reporter already called the bookstore."

Keith swore under his breath.

"Lorna didn't give them any information, thankfully." Todd looked at Keith. "What am I going to do?"

Keith could only shake his head.

Todd stood and began to pace, threading his fingers through his hair and balling his fists against his scalp. "I can't have people come to the bookstore all over again, Keith. It was bad enough back then."

I didn't know how to comfort him. To publicly relive the tragedy was Todd's nightmare. He'd spent so much time trying to let go of his past. For the media to invade the most tender part of him and expose his wounds all over again must've felt like a bomb going off in his heart.

I looked to Keith, expecting solidarity or some sort of united front to help Todd come back to center—but Keith was melting down too. His face had turned bright red. And of course—*of course*. Penny was his sister. This was just as invasive to him as it was to Todd, at least when it came to dredging up the past.

I racked my brain as to how to help, comfort, problem solve. I loved these two men more than anyone else in the world. I *hated* to think that I had brought them this unwanted attention. I didn't know how to help them. All I knew was how to run.

But perhaps, this time, running could work?

"Why don't we go on a vacation?" I asked. "God knows you both need one. Why don't we get away and let the bullshit blow over?"

"I don't know, Ann," Todd said slowly. "I should probably be at the bookstore."

"Why? So you can field calls from reporters?"

"Will distance really make a difference?" he asked.

"You're talking to the expert of running away from problems." I pointed to myself. "Let's go somewhere together. Like old times. Let's re-create Greece!"

Keith ran a hand over his face. "You might be right about lying low," he said. "But I need to be in New York with Barbara and Iris. It'll be quiet enough there. You two should go."

Todd stopped pacing and stared at him. "Seriously?"

Keith and I both nodded. "Seriously," we said.

"What about Lorna? She can't deal with all of it on her own."

"She's been working for your family for thirty years, I think she'll manage," Keith said.

"Where would we go?" Todd asked me, and I was relieved that he was actually considering it.

"Anywhere you like."

"I want to go somewhere you haven't been," Todd said. "Somewhere new for both of us."

"Is there anywhere left?" Keith quipped.

I already had an idea. "Actually, there is."

ANN

Six weeks after the movie premiere, the tabloid gossip had settled, and strangely, the bookstore was thriving. Lorna—bless her—was still handling phone calls from angry, overzealous fans of *Chasing Shadows*, people who claimed Todd was the reason I hadn't published anything new—but that was the extent of the drama. Penny had not been a tragedy just for Todd and the Whitakers; that hospital fire had killed others, too, and due to all the public attention, the bookstore saw a surge of local support. Lorna had to hire another employee to help through the holiday season, and aside from receiving a few nasty phone messages from out-of-towners, Todd's team managed just fine.

I kept telling Todd that we could stay in Thailand forever if we wanted to. That's the thing about travel: your normal world feels far away and inconsequential compared to what's up close in front of you. And that only makes it easier to keep going. We lived in a dreamland of togetherness, both ignoring the future and promising each other forever.

First, we went south to see the teal water. We rented a villa for next to nothing on Koh Yao Noi, a quaint island not far from the bling and bustle of Phuket. It was a fantasy place, lush and tangled with vines, with beaches that were powdery and pristine. Rock formations jutted out of clear shallow ocean, narrow and vertical. They looked like ancient stone-head statues, crowned in waxy leaves.

And the *water*—it was otherworldly. A hue of teal so postcard perfect, I was disbelieving. But it was not the only shade of blue. When the sky was overcast or the sun had not yet punctured the surface of the morning, we saw lavender gray and cornflower ripple across the ocean's calm surface. Under the high sun, we boarded fishing boats and walked beaches, witnessing coastal cerulean, jungle azure, deep pools of peacock and sapphire. We swam in turquoise, indigo, aquamarine.

The land, the ocean: it was not unlike my brief glimpse of Tahiti—except now I was seeing it all with Todd by my side, and in that way, there was no better place on earth. I'd traveled my whole life, but this was by far the most magnificent. The company made it so.

Under the diaphanous veil of our mosquito net, nestled among colorful pillows and fresh-smelling sheets, Todd whispered, "Can it be like this forever?"

"Of course."

He stroked my hair. "But at some point—I mean, back home, when the buzz dies down, we—"

"Shhh." I knew what he was about to say. At some point, we'd have to make a decision. Rome or Colorado. Together or apart. But we were postcoital in paradise; this was not the time to discuss it. I wanted to believe that we were the only two people in the world.

Todd didn't bring up the issue again—not while we were in the islands.

We stayed for a full month before venturing to the mainland. With a short flight, we traded blue water for green jungle. The elephant hospital Todd had mentioned when we first met was nestled in the hills of Chiang Mai. Todd stroked the elephants' rough trunks, fed them bananas, and spoke with their caretakers. I purchased a disposable camera and filled it with photos of Todd with an elephant's nose on his cheek, Todd touching a speckled ear, Todd in sandals on an elephant's back, grinning so hard I thought his face would split in two. We looked into the elephants' wise eyes and *knew* we glimpsed an ancient knowledge, a gentle intelligence beyond our own. It was thrilling and humbling, and somehow we'd managed to experience these profound moments together.

Could the rest of our lives be like this? Exploring the world and finding home not in one place but in each other? It all felt too good to be true.

Late December, as Todd brushed his teeth over the sink, he spoke through foamy toothpaste, unable to contain his joy. Todd had befriended the elephants' caretakers—called *mahouts*—and had gotten to help with nontourist activities all day. He was relaying the play-by-play of the elephant bath he'd helped with, even though I'd witnessed the whole thing.

I was propped up in bed, only half listening, counting backward, picturing weeks on the calendar in my head. I was wondering the last time I'd had a period.

Todd spit into the sink, wiped his mouth on a towel, and stalked toward me. He was naked—thin and tan from weeks of exploration in the sun. He paused at the foot of the bed and, like a cat, climbed up my body on his hands and knees.

The calendar in my mind surpassed a month, five weeks, six. It finally stopped at eight weeks and two days.

Todd kissed me, touched me, whispered to me. "I've never been so happy."

I re-counted, my body on autopilot. Eight weeks and two days since my last period.

"Todd," I whispered against his mouth.

He mistook my meaning. "Oh, Copper," he breathed.

"I—" Should I tell him? "Todd, I—" I couldn't, not yet.

He stopped stroking my hip and leaned back. He was clearly ready for me. I felt my body ache at the sight, ache for *him*, as it had ached for so, so long. But my body wasn't the issue—it was my mind that was suddenly racing, harried, distracted.

Todd's eyebrows creased. "Are you all right?"

My gaze caressed his bare form. Todd was a beautiful man. But beyond his beauty, he was a kind man. I saw the care and attention on his face, his immediate concern when he heard the strain in my voice. Over the course of this blissful time of travel, I had fallen more in love with Todd than I had ever thought possible.

The prospect of becoming a mother made me anxious—for one, my age concerned me—but becoming a mother with *Todd* felt as natural as breathing. With Dimitri, a future of matrimony and children seemed foreign and strange, but with Todd . . . with Todd, everything felt right. And despite the tangled knot of his past, I sensed that he'd be happy when I told him.

Nonetheless, the words stalled on my tongue. I wanted to take a test and confirm it first. I needed to throw out my cigarettes. So instead of speaking my truth or my worry, I held the little nugget of hope in my belly, safe and golden.

"I'm fine," I whispered. "More than fine."

I reached for Todd and drew him into a long, lingering kiss.

MAGGIE

Ann continues to speak, but Maggie hangs on her pregnancy news like a lifeline. *Her* lifeline. Ann isn't looking at Maggie—she's staring at the recorder. A part of Maggie wants to interrupt, ask the question. It's bobbing in the water like a life ring, red striped and stamped with the letters *r-e-s-c-u-e*.

Did Tracey lie to Maggie, after all? Is Ann Fawkes her mother?

She doesn't interrupt. She doesn't reach for the buoy. She waits for it to float closer. She waits for Ann to offer it up herself.

ANN

We decided to travel to the capital for New Year's Eve, seeking big-city celebrations to launch us into the new millennium. We'd spent nearly two months in seaside villages, silent beaches, tranquil jungle havens— healing places. Bangkok was all neon and noise. The streets smelled rancid and fire grilled, spiced and perfumed. Trucks laden with cages full of squawking chickens honked at nimble auto-rickshaws. People bartered and yelled and laughed.

Yet all of it seemed bland compared to the news I carried: the pregnancy test I had taken before leaving Chiang Mai was positive.

When I thought about having a child with Todd, an overwhelming elation washed over me . . . but then logistics would creep in. We wouldn't be able to ignore the differences that had torn us apart before. We'd have to answer our previously unanswerable questions: Would Todd agree to raise our child in Rome, or would he insist we live in the United States? Who would make the sacrifice, and would they resent the other? Could we stitch our lives together on behalf of a baby and still harbor the same love and affection for each other?

And that old familiar worry: Could I measure up to Penny?

So I didn't tell him, not yet. I decided to wait, process, and potentially see a doctor—just to be 100 percent certain. In the meantime, I lied and announced I was quitting smoking as an early New Year's resolution. I carried our child like a secret through the busy markets, savoring the effortless bliss Todd and I had cultivated—holding hands, trying each other's food, laughing.

But I couldn't stop nature.

At five in the morning on December 31, 1999, I burst out of bed and scrambled into our bathroom to retch. Todd hurried in after me, holding my hair, rubbing my back. I was hot and nauseous, my soft moans echoing in the bowl of the toilet. The tile was hard on my knees. My body shook as I heaved and heaved. Twenty minutes passed, and when I was empty, I stood and turned on the tap, splashing cold water on my face. Todd disappeared and reappeared with a water bottle in hand, and I swished and spit, cleaning out my mouth.

"You didn't drink the tap water, did you?"

I shook my head.

Todd met my eyes in the mirror. "Do you think it's food poisoning?"

"I don't know," I lied. "Would you mind getting me some crackers and ginger ale from the 7-Eleven down the street?"

He nodded and kissed my forehead. "Be right back."

It was morning sickness. I crawled back into bed to rest. My abdominals were sore from clenching, and I felt mildly fatigued—but also better. Clear headed. After ten minutes trying to get back to sleep, I decided to get up and shower.

Standing under the hot water, I held my still-flat stomach, stroking the smooth skin with my fingers. I hoped it was a girl. I imagined it as a girl. She was probably the size of a pea—but she was *our* pea. Half mine and half Todd's. I began to weep over the beauty of that thought.

Todd and I would figure it out—of course we would. But first I had to tell him.

That night was New Year's Eve. I resolved to tell him then, during the celebrations. It seemed like the perfect way to start the new year.

We took it easy that day, visiting temples and markets close to the hotel. At 9:00 p.m., we caught a three-wheeled taxi—called a *tuk-tuk*—to Khaosan Road, a long strip of colored lights, shoulder-to-shoulder tourists, and vendors hawking their goods. We'd heard the best celebration was there, so we wiggled our way into the throngs of people. Celebratory air horns honked, music blared from open doors, and people shouted in glee. Sparklers fizzed all around. The air was thick with noise and smoke and body odor; though the sun had gone down hours ago, the air shimmered with lingering heat.

My heart was racing, but not because of the sensory overload; I was thrilled simply because Todd was there to hold my hand. I perused silk scarves, deliberated over cheap jewelry, and plucked at expertly made instruments. We grabbed snacks in a fluorescent grocery store and sucked down bottles of Fanta as we were jostled along, lifting our gazes to the strings of lanterns that crisscrossed the street, the neon signs blinking over our heads, and the smoggy sky above.

We were just finishing our snacks when we rounded a corner and found ourselves under yet another awning. Silver and gold earrings were laid out on dirty velvet, not the hoops and zirconium of other booths but royal-looking antique baubles that were dull and scratched but ornate. I touched a pair of gold circles; they had scalloped edges and were the size of euro coins, with dark-red stones nestled in their centers.

The shopkeeper smiled at me and bobbed his head. "You like?" He was a small man with graying hair and delicate hands. He gestured to a mirror, and I held the earrings against my face.

"Twenty baht," he said.

I turned, hoping to show Todd my find. I expected him to be right behind me, but he was at the opposite end of the table, pointing to a ring display. A woman I assumed was the shopkeeper's wife held up ten fingers, spreading them and closing them into fists five times. Todd nodded in understanding.

I set the earrings down and approached him.

"What do you think of this?" Todd pointed at a ring with a blue stone. It had a vintage halo setting and a tooled silver band. Elegant, regal.

I considered the ring, then his face. He had a sincere expression—creased brows over glittering eyes, a half smile that picked up the right corner of his mouth.

Was he proposing?

I stilled, and the people around us faded. I saw a vision of our future: myself in a hospital bed, nestled in Todd's arms, our baby curled on my bare chest. She had Todd's eyes, my nose, his mouth, my hair. A chin and eyebrows all her own. As bright as the sparklers around us, I could see Todd bouncing her on his knee, lifting her up above his head, playing peekaboo. Teaching her how to ride a bike, drive a car.

I had to tell him. I couldn't wait until midnight. I couldn't wait a moment longer. If he wanted to marry me, he needed to know. My heart swelled like a balloon, carrying me high, high above the earth.

"Well, what do you think?" Todd pressed.

"I think I'm pregnant."

"You—what?"

I grinned. I expected him to hug me, to shout with joy, to kiss my cheeks and moistened eyelashes. But instead, Todd grasped my arm and pulled me away from the booth, ducking into an alleyway.

"Ann, are you serious?"

I was floating in the clouds. "Isn't it wonderful?"

"Wonderful?" He cleared his throat. "It's certainly a surprise."

"And so is the ring," I said. "Should we go back to the booth?"

His hands found my waist, and he pushed me back slightly, so he could look into my eyes. "What are you talking about?"

"The ring?" I asked.

He was shaking his head. "Oh, you thought—" His eyes widened, and his hand flew up to his mouth. "Ann, you thought I was proposing?"

"Weren't you?" My body didn't know yet to feel disappointed, to sink. It was as if my balloon had stopped rising and was hovering a mile above the ground, still high in the clouds.

Todd shook his head. "Oh, sweetheart, Keith asked me to get Una a birthday gift, remember? We discussed it this morning. I was . . ." He trailed off and hung his head. When he looked up again, his brows had knitted further, shadowing his eyes. "Are you really pregnant?"

That's when I saw it: disappointment.

"I'm late," I managed, staring into his face, hoping I was seeing it wrong, but—no. He was frowning now. There was no way to misinterpret that.

"How long have you suspected?"

"Only a few days."

Both his hands lifted to his head, where he pressed his palms into his temples. "Have you taken a test?"

"I took a test in Chiang Mai," I said, and added, "it was positive."

"You need to see a doctor, right? You can't know for sure until you see a doctor." Todd was pacing now. "Pregnancy tests are wrong all the time. They yield false positives."

"Todd, I'm certain."

Perhaps he was just surprised. Perhaps he was just considering all the complicated aspects and not the happy ones. After all, I'd done the same thing when I'd first figured it out.

I stepped forward and grasped his wrists, urging him to lower his arms. "We're going to have a baby," I said, staring at the neon reflections in his irises. The heat of the crowded evening pressed against us, and I began to sweat. I was no longer so weightless. My voice was thin. "Sweetheart, aren't you glad?"

For a moment, Todd's face was still as stone . . . and then it quaked. His lower lip quivered, and he began shaking his head, back and forth, back and forth. No, he was not glad. He wasn't glad at all. "I . . . I can't . . . Ann . . ."

My heart popped, and suddenly my helium was gone. I was plummeting toward the earth from thousands of feet up. "Why not?" I asked. "Don't you think we could have a family together? Don't you love me?"

"Don't do that," Todd said. "Don't *do* that, Ann."

"Don't do what?"

"Don't guilt-trip me."

I blanched. "I'm not trying to guilt-trip you. I'm *happy*. I was surprised and worried at first—but once you think about it, you might—"

"You don't understand!" Todd yelled, his voice straining.

I jumped back, startled.

He drew a breath. "I'm sorry, it's just—you don't—I can *never* have a child again. Never. Not after . . ." A sob escaped his lips, and he balled his fists, staring up at the night sky.

"I can't *will* it not to happen," I said quietly. "Why can't you see the good in this, Todd? This will bring us together."

"Are we not close enough as it is?"

My eyes filled with tears.

"I mean, *fuck*. If you're still feeling distance between us, that's your problem, not mine. You don't bring a baby into the world to repair a relationship. A baby sure as hell isn't going to fill that void."

I gritted my teeth. "You can't blame me for feeling distanced," I said, my words tight. "You've held back since the moment we met."

"I'm not holding back now," Todd said, spreading his arms. "We've been together every day for the past six weeks. I'm *here*. Right here."

"Then raise this child with me," I said.

"I can't do it again. I can't *lose*—" He broke off.

"You won't lose *us*," I said, touching his face. "You won't."

But when I looked into his eyes, I could tell I'd already lost him.

"I'm sorry," he said, removing my hands from his cheeks. He squeezed my fingers, then released them. "I am not prepared to love like that ever again."

There. The impact. My heart hit the ground.

But rather than feel broken, I grew angry.

"You can't *love* like that again?" I said. "You can't love me, or our child, as much as you loved your previous family?"

"I love you, Ann, I do. But there will always be a part of me that is locked up, locked away," he said. "There will always be a part of me that is terrified to . . . because if I lost . . ." He shook his head. "It would wreck me. Forever."

"Then why the fuck are you here?" My voice was ice. "Why would you string me along for fifteen years of my life?"

"Don't make me do this."

"Do what?" I asked. "Break up with me? Or ask me to get an abortion?"

A tear slid down his cheek, but I was steel by then.

He reached for me, but I stepped back.

"I would never pressure you to. . . I'm not a monster," Todd said, low.

"Then what are you, Todd? If you're not asking me to get an abortion, then what exactly are you saying when you tell me you can't do this?"

"I don't know." He ran his fingers into his hair, tugging. "I don't know—this is a shock. I . . . I just went through a miscarriage. I need a chance to think."

I wiped my wrist across my forehead, feeling hot and snotty and raw. "Goodbye," I said, hurrying down the alley.

"Ann, wait."

I ducked into the crowd, zigzagging through the chaos. Fireworks were going off somewhere else in the city, and people were cheering. I ran with tears in my eyes, the people and the lights blurring. I shoved shoulders and elbowed my way to the end of the road. I hopped into a *tuk-tuk* and urged the man to drive.

The smog of the city blew on my face as we wove through traffic, swerving around cars, pedestrians, scooters, and tour buses. I felt sick again, but it wasn't the same nausea as that morning—it was acidic, churning sorrow. It ached and fizzed up my throat, and I swallowed it back down. I was no stranger to disappointment. I told myself I could handle it, even as I was falling apart.

My driver merged with traffic, whizzing past a stalled produce truck. Engine fumes filled my nostrils. I wiped away my tears, clenching my jaw. I didn't see a way Todd and I could reconcile after something like this. I didn't see how we could—

BOOOOOOM.

A sudden blast erupted. The taxi jerked sideways. I grasped the bar by my head, holding on as the world tilted. I was floating. A string of beads hanging from the rearview mirror lifted, independent of gravity. My hair rose up around my face; my driver's arms waved in slow motion.

Then:

Pavement.

Pain.

Ears ringing.

Flames and smoke plumed into the sky. Sirens wailed, but all I sensed were the vibrations in my chest, the blinking of lights against my eyelids. My stomach hurt. The street felt gritty under my cheek. I realized my left leg was frozen, pinned underneath the frame of the *tuk-tuk*'s roof. It ached dully, as if it wasn't even mine. The driver lay unconscious nearby, thrown from the vehicle completely. It hurt to lift my head; blood seeped into my eye from a blossom of pain on my temple. With shaky hands, I pushed myself up off the tar and yanked my leg free.

The exertion caused a lightning bolt to crack through my abdomen. Tremor-like cramps followed, and I lay back, terrified, trying to calm myself. A sudden gush warmed between my legs. I looked down. Blood spread on my thighs, my dress. I gasped, a sound both hoarse and guttural, a sound I didn't recognize as my own. Then the world tipped again, and I slumped.

MAGGIE

San Juan Island, Washington State, USA
Friday, January 12, 2024

"Hold on," Maggie interrupts. "You lost . . . ?"

Ann nods, tears glittering on her eyelashes.

"So I'm not . . . ?"

She tips her head to one side, her mouth pressing into a sympathetic line. "Oh, Maggie," Ann says, her voice watery with emotion. "It would be an honor to be your mother. But—I'm sorry, dear—I'm not. And that's the truth."

Maggie wipes her eyes with shaking fingers. "What happens next?"

ANN

I awoke to the sound of a news broadcast, Thai voices nasal and quick. I heard a recording of sirens and chaos. The room beyond my eyelids was bright, and I squeezed my eyes shut even tighter, wanting to block it out. My body felt numb in the unbearable sort of way—the scary sort of way.

"I see her eyes moving," a distant voice said. It echoed slightly off the walls. "Ann?" A shadow passed across my face, and I cracked one eye open, wary of the brightness.

"The light." My throat snagged; it hurt my chest to speak. "Turn off . . . the light."

He stood, the room went dim, the TV muted, and then he returned to me. "Better?"

I blinked, and Todd came into focus.

"There you are," he said, touching my cheek. His hand was warm. "Copper."

I shivered. I was in a drab hospital bed, and the room was so, so cold. "What happened?" I croaked.

"A bombing," Todd said. "The police are still trying to figure things out. Apparently bombs went off in multiple locations. I heard the explosion all the way from Khaosan Road; they evacuated the street. It was chaos."

"A bombing?"

"Some sort of political unrest. That's all I've been able to glean."

"Jesus," I whispered. Memories of fire and smoke and pavement flashed across my vision. Then blood. Too much blood.

I recalled my conversation with Todd, my heart breaking in the back seat of the *tuk-tuk* before it swerved off the road.

My hand shot to my stomach, and a tense ache combusted inside me. "The baby," I said, tears filling my eyes.

Todd reached for my hand, but I pulled back, curling my fist into my chest.

"The baby," I repeated, more forcefully, but I already knew the answer.

"Sweetheart . . . I'm so sorry." His voice was gentle, his brow furrowed in compassion and concern. But it was his clear gaze that tore through me worse than any pain I'd ever felt, worse than the pain of a bombing, worse than the pain of losing our child.

What I saw in his gaze was the smallest flicker of relief.

Our baby was gone, and perhaps he was sad on my behalf and worried for my health, but he was also relieved. And I knew in that moment that all I'd ever see on Todd's face—for the rest of my life—would be that horrible, awful relief.

"Ann, what I said earlier . . ." He removed his glasses and rubbed his eyes. "I was wrong. I was in shock—"

"You're relieved, though," I said. "Right now, you're relieved."

"I'm relieved you're all right," he said.

"But also . . ."

Todd stroked my arm ever so briefly before his fingers fell back to his side. "Ann, at some point, our trip here will end. Then what? I'll return to Colorado to run my business, and you'll go back to Rome. It's the same impasse as before. How could we parent a child five thousand miles apart?"

Ignoring the pain in my abdomen, I sat up straighter and looked into Todd's eyes. "You've been choosing the past over your future—*our* future—for as long as I've known you."

"What's that supposed to mean?"

"Do you really want to run a bookstore forever? Live in your parents' house, with your parents' furniture, and run your parents' business? Do you want to live *their* dream forever?"

"I love the bookstore."

"More than you love the life we could have together?"

"But I'm not going to throw my life away for—"

"Me?"

He pressed his lips into a thin line. "I am really, truly sorry about the baby, but . . ." He shook his head.

I quaked. Todd would never let go of the past. And if he couldn't let go, he'd never be able to embrace me. Not fully. I was tired of competing with his grief and losing. I couldn't win against a memory.

My words were a whisper, but they came with force: "Get out."

"What?"

"Get. Out."

"Ann—"

"If that's truly how you feel, I don't ever want to see your face again."

ANN

Rome, Italy
April–June 2000

I'll never forget the headline: Unraveling the Mystery of Ann Fawkes: The Reclusive Author Opens Up about Love and Life Overseas. It sounds so harmless, doesn't it?

As you know, Maggie, the press caught on to the bombing and my hospitalization in Thailand. Todd and I had gone our separate ways, and I was back in Rome—at turns despondent and filled with an inconsolable rage over what had happened. Keith and Carmella kept encouraging me to move on, and I was *trying*, but then April came, and Keith rang from his business phone.

My publicist was also on the line, which clued me in to the bad news from the start. The short of it: I was to take an interview with a prominent magazine—to let a sleeping dog lie, I'll omit their name here—to get ahead of the story. After the debacle at my premiere and subsequent tabloid buzz, they didn't want the drama to spin out of control.

So I agreed.

I met the reporter at a nice hotel bar in New York and treated her to a couple gimlets. She turned on her recorder and rested it between us. The interview started out like a game of tennis: tense, but equally matched.

The reporter asked about my mother, and I spoke of her tragic life and even more tragic death, and how I hadn't known about the cancer until the week she died.

The reporter asked about my travels, and I told her many glamorous and gritty stories about the world: my home in Rome, the volunteer teaching, and where I planned to go next (South Africa on assignment for *Travel + Leisure*).

The reporter asked about my fiction writing, and I told her the dullest version of the truth: there was talk of compiling my short stories into a collection, but the movie had taken precedence over the past year, and my focus had been elsewhere.

The reporter then asked about Todd, and when she called him by name—well, there's no other way for me to put it—I panicked. I gulped my drink, and the gin and lime blazed a sour river down my esophagus. I believe I coughed; I remember the reporter offered me a cocktail napkin, which I took.

"Did I catch you off guard?" she asked, and maybe she looked a little pleased with herself, though I'm sure my memory is skewing the details against her.

"Perhaps you're unaware of the fact that I don't talk about my love life on the record," I said.

"After all that drama at the premiere, don't you want to set the record straight?"

I wiped my mouth with the napkin and slid it back across the bar to rest in front of her again, as if I'd merely borrowed it. For a beat, the reporter stared down at it, then tracked the recorder between us, then met my eyes again.

"What about the bombing in Thailand? He was there with you, wasn't he?"

Though it was jarring to hear Todd's name come out of her mouth so matter-of-factly, I knew *this* question was coming, because my team had prepared me. After all, the root of her query—Thailand—was the reason I had taken the interview in the first place.

I sat a little taller on my barstool. "Yes, we were there celebrating the New Year when multiple bombs went off in the city. I was in a taxi accident and ended up spending a night in the hospital. I appreciate your *concern*"—I paused to allow the venom of my tone to permeate—"but as you can see, I've recovered."

She appeared nonplussed, save for a quick sip of her gimlet. Then the gears of her thoughts seemed to catch on something. She set her glass down with a soft, two-note clatter. "A whole night? What injuries did you incur, if you don't mind my asking?"

"I—" The memory gripped me like a waking nightmare, of which I had no control. The explosion, the way the world tilted, the impact of pavement, the blood between my legs. I tried to blink it out of my mind's eye, but the vision wouldn't dissipate.

I'm still not certain what came over me, Maggie. I took the interview barely four months after my miscarriage, and I was still in grief over losing a baby, Todd, and the future I had thought was finally within reach. I could've lied and told the reporter all my injuries were minor, but I know she wouldn't let me evade so easily. I could've told her the partial truth, that I sprained my ankle and had a minor concussion. I could've said a lot of things. The reporter's question was a trap, I knew, but by my logic that night, the only way out of that trap was to tell the truth.

"I had a miscarriage," I said.

I must admit the shock on her face was worth the bitter truth. Thus far, the interview had been tense—unnecessarily ruthless, to be honest, when everyone knew I didn't owe my private life to anyone, that just by showing up I was affording the magazine a luxury—but this reveal visibly surprised her. With one word, we were suddenly both off balance.

"You—due to the car accident?"

"*Tuk-tuk.*"

"What?"

"It was a *tuk-tuk* accident. An auto-rickshaw. Not a car." I don't know why I fixated on that detail—I was flailing in the sudden exposure. I wanted to be clear with her about the details—even the minutiae.

"Wow." The reporter, for all her faults then and in the future, appeared to genuinely sympathize. I still occasionally wonder if it was her or her editor who spliced my words. "I'm so sorry for your loss."

"Thank you."

"Did Todd know about the baby?"

I hesitated. "Yes."

"Where is he now?"

My god, Maggie, I wanted to cry. Tears stung the corners of my eyes, but I refused to let one fall. This reporter didn't deserve my emotion. She hadn't earned it. But there I was, sitting in a hotel bar in New York, desperately waiting for the moment I could leave to get dinner with Keith before my flight back to Rome, wondering if my life would ever look like *normalcy* or *contentment* after a long road of getting neither. And sure, I was at fault for so much of my own suffering, but that interview—I didn't deserve that.

"He's in Colorado, running his bookstore," I said.

"Are you—"

"Listen, I'm going to level with you, all right?" I didn't want to remain off balance. Better to go bold than appear weak. "When the tabloids decided to misrepresent me and Todd at my movie premiere, we both faced harassment and ridicule. So we took a vacation. That's understandable, isn't it?" I paused, but not long enough for her to respond. "In Thailand, I learned I was pregnant. I lost our child in an auto-rickshaw accident—the result of a bombing. In the aftermath, I was devastated and angry. Todd and I had a fight. I told him to get out, and he left." I leaned toward her recorder and stared into its red blinking eye to enunciate: "That's all I'm going to say on the matter."

I slid off my barstool. "I believe I've given you plenty of juicy details to work with, but make no mistake: the public might own my work, but it doesn't own *me*. You think I want my pains and insecurities broadcasted?" I placed a hundred-dollar bill next to our finished drinks on the bar. "I want privacy. I want respect. Not as a writer, but as Ann. The woman. The *person*. I hope you and your superiors do well with this interview, because it's the last one I'll ever give. I've given enough."

I exited the bar.

I held it together for about a block before I broke down, smearing the tears on my cheeks with my sleeve as I hurried to the restaurant. When Keith asked how it went, I told him everything that had happened. He said it wasn't so bad. That was the point, anyway: to set the record straight. The interview might have been a disaster, but at least I'd told the truth.

If only they'd been interested in publishing the truth.

Come June, the article dropped.

Sitting in my apartment in Rome, with the magazine draped across my lap and Carmella rubbing my back, I tried to convince myself that it really wasn't so bad. The magazine had spun a story that was at turns epic and enthralling. They'd printed all my best stories: the truth about my mother, a few fun anecdotes from my travels, even the facts of the movie premiere. For the most part, I sounded mysterious and likable (and this made the magazine sound important, for having the clout to capture my honesty).

The last section was what did me in.

The reporter—in that conversational first-person perspective of an immersive interview—wrote that she then asked me about my personal life. She waxed poetic about how I opened up, the gracefulness of my candor, blah blah blah. Then landed on the ultimate misquote:

"I lost our child [. . .] and he left."

I despised those brackets. The missing multitudes. The context omitted and the implications introduced. Todd hadn't left because I had a miscarriage—he left because I told him to. That was the difference. And that difference was everything.

(Later, under threat of lawsuit, the magazine claimed they cut the article for space. I ultimately didn't sue—by then, the damage was done—but the reporter and editor *did* retire shortly thereafter.)

Todd called me a week after the article published. I hadn't heard from him since Thailand. There was no preamble, no polite small talk.

"Do you have any idea what you've done?" That's how he began.

"Todd, I am so—"

"Save it."

I had never heard him sound so angry—*livid*. Though there were thousands of miles between us, I cringed. The article had made *him* the bad guy, and I had never intended that—nor did I believe it. I had rehearsed my apology a million times, but I hadn't yet called.

"What were you thinking? Is that how you remember Thailand happening? You *told* me to leave."

"I know I did. They—"

"Oh, Keith relayed the whole misprint explanation. What I don't get is why you were talking about me in the first place. Do you have no respect for my privacy?"

That question stung.

Todd continued. "You suck everyone into your vortex and expect us to survive it, but Ann, there's no surviving your bullshit."

"I don't know what to say," I said, and that last word dripped with liquid shame.

"The bookstore was vandalized last night," he said. "I arrived to broken glass everywhere. The front windows, the door. A copy of your article was stapled to the doorframe with the words 'woman hater' written across it in Sharpie."

I sank to my mattress. "You're kidding."

"I wish."

"I'm sorry, Todd." I had spent my whole life wondering why other people were constantly letting me down, but maybe I was the letdown. The fuckup. The failure. Maybe it was my fault that people never stuck around. I was reckless, and selfish, and withholding. Just like my mother. "I am so, *so* sorry. I'll pay for all the damages."

"I don't want your money. I want my life back."

"I didn't mean for this to—"

"You think I give a shit what you meant?" Todd asked. "I know you were hurting that night, but so was I. Not for the life of me did I ever expect you to air our business to the public like this. But I guess I was stupid to think that that night could simply remain ours."

"Please, Todd, you have to understand—"

"I don't have to do anything for you."

The agony of his anger bored into my stomach. "Forgive me," I said, curling forward. "Please, Todd, you have to forgive me for this. I'm begging you. I never intended for any of this to—"

"I will never forgive you. *Never*," he said and ended the call.

MAGGIE

Maggie pauses the recorder. "Wow, Ann, I—"

There's a knock on the door.

Both Maggie and Ann turn, startled.

"Were you expecting someone?" Maggie asks.

The day has aged. They've been sitting on the couch since five, and it must be past noon now.

"I wasn't," Ann says.

Maggie's hunger makes her wonder: "Not Matt with some food?"

"I wish," Ann says. "But I forgot to make an order."

The doorbell rings, and Ann hurries to answer it. Maggie stands, trailing Ann, curious but also distracted by the intensity of Ann's story. After the past forty-eight hours of revelations, her heart is as raw and delicate as a peeled peach.

Ann opens the door, and at first Maggie doesn't believe who is standing there. Perhaps it's sleep deprivation. Or a trick of light from the sunshine beaming through the foyer skylights, casting a glare. But as Maggie warily approaches, the woman at the door only appears more real, and maybe she's here, after all, only no, she should be in Colorado, so why, why, why is *Tracey* in Washington, standing on Ann's front porch?

"Mom," Maggie whispers. "What are you doing here?"

"Hi, dear." Her body is rigid, but there's a sheen in her eyes.

Ann looks just as surprised as Maggie feels, her face pale, her head cocked, blinking. "Tracey. It's been a long time." How is Ann's voice so level? How does she sound so polite and unfazed?

"Do I get a hug?" Tracey asks Maggie, spreading her hands.

Despite her anger, Maggie falls into Tracey's embrace, and it feels like home. Tracey's soft arms envelop her, squishing her against a full chest and tummy, wrapping her in the kind of maternal comfort only the woman who raised her can offer.

When they pull apart, Ann interjects, "Well, come in. Please, sit down. Would you like coffee? Tea?"

Tracey's mouth is pinched. "Water, thank you."

"What are you doing here?" Maggie repeats, walking Tracey to the couch.

Ann fills a glass in the kitchen and brings it over. The three of them sit, with Maggie in the middle. Tracey's hair is a bit staticky, piled up in a bun, and it occurs to Maggie that she probably came straight from the airport. Her parents told Maggie about Todd only three nights ago; Tracey must've booked a flight almost immediately.

"I can't believe—"

"You weren't answering our calls," Tracey says stiffly, softly. "What has she told you?"

Ann frowns. "Nothing about *you*."

Tracey snorts, a single rush of defiant air. "I find that hard to believe."

"Still can't stand me?"

Tracey flinches.

"What's going on?" Maggie cuts in. The tension between them is like a steel cable about to snap.

Both women hush, watching each other with narrowed eyes. The silence builds, the steel cable practically groaning.

Maggie is the first to break. "Someone say *something*!"

Tracey startles, leaning back. Ann's eyes dance.

"It's not my place to tell her," Ann says.

Inside Maggie's chest, shock, disbelief, and fear converge.

Tracey stands and starts pacing. "You know I never liked you," Tracey says to Ann. "Keith was always going on about you. Working his ass off only to have you shirk your responsibilities. You always acted so *untouchable*."

"Now hold on, that's not fair," Maggie interjects, but Tracey is a mountain with magma burning at her core. It's a fire Maggie never knew existed, now rising to the surface, an eruption mounting.

Tracey fixes Ann with a searing glare. "You just *had* to wedge your way into everything with no regard for . . . for . . ." Her eyes glisten with rage, and she stutters over her thought.

Ann rolls her eyes. "You're a hypocrite."

"You're a liar."

"There is only one lie I've uttered," Ann says coolly. "*One.* Unlike you, who has been lying to Maggie her entire life."

Tracey is visibly shaking, but with anger or fear, Maggie can't tell.

Ann continues. "You paint *me* as the liar, but your family has always been full of *sh*—"

"Stop," Maggie bites out. "Both of you."

Tracey sinks to the couch again, grasps Maggie's hand, and squeezes it tight. "Dear, I didn't want to hurt you. I hate to do this now . . . and *here*." Tracey sighs, as if she's fortifying herself. Tears wobble along her lower lashes, and Maggie's heart hitches. "Maggie, dear," Tracey whispers. "Sweetheart, I'm your mother. Your biological mother."

Disbelief pools in Maggie's lungs, making it hard to breathe. She glances at Ann—expecting rage at Tracey's implication, that Todd and she were *together*—but all Maggie sees is relief on Ann's face. Relief, because this must be the final lie—and the final truth. Even though it doesn't make sense.

"How?" Maggie sputters.

This answer doesn't feel like a life ring—this feels like drowning. Betrayal drags her down. She tries to make sense of the confession, but there's no sense to be found. "How?" she repeats, because, for the life of her, the truth is unfathomable. The truth is salt water, filling her lungs, burning her eyes, making her choke.

TRACEY

Colorado Springs, Colorado, USA
August 1999

The best and worst thing I ever did was sleep with Todd.

It was the best because I got you, Maggie, and you are the light of my life.

It was the worst because I hurt Bob and my family, and defiled Penny's memory.

I want you to know that we all love you dearly. We only kept this from you because, well, at first you were too young to understand the nuance of what happened. And then we were afraid you'd be so hurt that you'd never forgive us. And I guess if that's how you feel at the end of this, I have no right to ask different of you. I only ask that you don't punish Bob for my mistake—he's been punished enough.

The circumstances that led me to the bar that night were long and tangled. I'd had a nasty fight with Bob, but it was years in the making. We'd been trying to conceive practically since we got married, and it wasn't working. I was ready for the next step—doctors, sperm donors, adoption, *anything*—but he wouldn't even see a specialist. Our sweet

Bob—he's a man of few words, but he'll do anything for his family. Yet this was something he couldn't do on his own. I don't think he could handle what he considered to be his biggest failure.

But at the time, I didn't understand Bob's resistance to getting help. I wanted answers, and he wanted the problem to disappear. I thought he was being insensitive, evasive, cold; he was struggling under the weight of duty, shame, and my imposed expectations. The issue was personal and emotional, and therefore our fights were also personal and emotional.

Do you ever feel as though your problems are in your house, hanging in the air like smoke? That's how I felt that night. The rage, disappointment, and blame that Bob and I had kindled—it was smoke in the air. I was gasping and couldn't breathe. So I stormed out and went to the closest bar I could find—for a drink, but more importantly, for distance. Fresh air.

Here's a vile truth I never thought I would have to admit: a part of me wanted to get back at Bob. For the past year, I had been noticing other men. At first it was harmless. A glance at a handsome man in the grocery store or a preoccupation with the tattoos of a guy at the gym. But as the marital fights grew more contentious, my glances lingered, and my mental curiosities grew vivid. I fixated and fantasized.

I am so ashamed to admit this to you, Maggie, but you have to know: I never planned to act on those feelings. I thought it was merely the thrill of temptation—desperate thoughts I indulged when I was alone or couldn't sleep. I worried that Bob would never face our problems head on. I was angry and powerless. Sometimes I wondered if an affair would wake him up. Force a change. It wasn't right for me to think this way, to imagine acting out to get his attention, but when an animal is stuck in a trap, there reaches a point when they'll chew off their own leg to see freedom again. That's how desperate I felt; my desperation made me self-destructive.

On the short drive to the bar, I drove behind a Camry going five under the speed limit. There was a **BABY ON BOARD** sign in their rear window. It reminded me of when Penny found out she was pregnant and how fretful she was. I had been so jealous. All I wanted was a family—even then—and suddenly Penny had one but wasn't sure she even wanted to keep it. I loved Penny fiercely, but seeing her have everything I wanted just dropped in her lap . . . it was hard to take.

Still, back then, I did all I could to support her. I threw her a baby shower, set up her registry, researched the best strollers, and bought her a **BABY ON BOARD** sign for her car. Penny even asked me to be the godmother.

The gesture of consolation stung.

And then, of course, I didn't even get *that*. When I lost my sister, my first thought wasn't shock over the tragedy of it. My first thought was that I wouldn't even be a godmother. You can't control your thoughts amid a tragedy like that, but *oh*, the guilt of my first thought corroded my heart. I'd loved Penny dearly, as you know. And I've struggled with my grief ever since, just as Todd did. But that doesn't change the fact that I had a selfish mind on the day she died.

When I saw the **BABY ON BOARD** sign in that Camry, I sped around it. In light of my argument with Bob, it felt like a taunt, but it also reminded me of Penny, and that guilt unhinged me just a little. Just enough. I sank into another daydream of kissing a stranger. As far as I was concerned, it was just another fantasy to occupy my torment while I drove.

I didn't expect to see Todd sitting in a dark corner of the bar. Relieved to see a familiar face—thinking he'd keep me from doing something stupid—I collapsed into the chair opposite his. Todd had broken up with his girlfriend because he was still hung up on Ann, and he was drinking to forget. I told him I was drinking to forget too. He handed me his whiskey, and I knocked it back. Then more appeared, and I knocked those back too. And soon we were spilling our feelings.

Soon, our broken hearts morphed into a mutual understanding. Two childhood friends, drunk and broken and desperate for comfort.

We connected over our shared sorrows in the worst possible way. And this is the part where we made a mistake. A fucked-up mistake.

I cheated on my husband with my dead sister's widower. It's a horrible, ugly fact that will forever weigh on my conscience. The only reason I don't regret that night is you, Maggie. I hate that you came from pain and sorrow and mistakes, but you will *always* remain a blessing. I love you more than anything.

That night, I returned home saturated with self-reproach. I might've wanted Bob to wake up, but not like this. I resolved to lock this skeleton in the closet. I reasoned that the emotional rot of guilt—forever—would be an apt punishment. But as you know, this wasn't a mistake I could so easily forget.

Weeks later, my period was late, and I knew—I *knew*—that it was Todd's. I had no one else to talk to about our dirty secret, so I called him. He bailed on his trip to Tahiti with Ann, even though I told him not to. A few days later, I was regretting telling him at all; I didn't want anything to do with Todd. I hated him for being there at that bar—for being just as weak as I was that night.

That's when I lied to him, Maggie. I told Todd that I lost you, hoping to save us both some shame and regret.

Then I came clean to my husband.

Bob and I moved forward, because we wanted a child and because Bob is a saint. That's the only way I can explain it. He could've left me. He could've walked away. But remember when I said that Bob would do anything for his family? Well, he did the impossible thing: he forgave me. He stepped in, and we never spoke to Todd again—or at least, we tried.

Five years later, Ann was the one who figured it out. She saw your picture in some correspondence with Keith, and she recognized Todd's eyes—you have Todd's eyes, Maggie. And since Todd had told Ann about our affair and my "miscarriage," Ann put the story together—the timeline, the lies, everything.

Though they were no longer together, she called me and urged me to come clean to Todd, but I wouldn't. I didn't want to blow up the life Bob and I had built for you, Maggie, because it was a happy life, and at the time, Bob and I had been naive enough to think that we had put all the secrets behind us.

This weighed on Ann, though.

She betrayed me and risked *your* happiness, Maggie, by confiding in Keith. And once Keith knew the truth, it was a huge mess, because of course he confronted Todd. For a while the whole family was angry and hurting and messy—and how could I blame anyone for feeling that way? I had disrespected everyone I loved by keeping that secret.

I was humiliated and furious with Ann. I still am.

But I'm even angrier with myself, for hurting so many people with my lies. Most of all you.

I don't know if you remember, but Todd came to meet you, once, at a family barbecue. He didn't stay long. After his loss, Todd was terrified of committing. You didn't deserve his uncertainty, so that afternoon, I told him he had to stay away. We agreed to give you an uncomplicated childhood. Todd was a good man, Maggie. He had his flaws, but he stayed out of your life for good reasons—or at least, good intentions.

When you called me a few nights ago, I told you about Todd to stall you—to save time—so that I could tell you the whole truth in person. Because Maggie, I know it must seem unforgivable, but we lied *for* you. We thought we were doing the right thing, protecting you from this awful secret. I was terrified you'd hate me as I hated myself. I wanted to spare you the awfulness—we all did—and I admit I wanted to spare myself from the shame too. But I realize now that we were harming you, and for that, I am so sorry.

That's all of it. That's the truth.

I know I was wrong to keep secrets.

I know I was wrong to lie.

Of course, it's too late now.

My only hope is that you'll find it in your heart to forgive me. Because even if you denounce me as your mother, I'm still the woman who raised you, and I will always—*always*—love you.

MAGGIE

Colorado Springs, Colorado, USA
Sunday, January 14, 2024

Maggie thought that when she got on the plane, she'd feel ready. Then she thought when she got *off* the plane, she'd feel ready. Now, she's standing outside a coffee shop in her hometown, and she's still not ready. Not ready to step through the door and sit down across from Bob, who is stiffly waiting and has not yet spotted her outside. Not ready to face this new reality and rewrite her life.

She hasn't forgiven Tracey—that would be a lie, and she's done with lies. She has, however, found a little empathy. Because, as she's learned over the course of Ann's story, grief does strange things to a person.

Maggie draws a long breath of cold Colorado air into her lungs. The sky is a deep, clear blue; there's ice on the sidewalk, snow piled in the street gutters. The crisp winter air smells like home: sledding and making snow angels with Bob, sipping hot cocoa and wearing Christmas pajamas with Tracey.

Maggie has every right to be angry, but where has anger gotten this family? Tracey carried her anger—toward herself, toward Ann, toward Todd—for twenty-four years, and that helped no one. Maggie could conjure her own and let it fester inside her forever, but standing here on the sidewalk, she doesn't want to be angry. Her childhood memories might be framed by lies, but they are nonetheless happy.

Maggie steps inside the coffee shop, the door jingling. Bob looks up from his untouched mug, and his eyes crease. At first Maggie suspects it's from the bright sunlight streaming through the window, but then tears fall. She's never seen Bob cry. She's seen his balled fists when he's frustrated, the subtle furrow of his focused brow, the slight lift of his shoulders when admitting to Tracey that he ruined their appetites by taking Maggie for after-school milkshakes—but tears. Those are new.

He stands, they embrace, and it's a strong one. Bob's arms shake a little, but he squeezes hard, stealing Maggie's breath in the way he has always hugged her, ever since she was little.

"Sit down, dear, sit down," he says, gesturing to the seat across from his own. "Do you want a coffee?"

"I'm all right."

"Do you want mine? I think they gave me almond milk." He makes a face.

Maggie can't help a smile, but it quickly fades. "No, thanks."

"Your mother wanted to be here."

"I hope she understands why I'm still . . ."

Bob grasps her hand. His palm is calloused and wrinkled, but strong—just as she remembers. It's the hand that steadied her when she was learning to walk, the hand that led her into school on the first day of kindergarten, and the hand that will someday lead her down the aisle. Her father's hand.

"I'm sorry," he says. "*We're* sorry."

Since Tracey's admission to Maggie rehashed the whole ordeal, the Whitaker Family text thread has remained silent. Maggie wonders if the family will ever recover from this final secret, now exposed. She fears her presence will only remind them of Tracey's shame. It's an old wound that never properly healed, now reopened.

When Maggie was a child and Ann exposed the truth, Keith and Barbara, Natalie and Jackson, Tracey and Bob, and Todd and Ann had been the only ones to know. According to Tracey, Keith had done what he could to keep the family together, all three Whitaker siblings moving forward with Tracey's lie. The least painful path, they all decided. But the news irreversibly changed Keith's friendships, and a rift grew between Keith, Todd, and Ann.

Keith was the most loving, forgiving person Maggie knew. If Keith was so affected by the news back then, how can the rest of the Whitakers expect resolution now?

"We lied to you and betrayed your trust," Bob continues. "I, of anyone, should've known better than to entertain more secrets—even well-intentioned ones. But at the time, I was so hurt by what Tracey did, and I wanted to protect you from it."

Of everyone involved in this mess, it's Bob whose strength and loyalty stun Maggie the most. "How did you . . ." Maggie trails off, shaking her head.

"Stay?" he finishes for her. "I'm a stubborn man, Maggie. It's my strength and my weakness." A pause. "Therapy helped."

Maggie shakes her head. "I don't see how I can move past this."

Bob's face falls, and he stares at his unwanted coffee for a moment. But then he meets her eyes, and squeezes her hand again, and says, "I think we all have to accept that things will never be as they once were." He tips his head, a sad but hopeful smile forming. "But that's okay because we can forge a new path together. If that's what you decide you want."

Whenever Ann spoke of her own mother, Maggie heard the regret in her voice, the what-ifs and amends never made. Perhaps Bob is right: they shouldn't try to repair the past—but they *can* try to build a more honest future.

Maybe. "I still have a lot of feelings to process," Maggie explains. "But I want to work through it—with you."

Her parents, for all their faults, blessed Maggie with a childhood of warmth and love. And while she wouldn't have chosen the deceit for herself, she knows that love was at the heart of their decisions. Maggie always believed that forgiveness came at the end of a long repenting road—but now she thinks forgiveness is a beginning. It isn't a signal that the healing is done but an invitation to heal together.

There's a lot to rebuild—but for Maggie, this family is worth the effort.

"We have no expectations," Bob says. "We only want what's best for you—even if you decide that distance is best."

If Maggie has learned anything from Ann, it's that while distance can provide perspective, it doesn't solve trials of the heart.

Now it's her turn to squeeze Bob's hand. "I want to figure it out together."

Outside the coffee shop, Maggie gives Bob the address of her friend's apartment where she's staying; she's not ready to stay in her old bedroom just yet, but they agree to a family dinner the following night.

When he hugs her goodbye, it feels as if he might never let Maggie go. It doesn't fix the damage done, but it *does* ease the pain. And for now, that's enough.

"I love you, Dad," Maggie says.

"I'm not sure I deserve that title."

Maggie steps back. "Are you kidding? You've been here for me since before I was born," she says, staring into his red-ringed eyes. "You forgave Mom and stepped in one hundred percent. You're Bob McCallum, and I am Maggie Whitaker-McCallum. The truth doesn't change that."

Her father pulls her close again, weeping, but Maggie knows his tears are, ultimately, filled with gratitude.

MAGGIE

When Maggie pulls up to Ann's house on San Juan Island, she isn't surprised to see the bakery's delivery van parked out front. Gathering her purse, voice recorder, and notebook off the passenger seat, she slides out into the sunshine. The now-familiar brine of the ocean wafts through the trees, mingling with the sweetness of pine sap. The sky is bright and feathered with clouds, and the steam of her breath curls around her face.

"Afternoon," Matt says, walking toward her from Ann's porch.

"What did you bring us?"

The masculine angles of his face widen into a big smile. "Ann's favorite. It's a surprise."

"Just out of curiosity, how much does Ann spend on pastries per year?" She holds up her notebook. "I'd like to include the figures in my exposé."

He leans closer to stage-whisper, "She doesn't pay."

"Now there's a scoop."

"No, seriously. You know she owns the bakery, right?"

"She what?"

"Well, co-owns."

"Hold on—"

Matt's walking away now, back toward his van. "Ask her about it."

Maggie rolls her eyes, but she's still smiling as she takes Ann's porch steps two at a time.

Ann opens the door before Maggie can knock. "*Finally*," she says, opening her arms, and Maggie realizes—awkwardly—that Ann is going in for a hug.

The embrace is light and airy but warm—sincere.

"How was your flight?"

Before Maggie left Washington, she called Grant and explained her predicament. She apologized for the sudden hiatus from work and, at Ann's insistence, agreed to return to Washington in a couple of weeks to complete the interviews. Maggie flew into Seattle from Denver the previous night; this time, she didn't take any wrong turns on the drive to San Juan.

"Easy enough," Maggie replies, following Ann inside. "Matt said you own the bakery? How did I miss that?"

"I never told you," Ann says with a smirk. "It's part of the last chapter in my story."

"Should we get started?"

"Gosh, no, not yet. We have to eat first." Ann hurries into the kitchen and presents Maggie with a plate of doughnuts. "My favorite."

Maggie chuckles. "Why was I expecting 'Ann's favorite' to be something more . . . sophisticated?"

Ann carries the tray over to the wingbacks. Outside the big windows, the sea glitters gold with sunlight, rippling like satin.

"You've been fooled by my glamorous stories of French pastries and Italian espresso. You forget that I am an American. A *poor* American, by origin. My mother and I used to eat doughnuts every Sunday morning. She'd buy us two each with her tip money."

Maggie selects a big swollen chocolate-topped doughnut and takes a bite.

"Good choice," Ann says.

Custard spills out, dripping onto Maggie's chin, and she grabs a tea saucer from the tray to catch any globs before they fall into her lap. Ann hands her a napkin.

"Fabulous, right?"

Maggie nods, wiping her smile free of custard.

She can't believe she's back in Ann's living room. The last time she was here, her whole life story was rewritten. The past three weeks in Colorado were intense. Her first dinner with her parents was volatile, but after two more awkward visits and a family counseling session, Maggie finally felt her heart ease and warm toward her mother again. They still have a long road ahead, but Maggie knows they'll get there together.

The rest of her visit was filled with family. Barbara and Iris came to see her, as well as Natalie and Jackson and Maggie's closest cousins, Ronnie and Fiona. The Whitakers spent their time clearing the air. The meals and outings didn't feel the same without Keith, but they were pleasant in a new sort of way: they were honest. And Maggie finally felt like she belonged.

But now, inside Ann's home again, thoughts of the podcast start swirling. Her conversation with Grant this morning was encouraging, but she can't help but feel nervous . . . and a little sad. This is their last sit-down. The final interview. Brit has already started splicing earlier recordings. Ann used a local studio while Maggie was on her family hiatus to record the bits of the story that they missed the first time—and the aftermath of Tahiti and the movie premiere, where Ann purposely omitted Tracey's name from Todd's admission. The podcast probably could have interviewed Ann remotely for the last chapter, too, but Grant insisted Maggie go in person, citing some ineffable magic quality in Ann's voice when Maggie is in the room. Maggie can't hear it, but even Brit swore to the difference.

"What's wrong?" Ann asks. "It can't possibly be the doughnut."

"Ha. No, I'm . . ." Maggie stares at Ann, admiring her golden eyes and the faint freckles across the bridge of her nose. "I'm savoring this."

Ann leans back, mouth puckering slightly. "I'm going to miss this too," she says. "I'd very much like to stay in touch. To be . . . friends."

"Is it strange," Maggie begins, "knowing that I'm Todd's daughter?"

"The moment I saw you on my doorstep, I knew that you weren't just *a* Maggie, you were *the* Maggie," Ann says. "Like Tracey mentioned, it was your eyes. And your lips, a little bit. You have Tracey's nose, but the way you frown in thought is all Todd."

Maggie must be frowning that way now, because Ann grins.

"Why didn't you say something?"

"It wasn't my place. I had done enough damage to your family."

"So our first interview . . ."

"I panicked. I didn't want to involve myself all over again." She shrugs with one shoulder. "But then you admitted your relation to Keith—and spoke of that *feeling* you had about needing to talk—and I knew I couldn't simply turn you out."

"You *had* to know that your story would surface . . . questions. Plot holes."

"That first afternoon, after you left, I was shaken. I called Tracey." Ann spots the surprise on Maggie's face. "I know, I'm sneaky, aren't I?"

"What did she say?"

"She didn't pick up. I left a message and told her it was time to tell you. I wasn't going to do it, but the story might unearth some things, and she better prepare to lay it all on the table."

"Wow."

"I know." Ann smiles a wan little smile. "I don't blame Tracey for disliking me—I would, too, if I were her. The fatal flaw of your family is their ability to shove their emotions down." She shrugs. "I lived a lot of my life stifling my emotions, feeling shameful over them. But the best, most defining moments of my life—as you now know—are the ones where I practiced radical honesty with myself and the people around me. Tracey resents that quality in me because it's disruptive. I never took pleasure in being that sort of catalyst for her. But here I am, me, Ann. I like to think that my presence in the Whitakers' lives has, overall, been positive."

"Do you have any regrets?" Maggie wants to know.

"Regret is poison to the soul at my age." Ann takes an unceremonious bite of a jelly doughnut—her second, after polishing off a simple glazed one—and jelly squirts out, a glop landing on her jeans. "Oh, shoot. You'd think I'd be better at this by now." She wipes the jelly off with her index finger, then walks to the kitchen to rinse her hands and dab at her pants with a wet paper towel.

Maggie walks over to lean against the kitchen island. "If you knew about the waves you were about to cause, why did you do this story?"

"Because . . . a lot of things. I wasn't lying when I said that it was time to tell my whole story. This podcast was a way to honor Keith and Todd. Remember them." She pauses thoughtfully. "And it's the story of your father. You deserved to hear it—even if it was colored by my bias."

"Oh." The backs of Maggie's eyes begin to sting, her vision getting a little blurry. "I'm sorry, I'm getting emotional."

"It's fine, dear." Ann ushers her to the wingbacks once again, a dark spot fading on her jeans. "In the last few years, I've lost my best friend and the love of my life. Without Keith and Todd . . . the world feels very empty. It has been a delight recounting the memories with you. Even the painful ones."

Settled in her chair again, Maggie takes a sip of the tea Ann prepared. "I saw Barbara. She asked for your address."

Ann's cheeks crease, a hopeful brightening. "Did she?"

"She wants to send you some of Keith's mementos. And maybe arrange a visit? Natalie too. They said they always liked you, despite everything."

"I would love that," Ann says with a watery little cough.

369

Maggie selects a festive, rainbow-sprinkled doughnut from the tray, hoping the cheery treat will keep her voice from breaking. "I don't think I ever thanked you."

"For what?"

"For being honest with me. For changing my life—" She breaks on the last word anyway.

Ann reaches forward, steadying Maggie's quivering hands. When Maggie looks up, she sees tears in the corners of Ann's eyes, too, making their color an even more vibrant amber. "While we're doing this thanking thing, I think I ought to thank you too."

"Why?"

"I've been trying to write Todd's story for years, but there was always something missing. You being here, encouraging me, listening . . . you were the missing piece. These interviews are a gift—even the illegally recorded bit." She winks, and a tear drops into her lap. "I am eternally grateful."

Maggie squeezes Ann's hand, then sinks back into her chair. For a moment, they sit in silence. This is their final interview. Best to savor it.

ANN

After the article dropped and Todd vowed to never forgive me, Rome—
the city I once thought had romance in every corner—became a black-
and-white noir. I moved through the world as if the world wasn't there.
My correspondence with Keith dwindled; my short stories became thin
and unpublishable; I stopped taking article assignments. I spent too
much time in my apartment, smoking cigarettes and staring at myself
in the mirror, horrified by the wrinkles and gray hairs that had emerged
while I wasn't paying attention. The older I became, the further from
love and family I seemed to get.

That was the sad-sack story I was telling myself.

Not even bubbly Carmella could pull me out of my funk. She'd
married one of her vendors (a longtime flirtation) and no longer had
time to run her restaurant, have a husband, *and* look after her wreck of
a bridesmaid. We still met up for cappuccinos in the mornings, but she
eventually stopped asking how I was. She knew how I was: inconsolable.
Miserable. So she spoke of other things: the food-tour schedule, fresh
produce she was excited about, the woes of acclimating to living with a

"messy man." I listened politely and felt so, so happy for her—and so, so sorry for myself.

Then, shortly after the anniversary of my mother's death, a package arrived. The brown shipping envelope was torn on one side, revealing the Bubble Wrap interior. I didn't recognize the name or return address. With care and curiosity, I opened the envelope from the perforation and slid out a book. Upon realizing what it was, I dropped the packaging where I stood in the center of my apartment.

The book was a well-loved first-edition hardback of *Chasing Shadows*.

Gently, I opened it—the spine creaking as I did—and thumbed through the sun-stained pages. Their state shocked me. Delicate pencil notes crowded the margins like clematis vines climbing a trellis of words. The pencil had bracketed paragraphs, underscored passages, and marked lines as *beautiful* or *wow!* There were stars next to key moments, hearts and arrows by the scenes when Jane and Frank were happy, and little cartoon water drops—or tears?—in the margins beside particularly trying mother-daughter scenes.

The graphite appreciation astounded me. Pride blossomed in my heart.

As the pages fluttered through my fingers, I landed on a makeshift bookmark: a receipt. The ink was gray—barely readable—but its origin gave me pause. Listed at the top was the bookstore in Denver where I'd given the final reading of my tour—the reading my mother had failed to attend. The receipt's purchase date was listed for that exact day.

I traced the waxy receipt paper with my finger, churning this fact through the fallow ground of my mind. Come to think of it, the handwriting in the book looked familiar. Slanted and perhaps more compact, but familiar. I'd seen it on Christmas and birthday cards. Permission slips for school trips. Dollar amounts on bounced checks.

In the rush of realization, I flung backward through the book until I landed on the title page. It was signed by me, a special note written to a random reader in a moment of personal disappointment.

> Pam,
> Tucked within life's greatest letdowns are the gold nuggets of love, laughter, and family. May you find all three more often than you lose them.
> Ann Fawkes

I recalled writing that special note, the note for a woman who had my mother's name, who couldn't make it to the reading, so her husband went instead. He had looked so out of place—a work shirt smudged with grease, a scruffy face.

Could it have been . . . ?

I pinched the thick stack of pages and bent them through my fingers, flipping rapidly through, searching for clues. When nothing else turned up, I set the book down and retrieved the envelope to check for anything left inside. Sure enough, crumpled at the bottom was a single piece of lined stationery.

> To Ann,
> You don't know me but I'm William "Bill" Price's son, Jeremy. My father passed away a few months ago and I found this copy of your book in a box in his attic labeled "Pamela."
> I don't think you ever met my father, but boy, did he love your mom. He was there through all the chemo and he was there when she died. She was everything to him.
> I know you had a rocky relationship with her and I don't mean to bring all this up to hurt your feelings so apologies if it does, but your mom was always a kind and

supportive woman to me and my dad. I was in college when they got together and she turned his life around (they were each other's reasons for getting sober), and that made my life better, too.

Your mother believed in my father when no one else did. She gave him all the money you left her so he could start his garage. I know you were angry about this so I'm writing to tell you that the garage was worth the trouble. Its success has brought my family many blessings. My father passed it along to me before he died. It's my honor to fill his shoes and support my wife and kids with his legacy. I know I'm just a stranger to you, and maybe part of a bad memory too, but I wanted to thank you for your part in making the garage a reality.

Anyways, this was your mom's copy of *Chasing Shadows*. I figured you would want it. She was real torn up that she couldn't make it to your signing. She had just started chemo and it was taking a toll, so Bill went to get it signed. He didn't tell you who he was on account of not wanting to ruin your big night, but Pam was elated when he brought the book home. She treasured it like nothing else. Bill used to read it to her when she was holed up in the hospital, and she died with it on her lap. She was proud of her daughter. Don't know if she ever told you that, but now you have the proof.

Take care,
Jeremy Price

It's strange to suddenly receive everything you've wished for, all your life.

Acceptance.

Love.

Pride.

I didn't know what to do with that stark perspective. All of a sudden, the lens had zoomed way out, and I was Dorothy realizing I'd had all those things all along. Except unlike Dorothy, I couldn't go home, because home was long gone. Home had died of liver cancer in August 1990.

For years, I'd wondered with disdain why my mother hadn't seized the opportunity to travel *with* me rather than criticize me. Now, I understood her courage: She hadn't run from dissatisfaction and hardship, as I had. She struggled—for years and years—but ultimately, she had faced it. And by facing it, she had found true happiness.

I clutched the book to my chest and didn't let it go for a long, long while. Tears misted my eyes, and I vowed to write Jeremy back, to thank him for this immeasurable gift. I vowed to do better by the people I loved. To write Keith, to celebrate Carmella's happiness, and to honor my own legacy by picking up my pen again. I vowed to stop expecting to be disappointed by the people I loved and by myself; to instead expect *more—ask* for more—so I might live a more fulfilling existence. By my mother's example, I vowed to stop running and finally face my fears and flaws. If she could transform her life for the better, then maybe there was hope for me too.

After this reflection, I walked straight to my desk. I set my mother's book upright in front of me, opened my notebook, and began to write.

There's a reason my new collection is titled *Letters I Should Have Written*. Not all of them are in true letter form, but most are. It's a collection of short stories from my travels: all the many letters I should have sent home to my mother, who would've loved to live vicariously through her daughter, had her daughter not been too selfish to see the current of love thrumming beneath all that desperate, well-meaning failure.

MAGGIE

For Mom.
—*Dedication,* Letters I Should Have Written, *by Ann Fawkes*

San Juan Island, Washington State, USA
Thursday, February 1, 2024

Maggie brushes her fingers across the advance copy of Ann's new story collection. The cover is a pale blue, overlaid with embossed lettering in a fine scrawl.

"That's a close-up of some writing she did in the margins of *Chasing Shadows,*" Ann says, pointing to details.

"It's beautiful," Maggie replies. "I'm sorry she's not here to see it for herself."

"Me too," Ann says. "But I know she'd be proud."

ANN

San Juan Island, Washington State, USA
2000–2015

I lived a whole lifetime in the years that followed.

Shortly after I received his note, I visited Jeremy. He showed me the garage, and I was blown away by how big an operation it was, with ten employees and a nice lobby. We drove past the home my mother and Bill had purchased together, a modest foursquare with a backyard and a purple mailbox—her favorite color. They didn't live there long before my mother passed, but I was glad she spent her last years in a proper home.

It was on that trip that I decided to make amends with America. As I walked the suburban streets outside Denver, I gradually realized I had held that grudge out of pain that had nothing to do with the place. A couple walking a golden retriever smiled as they passed. A woman jogging while pushing a stroller offered a quick wave. Cars drove slowly, and nobody seemed loud or abrasive anymore. I'd been searching for home in places when home was in my heart. It was in the people I loved, and in myself.

What would my life have been like had I figured this all out sooner?

Upon my return to Rome, I dove headfirst into being a better friend to Carmella. I reconnected with Bertie, and we dated for a while. I tutored restaurateurs and waiters for free and wrote the rest of my days away.

Then a new opportunity arose: Carmella's brother-in-law was an American, and his parents had a house in Washington State, on San Juan Island, an island so northerly that they had a view of BC, Canada, off their back porch. They were going to spend the summer in Italy, and they needed a house sitter.

"I like it here, Carmella," I said when she came to me with the offer.

"You might like it there too," she said.

I continued the conversation in Italian. "I like staying in one place, though."

"No, you don't. You're Ann. You love travel. You love to explore new places."

"I'm not sure I'll like Washington."

With her hands on her hips, she asked pointedly, "Have you visited Washington?"

"I have not," I said.

"Then you can't say you don't like it," she reasoned. "You will go."

So I went . . .

. . . and I stayed.

Damn it if Carmella didn't know me so well by then. I immediately fell in love with Washington's moody skies and regal evergreens, and the whales that feed just off Lime Kiln Point. I enjoyed the seclusion from the rest of the world, the tight-knit island community. I liked that everyone knew everyone—by the end of my first summer house sitting, I knew everyone too. It gave me a sense of belonging to walk into a coffee shop and know the barista by name, to recognize people's cars and wave at them as they drove past. I'd experienced some of this in Trastevere, but on San Juan, the community was a way of life.

The trip reawakened the true source of my wanderlust: my romanticism. The change of scenery reminded me that the world could still feel new and exciting. Rome would always be my first love, but maybe it was time to branch out again. To start anew.

I was elated when Carmella's in-laws decided to retire in Italy. They'd fallen for Rome as I had fallen for San Juan Island. I told them to stay in my apartment and feed my stoop cats until they found a more permanent place; they sold me their house. By New Year's Eve, they had shipped my meager possessions from Rome to Washington, and I started a new chapter.

Amid opening *another* restaurant, Carmella tried her hand at letter writing with me, and we spent a lot of money on overseas calls. I continued to write and maintained an email correspondence with Keith. I didn't ask after Todd, and Keith didn't mention him.

I was forty-six when Keith offhandedly shared your photo with me, Maggie. It was a family photo from your fifth birthday party. I recognized Todd's likeness in you immediately, and, well, Tracey explained the rest. The only thing I'll add is this: Todd deserved to know about you. And, despite everything, I knew I would never stop caring about Todd. So, I intervened. And despite the rift it caused between me and Keith and the rest of the Whitakers, that is one thing I don't regret doing.

But that was my only interaction with the Whitakers regarding you. I had recently started dating a nice divorcé who had a sweet seven-year-old son. Scott owned the bakery downtown and made fresh bread with my initials scored on the top. He'd never read my book, didn't care for travel, and didn't think I was particularly interesting for being a nomad most of my life. He loved me for the woman I was in Washington—the woman who no longer smoked, who instead had a garden, walked on the beach, read by the fire. The woman who had lived a whole life before him yet was happy having his companionship *now*. It wasn't a passionate or furious love—it was a simple, contented, straightforward love.

Scott was exactly what I needed.

We spent seven wonderful years together before he passed away of a heart attack in 2012. He left his business and his estate to me and his son, Matt. He left me feeling empty but deeply grateful for the time we'd had together. I was there for Matt in his grief, and then I went back to living alone.

I continued to write with enthusiasm. Whenever I was alone with my thoughts, the words began to flow like a spring from a mountain. When I was younger, my relationship with my work had been so unhealthy; I thought that I was capable of creating great work only if I was in pain, but in reality, I'd been using my writing as a form of cathartic wallowing. It was in the years after Scott's death that I realized I could write away the pain—and keep going, even in bliss. I no longer reserved my creativity for times of suffering; my work gained depth by acknowledging joy.

So did my life.

It was a chilly day in March 2015 when everything changed again. I opened my mailbox to find a single envelope, and it was like receiving a letter from the past. I recognized the handwriting immediately and tore it open while I was still standing in the driveway. A crisp winter-frost wind ruffled my hair; I wore only a thin pair of leggings and a sweater, and I shivered as I unfolded the letter.

> *Dear Ann,*
> *I've been thinking about you lately. I know it has been a*
> *long time since we last spoke—a decade, is it?—and I'm*

sure this letter seems out of the blue. Did you notice we just surpassed the thirty-year anniversary of our first meeting? I thought about calling you last fall but didn't think you'd want to hear from me.

Then, last month, Keith came home to Colorado for his mother's funeral, and after a few beers, your name came up. Keith mentioned that you two have all but lost touch, and this news saddened me. I know your role with Maggie is to blame; I'm sorry to have come between you two. I'm also sorry that I never properly thanked you for bringing Maggie's existence to light. I can't imagine it was easy for you to advocate for me like that; in fact, your act of compassion astounded me. I wanted to thank you then, but I never found the right words — I hope these painfully late ones will do.

Reminiscing with Keith brought a lot of feelings back to the surface. Feelings I should've shared with you way back when. I've always been afraid of how much I love you. Afraid of losing you. I know it doesn't make any sense, but that fear made me want to push you away. That night in Bangkok . . . I was so afraid, Ann. I was downright terrified that history would repeat itself. I was wrong to imply that I couldn't love you like I loved Penny — the truth is that I loved you more. I knew that if I lost you, there would be no coming back.

I let my grief get in the way of us. I know this isn't news to you, but here I am admitting it — finally. I should've let you in. Your love and vulnerability were my most treasured gifts, and I should've been the partner to you that you had been to me.

I have many regrets in this life, but my most painful regret is hurting you.

I'm not sure you knew this, but after Bangkok and the article drama, I sold the bookstore. It was a bitter transition, but I didn't want to drag my parents' legacy down with the bad press. Then I learned of Maggie, and her existence forced a change in me. There's no other way to put it. I realized I'd been holding on to the past so hard that I'd let my future escape me. You were right about that, Ann. You were right all along. I'm sorry it took so much strife to force me to face the truth.

Shortly after Tracey cut me off from Maggie, I sold my parents' house, bought a new place in Loveland, and finished my psychology degree to become a counselor. I feel like a new man, save for one thing: I still care for you.

So here I am, writing you a letter again—a letter that I'm sure is too little too late. But I'm getting too old to keep my feelings to myself. I'm getting too old for timidness. As far as I see it, I don't have time to hide behind my grief anymore. Life isn't worth living unless I can love with everything I've got—and I want to give all I've got to you, Copper.

I'm sorry it took me so goddamn long to realize it.

This is how I feel. How do you feel?

Ever yours,

Todd

I raised my eyes from the letter and stared into the granite sky. The clouds were low and heavy. I heard the sea crashing behind my house, beyond the cliff. My vision sank to my slippers, the ground. My garden was bare, save for some early spring crocuses poking through the hard soil. The wind continued to blow, rocking me.

It amazed me how quickly his letter brought me back to our long, winding journey together. I thought I had let the part of me that loved Todd—the passionate, hurt, irrational part—go dormant. I had spent over a decade *not* thinking about him. But suddenly the ground was thawing, and parts of me that I thought had died for good were coming back to life. My roots stirred. My leaves greened. I reread his letter and felt my heart bloom like the crocus—brilliant and fresh in a land that had once been so cold and cruel, so inhospitable. It occurred to me that perhaps it wasn't a matter of pain and heartbreak—it was a matter of timing. Thailand had been our autumn. This silence had been our winter.

Now, it was suddenly spring, and the things that had once stood in our way—differences that were once so huge—didn't seem so mighty anymore. In fact, they seemed inconsequential.

I rushed inside and wrote him a letter in return.

Todd,

What a strange thirty years it's been. Filled with so much love and heartbreak you'd think I'd never want to hear from you again. But the funny thing is that I see your sudden letters in my mailbox and I'm always—always—glad.

Thank you for writing to me. Thank you for this apology. I forgive you, of course. And I hope you'll forgive me, too, for all of it. But especially for being so afraid of you. Because that's what I was: afraid. I was always so terrified of losing you that I often held you at arm's length (we're one and the same in that way), but frankly, that was stupid. You say you're too old to be timid; I'm too old to be stupid.

More to the point, you asked how I feel, so here it is: How would you like to move to Washington State?

I'm living on an island away from the hustle and bustle of everything, and I think you would like it very much.
Love,
Ann

Within the week, I'd received his reply.

Dear Ann,
Send me the address and give me a month.
Todd

MAGGIE

For that voice inside you telling you to believe.
—*Dedication,* Chasing Shadows, *by Ann Fawkes*

San Juan Island, Washington State, USA
Thursday, February 1, 2024

"So he came?"

"He did."

"And the public never knew."

"No one needed to know but us."

"How did you keep him a secret?"

Ann chuckles. "Few people actually knew what he looked like. They knew his name and his business, but not so much his face."

"What did Keith think?"

"Oh, he mostly stayed out of it. He did visit once, though. It was the last time I saw him. He said he loved me, and he was glad for our friendship, and that he was happy for Todd and me. We kept in touch after that, swapping occasional letters and phone calls." Her mouth quirks. "It wasn't the same as before, but when he died . . . things were all right, between us."

Maggie sighs, wishing Keith were still alive. Wishing a lot of things were different, but also at peace with how they are now. "What was it like, seeing Todd after all that time?"

"Melancholy."

The sun is zinging through the trees, edging through the windows. Soon, Ann's whole living room will erupt with light—but for now, only a few beams glimmer in through the glass.

"How so?"

"His age, for one. He'd aged a lot since the last time I saw him—so had I—and seeing him . . . I *felt* the time that'd passed. The time we wasted. All the deliberation, all the *not* saying what we really wanted. We wasted a lot of time, Maggie, and seeing the unfamiliar wrinkles on his face and the gray in his hair . . . it made me realize what fools we were."

"But you were glad to see him?"

Ann doesn't smile, but her eyes light up as if from the inside. "We made the most of our final years together."

Maggie sips her third cup of tea, waiting for Ann to continue.

"Don't get me wrong, I was elated to see him," Ann says. "Overjoyed. Humbled. Grateful. We spent our first week in bed, talking and apologizing and making love. We had a lot of catching up to do. I suppose the best way to explain it is that this chapter of 'Todd and Ann' was easy. We cherished each other, because suddenly we realized we weren't the immortal youngsters we once were. I feel lucky for the time we spent together, and also like I earned it, if that makes sense. But I still wish we'd forgiven each other sooner."

Maggie has no follow-up response to that statement. She's still in awe that she's here in the first place, talking to Ann, hearing this story. She also has no idea how the podcast will come together. It feels too big a story to properly tell.

"What is it?" Ann asks, studying Maggie's face.

"I have no idea how I'm going to piece this thing together."

"I do," Ann says.

"You do?"

Just then, the light bursts through the windows, and the whole room brightens.

"This is as much *my* episode as *yours*, Maggie."

"What do you mean?"

"To tell *my* story, and Todd's story, you have to tell *your* story too. You have to be a presence in the episode."

Maggie recoils at the thought. It sounds impossible, unwieldy, and far too vulnerable. "I don't know if Grant will go for that."

"He will."

"And how are you so sure?"

"Because I called him."

"You . . ." Maggie trails off, irritated at first but growing amused. "Of course you did."

Ann flashes a mischievous Cheshire cat smile.

"I don't know, my family . . ."

"It's just a suggestion," she says, raising her palms. "But I think you'll come to the same conclusion."

"I'll consider it." Maggie wavers. "So . . . is this it? Are we actually done?"

"Not quite," Ann says. "I have one more surprise, but it's just for you."

She turns off the recorder, leaving it on the table as she leads Maggie through the house, down an unlit hallway, into her office. There are bookshelves, boxes, and a love seat shoved into a corner. Front and center—and most notable—is the worn wooden desk. On it rests a Brother typewriter—likely the one on which Ann first typed *Chasing Shadows*—plus a MacBook Air, a tabletop lamp, notebooks, papers, a corkscrew, and a small turquoise horse.

Ann doesn't linger. She ushers Maggie to the boxes in the corner: the letters from Keith and Todd that Ann showed her weeks before.

Maggie's attention darts from label to label, the relics of Ann's life, distracted until Ann pushes a shoebox into her arms.

"What's this?" Maggie asks.

"A gift. Open it."

Maggie lifts the cardboard lid and peers inside. It's filled with papers, some folded, some not. She recognizes Todd's handwriting, but when she lifts the top sheet out of the box, her breath hitches.

Dear Maggie, it reads.

"What is this?" she repeats, staring at the paper, throat constricting.

"A letter," Ann says. "Well, many letters."

"I . . ." Maggie trails off, reading.

> *Dear Maggie,*
> *I only just learned about your existence, yet I am filled with guilt. How could I not know you were here on earth? How could I not know what you look like, the sound of your voice, the lilt of your laugh? I don't know what foods you enjoy, or the subjects that interest you, or . . . anything.*
>
> *How can you be mine when I know nothing about you?*

Maggie stifles a choked little whimper, an involuntary release of vocal pressure.

"After everything that happened, I tried to give them to Tracey, so she could one day give them to you," Ann explains. "But she would have nothing to do with them, and since you didn't know who you were to Todd, I . . ."

"Kept them," Maggie says. "All this time."

A nod.

Maggie thumbs through the letters, landing on another.

Dear Maggie,

Today I met you for the first time, and I believe it was my last. I thought we'd have some deep connection when we met. I expected to be bowled over with feeling but . . . I wasn't. You might be "of" me, but you are not mine. I might be your father, but I am not your dad. You are Tracey's and Bob's. You are your own.

And that's okay.

Nonetheless, I've decided to write you these letters, in case you ever wonder about the man named Todd Langley who loved you from afar.

"I don't . . ." Maggie shakes her head, her vision flooded.

Ann pulls her into a half embrace, her arm around Maggie's shoulders. "I never read them. He told me I could, but it didn't feel right. They're for you. Do with them what you wish."

Maggie slides the lid back on the shoebox and clutches it to her chest. "I want to keep them to myself, I think."

Ann squeezes Maggie's arm. "That's a fine plan."

ANN

San Juan Island, Washington State, USA
May 2019

Planted at the patio table on my deck overlooking the Haro Strait, I set
down my pen and flexed my cramped fingers. A crisp wind kicked up
from the sea far below, threatening to extinguish the candle in the center
of the table. The air smelled of pine resin and rain. Summer was around
the corner in the Pacific Northwest, but for now the balmy afternoons
still succumbed to evenings made for fleece and wool.

I'd been bent over my notebook for hours, trying to tie two ideas
together by way of a metaphor that just wasn't working. I knew by
then that such quagmires couldn't be rushed or forced, but that hadn't
stopped me from obsessing over words all afternoon. Some things never
changed, but I'd come to enjoy the wrestling match of syntax, truth
grappling with fiction.

Behind me, the sliding glass door creaked. When I looked back,
Todd was there, two wineglasses grasped in one hand, stems crossed. In
his other hand: a bottle with a blue label.

"You look like you could use a break." He settled into the chair
across from me, and I moved my notebook to the side to make way for
his offering.

"I'm not sure if I need a break or new story entirely."

Todd uncorked and poured. "Why don't you get Keith's opinion?"

I shook my head. "Friends don't let friends read first drafts." I took up my glass, sniffing the familiar white. "Besides, this is my problem to solve."

"Am I interrupting?"

I rested my palm atop his chilly fingers and squeezed. "Not at all."

Since he'd moved to San Juan, we'd fallen into an easy rhythm. He was the sea to my beach, after all; we had drawn together and apart for thirty-five years, and I knew better than to push him away now. Our present existence was a high tide, and I would take every moment I could get—even if it meant setting my writing aside for the night.

Todd settled in, stretching his legs out underneath the table—and his foot knocked the wobbly wire base. Our wineglasses teetered; I managed to lift them before they toppled off the deck.

I chuckled at his clumsiness.

"I thought I'd grown out of spilling your wine," Todd said, cheeks flushing.

"Good thing I still find it charming."

Todd shook his head, tucking his feet underneath his chair. "Any more thoughts about summer travels?"

"Why don't we stay home this summer? Let Carmella come to us?"

"I like that idea."

I lifted the wine to my lips, belatedly realizing that I'd tasted this before—a long time ago. I twisted the bottle to examine the label. When I looked up again, Todd was grinning.

How he had managed to track down a bottle of Assyrtiko wine, I wasn't sure—but I chose not to ask, simply for the sake of novelty. By then, mundane musings were the full extent of mystery that I could palate: the surprising notes of flint and honeysuckle in the wine, how it tasted of Santorini and yearning; the way the blue in Todd's irises deepened as the evening swept in; how my heart still trilled like a songbird in his presence; and how his gaze remained ever trained on me, as if I was the only person in the world who mattered.

"What is it, Copper?" Todd asked.

I blinked, refocusing on that handsome face of his. "Nothing," I said. "I'm just content."

The corners of his eyes crinkled, and then he hefted the bottle of wine, refilling my glass. And it occurred to me that finally, *finally*, I was no longer waiting for him, but savoring him.

MAGGIE

Colorado Springs, Colorado, USA
Saturday, May 4, 2024

Iris is tending the grill like her father used to, the only Whitaker to inherit Keith's skill with charcoal—but that doesn't stop Bob, Barrett, and Uncle Jackson from hovering. The scent of brats and veggie burgers wafts through the backyard, making Maggie's mouth water as she sits with her cousins Fiona and Beatrice on the lawn, surrounded by the familiar sights and sounds of childhood.

Until today, she hadn't visited this backyard in years. Maggie expected it to feel like entering a funeral, a solemn affair, but when she'd pushed through the creaky side gate with a plate of cookies in hand, seeing everyone here . . . well, it had felt like a celebration, little fireworks going off in her chest, people cheering and hugging her in welcome.

In many ways, the place looks the same: the same pool, with the one cracked tile that Keith used to use as a starting point for cannonballs; the same three picnic tables, lined up banquet-style; the same old playset with the staticky plastic slide, the bolts of which used to burn the kids' bare legs in the summertime.

But the backyard has changed in the years since Maggie has visited too. Barbara added new planter boxes, umbrellas for the tables, string lights. Glancing at the shaded patio set where Barbara, Tracey, and Natalie now sit, Maggie wonders how many of these new features Barbara bought just for this occasion: their first reunion without Keith.

When Fiona and Bea leave Maggie in search of more lemonade, Maggie checks her phone. There's an unread notification in Keith's Fanclub, a new text thread she created. Previous messages go all the way back to February this year, when the foundation of Maggie's life was imploding; in the months since, amid the efforts to rebuild—family counseling sessions and visits home—the new thread has been a refuge of jokes and memories and love, with all her favorite people.

The newest message reads: Almost there, hit some traffic, with the initials *AF* listed next to the text bubble. The message was sent fifteen minutes ago.

Pulse jumping, Maggie is sliding her phone back into her pocket when she hears the rumble of an engine and the crunch of gravel beyond the fence. Everyone else hears it, too, a hush falling over the group, save for the thump of the wireless speakers still playing music from Barrett's phone. Maggie stands, and she's halfway to the gate when it squeaks open, and then there's Ann walking through with a bottle of wine in hand.

Maggie approaches her, offering her a quick hug in greeting. Ann's slight form feels wooden in Maggie's arms, and when they pull away from each other, she can see the worry creasing Ann's eyes. But before Maggie can offer words of encouragement, Ann's gaze flicks past her.

"Welcome, Ann," Barbara says, brushing past Maggie for her own turn embracing Ann. Even with everyone watching, Maggie can tell the hug is sincere; Ann's eyes close briefly in an expression akin to relief, and Barbara's cheeks are flushed pink with emotion when they pull apart.

"Thank you"—Ann coughs, clearing her throat—"so much, for having me here today."

Natalie is next in line, grasping Ann's shoulders and eyeing her with a scrutinizing glare. "You haven't aged a bit," Natalie complains, scowling. "No fair."

Ann laughs, some of the awkwardness dissipating.

But then Tracey is walking forward, and to Maggie's—and apparently Ann's—surprise, she hugs Ann too. It's brief, airy, and stiff—but it's a hug, nonetheless.

In therapy, Tracey has been working through old grudges and resentments. Two days ago, during a family session, the therapist suggested Tracey practice exercising empathy for Ann. Much of their grief is shared, after all.

"We're glad you could make it," Tracey says, a bit tensely, but Maggie knows she's trying.

Ann presses her lips together, meeting all four of their gazes in turn: Barbara, Natalie, Maggie, and back to Tracey. "Me too. Truly."

"I bet Keith is beaming right now," Barbara says.

Natalie loops her arm through Ann's, leading her toward the kitchen—presumably to open the wine. "You *must* tell me what kind of eye cream you use."

Barbara and Tracey follow, and to Maggie's surprise, Tracey quips, "It's probably the Mediterranean diet she ate for so long."

Ann chuckles. "You mean all the carbonara, pastries, and cigarettes were good for me?"

And just like that, the four of them disappear into the house.

Maggie remains outside, her sneakers planted on the walkway.

"Now, that's a sight I'd never thought I'd see," Bob says, wrapping an arm over Maggie's shoulders. "I think you fostered a miracle today."

"I didn't know Mom had such willpower," Maggie says.

"That's not willpower, dear, that's forgiveness."

Maggie chokes on any potential response, instead opting to lean into her father a little more.

"Food's ready!" Iris calls, carrying a big plate of grilled sausages and patties toward the picnic tables.

The four women emerge from the kitchen, wine bottle on ice, glasses in hand. Everyone finds a seat at the worn picnic tables, the gingham tablecloths fluttering gently in the not-yet-summer breeze. Maggie ends up sandwiched between her mother and Ann, with Bob across from her. She looks around the table, feeling Keith's absence a little extra, now that they're all seated.

A pause builds, like the intake of breath before song, and Maggie—timid, mild Maggie, with her heart pattering—does something she never would've done six months ago.

She stands, raising a glass, and clears her throat. "I just wanted to thank you"—she meets Bob's eyes, her mother's, Ann's—"thank you *all* for coming. For being here for Keith, even though Keith himself couldn't be here."

"He's here in our hearts," Barbara says, eyes shining.

Maggie smiles down at her, swallowing a lump of emotion. "He would be so happy"—her voice goes high—"to see us all here together, in spite of the circumstances that almost tore us apart." Maggie touches Tracey's shoulder, a peace offering. "There is nowhere I'd rather be." She raises her glass. "To Keith."

"To Keith," they all say in unison, and drink.

Maggie sinks down to the bench and takes a second sip of her wine, fanning her face. Tracey rubs her back, and Bob nudges her foot under the table. The family devolves into chatter, taking up their forks—but then, beside Maggie, Ann is rising from her seat, clutching her own wineglass.

"I'd like to make a toast of my own, if I may," Ann says, and her tone is breathy and small. After hearing the many intonations of Ann Fawkes throughout their interviews, Maggie recognizes the emotion immediately: reluctance.

The group hushes again, all eyes trained on the woman who disrupted their lives so thoroughly.

"We've been through a lot together, haven't we?" Ann begins. "Through awkward Christmases and shared pains. Keith had a way of bringing people together, a glue and a balm in one, uniting us and soothing us despite our differences of opinion." Ann shifts on her feet, and Maggie spots a slight tremble in her wrists. "I know many of you have wished away my presence, perhaps even wished I didn't exist. But I can't help but think that today—this—is exactly what Keith would've wanted. Regardless of how any of us feel about it."

To Maggie's great surprise, Tracey chuckles. Beneath the table, Maggie grasps her mother's hand, and Tracey folds both her palms over Maggie's fingers—fiercely, motheringly.

"I'd like to take this moment to say that I'm sorry," Ann goes on. "Not for what I did, exactly, but for the hurt my actions caused." Ann's golden eyes find Maggie, and she smiles down at her—fondly. "And I'd like to make a toast to the young woman beside me, who upended all our lives in the best possible way. Who bravely brought us all together and forced us to face the past, if only for the sake of a more honest future." Ann nudges Maggie's shoulder. "Maggie, would you please stand again?"

Maggie hesitates, glancing at her mother and father before rising beside Ann.

"Keith would be so proud of you," Ann says to her, then lower, "Todd too."

"We are all so proud," Bob adds.

Ann smiles at him, then lifts her wineglass a little higher. "To Maggie."

In unison, the family cries, "To Maggie!"

And for a moment, Maggie could swear she hears Keith's voice among the cheers.

Podcast: Stories Behind the Stories
   Episode #148: Ann Fawkes
   Air Date: June 2024
   ["Stories" jingle.]

HOST, ANITA SING: *You're listening to* Stories Behind the Stories. *I'm Anita Sing. In this episode, our guest host is Maggie Whitaker-McCallum, an editor and assistant producer who, by way of this story, earned herself a promotion to full-time producer here at* SBTS. *Maggie spoke with Ann Fawkes, author of the cult classic* Chasing Shadows *and the much-anticipated story collection* Letters I Should Have Written. *Their conversation started off as a regular interview, but Maggie soon learned that Ann's story is a peculiar one—peculiar, in part, because it overlaps with Maggie's life in surprising ways.*
   [Fade into a field recording clip.]
   ANN: *I didn't invite you here for a deeper take.*
   MAGGIE: *Then why* am *I here?*
   [Fade to Maggie in studio.]
   MAGGIE: *I'm Maggie, and this episode is a special one. Why? Because it literally changed my life.*

For a week in January, I sat down with my favorite author to discuss her life. Fans of Ann Fawkes know what a rare opportunity this was—a private person, Ann has never publicly opened up to this degree. But as the interview process got started, Ann and I soon realized that her tell-all was significant for another reason: her life intersected with mine. Throughout the interview, decades-old secrets about my own family were unearthed. Half truths became whole.
   One could call this episode a two-in-one. Because scribbled in the margins of the story of Ann Fawkes is the story of Maggie Whitaker-McCallum: intrepid journalist, loving niece, grateful daughter, and staunch believer in the power of gut feelings.

ACKNOWLEDGMENTS

Travel has always been a powerful source of inspiration for me.

The idea for this novel came to me in 2019, while I was on a jungle tour in Tahiti, French Polynesia (seriously). I had this image of a woman smoking a cigarette at a hotel patio table in a beautiful oceanside locale, realizing that she's been stood up. I wanted to write a sweeping love story, one that took place over decades of togetherness and distance. What keeps people coming back to one another, and what keeps them apart? Why are we so resistant to vulnerability, when it in fact leads to something we so deeply crave: intimacy? I wanted to explore these themes and more.

This book you're holding went through many (many, many) iterations, but I'm proud that a version of that initial idea remains the opening scene. Imagine me feverishly typing "plumeria and tropical rain" into the Notes app of my iPhone while bouncing in the back of a jeep somewhere along the Papenoo River. You never know when a book idea is going to hit you.

The irony of this travel novel was that six months after its inception, the world shut down. I edited this book all throughout 2020 and was grateful to travel vicariously through my characters over the many months of staying home. As I navigated the collective and individual grief of lockdowns, death, and uncertainty, the inspiring themes of the book—physical distance and emotional closeness—were at the forefront of my mind. When times are tough, I tend to lose myself in my writing—it's my security blanket—but this novel also provided a grounding sense of connection for me during the pandemic.

The locations in this book are near and dear to my heart. My husband and I honeymooned in Greece and Italy; I taught English in Thailand; San Juan Island is just a couple ferries away from my hometown; and Tahiti—well, you get the idea.

All this is to say I'd first like to acknowledge not a specific person but the places that inspired this novel and continue to inspire me as I explore this beautiful planet. Thank you to the pilots and cab drivers, the baristas and waiters, the tour guides and museum clerks, the shopkeepers and hotel staff. Thank you to anyone who has kept me company as I walked across cobblestone streets or wedged into the back of a *tuk-tuk*.

Next, I'd like to acknowledge my agent, Michelle, whose encouragement and expertise keeps my career on track. Thank you for being the very best partner in this business.

To Alicia, my editor at Lake Union: Thank you for championing this book. You make me a better author, and I'm so grateful to work with you.

A lot of people contribute to a book. This one wouldn't be possible without my copyeditor, Elyse; my proofreader, Stephanie; my invaluable author-support gal, Gabe; and the rest of the behind-the-scenes team of designers and marketers.

Sue and Steve, thank you for your continual enthusiasm and support. Apologies for making you wait so long for this book!

Emily, thank you for your friendship and book-buying enablement. Whether over coffee or cocktails, I love discussing books and travel with you. Thanks, also, to Samantha at the Imprint Bookstore in Port Townsend, Washington, for supporting local readers and authors like me.

Mom and Dad, thank you for joining us on that trip to French Polynesia. I am so grateful for your support of my dreams, whether they be swimming with whales or writing books or some other equally epic endeavor.

Not all those who support my writing career are human. Thank you to my cat, Emmie, who, for the past fifteen years, has sat beside me every morning while I write. (He's sitting beside me now!) Here's to many more writing mornings with you, buddy.

And to my husband, Joe: my forever adventure partner. Thank you for always letting me have the aisle seat, for finding cold medicine for me in Florence, for taking me to mind-blowing Greek ruins, for swimming with sharks alongside me, and for holding my hand wherever we go. I can't wait to see what adventures we go on next.

BOOK CLUB DISCUSSION QUESTIONS

1. *Halfway to You* explores emotional and physical distance in a romantic relationship. What do you think is more important: emotional or proximal closeness?

2. The characters in *Halfway to You* struggle with honesty—specifically, being honest and vulnerable with the people they love. Do you find it harder or easier to be honest with the people you love (as compared to acquaintances, strangers, etc.)? Why?

3. When Ann and Maggie first meet, Ann says that having a *feeling* about something is the "closest we get to divine intervention." Can you pinpoint any moments in your life where you made a decision based off a gut feeling? Were you ultimately glad you did?

4. Tracey and Bob lied to Maggie about her parentage first to protect her feelings and then continued with the lie to keep the peace. Do you think it's ever okay to lie to someone to protect their feelings?

5. Do you think Ann, upon receiving her inheritance, had a financial responsibility to her mother? How do you think Ann's relationship and resolution with her mother

would've been different had she asked her mother to travel with her on that first trip to Europe?

6. After Todd's rejection in Greece, Ann made it a point to never push too hard for personal or intimate details, for fear that he would leave again. Do you think Todd was right to withhold painful details about his past? Do you think Ann could've asked for more vulnerability on Todd's part? Should partners share everything with each other?

7. Ann started writing as a way to process difficult emotions but later describes her relationship with her craft as "unhealthy . . . cathartic wallowing," challenging the notion that art can be created only through pain. Do you think pain is required to create great art?

8. All the characters in the book struggle with letting fear and vulnerability stop them from living, loving, and going after their dreams. Can you think of a moment in your life when you overcame fear and your life improved for the better?

9. Have you been to any of the destinations in the book? Which one would you most like to visit and why?

ABOUT THE AUTHOR

Photo © 2019 Pinto Portrait

Jennifer Gold is an award-winning author of discussable book club fiction. Her novels feature themes of love, second chances, and self-discovery.

Her debut novel, *The Ingredients of Us*, won a 2020 Book Excellence Award and was a two-time 2020 International Book Awards finalist. Her second novel, *Keep Me Afloat*, received five award recognitions, including a CIBAs/SOMERSET Award First Place Winner honor.

When she's not writing, Gold can be found sipping coffee, enjoying the outdoors, or curling up with a book. Gold is a travel-obsessed romantic living in the Pacific Northwest with her husband and three cats.

Connect with her through jennifergoldauthor.com or her newsletter, which features sneak peeks of upcoming projects, photos from her travels, book recommendations, and more. Gold also loves connecting with fans on Instagram and TikTok (@jennifergoldauthor).